Contents

This book is dedicated to my daughter Jenne and son Vincent, by far my greatest gifts!

Beyond the Brushstrokes

Season of Indecision

Special Thanks

To my MUSE, Angel or spirit who spoke to me for over five years, repeating, "The sun was setting with intense orange and red hues as her car crested Sandpiper Hill." Hearing these words until I nearly lost my mind is what inspired this novel, and I look forward to our next collaboration.

A very special thanks to my daughter, Jenne, who provided a glimpse into the mind of women of similar age as Jadyn and for helping me with character voices and inspiring me. It wasn't possible to write this book without seeing your essence in aspects of Jadyn, which is why I chose your beautiful face when I designed the cover.

To my son Vincent, thank you for believing in me and bringing to light that writing is an art. Your simple words of advice were unclear to me for over a year. My realization of the meaning of your words and my acceptance of them breathed new life into my creativity and washed away my many fears of anticipated critiques from future readers.

To my mother, Lucille, one of my beta readers, so many thanks for never holding back suggestions of how the story should unfold. Even after you left our family to join the angels, your opinions never left my mind. I'm sure you smiled from heaven when I amended my story to align with some of your wishes. Mother truly knows best! I love you, Mommy!

To my father, Don, you weren't afraid to be my first critic and call my first draft pretentious. Your words were tough but very beneficial and taught me the full meaning of pretentious. and fueled my desire to improve my writing style. I know you're supporting me from heaven with mom, and I love you more!

To my dear Aunt Joan, thank you for your consistent encouragement. Our talks mean more to me than you will ever know. Your kind and wise words of advice, remain ever present within my mind.

To my sister Cat, thank you for your encouraging words regarding my writing style, and for reading along as I wrote my first draft. I know you've got some books in you which I hope to read one day.

To my sister, Therese, thank you for inspiring the angel box segment of the story. I thought about our past shared Christmases as I worked on those chapters. I love your dedication creating new traditions and keeping the old ones alive.

Thanks to my brother John for helping determine the book's genre.

To my niece, Michelle, thanks for reading as I wrote the initial version of this book, for your words of support and for sharing your feelings about the story and its characters. I'm most grateful you saved me from the embarrassment of naming one of my characters after a famous singer!

To Teri, my dear friend, thank you for listening while I read, reread, and read yet again chapter after chapter only to repeat the process too many times to count! As we shared our time together, your tears and laughter sang to my heart and will forever remain part of me..

To my friend Raygen, many thanks for the times we shared in real-time, which inspired scenes and words I used in this book; actual circumstances will remain our little secret.

Special thanks to my dearest friend Jenny. We've been friends for nearly our entire lifetime, and you have always been my biggest cheerleader! No doubt you will see content resembling some of our coming-of-age stories. Thank you for sharing your incredible memory of events and details and for reminding me of them as I wrote. My friend, we will forever walk the southern California beaches in my mind.

To Tammy, my dear friend who joined heaven's angels way too soon at only thirty-nine, for inspiring some of the content within this book. We sure had some good times!

To my daughter from another mother, Tiffany, thank you for listening while I read my novel as we drove from Colorado to Arizona. You helped me see why a part of the book bothered me. You helped the content follow a more logical path in one chapter, which repaired breaks and issues in others. I know we share the love of writing and hope to see your name grace the cover of a novel one day.

To my Middle School English teacher, Ms. Connelly, for telling me: "If you don't keep writing, I will hunt you down and kill you! Your belief in me, and those words never left me. I hope you get to read this. My fear of you scared me into writing it!

Special thanks to my final editor, Karleen Wood, for understanding my vision for this book and accepting my choices during our arduous editing sessions. You went above and beyond what I could have ever imagined possible. You pushed me to reach the potential I sought to achieve. Your belief in me and Beyond the Brushstrokes helped me through the many sleepless nights it took to review and complete the edits. You have become more than an editor, you're a true friend, and soul-sister.

Thank you, Matt Bird, for writing The Secrets of Story. Your book resonated with this writer. I will never forget what I learned by listening to your book over six times. You guided me through my dialog issues and helped me understand what is most important to say and what to leave out. Thanks to you, I listened to the editor mentioned below and rewrote my book. Doing this added a few years to my process but helped correct issues I knew existed but even though the readers who love me, found no issues.

Thanks to Peggy Lang, for doing a critical read on my first version, saying I could publish the version I presented to her, but if I dared to change my manuscript, I potentially could have a book worthy of a motion picture. All I needed to do was blow up my entire book! I did most everything she mentioned and hope she doesn't feel as tortured by this version should she dare to read it.

To all the commuters who became curious as I wrote on planes, trains and shuttles and begged to read this story. Many of you were frustrated as we went our separate ways, not knowing how the story ended. I hope you've found your way to this book and have your answers.

My final thank you goes to you, the reader, for overlooking my first novel's messiness without harsh judgment. With my fingers crossed, I hope you enjoy my story and its flaws.

Chapter 1

The Wedding Party

J adyn, enjoying the music and her short-lived solitude, gazed out at the Pacific from within a courtyard overlooking the ocean. Voices of Kendall's emerging wedding guests increased along with the music's volume. As if in a choreographed dance, they moved like butterflies to flowers, joyfully hugging, kissing, and swirling around one another, a contrast to her statuesque pose. She could feel the breeze created by their movement against her bare back, wearing her right high heel sandal like a bracelet, her bare right foot perched on top of her left, and her right hip leaning against a stone planter filled with flowers and palms. If onlookers were to catch a glimpse of Jadyn's appearance they would, for sure, think the party was just about to end.

If she didn't get a hold of herself, she knew her private battle of once joyful, now haunting memories threatened her best friend's celebration. So, Jadyn created a protective, isolating bubble, surrounding herself and shielding the wedding party and guests from her erratic, unstable emotions. If she could contain them, there was hope today would end as a flawless memory for Kendall.

She brought herself out from the depths of her anguish by visually painting over her memories as if they were on a canvas, a canvas needing to be whitewashed, camouflaging them, a clean slate. Using a paintbrush in her mind, she smeared white paint over the memories like a window washer's foamy scrubber and hoped living vicariously through Kendall would muffle the voices of her past so she could join in the celebration.

Jadyn, spaced out, completely detached from everything and everyone, wanting desperately to be happy, prayed for readiness to join the reception. She kept drifting in and out of her past and present. Drifting, like an unmoored ghost ship, floating on the open sea.

Thoughts of her hypothetical painting, and Kendall's new life, cut through the static in her mind, like lightning slicing through the night sky. She used her artist's mind to compare the blue-green hues of the ocean to the pastel blue sky and brushed over the stained canvas, erasing memories lurking below the imaginary white paint. She was frightened they'd seep through at the most inopportune moment, that they'd emerge from beneath the brushstrokes and reveal to everyone just how hopeless and broken she knew herself to be.

Chapter 2

Self Isolation

J adyn couldn't create enough space to silence the belittling words of Kendall's Aunt Miriam and Uncle Saul, nor could she block the creepy sensation of Miriam's disapproving gaze burning into the back of her head. Miriam's Critical thoughts, and the sudden crash of crystal shattering on the terracotta tile, tore through the imaginary force field she'd created. Jadyn felt compassion for the server who she feared may lose his job after losing hold of the full tray of champagne glasses in pieces at his feet. Its ear-piercing crash sounded like a shattering window, exposing to Jadyn she'd only created an illusion of distance.

The music softened as she took a gulp of champagne from her cool, moist flute and spoke to it as if a person, "You're so lucky you didn't end up broken on the ground like all the others."

Jadyn reflected on their fun, dancing into the early morning hours at the bachelorette party the night before. Rolling her eyes, she played back their morning schedule; and how they ran around at the behest of the photographer, who acted more like a fast-moving Border Collie than a human. Because she took part in all of it, Jadyn's feet were killing her. She twisted the strap on her shoe, strangling it, knowing there was still a cake to be cut, a garter-to-toss, dancing to be done, and her speech!

She recalled the photographer herding them around like goats on cliffs, using precariously placed boulders as a stage. She harshly criticized her, to Kendall's sister Sarah, saying, "This snap-happy shutterbug is really starting to bug me!" Jadyn had convinced herself and tried to convince Sarah; that the photographer was only trying to expand her portfolio until they were both humbled by Kendall's glowing face.

After discovering Kendall was delighted with the photographer, they happily assumed their positions in the herd and were glad to be led around like goats in high heels. Anything to make Sarah's little sister happy, anything to make Jadyn's best friend smile.

She wondered what Kendall and Levi were going through at the hands of this amazing award-winning photographer. Without a defensive end to block for them and no team to protect them, they were under her control. She visualized Kendall on the side of a cliff, hanging over the edge, her white dress shredded and dangling in the dirt.

Jadyn, so concerned with her pity filled thoughts, became mindless of the fact that she was balancing on one foot. She took repeating sips of her champagne, hoping it would calm her nerves. It was a bit too relaxing. Her muscles and tendons loosened, causing her ankle to give way, and the narrow heel on her sandal slipped out from beneath her. Champagne splashed all over her and all over her pinkish-peach maid of honor dress. Her goofy brain showed up saying, *turns out drinking champagne only made things worse! Go figure.*

Jadyn's one-leg jerky move caused a reaction in Saul. He leaned forward, nearly shooting champagne out of his nose, and blurted out, "Look, she's a drunk flamingo!"

His wife Miriam gulped the champagne in her flute as if taking a shot of tequila in a barroom toast and laughingly bellowed, "And all this time, I thought she was a mensch!" Then, without missing a step, she let out a wide-mouth belch, utterly devoid of embarrassment.

Saul didn't seem to notice before chiming in, "Seems trashy to me."

Their daughter Brittney heard them gossiping and asked, "Who's trashy?"

Saul pointed at Jadyn from behind her back.

Brittney's loud degrading words broke through the music, "Oh, her! She's the so-called maid of honor."

Miriam questioned, "Is that the girl Kendall brought to all of our family gatherings?"

Brittney nodded and grabbed a flute of champagne from a passing server's tray. She chugged, gasped for air, and answered, "T-Ya! She's a putz and basically Kendall's third wheel."

Miriam yelled, "Oy Vey!" banged her shoulder against Brittney's, and continued, "She was around so much, I was starting to believe Kendall was gay, and Jadyn was her lover!"

Brittney angrily put her hand on her hip and pushed it out. "She just showed up yesterday and is getting all the 'cred.' I'm the actual maid of honor! I did all the work!"

With low voices, her parents agreed, and Brittney continued ingratiating herself, "I even loaned her a pair of my hiking boots yesterday, so she could take the bridesmaid's hike, and all she did was kvetch and complain about how tight they were."

Saul supported Brittney, "Oh, Bubala, you're so kind."

Brittney snarled, "She is such a schmuck!"

Jadyn glared at Brittney and escaped to the bathroom with her shoeless right foot, hobbling like a car with a flat tire and drawing even more unwanted attention to herself. She decided she might as well deal with her aching feet now; all the guests had to wait till the photographer finished shooting Kendall and Levi anyhow.

Chapter 3

The Cleansing

J adyn opened the bathroom door with a swift and thrusting two-handed push! Relieved she had the bathroom to herself, she sighed and said, "Ahh! Thank God."

Feeling distracted and confused over exactly what the heck was up Brittney's butt, made it impossible for Jadyn to cycle through her remaining maid of honor duties.

With a pissed-off look, Jadyn slid off the sandal she'd been wearing on her wrist and tossed it to the floor. She imagined pulling hair from Brittney's head, yanking paper towels from the dispenser, pulling out one after the other in quick succession, right hand, left hand, right hand, left hand.

Jadyn pictured someone slipping on the water that was certain to splash on the floor, so she spread the paper towels beneath her. She slid off the other sandal, hopped up, and sat on the counter. With her feet in the sink, Jadyn squirted soap into her hand and started washing off the sticky-itchy residue attached like plastic wrap to her feet. Scrubbing, she looked at her reflection in the mirror and spoke to herself, "If only I hadn't played around in the ocean, then I wouldn't be sitting here at risk of embarrassing myself."

Jadyn replayed the ceremony, and how the waves called to her as they stood beneath the pinkish-peach peonies and yellow sunflowers delicately woven into the white lace fabric threaded into the Weeping Willow branches of the Wedding Arch.

She recalled how the sand was surely scratching the shiny wooden surface they stood upon as she tried to not slip and fall in front of everyone and how beautiful Kendall's bouquet looked when she passed it to her before reading her vows to Levi. He flashed a smile and winked at Kendall before reading his vows. Jadyn felt her heart swell with joy for them and bleed for her.

After the ceremony ended, she ran into the shorebreak and danced in the foamy bubbles; it made her think of champagne. She knew it wouldn't be long before she was called to join the bridal party for photos. But she simply had to answer the ocean's call.

Jadyn's self-talk ended when two bridesmaids she'd just met at the rehearsal dinner the night before entered the bathroom. They staggered in wearing their yellow bridesmaid dresses, obviously feeling no pain from their champagne. The sight of her sitting on the counter made the word *awkward!* scream in all their minds. When they saw Jadyn's fingers sliding between her toes beneath the cool running water, they couldn't hold back outbursts of hysterical laughter.

She greeted them with all the dignity she had, "Hi, Jackie. Hi, Tanya." Both, disgusted at the sight of her, only nodded, and neither told Jadyn her dress lay submerged in the grungy, soapy foam. Jadyn was beyond embarrassed and mortified they'd seen her washing her feet in the sink like a dirty debutante!

Jackie leaned against the counter with her chin forward, close to the mirror, retouching her lipstick. She abruptly jumped backward, exposing a large wet spot on her stomach, "What the… !" Pissed off, glaring at Jadyn's reflection, she scowled. "Need a wipe for that?"

Jadyn thought, *just great! Another reason for people to hate me!*

Tanya peered at Jadyn and Jackie's interaction from within the open stall. With her puffy yellow dress tucked under one arm and panties at her ankles, she dropped onto the toilet. Holding tight to the door, drunkenly swinging it side to side, Tanya gave Jackie a nasty eye-rolling look and yelled, "Oh, my God, your dress!"

Jadyn offered a sincere "Sorry," and aware it wouldn't be enough to keep them from gossiping about her, jumped off the counter, wiped the water from it, and dried her feet. Thinking Jadyn was deplorable, Jackie and Tanya walked out the slowly closing door. With chins raised and loud, complaining voices, Tanya said, "Why Kendall chose her to be maid of honor is beyond me!"

Jackie agreed, "It's a mystery to me too! She doesn't appear to have any class at all."

Jadyn heard their vile remarks and wondered how Kendall could consider them friends; they were anything but friendly. She lit up when the bandleader's voice broke through their mean chatter announcing Kendall and Levi had arrived!

Lowering her tense and defensive shoulders, she said, "Ahh! Finally!" and walked out to welcome them, praying their presence would make everyone behave.

Chapter 4

Toasted

Terror marked Jadyn's face as she found her seat at the head table and discovered the tuxedo-wearing servers spreading out like black ants, filtering around the tables and guests. They were gracefully moving like ballroom dancers, pouring champagne, signaling the toasts were next, and creating fear in Jadyn. She dreaded standing in front of everyone. After all, many of them apparently hate her. Why? Jadyn didn't know why. She'd concentrated with all she had on her perfect speech. Jadyn memorized it over weeks of practice.

With panic rising, she searched her mind. Pushing back her fear like cobwebs in a darkened cave, trying to comprehend that she'd completely lost the words she'd so lovingly and carefully put together for Kendall. Her words were hiding somewhere inside her drunken mind, swimming around, blurred and jumbled, making it impossible to rehearse! Unwilling to accept failure and drunk, she had a full-blown panic attack!

Fear of disappointing Kendall enveloped her, like sinking into a hot tub on a chilly night, and all she could think of was, *I need more champagne!*

Jacob, Levi's oldest friend and a successful attorney at only thirty-one, took to the mic first. He dipped his finger into the champagne flute and ran it along the rim, causing an eerie high-pitched shrill to silence the guests making everyone focus on him. Jacob raised his glass, facing the now Mr. and Mrs. Schmidt, and Jadyn looked up at him as he began speaking.

She imagined he acted the same in the courtroom, demanding the room, no word unchecked, each topic powerful and well versed. His eloquence, a sharp contrast to Jadyn's unready mind. She knew everyone would notice, making her even more stressed. With his voice playing in the background, she frantically attempted to recall her speech. Each of his perfectly spoken words grew louder than her fading memory, but not her rising fear!

He spoke confidently, "I've known Levi since I was taller than him; not sure when he grew taller than me, but I've looked up to him ever since. I had no choice." The guests laughed.

"It will surprise many of you to learn that Levi and I met as kids on the Little League field. He was there by choice, and I, well, I was trying to negotiate with the coach to be the scorekeeper." Levi pointed at Jacob and laughed along with the guests. Jacob pointed back at Levi and winked.

"Levi and I may not have sports in common, but we do have mutual respect. Without him, I may never have completed law school. He was always there with an energy drink when I needed one. Let me tell you, it was his fault I needed one because he made me go to all the parties. Had he not, I wouldn't have met my Wifey, Naomi. We now have wickedly badass wives who make baller sandwiches in common!"

Kendall and Naomi laughed along with the guests. "All kidding aside, I know everyone here couldn't be happier that Levi chose Kendall to be his beautiful bride!"

Levi turned, smiling at Kendall as Jacob continued, "I knew you were a keeper when you laughed at all my jokes and how you make Levi happy in *so* many ways."

He impersonated Groucho Marx, raising his eyebrows and motioning with an imaginary cigar, "Ways I never would."

The guests erupted in laughter! And a bridesmaid screeched out, "I'm going to pee myself!"

Kendall's Aunt Miriam asked, "What's everyone laughing about?" Uncle Saul shrugged his shoulders and returned a befuddled Grinch mouth look.

The room quieted; Jacob considered this a perfect opening to continue speaking. "I know this union will last just as our friendship has lasted, standing the test of time. Come on, everyone, let's toast the bride and groom!"

The room thundered with cheers!

Jacob walked to Jadyn and passed her the mic, holding it like a Harry Potter wand. For Jadyn, the room dissolved into darkness, and the walls closed in around her as if she were in a trash compactor.

She shuddered, wishing she could refuse the wand. If only it could take her back in time to when she remembered her speech; instead of shining upon her for all to see, she'd lost her words, exposing her as an imposter. She tried positive imagery, envisioning herself a wizard, like Harry Potter's Hermione, failing miserably, only to end up like a deer in the headlights, pathetic, weak, a wizard with a broken wand. Jadyn forced a smile she hoped was believable, reluctantly grabbed the mic with both hands, stood frozen, gazing at Kendall's waiting eyes, and with trembling hands and voice, she said, "Kendall and I have shared some wonderful times, many I can remember, and some are hard to recall because, let me tell you, we also shared a lot of wine! Ha-ha! She's the best friend a girl could ever have, and her new husband Levi, who occupies most of her time, is the luckiest man alive to have taken her off the market. If you've seen the ring, you *know* he loves her!"

Kendall kicked Jadyn's shoe, causing her to fall against the table, tipping over champagne glasses, making Jadyn blurt out, "Oh shit!" Her expletive was loud and clear. She collected herself, looked up, smiled, and said, "Oh, Schmidt! Cheers to the Schmidts! Here's to the Schmidts! Cheers!"

A mixture of cheers and whispers, laughter, and judgment confirmed Jadyn's fearful thoughts.

Wishing she could just drop the mic and run, Jadyn passed it to the groom's father. She hid her face in Kendall's veil and gave her a tight squeeze. Brittney stood with her champagne glass raised and yelled out, "Brilliant words from the maid of dis-honor!"

Jadyn felt Brittney's words punch her in the stomach, feeling all eyes on her and knowing everyone agreed with Brittney. She looked at Kendall with a pained expression and tears welling in her eyes before pulling away and running to the bathroom.

Kendall sat hard, leaned over Jadyn's empty chair towards her annoying younger cousin Brittney, and sternly said, "Why are you acting so schmaltzy? You're ruining my reception. You don't even know her. You're being so mean. She's my oldest and best friend, and she's amazing!"

Brittney fought back, "She is not amazing; she

ruined my life! Not to mention her speech was awful!"

Kendall, at a loss for words, not knowing why Brittney was so verklempt or why she harbored such vitriol for Jadyn, reached the limit of her patience. Unwilling to deal with her anymore, she gave Brittney a disgusted look and lashed out, "Whatever." She composed herself, turned away from Brittney, and saw her older sister Sarah standing beside her with the microphone. Her sister and comrade in arms cupped her hand over the microphone and whispered, "What the heck is wrong with Brittney?"

Fifteen minutes later, after their father finished the final speech, Kendall and Sarah grabbed each other's hands and quickly ran to the bathroom to check on Jadyn.

Chapter 5

Unstable Love

Kendall and Sarah entered the bathroom, and Jadyn quickly begged them, "Don't be nice to me. I finally stopped crying!" Sarah didn't listen. She loved Jadyn and treated her like a baby sister. She held her and kissed her cheek, asking, "Do you have any idea why Brittney is treating you so bad?"

Hearing the love in her voice and seeing the compassion in Kendall's eyes as she joined in, "Do you? I just don't understand why she's being so mean to you. I'm so sorry."

Those words and their loving faces opened the floodgates! Jadyn sobbed, "I keep putting on mascara and crying it off again, and no matter how many times I've applied my makeup, I can't cover up my swollen eyes or red nose."

Kendall stood beside Jadyn with her hand on her shoulder and spoke to her with compassion and understanding. "Oh my God. Stop. Please stop. Put your makeup away. It's time to call it quits."

Jadyn wiped the black smears off her cheeks and looked at Kendall in the mirror. "I can't give up. It's your wedding day."

Kendall teased Jadyn, hoping she'd feel better, "Babe, you're a hot mess."

Jadyn resisted, "It's your wedding day. I can't disappoint you."

Kendall positioned herself in front of Jadyn and looked her in the eye. "I don't know how I'd be feeling if I were in your shoes. I can only imagine how you're feeling. If you can't get it together and you want to leave, you're forgiven. All the important photos have been taken, and your duties are done. There's nothing left for you to do."

The DJ interrupted Kendall, announcing, "it's time for the cake cutting; where's the bride?"

She gave Jadyn a one-arm hug, "Love you," and Sarah said, "Bunches!" and they headed back to reception.

Jadyn gathered her belongings and crept away during the cake cutting. She desperately hoped nobody would see her take this pathetic walk of shame. She got into her SUV, thinking *there's no such thing as a smart drunk,* turned the key, and drove down the Pacific Coast Highway, anyway.

Chapter 6

Fallen Bouquet

The cake plates were nearly cleared, and it was time for the bouquet toss; Kendall set her bouquet in flight with angry inertia. She threw it so hard that when it struck Brittney's chest, the delicate petals broke off and rained onto the terracotta tile. Brittney didn't even try to catch it. Like a dead bird falling from the sky, she let the bouquet tumble and fall to the floor on top of the broken-off petals. Everyone looked at Brittney with disturbing glances as she turned to walk away, only to be stopped by Kendall. She gripped Brittney's arm *tightly* and grabbed the broken bouquet with the other.

Kendall continued to punish Brittney by shoving the tattered bouquet into her chest. Looking like an angry lioness growling, and teeth clenched, she admonished her behavior, saying, "I watched you! You didn't even try to catch it! It hit you; It's yours!"

She pleaded with, "I don't want to marry him! He doesn't love me; he loves her!"

Brittney's refusal of the bouquet and how literal she took this tradition took Kendall by surprise. Shocking behavior, even for Brittney, acting like a fool in front of all the guests. Kendall, confused and pissed off, asked, "Loves who?!"

Brittney furiously yelled with teeth clenched, "Your maid of honor, that's who!"

Chapter 7

Walk of Shame

Jadyn drove slowly and carefully as she pulled into a vacant space in the parking lot, not even close to the blotchy fading lines. She climbed out of her SUV and gave it all she had to get to the sand fast. She walked off-balance over the crumbling concrete, stepping predominantly on the toes of her shoes, staggering with an exaggerated sway in her hips.

From where Cole stood, her figure was a tempting silhouette. He thought she looked angelic and out of place in her translucent, diaphanous gown. "Wow!" He whispered, with eyes fixed on her. His mind took off running without him. He had a narrator in his head describing her. *There she is, barely walking, more like staggering, yet dreamlike, with blonde hair blowing gently in the wind as the high tide, low and slow waves softly lap on the shore beside her.*

Cole smiled big as he watched Jadyn hop on her left foot, bending forward and reaching behind her to remove her right shoe. Jadyn fully extended her fingers as she mostly missed her target, and it appeared she would never accomplish this simple task. He almost cheered when she pulled the shoe from her raised foot as it met the still-warm sand. His brows raised, and Cole covered his mouth to silence his laughter when her attempts to remove her left shoe brought her to the sand with an embarrassing thud. She frantically looked around, tossing her head right, left, and behind to see if anyone had witnessed her ineptness.

Jadyn laughed much higher and louder than she'd planned, "Ha-ha-ha! too much champagne for me!" Her laughter quickly turned to outright sobbing, followed by a lot of yelling, "Why God! Why!" She screamed as if muzzled for years and was finally allowed to speak her mind. Anyone else would know better than to walk into her pity party, but Cole couldn't see clearly, not even close.

He squatted behind an assortment of small shrubs below a buzzing streetlamp, looking and feeling like a stalker or a creepy peeping Tom. Cole tried to convince himself it wasn't wrong to keep watching her, "I didn't plan to be here. Maybe it's fate."

Jadyn continued crying, with shoes strewn about and legs bent, like a defiant toddler who failed to reach the cookie jar. Her dramatic self-loathing and tear-filled rant were disturbing yet oddly intriguing to Cole. He began pacing, taking one step in either direction, questioning his desire. *Why do you want to meet her? She's yelling and crying and a mess! What about all that drama is appealing?*

Jadyn slid her fingers through the loose, dry sand bordering the cool, wet sand beneath her. She sifted through it until she discovered a smooth, paintbrush-shaped piece of driftwood. Its texture instantly inspired Jadyn and made her want to draw. Her hair fell around her face as she leaned forward on her knees and carved into the damp, pliable sand. He found her artistic process breathtaking to watch. In just seconds, she created an amazing work of art. She bled out her sorrow into the sand, an outpouring of emotion, a release of creativity, and a drawing worthy of being protected from dissolving into the rising tide's upcoming repeat appearance. It must have cried out when she turned her back on it and walked away, as if a mistake, and without a witness of its birth, like it never existed.

Cole finally convinced himself to go to her, thinking, *who is this crying, pitiful, beautiful woman? Clearly, she needs help.*

He began walking toward her with his bike by his side as if it were his faithful steed, acting out scenarios and gesturing with his free hand. He looked like a complete fool. If only Cole were aware of it.

The sun crested the ocean, and typical of a sunset in May, fog formed along the shoreline, swirling around her slowly moving silhouette, making her appear almost dreamlike in its mist.

Jadyn stopped walking and sat calmly with legs crossed, quiet and oblivious to everything except the surreal vastness of the sky framing the slow undulating dark sea. She thought it looked as though God himself airbrushed it, a sky oozing with vibrant colors, more colors blending than she'd ever witnessed. Jadyn knew these unimaginable colors would haunt her memory just as sorrowful thoughts crept in and out of the shadows within her mind. Shades of yellow and orange contrasted the mostly light-blue sky. A string of pelicans floated with un-flapping wings, just inches over the water, heading up the coast. Jadyn wondered if Kendall would see them in flight as they would surely glide by her reception. If only they had cameras attached to them, like drones, to peer into the party and check in on Kendall.

Jadyn shuddered when a sudden chill grabbed the

back of her neck like unwanted fingers touching her. She considered grabbing her sweater from the SUV but opted to punish herself, saying under her breath, "You don't deserve to be warm. Get up and walk if you're cold!"

Jadyn clumsily got up, staggering bare-shouldered to the water. Her buzz from the champagne she'd chugged earlier hadn't come close to wearing off. She continued admiring with an artist's jealousy, the sun peeking out above the glasslike water's edge.

Cole turned his back on Jadyn to hide the flash of his cell phone's camera as he snapped a picture of her drawing. He wasn't about to allow it to be forgotten and couldn't understand how she could leave it to be washed away. He pocketed the phone and patted it with satisfaction, knowing he had a keepsake of her talent to carry with him.

Cole was glad no one saw him and continued following Jadyn to be sure she remained safe.

Fragmented colors of the setting sun glowed through each recurring wave, breaking apart in the pooling, foamy breakwater, forever changing, soon to disappear. Jadyn thought it likened to viewing the world through a kaleidoscope lens, watching the colors dance until each bubble became sucked into the soggy sand, leaving it scarred with ghostly outlines of salt.

She dug in with her toes, creating a hole in the sand, and fast-moving sand crabs emerged, quickly swimming in the water after each wave exposed them. Jadyn looked into the water like a crystal ball, fondly recalling a childhood memory of her father holding her hand as they walked along the seashore. It filled her with amazement when he stopped to show her how to reveal what lay beneath what looked like bullet holes in the wet sand. The ocean's soothing repetitive motion pulled Jadyn into deep meditative concentration.

A group of drunken vagrants suddenly and unexpectedly appeared from behind a lifeguard station a few yards from Jadyn. The men carried bags, hiding bottles in hand, and tore her private thoughts apart as they noisily staggered toward her. After hearing one slur, "Hey, Chica, what brings you to our stretch of beach?" She stopped playing in the water and considered her escape options. Jadyn cringed! Karate moves played in her mind as she stepped back and tried to come up with a great retort to his unwelcome comment. She knew saying, *leave me alone* was not a good option, so she forced a smile instead and yelled, "Honey, where'd you go? Come on! Quit hiding from me, silly man!" Before turning away from them and, without looking back, she began running, only to be surprised by a man running toward her from out of nowhere!

Jadyn's breath caught in her throat, and fear marked her face when Cole overreacted, grabbed her waist with both hands, and aggressively pulled her to him. He frantically shouted, "Sorry guys, this beauty's with me! Have a good night!"

A man larger than the rest dismissively raised a hand with an angry expression and yelled back, "Ya, ya! Alright! We hear ya!" he swung his raised arm around as if to scoop up his cohorts. Each of the men looked at their apparent leader argumentatively as they turned to walk back to where they slithered out, shaking their heads in disappointment. Like a pack of hyenas, they looked back as if considering an attack, with disorganized steps and complaining voices sounding like dogs barking, almost growling.

Chapter 8

Collisions

Not having even seen the face of the man still holding her, Jadyn's body reacted without her control, fists clenched so tight she thought her fingernails would soon draw blood. She couldn't catch a full breath. Her muscles were stiff. She feared she would break if she moved against the strength of just who had their hands on her?! *Did he just save me? Or is he also a threat?*

Her thoughts only increased the fear, and she released a scream! She ended with a playful sound for fear those disgusting men would return. Jadyn struggled to understand which emotion to embrace: gratitude, rage, or terror?

Disoriented yet aware only a few seconds had passed, she glanced back to ensure the creepy men were far enough away to no longer be an immediate threat and switched her focus to Cole. She gathered her strength, wiggled, twisted, and finally turned to face him, yelling, "Take your hands off me!" She forcefully pushed his hands off her waist, took a step back, and tried to intimidate him with a karate pose.

Cole could barely stand how cute she looked. "Ha-ha-ha! Relax, Rambo, I'm no threat."

His knee-jerk response pissed her off till she saw his face, providing some relief. If only her still vibrating body would settle. Still simmering with lingering fear, she mindlessly blurted out, "Asshole!"

Cole playfully defended himself, saying, "Didn't mean to scare you, but I'd say I'm an ass-saver, not an ass-hole! You're welcome."

She kept pretending to be tough. The more she did, the cuter she appeared, and the more Cole laughed at her!

Jadyn is caught in a Catch-22 with no hope of escape.

She scolded him with conviction, "You're welcome? You want me to thank you? *Okay,* fine! Thanks for scaring the living hell out of me!"

Cole thought she acted unhinged. "Aren't you being a tad dramatic?"

Teetering on the edge of anger, she yelled, "Dramatic! You want dramatic? I'll show you, dramatic!" She flung her hair with attitude and open palmed, pushed against his shoulder.

Cole laughed harder. "Drama queen!"

Jadyn's tight lips and scowl let him know he was about to really get it, "Next time you think you need to save someone, ask if they want saving!"

The gloves are now off! Cole blurted out, "Noted!" and teased, "My mistake! You and those dudes would have ended up great friends!"

Jadyn, outmatched by him, searched for a snarky comeback.

He was too quick for her and continued defending his actions. "Come on! I am genuinely concerned about your well-being. I've heard of people killed on this beach. Just saying!" Secretly enjoying her dramatic rant, hoping she'd follow him as he walked back to his bike, he hid his intentions.

Jadyn knew to be cautious yet really enjoyed their playful back and forth, "You know, trying to scare me into walking with you won't work."

Still walking a few steps ahead, Cole raised one hand and yelled, "I *was* just being a *nice* guy. You don't have to be such a...."

Jadyn interrupted with an attitude, "A what? Are you calling me a bitch?"

Cole noticed her voice sounded distant. Concerned, he turned and saw she stopped walking and yelled, "A pain in the ass who believes I'm an asshole!" Cole was pretty proud of himself after saying all that. He figured she'd for sure keep walking with him, walked faster than before, and declared to her, "I am a hero, not an asshole."

Jadyn ran a few steps, "Sorry. You're right. I should have thanked you." Realizing how pathetic she sounded, she rolled her eyes, "Thank you for scaring the shit out of me!"

Cole, still walking, said, "You're like a dog with a bone, woman!"

Jadyn finally admitted Cole saved her, "Okay, okay, I was terrified before you showed up! Thank you for *real* this time. Pretty sure my life would've flashed before my eyes tonight."

Cole faced her. "I'm glad I could help."

She squeezed his arm and asked, "So, Mr. Hero, are you going to walk me to my SUV?"

Cole asked, "Exactly who am I walking?"

She smartly questioned him, "You mean whom, right?"

Cole yelled out, "You ball-buster!"

Jadyn said, "Yep! You can call me Ms. Ball-buster!"

Jadyn felt her ring finger with her thumb, laughing, "I have a fun idea; let's not tell each other our real names. You game?"

Cole wondered why she wouldn't want him to know her real name. "If you say so." With a furrowed forehead, he searched his mind for a fake name.

Jadyn recalled the legend of Katarina and Arturo, how they longed to be together, and felt it befitted her life, "Call me Katarina!"

Cole questioned her, "Come again?"

She playfully explained, "My name is Katarina, and you are?"

He gave in with a pained and wrinkled forehead, saying, "Huey."

She laughed loudly, "Ha! What a manly name! Isn't it a cartoon character's name?"

Wondering if he was having fun or not, he said, "wow, aren't you full of it?"

She giggled and offered, "You have this odd effect on me. I can't help myself! Sorry!"

Cole scolded Jadyn, "Nothing *good* to say, remember? Huey is the Hawaiian God of surfers. If it isn't pleasing to you, Katarina, how about Rodolfo?"

She wrinkled her nose and asked, "Where'd you get Rodolfo from?"

Jadyn sensed Cole's patience waning as he said, "From the dark reaches of my, *I don't care what you call me,* if Huey isn't good enough for you, *mind.*"

Giggling, she said, "Sorry, I take it you're not enjoying this as much as me?"

He just shrugged one shoulder and said, "No problem," before continuing their walk to her SUV and his bicycle. Jadyn slowed, matching Cole's pace. She felt her body-temperature drop and longed for the sweater sitting on her front seat.

With arms wrapped around her, she shivered, "Burr, the sand is freezing!"

He came back with, "If your feet are cold, Katarina, walk in the water."

She said, "you're full of it," and then, in disbelief, "Yeah, right!?"

Cole insisted, "Do it. You'll see I'm right."

She did as instructed, "wow, how strange?"

Pleased with himself, "Told ya."

Jadyn loved learning, "Why did that work?"

Not knowing himself, he replied, "I believe life is way more interesting when you don't have all the answers."

Jadyn jumped in, "Like not knowing each other's real names?"

Cole gave in, "OK, I get it."

She raised her dress. Cole teased, "You have an odd way of dressing for the beach."

She smiled and said in agreement, "You like?"

Water splashed to her waist. She could feel the weight of the fabric clinging to her skin, reminding her of Cole's warm hands on her earlier. Unable to look away, he cleared his throat with exaggerated open eyes and laughingly said, "You, Katarina, look like a soggy dog."

Jadyn smiled big, "You think so? Awe! Thank you, Woof Dolfo!" As the words left her lips, her inner voice screamed, *this is getting way too familiar!*

As they continued walking, Jadyn enjoyed secret pleasures each time the water descended back into the Pacific. The thrusting force of each wave's path grabbing at her ankles, combined with the sinking cool, wet sand sliding between her toes, felt stimulating. With each quicksand-like step, her face and private thoughts grew hotter.

Jadyn knew she shouldn't think about him this way and hoped it was too dark for him to see the passion painted on her face. Cole broke the awkward silence. Recounting a news story about a local girl's assault a few yards from where their lives collided. Cole described the event with a lower tone in his voice, "She was only seventeen and forever changed by a Creep! Things like this make me question whether children are part of my future. I mean, how do you let your daughter leave the house? If I were there, that sicko wouldn't have walked away from anything again." He spoke passionately, and his now heavy steps quickened.

Jadyn sped up. Her toes struck the water's surface, causing her to lunge forward. Her mind reeled, envisioning falling face-first into the surf, so she sprang out of the water and over to Cole.

Chapter 9

Awkward Plans

By the time they reached the pavement, Jadyn was freezing again. As she brushed the sand off her already miserable, painful feet, she felt it cut into her tender skin. She dreaded putting her shoes back on, but the broken concrete would surely be unbearable without them, so she reluctantly began sliding them on. Jadyn was more than a little wobbly with nothing to hold onto, and Cole pretended not to notice until she nearly fell over. Amused and enjoying watching her struggle, he finally extended his arm and absentmindedly said, "Hey. Hold on, you don't wanna fall again."

She caught what he just said, "Oh, my God! You were watching me for a long time!" She couldn't resist teasing, "Stalker!" Cole rolled his eyes.

He was amused by how pleased she was with herself and continued the fight by raising his hands in the, *don't arrest me* position, saying, "You caught me! *Come on,* it's not like I planned this! After all, you were making *a lot* of noise!" Feeling a win with his dig at her earlier behavior, he went on, "Of course, I've already described how you look."

Excited, knowing she had the perfect snarky comeback, she teased him, "If you say so, Tom!" The look on Cole's face made her laugh, and she let out a little snort, embarrassing herself.

Cole was merciless, "Ha! How ladylike!"

After managing to pull up the strap on her sandal, she thought, *one foot done, one to go.* Jadyn felt conflicted and a bit turned on as she explored the strength of his forearm with her fingers. Still slumped over, Jadyn switched to the other foot. Her pinky gave way and let go of the wet, sandy hem of her dress. As it dropped, she felt it scratch her sand-laced legs, and a sizable clump fell onto her toes like a dump truck releasing its load. She rolled her eyes before scooping the sand from between her toes and brushing it off. Feeling ridiculous, Jadyn nervously looked at him and broke the awkward silence, "Thanks, Rodolfo."

Cole said, "No problem," and shook his head, fighting the urge to kiss her. He was lost in the color of her painted toenails as she stood up and released her grip from his arm. When her fingers slid away, his face fell slightly in disappointment, and he thought, *come on, Huey, you just met this chick.*

After finishing with what seemed to Jadyn as an endless job of dealing with her needy feet, Jadyn started walking ahead of Cole to her SUV. She was pissed off at the drunk version of herself for parking so far from the sand.

Guilt washed over her as she reflected on how inebriated and despicably irresponsible, she acted driving away from the reception in that condition. Relieved, her buzz was dissolving, clearing her mind, and giving back her coordination, but it only made her more aware of just how painful it was walking over the pebbles littering the weathered pavement.

Cole could see her walking like a dog's first steps on cold, wet grass, and knew carrying her the rest of the way would be inappropriate, so he extended his arm, "Use me as a crutch."

Jadyn released a snorty giggle, "Crutch would've been a great name!"

He gave her a "you're *not funny*" look, "Don't even go there!"

She gave in, "Ha-ha, okay," and clicked to unlock the door. With her hand still gripping his arm, Cole grabbed the handle and opened her door.

Jadyn was intrigued with Cole and hoped he'd join her if she asked, "I'm starving! Where's a good place to eat?"

He gave her a once-over examination, "Looking like that?"

With a crooked smile, she joked, "Are you saying you'd be embarrassed to eat with me looking like this?"

He raised one shoulder with a quick shrug and tipped his head to the side, "I'd suffer through a meal with you."

Jadyn responded, "Well, your torture will have to wait till I change out of this dress. Unless you really don't *mind* being seen with me looking like this."

He couldn't wait to see her reaction as he asked, "You mean this soggy-raccoon look you've got goin' on?"

As she lowered the SUV's visor, Jadyn realized she hadn't looked at herself since Kendall encouraged her to leave the reception. She covered her mascara-smeared face and asked him, "Just tell me where?"

Cole was concerned, "Sure you're okay to drive?"

She flicked hair from her neck with the tips of her fingers, crossed her arms, and snapped, "I got here, didn't I?"

Cole thought, *Think of something fast!* He knew she'd be driving off no matter what. He checked his attitude. *Don't be a jerk.* He didn't want to risk not seeing this sassy woman again. He spoke to her through the closed window and door, his voice ascending, "My bad! What can I say? You're growing on me!" He hoped she'd make it safely to her room.

Cole thought for sure he'd blown it when she turned on the engine. She surprised him when she opened her window and said, "Don't you tell me what to do, Rodolfo."

Her smile let him know he was reprieved, so he continued, "A couple miles north of here; there's a place with blue and white...."

Jadyn excitedly and rhythmically banged her steering wheel and cut in, saying, "Breakers with the blue and white awnings?" Cole nodded.

He decided her cuteness didn't exclude her from having manners saying, "You're one of those girls."

She looked inquisitively at him, "What kind of girl am I?"

He hoped she wouldn't get mad, "The interrupting kind."

Jadyn spoke through snorty laughter, "Sorry. I know. I know. You nailed me. Go on."

He said, "Yeah, Breakers." and quickly teased, "How much time do you need to fix - *this*?" The gesturing wave of his nonexistent wand-yielding hand made her laugh.

She debated how much time she needed. Her stomach had been growling since she warmed her feet in the ocean and burned from the alcohol sitting in its empty void, so waiting much longer to eat was out of the question. She also felt the day literally crawling on her skin and desperately needed at least a quick shower. "It takes an hour, smartass."

He laughingly said, "If you say so, Katarina! See you in an hour - fifteen!"

Cole spun his bike around, threw his leg over the seat, and began to ride in one smooth motion. He looked back at her from beneath his armpit, thinking Jadyn wouldn't see, but she caught his gaze and smiled back before driving to her hotel, feeling dirty and guilty the entire way.

Chapter 10

Bike Ride & the Tide

F ew stragglers remained on the darkening beach as Cole rode away on the concrete path cutting like a river through the sand. She watched him travel beneath the towering lights lining the path and through ghostly shadows of the gently rustling palm trees lining it until he dissolved into the landscape. She felt her ring finger with her thumb, looked at it, grasped the steering wheel, and drove to her motel.

Cole couldn't hear the trees swishing in the soft breeze nor the rising waves lapping at the shoreline. The sound of sand crunching beneath his tires made it impossible to hear anything else.

Riding fast, Cole sat on the seat of his bike only once. He remained standing on the pedals as he approached an old bike rack covered with erosion and peeling rust-peppered gray paint. He ended his ride as smoothly as it began, swinging his right leg around, joining his left, and skillfully coasting the remaining three feet into an empty stall. The metal pipes of the bike rack clanked as his lock struck them. After spinning the dial to secure it, he hopped up the three cement steps leading to his beachfront apartment building.

Cole pulled the heavy glass door open and, before it fully closed, had already ascended the two floors to his apartment. He easily skipped every other step, and the old wooden floorboards squeaked with each release to greet him.

Cole approached Randy, his younger friend, and neighbor from apartment 2B. Randy awkwardly bent forward, fighting to keep the six-pack he cradled in his arm from slipping, "If the beer's too much for ya, I can take it."

Randy thought if only he could find his damn keys, he'd be offering Cole a beer instead of talking to him from through his fallen hair.

Cole knew better than to ask what he was searching for in his shorts' pocket but couldn't resist, "Whatcha diggin' for?"

Randy gave up the search and stood facing Cole, "Dude, you look like you just rode a killer wave. What's up?"

Cole ignored the question with a quick, "Nothing."

Randy pushed, "Come on. Spill!"

Smirking, Cole bargained, "I'll tell you for one of those beers."

Randy, happy to stop foraging through his pockets, said, "Lead the way."

Chapter 11

Bro's & Beers

Cole dangled *his* keys, mocking him before unlocking *his* door directly across from Randy's still-locked door.

They entered apartment 2C. Cole decorated his place with trophies he'd won, photos of him surfing, and others of him receiving awards. They each stepped zigzagging around Cole's overly excited calico cat, Paws.

Paws jumped on Cole's lap as they sat on a couple of low beach chairs in front of a table fashioned from a beat-up surfboard positioned atop a large piece of driftwood and strapped together with bungee cords.

Randy reached into his pocket to pull out his blue Bic lighter, only to discover the once-hidden keys. Looking a bit confused, he raised his chin and tossed his keys onto the board as if declaring victory.

Cole teased Randy, "You can't keep your pockets organized, but you pop off beer bottle caps with your lighter like a gladiator!"

Randy smiled in agreement, sat back, put his feet on the surfboard, and slid the defeated keys aside with his heel before challenging Cole, "I'm all paid up. Spill."

Cole drank nearly half the bottle, belched, and teased, "You gave me one for this hand; I need one for my other."

They laughed, and he went on, "I met a very odd and very hot girl tonight. I'd tell you her name if I

knew it. She's got long blonde hair and a wicked smile."
He turned on his cell, saying, "Check out this sick
drawing she drew in the sand." He pleasantly recalled
her drawing it. "We're grabbing something to eat at
Breakers, in…." He looked at the clock on his cell and
continued, "thirty."

Randy scooped up his keys and started to stand,
saying, "I'll get going."

Cole slid the remaining beers away from Randy, and
questioned him, "Why?"

Randy closed one eye, seeming to struggle with his
last gulp of beer, and asked, "Aren't you gonna shower?"

Cole came back with, "Women are always late."

Surprised, Randy thought how stupid he sounded
and challenged him with, "Do you want to see her after
tonight?"

Cole considered his question, "Yeah. Sure."

Randy pointed his beer bottle at Cole and said,
"Being late would be lame."

Cole wanted to win this debate. He shared his belief,
"I haven't met a girl who wasn't late. Trust me; she
needs more than an hour to clean up. She's a mess!
I've got time to finish this beer." He clanked his bottle
against the neck of Randy's and sat back.

Randy shook his head, "I wouldn't chance-it."

Cole, not relenting, continued, "Trust me, Rand, this
girl is not the organized type."

Randy scooped his keys off the board like a child
playing a game of Jax and fisted them, saying, "If you say
so, but now you're down to twenty minutes."

Cole shot up, "You've convinced me. Thanks for the
brewsky. Next one's on me."

Chapter 12

Tiny Cars & Key Chains

After closing the door behind Randy, he walked the short distance through his bedroom to the bathroom, stepped out of his swim shorts, and flung them with his toes into a broken white plastic hamper.

The skin on his well-formed buttocks starkly contrasted with the dark caramel color of his tanned, muscular back and thighs. His brown hair was bleached with streaks of blonde painted by hours in the sun.

As Cole leaned under the water's flow to rinse his hair, droplets ricocheted off his shoulders over the glass door into the room. He rushed to rinse off the sand-filled bubbles sliding through the hairs on his legs and shut off the shower just as they merged with the pooling water at his flip-flop, tan-lined feet.

Paws jumped off the counter with a brash meow and belligerent scowl as the water rained from Cole's fingertips on her. He laughed, "Shouldn't have used my towel as a bed. Out of my way, cat." His mind finished his sentence with, "Arina." Smiling in the mirror, he continued, "Katarina," and wrapped the towel around his waist.

Cole's shoulder-length hair released glittering beads of water onto his back as he shaved, patted cologne on his neck, and brushed his teeth. He flung his head forward and back to dry it, adding to the cascading water on his mirror. His movement caused the towel to fall to the floor, where he ultimately left it.

Cole was quick to dress despite Paws persistent meowing and disruptive rubbing across his shins. He was feeling as much desire for Katarina as Paws did for food. With understanding, he opened a can of cat food and dropped it into her bowl with one quick jerk of his wrist. He stroked her soft fur saying, with a soft loving tone, "There you go, girl."

Cole dropped both hands by his sides, grunted, and grabbed a purple rabbit's foot keychain. He gripped it tight, squeezed hard as if to kill it again, and picked up his cell to see he was already five minutes late. Cole locked his apartment door and headed to his building's poorly lit parking lot. He looked around and hesitantly slid the single key dangling from the foot into the lock of a purple and white Mini Cooper, complaining, "Damn it! How am I supposed to get in and drive this clown car?"

Cole opened the door and slid the seat as far back as it would go. He searched for more space behind it, wishing he could take the seat completely out. He grimaced and carefully negotiated himself into the driver's seat by shifting his hips from side to side and spreading his knees apart. Feeling awkward and embarrassed, he turned the ignition and brought the Mini Cooper to life. Cole felt the sensation of more space as he lowered the rag-top on the convertible and vowed; *Katarina cannot see me get out of this!*

Cole pulled his leg inside, closed the tiny door, and drove the seemingly endless 2.8 miles to Breakers.

Chapter 13

The Undressing

In mere seconds of entering her motel room, Jadyn tossed the shoes she took off before driving away from Cole across the room. She unzipped and frantically tore off the dress as if it were covered with maggots. She struggled to break the tight hold it had on her damp skin, releasing clumps of sand once embedded within the soggy, matted, and partially torn hemline. Sandy clumps dropped and spread like little explosions onto the once clean wooden floorboards. She felt as if she'd been in a war with the dress. When it finally dropped, Jadyn slid it to the wall with a kick, sending it with finality over to the shoes, relieved knowing both would never be worn by her again!

Jadyn entered the bathroom, searching with her fingernail for the edge of the adhesive-backed stick-on bra she had worn all day; wearing it was far worse than she'd imagined. She knew this war of the bridal clothing wouldn't end until she finished peeling each off and feared they would rip her nipples off in retaliation! Once the torturous removal process was complete, she caressed her breasts, gently sliding her fingers over the red, raw, stinging skin she'd sacrificed for deeper cleavage.

Usually Jadyn didn't allow vanity to dictate her decisions, but the dress didn't leave room for a bra, and all of Kendall's other bridesmaids had fake tits.

Even though Jadyn had solid D-cups, it was the stick-on bra, or she risked looking like a boy forever in all the photographs. Seeing their well-over double-Ds made her wonder how big their cups actually were. She held onto her breasts, imagining having their larger boobs and riding Kharibia in a full gallop. They would undoubtedly be bouncing around uncontrollably like overfilled water balloons. This vision made her appreciate the breasts God gave her as she spoke to them in the mirror, "Sorry girls, I promise never to put you through this again." She questioned if it was worth the pain and stepped into the shower.

Jadyn stood with her face in the force of the hot water for a full minute. She questioned her choices as she cleansed herself of not only the grime but the guilt she felt looming and growing within her. She thought about not showing up. *Should I or shouldn't I?*

Jadyn was starving for food and starving for the touch of a man as she checked her legs and armpits and questioned her morals. She chose to shrug off those morals and brushed aside the angel to accept the little devil sitting on her shoulder whispering in her ear, "go have fun!"

Feeling renewed, Jadyn grabbed her blue jeans, held them close, inhaled her laundry detergent's lavender aroma, and slid them over her thong. Jadyn smiled as she grabbed her favorite bra and slid it over her still-sore breasts. She felt more like herself as she finished dressing in a simple white cami and slip-on tennies.

Jadyn grabbed her ring finger, rubbed it as if spinning a ring around, and unzipped her makeup bag. She pulled out mascara and added just a little to her lashes, a small amount of blush on her cheeks, and some lip gloss. With a look of worry, Jadyn tapped her cell to check the time. She closed her eyes, took a cleansing breath, and declared, "ready or not!" Jadyn fisted her cardigan, pulled the keys from her purse, slid it on her shoulder, glanced in the mirror, and headed for the door.

Chapter 14

Good Samaritan

Jadyn clicked the key fob several times, and when her SUV didn't chirp back, she unlocked the door using the key. Once inside and seated, she got a sinking feeling the battery was dead. As she turned the key and heard the unmistakable clicking sound confirming it was dead, she realized Rodolfo was right about her condition. Why else had she switched off the automatic lights feature? She banged her head against the seat and closed her eyes tight until the sound of keys tapping against her window startled her and made her jump. She turned to look at a gentleman with deep smile lines etched on his smiling face with keys in hand and gentle offering eyes. She looked at him with a questioning expression. He raised his other hand, revealing battery cables, and yelled so she could hear through the closed window, "Pop the hood, and I'll get you on your way."

"Thank you so much!" Jadyn said, smiling as she pulled the hood release lever and, having no power to lower the window, opened the door. A brief five minutes passed before the good Samaritan yelled, "Turn the key!"

The engine turned over, releasing the tension like steam from an overheated radiator. He dropped the hood and gave her a simultaneous wink and two-finger salute, a perfect send-off. Like a sergeant's orders, his approval gave her permission to meet up with Cole.

"Thank you, thank you!" Jadyn said with an exaggerated mouth so he could see her words just in case he couldn't hear her through the windshield and the sound of her now-running engine.

His thick Texan accent was perfect for a hero's response, "My pleasure; it was no trouble at all. You remind me of my granddaughter; I'd want the same for her."

With a begging expression, he held his cell phone to her window. She lowered it. In return, he asked a favor, "I'm fixin' to meet up with someone at a place called Moon Shadows. His text said *HS on PCH*. Do you have any idea what it means? I'm an old man, and you kids have this new lingo; honestly, it escapes me." He laughed at himself, "I used to think of myself as intelligent, but this smartphone puts me in my place each time I use it."

She giggled and explained, "I think he's telling you to head south on PCH. It's short for Pacific Coast Highway," She pointed to the street he drove on to enter the parking lot, right there, "It's the highway running along the ocean, also known as Highway 1."

He nodded and, open-mouth, smiled, "Ah, I see, the first highway from the Pacific Ocean, got it. Thank you, little lady. Be safe, and have a good night."

Jadyn smiled, wished him a good night, backed up, and drove north out of the parking lot, to Breakers and to Cole.

Chapter 15

Anticipation

Breaker's door was grand. It stood eight feet tall, was made of four-inch thick solid wood, and was impossible to see through. In spite of it, Jadyn kept staring, wishing it would turn to glass.

Feeling antsy and on display for longer than she could stand, Jadyn stood and walked from the lobby to the patio bar. It felt better than sitting beneath the bright lights of the lobby entry, and now she might get to see him drive into the parking lot.

After the day she had, the salty air, the sound of the waves, and the bar's music were welcome and soothing. If Cole didn't show up, Jadyn decided she would eat alone at the bar top. She reviewed the menu and kept glancing at the parking lot over the bar area's low wooden fence. Jadyn slowly sipped her club soda from a tall, moist glass with *Breakers, Home of the Best Drink Makers*, embossed on it. She thought the overabundance of lemon and lime wedges cut and set along the rim resembled seagulls perched on a railing as she squeezed and added them one by one into the jacuzzi-like bubbles.

Chapter 16

Who's Late?

From the corner of her eye, Jadyn caught a glimpse of a purple Mini Cooper entering the parking lot. She could see Cole behind the steering wheel as it rolled beneath the lights. Jadyn tightly gripped her fingers around the glass as if it could stop the soda from spewing out of her mouth and nostrils, laughing loudly!

Her mind reeled with devilish thoughts as she plotted ways to tease him about his choice of car. Jadyn, relating to how Cole spied on her earlier, was embarrassed realizing their roles had changed, and it was her turn to be a *Peeping Tina*. She wondered aloud, "Is it his girlfriend's? Or, oh, my God, his wife's?" She grabbed the last lemon and squeezed it hard, sending the stinging droplets into her eye, blurring his walk to the restaurant door.

Jadyn patted her eye with a damp cocktail napkin, hoping the mascara wouldn't smear, saying under her breath, "This isn't a date! We're not on a damn date!" She nervously rubbed her thumb over her ring finger, looking through and around the crowd of drinkers waiting their turn to order. Jadyn tried to look cool as she felt anxiety building, waiting for him to find her.

Meanwhile, Cole entered Breakers. His flip-flops slid on the sand scattered near the entrance making him feel like they were flippers and he was on ice. He shuffled his way to the wooden hostess stand where

Christina stood on tippy toes looking up at Cole even though she wore three-inch heels. As he approached, she thought, *what the F?*

Laughing, Christina asked, "Drink - much - Cole?!"

"I'm NOT drunk, and I'm NOT Cole tonight. Tonight I'm Rodolfo!" he said, waving his hand like a conductor and ending with a wink, "Table for two, Christina, or should I call you Tinkerbell."

"Don't include me in this game you're playing unless you call me Christina Aguilera."

"Okay, *Genie in a Bottle.*"

"I'd rather be a Genie in a Bottle than some fairy flying around." Tired of their exchange, Christina fake-smiled and rolled her eyes, "Meeting a blonde chick tonight?"

He felt a rapid sinking feeling in his stomach like an elevator falling fast when he realized Jadyn wasn't late; he was the one who was late, and now even later, after wasting all this time with Christina.

He looked around the lobby like a searchlight from a lighthouse, asking, "Did she bail?"

Christina motioned with her head, "No, she's sitting at the patio bar."

Chapter 17

Breakers

Cole couldn't silence the sound of Randy's voice playing like an old record, skipping and repeating in his mind as he walked outside, hoping he hadn't blown it. Scanning the bar top for her, he bobbed his head over the standing-room-only patio, finally discovering her eyes on him. Jadyn tipped her head to one side and punched the air as if to hit him. He knew she'd be giving him hell for being late and was looking forward to it. He walked up to receive his punishment, "Sorry for being late. I had a little car trouble."

She thought about telling him about her car trouble but instead came back with, "Definitely little!"

Cole smiled and pulled the bar menu from her hand and tapped her head with it, "You're relentless!"

She laughed and grabbed his wrist, "You can't arrive in a miniature car and not expect some ribbing. It's purple!"

"Your table's ready, Rodolfo!" Christina said for the second time, a bit annoyed, knowing if she could just say Cole, he'd hear her. But she played along, repeating it even louder and bumping him with her hip. "Rodolfo, we're ready to seat you now!" Finally, noticing something besides Jadyn, he responded with a wink and a big smile, "Thanks."

"I love this place," escaped Jadyn's lips as Christina

led them to their table. She walked beside Cole, breathing in the oceanic perfume of wet salt blending with the aroma of garlic and fish cooking in the kitchen. Her stomach growled as the smells reached her, reminding her she only had chocolate-covered strawberries and Mimosas for breakfast.

The sound of the waves lapping at the shore kept her grounded as they passed flickering candle flames reflecting on high-gloss resin tabletops made to look like the shoreline by an artist. She looked up at the dark wooden rafters and admired the beach artifacts, old signs, surfboards, and torn fishing nets hanging from them, as if ornaments on a Christmas tree.

They were seated at a booth with chairs facing the wall and a bench seat facing the windows. Cole sat beside Jadyn on the bench rather than on one of the chairs. He looked at her and asked with eyebrows raised, "Like the view?"

She let out a soft breath, "I beyond like it." Cole found the sound of her voice sensual and longed to know her thoughts as he unintentionally placed his hand on her thigh. She looked at his hand with eyes wide open, and he quickly removed it. Jadyn enjoyed the embarrassment on his face, and hoped he wouldn't notice her flushed face glowing in the candle's light. Jadyn thought he knew she liked his faux pas, so she turned away to look out the open windows to distract him, but he couldn't take his eyes off her. Cole was unsure if she was sunburnt or feeling hot from his touch as the candle flickered and danced on her cheek.

As Jadyn watched the moonlight shining on the water, she asked, "Doesn't the moonlight look like milk on black tar?"

He cocked his head to one side, attempting to see it as she did, "I suppose."

Her shoulders relaxed and dropped. She rested her head, focusing on the romantic setting and how comfortable she felt with him.

She was clearly lost in thought, staring at the moon, and he longed to know what was on her mind. Cole felt terrible when he struck his glass with his fork, bringing her back from wherever she was; to wherever those thoughts had taken her. With her attention now on him, he grimaced, "Sorry."

Jadyn was stirred by him and distracted by the clanging sound for only seconds. Her unkind mind rewound and flashed back to Kendall's last words to her before leaving the reception, her face laden with disappointment, "You're forgiven." Jadyn had felt disgraced, even though Kendall was so kind and understanding, more understanding than Jadyn believed she deserved. Yet she also believed she deserved this time with Cole, a time without guilt breaking in, like a mudslide destroying a mountainside. Jadyn hungered for this night, this interaction, this forbidden story unfolding, and with no hope of a future with Cole, she attempted to maintain a positive mindset. Her face tightened as she reproachfully thought, *how did I just leave the reception? Damn champagne!* She mentally argued back; *you can't blame the champagne, Jadyn.*

Jadyn's cell phone vibrated. Cole looked as the phone lit up. He watched an amazing work of art flash on the screen for a split second and then disappear, replaced by an incoming text. Cole grew curious, wondering why Jadyn seemed so upset. Respectfully, he shifted his gaze, giving her privacy to respond to the text, which asked, *Are you alive or dead?*

Jadyn felt this was more than Kendall should have to ask on her wedding day. She knew she was doing considerably better than just *alive* and felt all the worse for it. Jadyn typed back, *Alive. Pretty sure you'd like to kill me about now,* followed by a *sad face emoji.*

Kendall replied, *red-face angry emoji, Brittney's a bitch. Glad to know you're OK.* Cole busied himself by scrolling through his phone. Jadyn glanced to see he was occupied. Relieved, she wrote, *Please don't worry about me. Have a fantastic night spoiling the hubs. Winking face emoji.*

Jadyn set her phone on the table and looked at Cole. His eyes met her haunting green eyes. They held glistening tears in their corners and compelled him to softly ask, "You okay? You don't look so good."

Looking at her cell's dark screen, she replied, "Sorry, I've got a lot on my mind."

Cole, wanting to uplift her, changed the subject saying, "I noticed an amazing picture on your phone when it first lit up."

She looked at the cell in her hands. "That's my friend Kendall. She's pretty; not sure I'd call her amazing, though."

Cole rolled his eyes, "No. I was talking about the background photo."

Jadyn turned on her phone and showed it to him, "This one?"

He placed his hand beneath hers and leaned in, trying to see it behind all the apps littering her screen. "Ya, what I can see of it."

She tapped to open a folder titled artwork, saying,

"It's one of my paintings."

Cole questioned, "A painting, like on a canvas? I'd love to see it better."

She said, "Okay," and handed him her cell.

His eyes grew wide as he flipped through her album with twenty or so images and complimented her, saying, "Wow. You're really good. Call my cell, so I can have your number." He gave her a cheesy smile.

Since he had a hold of her cell, Jadyn told him to text himself using it. Cole pulled up her texting app and texted right before a man interrupted, saying with a beautiful accent, "Good evening Cole; how's everything going?"

Cole groaned and held up his *wait-a-minute* finger at Drake, a second too late. He faced her, "You know my name! Fair is fair. Now you have to tell me yours!"

She giggled and said, "Oh, do I?"

Drake cleared his throat, fishing for an answer from Cole, "Well?"

Cole shrugged and smiled sheepishly at Drake, "Things are good. You?"

Drake raised a hand and pressed Cole, "Come on, introduce me to this lovely lady."

Cole sat up tall, "Would if I could. She won't tell me her real name." Cole looked at Jadyn and playfully said, "Katarina, meet Drake."

Drake's face lit up. Smiling, he spoke in solidarity to Jadyn, "Ah, Katarina! The one who longs for her, Arturo?"

"Yes!" She said, smiling big, jabbing Cole with her elbow.

Drake teased, "Well, Katarina, you call three times, and I'll be your Arturo," followed by his deep open-mouth laugh. "Hahaha."

Jadyn thought Drake was delightful as he leaned over and spoke playfully to Cole. She loved how the silver in his beard glistened in the candlelight, contrasting beautifully with his cinnamon-brown face and eyes.

Drake spoke with one hand on the table, the other on hers. He was crowned by light shining through his straw hat's loose and tattered weave. Her smile grew when she caught a glimpse of his beer belly peeking through spaces between the buttons of his bright aloha shirt. He was a colorful character, to say the least. He slid his hand off hers, extended his arm, and pointed across the room, "Care to dance?"

She chuckled as he raised his bushy, out-of-control eyebrows and winked at her. Knowing or hoping he wasn't serious, she replied, "My dogs are barking so loud right now; another time? I love your accent. Drake, if you don't mind me asking, where are you from?"

His very-white-bright, larger-than-average teeth were nearly perfect as he chuckled with a flirtatious smirk and winked, "You'll have to guess what makes me sound so sexy. And don't you tell her, Cole! Ha-ha-ha! I believe in you, young lady." Still chuckling, "Let me know when you figure it out!"

Drake turned to leave as if dancing with a woman in his arms and stumbled when his leather sandal caught between the wooden floorboards. He spun around and said in a half-serious tone, "I really gotta get around to fix-in' this floor."

Jadyn couldn't resist asking Cole under her breath, "Does he own this place?"

"Yup, hard to believe?"

"Just a bit. So, where's he from, *Cole*?" She looked up begging and tipped her head to one side, "Hmm, Cole, nice name."

He got a serious look on his face and countered, "Thanks. Now tell me yours."

She teased, "It sounds like you should be out on the prairie or something."

Frowning, yet delighted, he said, "Done yet?"

With a silent laugh, she ended with, "Okay, okay, I'm done. Tell me where he's from."

Cole tried to hide his smile, demanding, "Not so fast. It's your turn to tell me your name."

She knew she had to fess up. Wanting badly to learn where Drake's accent was from, she surrendered, "Jadyn."

He looked at the ceiling, "What'd you say?"

She repeated, smiling with a failed attempt at looking frustrated. "Jadyn."

Cole tried to see how far he could take this, "Say it again?"

Jadyn let him have it, "Fine, be a turd. Huey!"

He lifted his glass of water and toasted with it "I like it, it suits you, and I'm so glad I no longer have to say, Kat-arina."

She raised her chin and spoke defensively, "I think Katarina's a pretty name. Now, where's Drake from?"

Cole spoke with a stern tone, "Really? He kept me guessing for days, and you want me to tell you after just a few minutes?"

She flashed him a flirty smile. "Absolutely, yes!"

Cole gave in, "France."

Jadyn gave him a victory smile. "Pushover!" then, replayed the conversation with Drake, trying to detect the French influence until their server walked up to the table.

Gothic Girl popped into Jadyn's mind as she evaluated the server. She and Jadyn appeared to be about the same age. She wore her straight, jet-black hair in a ponytail and her bright blue eyes glowed against her deeply tanned face. She was dressed in a tie-dyed t-shirt and cutoff denim shorts, and Jadyn wasn't sure what to make of her, as she spoke to them with an order book in hand.

Jadyn was pleased to hear her voice, sounding just as she'd expected. "Hi-Yah Cole, how's it?"

Her Italian New York accent and mannerisms felt like a cliche and clashed with everything about the restaurant. In a good way, she decided, as she continued watching them interact like siblings.

Cole replied playfully, "Fine, what's new with you, Bailey?"

She spouted out, "Nuttin."

He motioned to her and said, "This is Jadyn," and looking at Jadyn, he said, "Bailey's from New York."

Jadyn watched Bailey say, "Brooklyn."

She smiled and asked, "Trying to get into acting?"

Bailey shook her head, "Nah, school."

Jadyn inquired deeper, "Like it here?"

Bailey looked up for a nanosecond and smiled, "Malibu's a lot better than Tar Beach."

"I've never heard of Tar Beach."

Bailey laughed, "Course not! It's the top of buildings, 'ya know. We spread out chairs and pretend we're at the shore laying out. Classy, eh?"

Jadyn giggled and said, "Very."

Bailey slid her pen out from behind her ear, tapped

it on her order pad, and urged, "Better speed this up. What's your poison?"

A voice in Jadyn's head screamed, *no champagne!* Her need for liquid courage was stronger than wanting to feel good in the morning, so she replied, "The Breakers' Mai-Tai Mule and the shrimp Alfredo. Can you put half in a To Go container?"

Bailey asked, "Before you eat?"

Jadyn nodded, "Yes. So I can give it to the homeless man outside without my germs."

Bailey smiled and asked Cole, "Beer?"

He nodded, "The lager on tap and the Lobster Roll."

Bailey flipped her order book closed, saying "gotcha," and bounced away to the beat of the music playing, making Jadyn more aware of it.

Jadyn turned back to look at Cole looking at her. He was impressed by her kindness, "How righteous."

She looked at him confused, "Hmm?"

He tapped his finger on the table, "How you planned ahead to give him your food."

Jadyn shrugged, "It's just something I like to do."

Cole then shared, "I really liked seeing you do that because I volunteer at a local food kitchen."

She smiled demurely at him and said, "Awesome," and realized maybe, just maybe, she could fall in love again.

Chapter 18

Toes in the Sand

Cole paid the check, even though Jadyn kept insisting she pay her portion. He spoke in anticipation of hearing her say no, yet hopeful, "Wanna go to the sand?"

She quickly said, "I was hoping you'd ask. Let's bring the man my extra food first."

Cole smiled and obliged.

With her good deed done, Cole proudly led Jadyn to a thickly painted and peeling wooden staircase descending to the waiting sand. He extended his arm, "Hold on. The stairs are slippery." He guided her to the last step and onto the sand, where she removed her shoes.

Breakers' music floated out from the bar and mixed with the sound of the lightly lapping waves. Cole, filled with romantic thoughts, asked Jadyn to dance. They were shadowed by several lights positioned beneath the windows they looked out of during dinner. Equally, they enjoyed seeing the light dance on the ripples up close, magnifying how it sparkled and spread out over the otherwise dark sea. Looking at the scattered rocks around her feet, she evaluated his dance request, "Here? Now?"

Cole kicked aside the rocks, grabbed her hand, and pulled her into him for a slow dance. His height forced her to dance on her toes; she sank into the sand, and her knees suddenly buckled. She thought, *I'm going down hard!* Cole held fast to her and set her gently on the sand.

Surprised and grateful for the smooth landing, Jadyn looked at him, still standing with the lights behind him, and said, "Thanks!"

Cole said, "No problem, I know a wipeout coming when I see one. You crouched just like a wahine. What made you drop?"

She rubbed the bottom of her foot, "I found the rock you missed. Great work on the dance floor."

He thought, *here we go again,* "At least I was here to catch you. "He leaned knuckles first and sat beside her, facing the nearly resting ocean.

He hoped to convince Jadyn to see him again. Perhaps she'd like to learn to surf? "It was my instructor's maneuver."

She probed, "Instructor?"

His posture changed, and he proudly stated, "Surfing. Wanna learn?"

She answered, "Not sure. It's a question I didn't expect to answer tonight." She turned to the water considering his question, and became distracted, "I love how the lights from the restaurant and the moon shimmer on the water, like a painting set in motion." She shook and squeezed her shoulders together to chase away the chill crawling up her back. Shivering, she embraced herself and rubbed her arms.

Cole patted the sand, "Come closer; I don't bite."

Jadyn moved a little closer. Not close enough for Cole. He grabbed her sleeve, pulled her over to him, and set her in front of his chest. He wrapped his arms around her for a second and bit her neck. He laughingly said, "Should've said, I don't bite… *hard.*"

Astonished and amused, she felt all the nerves in her neck tingle and reprimanded him, "Bratdracula!" If not for his arms holding hers, she would have hit him.

He owned it, "Yup." Cole thought *I shouldn't have bit her* and said, "I've always liked the way light plays on the water, never thought of it as art in motion."

Jadyn could tell this was his attempt to change the subject and followed Cole's lead, "Everything is art to me."

He liked hearing about her artistic passion, "That's a cool perspective."

Jadyn smiled, "Working in a gallery has made me way more artsy-fartsy. Every dog I see, every bird I see, the waves, the trees, your knees, literally everything I see is a painting waiting for me to paint it." She took a deep breath, "It's a dream come true. I'm even allowed to paint while I work."

He was pleased to hear her voice sound uplifted. "Nice! Life should be a dream come true." It was thrilling to Cole when her body dropped and loosened in his grasp.

Jadyn asked, "What do you do?"

He squeezed her, "Well, I wouldn't say I am an artist, but I can play guitar, and I surf pretty good."

He attempted to understand, not having any artistic knowledge, "I feel the same way about surfing; every wave I see, every lip I see, your lips, the walls, the face, your eyes, they all tempt me."

Jadyn teased, "So, you surf and play guitar for money?"

Cole proudly said, "Actually, I surf for money and play my guitar for fun."

She turned to examine his face for sincerity.

"Seriously?"

He returned, "Seriously."

It wasn't what she considered a real job, "Interesting job."

Cole detected a slightly judgmental tone in her voice, "There's a saying, *if you do what you love, you'll never work a day in your life.* I'm a firm believer. Surfing affords me a life I love."

She looked at him questioningly, "You're brave to do something so..."

Cole defended his job choice, "Are you going to start picking on me again?"

They both laughed, feeling comfortable with one another, and kept mentioning it. Both hoped this was the beginning of something special.

Cole fought the urge to ask why she'd been crying earlier. He knew or hoped she'd eventually tell him and asked, "How long will you be in the area?" He knew she'd fallen asleep when she didn't answer and lay heavy against his chest.

After a few minutes, her body suddenly jerked, and she awoke to his face near hers. With her heart pounding and feeling hot, she grabbed his head and pulled him to her. Guilty thoughts pushed through her desire for him. Jadyn abruptly stopped kissing him, stood, and brushed the sand off her hands, saying, "I really should go." Cole didn't argue. He thought she was special and worth the wait.

They arrived at her SUV, and she turned to face him, "Thanks, Cole. I had a wonderful time once you finally got here, that is."

When no comeback joke rebounded, she asked, "I'm going to work on my tan tomorrow; wanna join me?"

He felt a rush of excitement! Maintaining the appearance of calm, he replied, "Tomorrow's the start of Surf Qualifying in Surf City, aka Huntington Beach or *the zoo*, as I like to call it. It's an hour and a half south of here; you can come if you want."

She looked at him, questioning, "Sure you want me around during your event?"

He excitedly replied, "Yes, I'm sure. You can see Huey in action! This event is like a live-action film. With the nearly full moon and King Triton's help, I expect some record-breaking swells! No doubt a speed bump or two will show up, thinking they're qualified to compete and go over the falls into shore break! When you see the Pacific show them what's what, and they surprisingly emerge from the rock-tumbling water's grip, still alive and walking, Katarina, you will know Huey, the God of surfers, is real! And why it is a much better name than Rodolfo. Just saying."

Concerned and fearing for their safety, Jadyn smiled and said, "Sounds frightening."

Reading Jadyn's fearful expression, he reassured, "Make no mistake, it can get gnarly. Huey is a good and kind God, though! He'll set you up with the perfect wave at the perfect time, and I'll be there to catch you. I'll have your back." She gave him a, *I'm not so sure about that,* look.

He continued, "The falls you'll take, causing scratches to your body and your ego, are so worth it when you catch a glassy face and ride till the soup, you'll see—it's epic!"

Jadyn grew concerned, "You're not doing a good job selling me on this."

He tempted her, "I'm confident, with your obstinate

and competitive nature, that I can turn you into a dudette between sets. If you let me."

Jadyn could see his excitement rising like the waves she pictured crashing over her and bargained, "I don't know, it seems like a bad time to learn."

He knew if he challenged her ego, she would stop with the excuses. Cole said, "No pressure. I'll bring an extra board and suit just in case you decide to be brave."

Jadyn's groggy and aching head made her long for sleep. "Have to think about surfing; for sure, I'll be there to tan." She liked imagining Cole, in the zone, with Triton and Huey as angels, riding the waves with him. It all sounded poetic. After hearing him speak passionately, she understood how surfers could sit for seemingly endless hours just for a few good rides.

He smiled at her as she gazed through and past him at the ocean and began thinking of other ways to convince her to learn as she said, "Thanks."

He asked her, "For?" fishing for details.

"For dinner and drinks and for saving my life! Happy?"

"Yes. And you'll thank me for teaching you to ride a wave tomorrow."

She said, "We'll see," pushing him back with both hands against his firm, muscular chest and sliding into her seat. She closed the door, cracked her window, and smiled big at him.

He smiled back, placed his open palm against her partially open window for a moment, stepped back, and said, "See you tomorrow, Katarina!"

Jadyn yelled, "Call me! Be my alarm clock, Huey!" She waved with her free hand out the window and drove away.

He watched until she faded into the distance between them, with a dreamy-eyed expression he knew other men would find amusing, so he shook it off before turning back to the restaurant, where Drake stood watching from the bar. He motioned with his hand for Cole to come back inside, and with a quick eye roll and sarcastic smile, he went back inside for some anticipated ribbing.

Chapter 19

Sinker & Shots

Instead of the expected joking, Drake spoke in a fatherly tone, "Step into my office."

Despite the slamming door, Drake's dog, Sinker, didn't stir when they entered his office. Sinker was primarily gray and lay beneath Drake's desk with his nose extended towards Cole's feet. He could feel Sinker's warm breath against his skin as he looked at pictures of him on the wall. Sinker was once a magnificent shiny black lab with a white heart-shaped patch of fur on his chest. At some point in his life, he was blinded in one eye by a fishhook that found its way to his face, and he either lost most of his hearing or, most likely, has decided he's too old to be bothered.

Just as Drake was less than neat in his appearance, his office was littered with piles of paperwork and dirty plates from long-gone late-night meals. Drake removed a precariously placed stack of papers from his brown leather chair and looked around for a safe place to set it. He carefully placed it atop a rickety table just left of the slightly opened window. Cole sat in the chair, and they both watched in anticipation of the stacks' inevitable descent to the floor. When the stack collapsed, they both burst out in laughter, and Drake resounded, "To hell with them!"

Drake pulled moist-stringy cherry tobacco from a pouch and packed it into his hand-carved walnut pipe.

He puffed to light it and set it down, releasing a slow-moving ghostly trail of smoke streaming up like bubbles leaking from a dolphin's blowhole.

Drake looked at Cole with a parental gaze. He leaned back in his oversized black leather chair, which showed signs of multiple repairs using black duct tape. Many of the failed repairs had fallen loose and were now dangling, their sticky edges heavily bearded with an abundant amount of Sinker's hair. Drake put his feet on his old dog's back and said, "So, this girl's different, isn't she? If you want to learn from an old man who has had his share of relationships, I'm here for you."

Cole chuckled as he spouted out, "Yeah, right!" Cole knew Drake had married his one true love, Alannah. Photos of the two of them hung on his office wall and were also scattered throughout the restaurant, a testament to the love they shared over the years, images frozen in time.

Drake laughed and said, "Alright, you tell me all about your Katarina."

Cole said, "Turns out her name's Jadyn." He tossed the ball back to Drake, "How about you tell me what made your marriage so strong and long-lasting, old man."

Drake appeared to be transported to a different time and place as he recounted their whirlwind romance in the early sixties. "It was the time of free love and free expression. The first time I caught a glimpse of her on the grassy hill overlooking the ocean with the sunset shining all around her, it made her sparkle and glow with an iridescent luminescence. I couldn't look away. I suppose it was what *some* would call her aura; to me, Alannah was a guiding light shining from my personal lighthouse calling me home. Her top and skirt screamed hippie chick to me. When I saw the twinkle in her eyes, I was officially hooked. I decided if she'd have me, I'd remain loyal, steadfast, faithful, and committed to ensuring she knew every day she was loved.

Gathering his thoughts, Drake shifted in his chair, puffed his pipe, and after looking at Cole, continued speaking in a melancholy-sounding voice. "Thirty-two years of happiness, beautiful days, play, stormy nights, crankiness, sadness, and loss." He shook his head, briefly smiled, and continued, "Given the chance, I'd do it all over again. She was artistic and graceful. Even though she described herself as painfully shy, she stood out everywhere we went. I loved the experience of walking into a crowded room with her and how everyone seemed captured by my beautiful Alannah, especially animals and children. I suppose it's why God didn't give us the gift of children; Alannah was mother to all children."

A slow-moving tear released from Drake's eye and found its way to his chin, disappearing within his wiry beard, "Her auburn wavy hair was stunning and fell the full length of her back."

He cleared his throat and leaned forward with elbows on his desk to ensure he had Cole's attention. Drake braced himself for an emotional release. Having never told his story before, he had no idea how turbulent it would be to share it.

He sucked on his pipe, drawing in the sweet-smelling tobacco, and hesitantly said, "The unconditional love we shared intensified and grew stronger over the years. It was a strong love!" Reigning in his emotions, Drake spoke with labored and withdrawn words, "So strong, but not strong enough to win the fight against the insidious, cancerous invasion promising to steal the vibrant sparkle from her eyes. Damn chemo!"

Drake slammed his large open palm on the desk so hard it nearly scared the fur off Sinker and Cole off his chair! They heard Sinker's toenails scraping the wooden floor to gain traction for his escape. It sounded like a cartoon character, making them both laugh. The old dog exploded from beneath Drake's desk like a cannonball. He jumped headfirst through the doggie door and ran like hell.

Drake resounded, "Oh, my God! We need to do shots for Sinker! He's got life in him, after all!"

Drake pulled out a full bottle of Jack Daniels, slammed it on the desk with one hand, and clenched a couple of shot glasses with the other. The glasses clinked with the sound of billiard balls, announcing the presence of happy drinkers. He poured like a long-time bartender, filling the shot glasses to their brim, and slid Cole's to him without spilling a single drop!

Cole, impressed and intimidated, stated, "I'm more of a microbrew kinda guy."

Drake looked disappointed and asked, "Beer? Cole, I think of you as *mon fils*, my son, and I'm going to give you some fatherly advice. Beer is not a man's drink. Tonight you're a man. Tonight you learn why Sinatra asked to be buried with a bottle of Jack!" He raised his glass, laughed his baritone laugh, and shouted, "*a votre santé au vieux chien*... cheers to the old dog! Do you suppose he's been pretending to be blind and deaf all these years?"

In wonderment, Cole said, "He certainly had no

trouble finding his way out his doggie door."

Drake looked at his flapping door, "Wonder what else he's keeping from me. Whatcha think he does when I am not around?"

After their toast, Drake set the glass on the desk, lowered his head, and softly said, "It's been nine years since I enjoyed a toast with my sweet Alannah."

Drake pointed to a photo of Alannah standing on the shore, with the sunrise filtering through her windblown hair, and said, "The Chemo took more than her hair; it also took her strength and vigor. She lost much of her *joie de vivre*. Ahh, my Alannah, such a fighter. She didn't go hide. She replaced her fiery mane with colorful silk scarves. Which she wore proudly and spread happiness everywhere she went."

In support, Cole placed his hand on Drake's.

Without looking up, Drake continued, "And when she dwindled away to half her body weight, I still could only see my sweetheart, *mon seul vrai amour*, my one true love."

Drake wiped his eyes with his knuckle, and Cole fought his tears from forming. "True love's strength is why I didn't flip my boat and deliberately die with her. Between the two of us, we caught over thirty fish that day. We were talking about how good our dinner would be. My love rested on the boat's bow, humming her favorite song; her porcelain white skin glowed in the sunlight until her melodic serenade simply stopped. In an instant, I knew she'd crossed over, and my one true love was with the angels. I cried so loud the heavens could surely hear me.

I turned off the engine, dropped anchor, and held her in my arms until the sun sank below the horizon.

I begged God for the strength to bring her to shore. I contemplated tying our bodies together with the anchor's weight pulling us under to be forever joined at the bottom of the sea. I came damn close, might have gone through with it, but she had told me to live a long life for her; I couldn't disappoint my Alannah. I navigated my boat back to shore, trying to imagine my life without her."

He sucked in air to hold back tears, "And now her lifeless image is chiseled into my mind, a carved maidenhead, her spirit forever leading my voyages."

Cole gently said, "How horrible."

Drake recognized sympathy in Cole's eyes and wanted him to know the sadness they shared, in the end, was a small price to pay for years of love. "Love is a powerful drug. Once you take it in, it never leaves your system. Even if you intentionally walk away from someone you love, when you believe all love is gone, some will forever linger within your soul. I believe love can't die, not true love anyway."

He stood up fast and said, "Sorry. My point is, it only took a moment to know Alannah was to be my bride, and the look on your face tonight is the same look I had on my face the day she and I met." Drake leaned back in his chair and coaxed Cole for his thoughts about Jadyn, "One good sharing deserves another; your turn."

Cole contemplated his thoughts, envisioned the little time they'd spent together, and told him, "Jadyn is beautiful, artistic, smart, and funny, but something is bothering her. I have a bad feeling. I don't think we'll end up like you and Alannah."

Drake quickly said, "Aren't you gonna keep seeing her? It's all over your face. You're falling if you haven't already fallen for this girl."

Attempting to convince Drake and himself he was in control and not vulnerable, that he would take it just fine if she drove out of his life forever, he replied, "We've been on one date! I haven't fallen for her yet."

Cole braced himself for more innuendo and counsel when Drake got a 9 1 1 text from his bartender, abruptly ending their conversation.

Sinker heard Drake's footsteps and flew back inside. He nearly knocked Cole over on his way to his side.

Cole enjoyed seeing Sinker's unevenly swaying hips and wagging tail heading to Drake. Sinker's smiling face looking up and Drake's gentle palm patting his head as they walked to the bar warmed his heart. He was spared further questions for now but knew Drake would push the topic another day.

Cole stopped in the lobby to say goodbye to Christina and Bailey, then hopped into Malika's Mini Cooper and drove home, recalling his evening with Jadyn and Drake's words of wisdom.

Chapter 20

Morning After Call

J ust as Jadyn's dream was getting really good, the planets and stars were still visible in the inky night sky, and the sun wasn't even close to crossing the horizon. Too early for it or Jadyn to rise, she awoke to the sound of crickets chirping, or so she thought. Analyzing the sound was like opening a birdcage, freeing her dream, sending it back into the vastness of her subconscious to join dreams that previously escaped during other unexpected awakenings.

She tried to catch these elusive dreams and bring them into her conscious mind, like butterflies into a net. But they flutter away, to later tease her in flashes or as fragmented memories like words written on a whiteboard sporadically erased. There were small slices, just slivers of broken dreams created during her mind's nightly escape from reality, lost, yet not completely forgotten, like a past life memory haunting her.

With blurry dry-eyed vision from the previous day spent drinking, crying, and not sleeping well, she repeatedly blinked until the moisture she mined by doing this cleared her vision. Ultimately, the cobwebs clouding her mind receded, and Jadyn realized the chirping crickets as the sound of an incoming text. Her heart pounded hard, she was short of breath, and her chest was tight as her mind played different scenarios like a movie preview, reminding Jadyn of what awaited her at home.

A text before daylight was never good news. It always left her feeling destroyed, all joy obliterated, but this text was from Cole.

Wakey, wakey, Katarina! Time to break free from the norm with Huey! Ready?

With her humor and sarcasm left on her pillow, alongside her lost dream, she replied, *what time is it?*

He picked up on her not-so-subtle and definitely unexcited response and replied, *Change your mind?*

Jadyn spoke with a dry-scratchy voice as she also typed, *"Bout?"*

After reading her short reply, Cole decided a call would be best; he needed to hear her voice. When the phone's startling vibration made her jump, she answered, laughing. Cole was relieved to hear her laugh, and Jadyn was relieved she no longer had to focus on the screen with her messed-up morning eyes. Jadyn pretended she was happy he woke her and mumbled, "Hey, early-bird, catch the worm?"

He fished for her state of mind, "Depends on if you changed your mind about the qualifying event, have you?"

She drank some water, hoping to rinse away the pounding in her head, and offered, "I believe I have a hangover. Text me the address, and I'll come later. It's all day, right?"

Cole said with a light tone, "Yeah, I didn't figure you'd want to stay all day, but last night you asked me to call you in the morning."

"It's 4:30! If I knew, it would be o-dark thirty," she replied, her voice tapering off. She didn't want to admit how crappy she felt about her actions the day before, her excessive drinking, or her mixed feelings about going back home.

Cole checked the time and stood up, saying, "OK. I'll be ready for my student to arrive at around one o'clock. I'll only have one more run after you arrive. Plenty of time to get you on deck." He waited for her reaction, wondering if she'd fallen asleep or was ignoring him, and questioned, "Hello?"

Jadyn finally broke her silence after inhaling an entire bottle of water without breathing. As if diving deep, holding her breath, and finally breaching the water's surface, she gasped for much-needed air, inhaling loudly, and answered, "Not sure about me getting on a board, but I'll bring a book and a ton of water and see you then. Break a leg!"

"K, I'll text you the address and call you around 12:30 to navigate you to my towel. Don't forget sunscreen. I know it's only May, but you, pale-one, will burn."

Absent of humor and with a forced sleepy-sounding voice, she said, "Going back to sleep, see you later, Huey."

Jadyn wanted to feel happy and wanted to allow herself to feel excited. Still, she didn't feel deserving of either and desperately needed more sleep.

Chapter 21

Mandala throws

When Jadyn's alarm sounded, she'd already been in the bathroom getting ready and singing along with the song intended to wake her. She felt refreshed and excited after a nice chat with Kendall before she and Levi caught their honeymoon flight to Bora Bora. When she awoke to the sound of seagulls barking at one another on the roof, Jadyn made a conscious decision to be one hundred percent present in the day by taking time for yoga and her morning meditation before joining Cole.

Jadyn drove along the coast in search of coffee and a semi-private stretch of beach and noticed a merchant selling vibrant-colored and very artistic circular mandala throws. She and her small son were dressed in tie-dyed shirts and surrounded by customers.

The soft billowy throws hung on a line, waving like flags, beckoning her to buy one. As she pulled into the driveway, she felt it was serendipitous to see the merchant in the parking lot adjacent to the coffee shop.

Jadyn took her place in the drive-thru lane, thrilled and grinning to have this pleasurable, colorful view for the duration of her time spent in the lengthy line of cars. Her rear-view mirror reflected a woman's beleaguered face etched with melancholy and sorrow. This lone woman sat with her scarf-covered silver hair and lace-gloved hands gripping the steering wheel.

She intently focused on the distance between Jadyn's bumper and her cherry red convertible, a 1957 Buick Roadmaster. It was in pristine condition, and Jadyn imagined she must treasure it and the memories it held for her.

Finally, her turn at the window, a young man wearing a broad smile and Xavier on his name tag stuck his hand out for payment. His gracious and energetic demeanor made the already beautiful morning even more beautiful. Jadyn felt overwhelming gratitude, "I'd like to pay it forward for the lady behind me."

Xavier's eyes shined with appreciation, and his smile stretched even wider, "How kind of you! Yes! I *can* help you with that, and I will! Can't wait to see her face when she finds out! Thanks for making my day!"

She inserted the coffee into her cupholder and matched his enthusiasm, saying, "No. Thank you for making my day!"

Jadyn drove away, watching Xavier's face brighten even more when Olivia pulled up to the window. He declared, "The lady that just drove out paid for your order! Isn't that great?!"

Olivia looked at him in astonishment and, with a pleased smile, said, "Now, isn't that sweet of her. I would have loved to thank her personally."

He agreed, "Yes, ma'am, she was very kind. How's Mr. Charlie doing?"

Her eyes lowered, and her face dropped slightly, "My Charlie isn't doing well. He thinks I'm a delivery woman when I bring him his Sunday cup of Joe. I keep hoping he'll wake up, but the doctor doesn't hold much hope."

Xavier swept aside a tear on his cheek as he turned his head to hide his sadness. "I sure do miss seeing him

76

sitting beside you in this beautiful buggy of yours."

"I still tell him you said hi, anything to jog his memory. Right?"

Unsure what to say, he just smiled and handed her the tray with the cups, sugars, and creamer packs.

Olivia said, "Hey! You know what? I feel so much better after discovering she'd bought my coffee; I want to get in on this and buy the young man behind me his coffee if that's okay with you?"

Xavier blinked hard and smiled wide, "Sure thing, you sweet dear lady."

She smiled, "you are such a delightful young man."

He winked at her and said, "You're going to make me blush. Here's your credit card, and I will tell him it brought you joy to pay it forward and buy his latte today. See you next Sunday for our weekly date."

Jadyn parked. With coffee in hand, she exited her vehicle and sauntered to the outdoor shop. She slowly strolled, skimming with the fingertips of her free hand over the soft flowy fibers and made her decision. She selected and bought one infused with intense shades of red, yellow, and rich deep royal blue.

With her new throw beside her, she drove to a small stretch of beach. She parked on the roadside, locked her SUV, and walked toward the water with it rolled up and tucked beneath her armpit. Choosing a smooth section of sand where she felt safe, she saw only a woman reading a book nearby.

A gentle coastal breeze caught Jadyn's ethereal throw as she lifted it, spreading it out on the sand.

The colorful throw looked like a giant Macaw in flight to onlookers! Its fresh, mystical, outstretched appearance on the beach increased the level of spirituality vibrating within her. Jadyn positioned herself on the desirable, silky-smooth surface, ideal for practicing yoga and meditation, her own magic carpet, and blissfully executed both. With rhythmic echoes of the waves to focus on, Jadyn effortlessly reached the liquid violet deep in her mind's eye.

Jadyn sat cross-legged, with the view pouring into her open eyes, grateful her morning ritual was complete. Contented, centered, and staring at the waves. She was thinking ahead, picturing the zoo, and imagining Cole teaching her to surf. Excited and nervous, she rolled up her throw, gathered her nerves, and headed to her SUV.

Chapter 22

The Lesson

On Sunday, traffic isn't bad on PCH; it's more than a road to Jadyn, it's a trip down memory lane. She and Kendall shared many weekend getaways driving north, from Malibu to Santa Barbara, Monterey, or quaint Carmel. While the Pacific coastline whizzed by, consistent yet ever-changing, the two shared their innermost private thoughts, wishes, and dreams, unaware of the bond it created, forever tying them to one another and to the Pacific.

The artery-like highway moved as if in time with the blood flowing within Jadyn's veins, moving in ebbs and flows, as the pulsating ocean remained locked over her right shoulder, her view of its vast beauty broken only by million-dollar homes and businesses.

Jadyn drove south to Huntington Beach. Her SUV was like a giant cello, the open windows, the F-holes, releasing their haunting sound, turned up loud enough for everyone to hear it playing. Jadyn's emotions fluctuated as she swayed, deeply connected to the notes. She moved her free arm conducting the songs, dramatically swinging her imaginary baton. The waves were her performers; the gulls, sandpipers, and people enjoying the beach were her audience, and the Pacific her amphitheater.

Jadyn allowed herself to be pulled into the rich, deeply moving tones only a cello makes. She switched from an imaginary conductor to a cellist. Fingertips moving an imaginary bow, arm rotating, wrist as if a hinge, left, right, fast, slow, sliding the hairs over and across the vibrating strings. The unique, cry-like sound pulled out dark emotions deep within her, so she changed playlists.

When the sound of Sheryl Crow singing, All I Wanna Do, replaced the cello music, she found it funny and laughed. Jadyn joined in and sang the lyrics. "All I wanna do." Her cell phone rang, and still singing, "is have some fun," she answered.

Cole's excited voice flooded in, "So you wanna have some fun, do ya?"

Jadyn giggled with embarrassment, "Oh no, you heard me?"

He laughed with her, "Any idea when you'll get here?"

She smiled big, "I just entered the parking lot where you told me to park, and it looks like I'm getting lucky! Someone's actually pulling out of a spot close to the sand! You weren't kidding about it being a zoo!"

Cole contemplated how Jadyn proved him wrong again. His presumption about women always being late was no longer valid. He liked her dependable nature, smiled, and readied himself to navigate her from the parking space to his towel.

Jadyn stepped onto the soft, white Huntington Beach sand, much whiter and much softer than the rocky sand of Malibu. She slid off her sandals and walked blindly toward him. Cole quickly spotted Jadyn in the crowd, wearing a teal-colored, cotton summer dress unbuttoned up to her thighs. The spaghetti strap bodice exposed the straps of her bikini tied behind her neck. She struggled to walk with her oversized, impregnated beach bag flung over her shoulder. It kept rolling across her back from side to side, making her wobble side to side, reminding him of how she staggered in the sand the night before. He enjoyed watching her from afar, unaware his voyeuristic behavior made him once again a Peeping Tom.

Jadyn grew too close for him to hide from her any longer, so he tossed his phone onto the towel and grabbed a wetsuit he had lain beside him. The deflated suit looked like a dead seal as he waved it over his head long enough for her to see him. Overly excited, Cole awkwardly offered it to her without even a customary greeting or a simple hello.

Jadyn stood facing him, looked at her overflowing arms, then back at him, "Hello? See my hands? Not to mention, I just got here."

Jadyn faked annoyance to hide her arousal at seeing his glistening skin exposed by his unzipped, damp wetsuit. She stared through her dark sunglasses at the water droplets clinging to his chest hairs like dew drops hanging from grass the morning after rain.

Cole's also concealed eyes danced all over her form, making him not only feel but actually act stupidly. He finally helped her, "Sorry. Just pumped to see you surf."

Pleased to see him act off-balance for once, Jadyn brushed sand off the towel he provided and settled on it. On one knee, Cole flipped open his red and white plastic ice chest and offered, "I brought fruit, veggies, bottles of water, beer, Kombucha, and granola bars." He reached into the melting ice, stirred up the floating bottles, and pulled out a Ginger Kombucha for her.

Jadyn likened the water on him to the condensation

on the bottle's crimson-colored glass and accepted it, secretly hoping it would help settle her hung-over stomach. She removed her sunglasses with the other hand and said, "Thanks," hoping he would remove his. She desperately wanted to see his eyes in full sun.

Cole didn't take his glasses off. Instead, he explained, "You'll sunburn those pretty eyes if you don't keep your glasses on. You'll have to leave them behind once you're in the water." She loved how considerate he sounded; it's been a long time since anyone took care of her.

They sat side-by-side, watching participants gliding along the waves, hiding their awkwardness behind dark sunglasses. His bouncing leg advertised his patience waned, so she screwed her drink closed, plopped it back into the icy water, and announced, "Okay, I just sat over an hour getting here. I'm ready."

Cole watched as she pulled off her dress and tried to step into the wetsuit. She imagined this is how a squid wrapped around her would feel - a giant sucking tentacle sticking to her clean, dry skin! Sliding into it was simply impossible. She felt ridiculous, wiggling and squirming in front of him like a child trying to avoid being kissed by an overly affectionate relative.

Jadyn, feeling on display, blushed and turned her back towards Cole as if he couldn't see her. But, of course, he could and enjoyed watching every second of her awkwardness, if for no other reason than to have ammunition to tease her with later. She knew all too well his plan as she tried to reach the tab on the end of the zipper. A memory flashed in his mind of her trying to remove her shoe, and he decided this was way better than her clumsy display from last night! He imagined the ribbing he'd give her to defend himself from the machine gun discharge of words constantly shooting from her mouth.

Cole was clearly proud of the words he was about to release as he flashed her a long adorable, dramatic-cheeky smile, telegraphing a significant teasing was headed her way, "By the way, it's easier to get into a wetsuit—wet."

Jadyn pushed out her hip, gave him an annoyed look, and said, "Gee, thanks! By the way, why do you have a women's wetsuit?"

He playfully replied, "Jealous?"

Jadyn spoke with a firm yet mumbling speech, "Me? Never," as she struggled to zip it closed. "Seems stupid to put the zipper on the back."

He finished zipping it for her and, with humor still reflected in his tone, "It's better than *zip-ripped skin* from belly-down paddling." Jadyn imagined the pain and slid her hand over her belly, relieved she didn't have to learn the hard way.

Cole responded, "This is my sister's wettie. She left it inside her Mini Coop. I figure she owes me; she's helping her friend move with my truck. I had to borrow my buddy's truck to get the boards here."

Jadyn wiggled and squirmed in the tight pantyhose feeling suit and growled in frustration holding her hair, "Great! My hair's stuck in it!"

He laughed, saying, "Hang on, drama queen!" Cole unzipped it an inch and helped pull the hair from the suit's grip.

Jadyn felt the need to know more about his sister. After all, this is not a simple t-shirt. It felt more like a lingerie borrow, so she said, "I think I should at least know your sister's name."

She felt Cole's breath enter her ear, "Malika. Born in Hawaii, hence, the Hawaiian name my parents gave her. I was born here on the mainland. They named me after my great-uncle on my father's side. My mom loved the name. Said it sounded strong."

Jadyn grabbed Cole's bicep, grinned, and squeezed it, "I agree. Cole's a strong name. It fits you."

He flirted, "As my sister's suit suits you." He felt a rise of desire build, and he changed the subject, "Ready to get on deck, Barney?"

She creased her forehead and asked, "Barney?"

Cole smiled with his hand holding onto the upright surfboard. "Barney is what we experienced surfers call a Newb, you know, new surfers." His smile widened, and he pointed at her, "what you are."

She examined the board's waxy-yellow surface and asked, "am I supposed to carry it on my own with no help?"

Cole's playful yet judgy expression challenged Jadyn's pride. "All the wahine's carry their own boards." Looking forward to watching her struggle, Cole demonstrated. "It's a no-brainer, just put both hands on it, swing it around, and tuck it under like this."

His smile annoyed Jadyn. She challenged him, "I see, I get it." She decided not to drop the board under any circumstance. Determined to prove herself capable, even though clearly a newb to anyone watching, she successfully lifted the board and started to walk, impressing Cole. He congratulated her, "Good job! Follow me."

They carried the boards toward the water's edge and set them on the sand. Cole gave her more instruction and finally strapped the board's leash to her ankle, saying, "The only way to learn is to do it! Copy what I do. The toughest part is getting past the waves."

She listened and watched the surfers, bellies to the board, popping right over the tops of waves, and announced, "Looks easy to me."

Jadyn honestly believed this till a surfer barrel-rolled his board! He submerged himself upside-down, in and beneath the wave's lip, rolled back over, and magically appeared on the other side like a sea otter reemerging from the ocean with an oyster, chillin' and grinning! Her mouth dropped in surprise. Jadyn faced her adversary, admiring the surfer's fluid movement, longing to reach his skill level, pondering the board-mounting process. Cole laughed and yelled, "Easy! Ha-ha! I wouldn't expect you to say anything else!"

The sound of waves crashing and music blasting from huge speakers at a high-level party on the sand made teaching Jadyn a bigger challenge than he anticipated. "Remember! Go straight into the wave! Don't let it flip you like a pancake! If you do, the board will break your head open like a coconut! Catch you on the other side!"

She felt like her dog ran away from her as he downward dogged onto the board and stroked the water with only his arms until he and his surfboard crested the wave. He disappeared on the other side. She thought it looked like lovemaking when Cole raised his chest up for an instant and back to the board again. Great! Sex now clouded her mind. He sat straddling his board beyond the waves, facing her, waving her on, and watching her every move.

Fear rapidly rose in her chest! She strained to hear

him as he sat on his board, watching and talking to her. His mouth moved, but she couldn't hear any audible instructions. Waves as undulating walls towering and repeating made Jadyn consider texting Kendall, letting her know where to find her in case this would be the last thing she ever did. She clenched her teeth with an, I'm freezing smile, faking bravery, and Cole pushed, "Dudette, don't chicken out on me!"

Jadyn's first attempt to crest a wave left her feeling ridiculous. It pushed her sideways through the soup and spat her back onto the light cream-colored sand. Her wet, dripping, sandy, clumped hair and sandy seal-like black body advertised her ineptness. She blamed Cole for her crash. Jadyn couldn't blame him for the scorched skin she'd suffer later, yelling in defiance, "If you weren't watching, I'd have nailed it!"

He laughed loudly, arguing, "If I didn't watch, you'd have no witness, no one to catch you!"

Jadyn, thrilled to make it over the next wave, smiled big at Cole as he stroked the water over to her and took hold of her board. He knew she wanted to be congratulated, so he asked, "Feels good, doesn't it?"

With a cocky look and a head bob, Jadyn acted just as Cole suspected she would, saying, "I knew I'd get it! Now for the fun part!"

He stopped her from starting to paddle, "Whoa! Slow down, Barney! You first need to get up with the water below the board." After making her rise from belly to foot a few times, he asked, "Ready?"

Jadyn nodded, "Of course I am."

Shaking his head at her pride, still hoping she'd succeed, Cole let go of her board, "Do what I do, newb!"

With no apparent effort, Cole abruptly spun his

board around, paddled off, stood, and caught the wave. His sequence was successful, performed while laughing and an added pretentious wave goodbye. She knew he couldn't hear her yell, "Show off!" His smooth moves reminded her of how he rode away on his bike the evening they met.

Jadyn's eyes widened, and her heart pounded when she realized he'd left her to fend for herself. Straddling the board with panicky fearful thoughts racing, Jadyn knew she couldn't sink into the fear. She had to do something! After all, the ocean's pulsating movement couldn't be paused by remote control. This is real! This is do-or-die time! She couldn't fail; Cole's teasing would be torturous if she couldn't do this!

Her thoughts were like an angel and devil arguing, telling her to be brave and ride the next good-feeling wave or quit before starting, challenging her courage. She could use the surfboard like a lame boogie board, the surfer's walk of shame, an unacceptable outcome! Jadyn had to succeed and spoke encouragingly to herself, "I can do this! I can do this!" And on the third, "I can do this!" Jadyn got up screaming in celebration, woohoo!

To Cole's delight, Jadyn rode the wave with her butt sticking out further than it should've. She knew she looked silly, especially when she fell bum-first into the soup. He ran over and stood above her. Jadyn declared, "Told you I'd be good at this."

Dying to tease with a big-butt comment, he instead congratulated her, "Great first ride!"

She smiled proudly before bragging, "Try staying on a wild pony with no saddle. It's a lot harder than riding this surfboard."

Their playful banter continued, and after many humbling spills following her first ride, they paddled to shore.

She finally admitted learning to surf had been challenging, "You're a great teacher Huey. Best surfer out here today; I'm impressed. I'll never look at surfing the same again. Thanks for forcing me to learn."

With a cocky smile, he pushed his chest up and out, "Thanks for noticing! Gotta go!" He spun around and ran up the beach to the much bigger waves, where cameras sat, ready to film his final qualifying run. Jadyn wondered how he knew it was time for his turn, not seeing a watch on him or any visible clock.

She stood on her towel, bouncing to see over the crowd as Cole rode through, up and out of the tube. He danced with the wave, zigzagging along the lip, reminding her of their sandy dance. He finished with a confident, classic, hang-ten finish, arms by his side, surefooted and deserving of the loud resounding applause! Cole stepped off his board, shook his head, releasing the trapped water like a dog after a bath, ran through the soup, and disappeared into the crowd of spectators. His skills made Jadyn's skin hot and her face flush. Impressed and proud to be seen with him, yet questioning whether or not she should spend any more time with him. Jadyn made her decision.

Cole sprinted to her, his wetsuit unfastened, its arms flapping, and surfboard tucked under his arm, making it appear like it weighed less than a feather. His strength was impressive and visible, with his suit pulled open like a window revealing his six-pack all the way to his tan, tight lower belly. He smiled exuberantly and yelled, "Time to celebrate!"

At the sight of him, Jadyn expelled a large gasp and accepted she couldn't resist him. She asked, knowing the answer, "I take it you qualified?"

Chapter 23

Seagulls & Sandpipers

Cole had a look of urgency on his salt-laced face as he followed Jadyn to Malibu. Just as the sun kissed the welcoming Pacific and cast shades of orange onto the windows of lucky homeowners blessed with this nightly show when gulls join sandpipers and sunset lovers to witness the close of another day. Cole followed Jadyn into her motel parking lot, and they hurriedly ran across PCH so they could be part of this last sunset before Jadyn returned home to Sedona. Cole grabbed a towel and her hand before crossing through the traffic with excitement and a melancholy feeling building in his gut.

God did not disappoint. Clouds skimmed the horizon, filtering a rainbow of liquid light transformed with each passing minute of the sun's descent. The scene filled their hearts with more than they had already shared as they sat in silence. Their combined silent thoughts were broken only by the waves and their sighs of appreciation for what may be their last sunset together.

Darkness loomed as they held hands while walking back to her motel. They said a short goodbye before separating to get ready for their last dinner. For Cole, this was an actual date, not just two strangers sharing a meal. He was hopeful as he drove Randy's borrowed truck, the boards, and a six-pack to him.

In contrast, Jadyn was full of unsettled emotions stirring in her belly like a storm at sea, constantly pushing and pulling at her soul. Uncertainty of the moment troubled her. There was no way to predict the outcome of this new relationship. Her conflicted feelings for Cole made breathing difficult as she removed her wedding ring from the bedside drawer, only to quickly return it to its hidden box. She should have been wearing it when they met. She wasn't trying to hide it from him; it was her fear of losing the ring. The ring had fit perfectly a short time ago but now swirled around like a necklace on her thinner-than-ever finger. Jadyn knew how bad she would look to Cole if she told him about the ring right now. She also knew the time would come when she had to tell him.

Chapter 24

Wine to Dine

His knock was soft, just a couple taps with his knuckles, but it was still a shock, so she quickly closed the drawer, got up, and opened the door to greet him. "Almost ready," she said as she slid on her sandals and grabbed her cardigan. With his hand at the small of her back, he led her to the Mini Cooper and opened the door for her.

He faced her before closing the door and said, "You look nice."

She smiled and watched him walk in front of and around the car. Cole paused to adjust his long legs before he entered the tiny car. Butterflies swirled inside her nervous and cavernous stomach as Jadyn offered, "You barely fit in this car. Would you rather drive my SUV?"

"As long as you're comfortable, I'm fine. Besides, there's no wiggle room for you to wiggle away from me. We need to stop and grab a bottle of wine on the way; they don't have a liquor license."

He said with a wink, "We need to stop and grab a bottle of wine on the way; they don't have a liquor license."

She smiled back, "I don't know much about wine, so whichever one you pick is fine with me."

When they arrived at the market, all the parking spaces were occupied, so he parked out front, leaving Jadyn in the car, and ran inside. She was relieved no one gave her a dirty look as she waited.

As soon as he swung his door open, she said with surprise, "Wow, you were fast."

He enjoyed her accolade and looked as if he'd won a prize as he replied in confirmation, "Longer legs prevail."

Chapter 25

Gull's Nest

The Gull's Nest sandy-dirt parking area had a single spot remaining. Cole parked beneath the canopy of trees, vines, and flowers covering it. Jadyn excitedly peeked through slits between the wooden fence slats and caught a glimpse of firepits and twinkle lights.

Beyond the fence, smokey streams rose from smoldering embers into and through the trees until they dissolved into the dark sky.

Cole explained The Gull's Nest to Jadyn, "This is a favorite spot for locals to hide away from tourists spilling into the coastal region each day. This peaceful, cozy fifteen-table eatery offers entirely casual, patio-style outdoor seating. With no roof over the tables, they offer only take-out if it rains."

"Thank you for telling me." Jadyn looked around, analyzing the randomness of The Gull's Nest, and especially enjoyed its shimmering twinkle lights dripping from the Oak trees. The lights were draped over the tables and across the creek, illuminating the water and reminding Jadyn of tinsel on a Christmas tree.

After enduring hours of loud music at the surf tryouts, she welcomed the soothing romantic glow of the lights and the soft trickling sound of the stream running alongside the dining area. This unusual atmosphere complimented the soft music they had streaming through a single Bluetooth speaker set on the fence.

Cole held her hand and led Jadyn to the picnic table he'd called in and reserved. She loved how they had a painted rock to mark it *'reserved.'* She felt at home in this setting and with Cole.

He motioned for her to sit, "Feel free to sit, or you can walk with me if you want." He pointed at the order window. "I'm going to grab a couple of wine glasses and see about the fresh catch of the day.

Jadyn was feeling chilly and gazed at the smoke rising from the fire she hoped would warm her, "I'll stay here." Chills increasing on Jadyn's sunburnt skin grew in intensity with each passing minute. She tried to shake off the creepy-tingly feeling of fire ants ascending her back and attacking her shoulders with a barrage of stings. She stood near a fire pit as another battle raged on her skin. Jadyn couldn't decide which was better: allowing the chills to run amuck or accepting the brutal sting from the searing flames. Each time she got too close to the fire, she thought, *stupid woman!* Self-berating thoughts struck her like a hammer banging against her skull, reminding her she hadn't applied the damn sunscreen she had in her bag the entire time!

She walked closer to the fire and watched the hot embers sizzle and spark; she was mesmerized and startled when Cole came up behind her and placed his hands on her burnt and crispy feeling shoulders. He spoke with his cheek against hers, his mouth so close she could feel the warmth of his minty breath, "The fresh catch is Sea Bass, sound good?"

Jadyn spoke with a pained expression above the

streaming music, "Perfect!" and was afraid to move until his hands lifted off like a helicopter. He headed back to the window, ordered, and returned with a couple of plastic wine glasses and a corkscrew. He straddled the bench seat, sat, and served them each a glass, saying, "This is a small store of sorts. They fish daily and sell much of the catch to the restaurants in the area. Fish that isn't distributed is sold here. They made this patio area so people could wait their turn to order fresh fish to take home in comfort, and over time it transformed into this self-serve gourmet, campout-style restaurant. If they have fish, it opens; if they don't have enough, they close."

She smiled and said, "Sounds romantic."

Cole smiled and nodded in agreement as he lifted his glass to meet hers and toasted, "Here's to chance encounters."

Jadyn smiled and said, "clank," as their plastic glasses touched and they sipped the Pinot Grigio. It was crisp, clean, and chilly but warmed her as it moved through the empty void and headed straight to her head.

Wild rice and asparagus with Hollandaise Sauce accompanied the lightly cooked lemon and garlic butter-basted fish. Jadyn ate faster than Cole. He teased, "I like it when a woman isn't afraid to eat like a man."

She gave him a stern expression and lightly slapped his hand, scolding him, saying, "I do not eat like a man!"

He smiled and retaliated with a slight fingertip slap.

Jadyn went on, "And I'm not finished till the wine's gone."

It was evident to Cole she had a buzz, "Good thing I'm driving."

Noticing they were the last remaining customers, Cole stood, cleared their plates, wiped off the table, and asked Jadyn, "Ready?"

Feeling cold and opposed to the idea of leaving so soon, she said, "I'm sure they'd like us to leave, but I'd love to stay longer; I can see why they call it The Gull's Nest; it's lovely and cuddly. It kinda feels like you're inside a safe, nurturing nest. Thanks for sharing it with me."

Cole tenderly grasped Jadyn's soft, warm hand, and they reluctantly strolled to the parking lot.

Chapter 26

Angels don't Sleep

When they arrived at Jadyn's motel, Jadyn invited him into her room, even though the angel on her shoulder was nagging at her. She fought the feeling it was wrong and decided it was worse to not have him come inside.

Jadyn's motel room, lit by only a tiny glow from the alarm clock's digital display, was way too intimate for her. She nonchalantly hit the light switch with her elbow as the door closed behind them, making the room switch from dark to light, like a blinking eye.

Surveying the room and rubbing her cold tingly hand, Jadyn grew anxious, realizing her only options were to have him sit on the bed or a small chair.

He held her hand so tight the blood was pushed out of it. It felt cold when she pulled it out from his and walked to the thermostat. With her back to Cole, blowing hot breath into her hands, Jadyn complained, "my hands are so cold." She tightly squeezed her eyes, hoping he would be sitting in the chair, when she turned back around.

Still standing and watching her, he could see how extremely uncomfortable Jadyn was. She appeared lost in the small space, and Cole figured it was the perfect opportunity to tease, "Funny your hands didn't feel cold a minute ago."

She dropped onto the bed, sitting on her hands to

warm them, and as she feared he would, he sat beside her.

Cole reached his arm around her neck and began kissing her. She immediately realized she had trapped her hands – *not a smart move*. It reminded her of his arms wrapped around her the night before as they sat beneath the lights of Breakers. Jadyn fell back against his weight, and they tumbled backward onto the bed. She found herself in his arms with little defense and broke-out in an uncontrollable nervous belly laugh, with repeating snorts.

Cole raised up on one elbow and looked at her, asking, "What the heck is so funny?"

She couldn't tell if her sunburn hurt anymore. The wine had officially kicked in as she searched her mind for the angel's help, only to release the devil's words, "last night, my hands were ready to punch you, and now..."

Cole started feeling excited, like a dog begging for a treat, and asked, "Now what?"

She struggled with her desire for Cole. She understood it was wrong to think and, even worse, to say the quiet parts aloud, "Now, I'm glad they're trapped, and you can."

He pressed, "So I can, what?" He felt hot, and his breath became shallow as his excitement clamped tightly on his chest.

Jadyn wiggled her hands out from beneath her butt, feeling the comforter scratch her skin and her bare ring finger, then said sadly, "I don't know. I probably shouldn't say what I was thinking." Jadyn was relieved the angel won.

Cole, concerned, felt she looked more than a little

nervous, "Want me to stop?"

She didn't want him to stop. "Can you just hold me tonight?"

Cole thought, *if I kept my mouth shut, I'd be making love to her right now!* The gentleman in Cole was glad she opened up. He was grateful to spend more time with her no matter what they did. Cole softly asked, "All night?"

Jadyn answered with longing eyes, "Yes. All night if you can."

He thought about it for a second, "Sounds nice, sure, I'll stay."

She smiled and said, "Awesome, thanks," and closed the bathroom door and changed into yoga pants and a tank top. Cole heard her brush her teeth, wishing he could brush his. He ate a mint from his pocket and took off his shoes.

She felt butterflies in her stomach as she slid under the covers. Cole immediately spooned her, and she felt tingly all over. Unsure if it was her sunburn or desire and not really caring, which was true, Jadyn drank in the feeling of his embrace. He felt concerned about her secrecy. Their thoughts stilled, and the darkness gently pulled them both to sleep.

Chapter 27

The Open Box

C ole awoke with Jadyn still asleep in his arms, and when she moved as if sensing his awakening, he felt his body respond to hers. His face tightened as he pulled his hips back and away from her, "What time do you need to head out?"

Jadyn blinked herself to a waking state and sat up quickly, "Early. Like an hour ago. My mom wants me to go to the valley and see her before I head home." She winced, "I *hate* driving in the dark."

Realizing they weren't going to do more than they already had, he announced, "You get ready; I'll grab coffee." Feeling hungry, he asked, "Want food?"

She remembered her last talk with her mom, "Just coffee, mom's making breakfast."

When Cole returned to Jadyn, nearly ready, the door cracked open for him. He knocked anyway and said through the closed bathroom door, "Coffee delivery."

He could hear her talking on the phone, so he sat to wait on the bed. As he did, the ring box rolled over to him. Knowing it wasn't right, he opened it anyway. After seeing the diamond ring nestled inside, Cole slammed the box closed, thinking, *hell no!* He stood with an angry and confused look as she walked into the room smiling with her hand outstretched, saying, "Where's mine, coffee man?"

Cole didn't say anything as he placed the coffee in

her hand with the ring box perched on top.

She looked at it with fear rushing over her and back to him, concerned, "You looked inside?"

He looked sternly at her, "Yes!" and shifted to leave.

Jadyn was instantly filled with remorse, "I need more time! I can explain! It's complicated!"

Walking with a hand raised to dismiss her, "Complicated?! Really?! What a lame excuse!"

Struggling to sync her mouth with her brain, "It's not. I mean, I know it sounds like one, but...."

Walking with heavy feet to the Mini Cooper, he yelled, "But nothing!"

She repeated, "If I had more time. If I didn't have to go."

His dejected face brimmed with disappointment as he shot her one last look before getting into the car and reprimanding her, "Time? You could have told me yesterday or last night!"

Cole pulled out of the parking lot and angrily drove.

She was still talking. "You'll understand. I promise. I'll tell you soon. If you'll let me?"

Chapter 28

Coffee & Bagels

Frustrated, Jadyn tossed her bag in her SUV and drove to the gas station, where she texted Cole for the fifth time. *I'm leaving. Want me to call when I get home?*

With a burning sadness in her heart and longing etched across her face, she turned the key and drove to the valley. Jadyn knew she deserved his ghosting. She didn't deserve him in her life anyway.

Jadyn searched her mind for the best way to explain to Cole why she was there, alone, without her ring on her finger, and why she let him kiss her.

Jadyn reluctantly drove to her mother. They planned this before Kendall's wedding. It was too late to make any changes now. Her mom would be too disappointed and staying longer was out of the question. Her tight timeline to get back to Sedona prevented it; they expected her back at work.

Jadyn, troubled by her own emotions, was concerned about exposing her feelings. She knew her mom would sense any negative energy, and no way in hell was she going to talk to her about Cole.

She only had to maintain the appearance of being happy for as long as it took to eat a bagel and cream cheese. She decided she had time for one and coffee, lots of coffee, and more coffee to go!

Jadyn blew her mom a kiss as she drove away with

her coffee and accepted, she'd have a quiet, solitary long drive home, filled with memories of Cole flashing through her guilty mind and feeling ashamed.

Chapter 29

Driven to Lie

Driving with only her thoughts to keep her company, Jadyn kept trying to devise the best explanation to offer Cole. She found herself questioning her actions. *How could she explain away how she ended up on the beach that night? Worse, why did she give him hope of a relationship?* There was no way to paint this pretty, and she knew it.

Jadyn was adrift in a pool of negative thoughts, trying to swim away from the truth, but like a shark, it hunted her, forcing her to admit she was wrong. Her thoughts admonished and attacked her character as she searched her mind for something believable and tenable to offer Cole.

Jadyn's self-reflection released the floodgates holding back her memories, and like a tsunami, they flooded in. To escape, she reflected on her first time driving from her mother to Sedona, a little over two years and a lifetime of memories ago, when Jadyn's Aunt Theodosia opened up her world!

Theodosia invited her to spend the summer in Sedona under one condition, her mother's approval. Jadyn feared the inevitable conversation with her mother would be a loud, bordering on fighting, debate, as she yelled, "I'd love to!"

Before hanging up the call, Theodosia smiled and repeated, "Call me when you get a yes."

Jadyn bubbled with exciting visions of summer with her aunt and spoke to herself, "What a fantastic opportunity! Mom just has to agree! This is the perfect time! The perfect place! Please, God, let her say yes!"

Jadyn had no way of knowing this was a plan concocted by her mother and aunt. During a face-time call, the two of them pinky-swore secrecy. No matter what, they'd never let her know about their conspiracy. They were scheming to help motivate Jadyn and to open her vision to a world of opportunity. This plot between twins, albeit sneaky, was an experiment born out of love.

Jadyn needed a gentle push to move forward in her life. Perhaps if they shed light on the possibility of life as an artist, it would resonate with her. They weren't sure. But it was clear to both of them she lacked passion and had no fire burning for any particular life journey. They also agreed that Jadyn would feel manipulated if she got wind of them working together. She may not know her path, but she always fought hard for her independence. If Jadyn were to find out what they were up to, she might not follow her own life's path.

Even though they were twins, they appeared to have little in common. Jadyn's mother, Sophia, chose a traditional career, one forcing her to dress for success as she liked to describe it, certainly not the outdoorsy type, and to Jadyn, she appeared a bit up tight. Jadyn identifies more with her aunt than her mother and often feels guilty about it.

Her eccentric Aunt Teddy, a pet name bestowed by Jadyn, dresses primarily in Avant Garde, artistic, whimsical clothing, sculpts clay and metals, loves her garden, and is one of the most authentic people in her life.

Jadyn was surprised at the ease of the conversation with her mother. Especially with the breakup of her parents' marriage being so fresh, it went almost too well. Her mother even encouraged Jadyn saying, "Carpe diem!"

Sophia knew her daughter needed to escape her glum house and how depressing she'd been. A creative respite was perfect. After years of school, which never inspired greatness in her, Jadyn needed to get her head straight and figure out her life's plan.

Sophia wished Jadyn a wonderful time as she drove off to Teddy and smiled with a satisfied look of accomplishment. She pulled out the cell from her pocket and texted Theodosia. *Our plan has begun, the bird has flown the nest! L O L!*

Chapter 30

Sands of Time

Hour by hour, she became connected, inspired, and pulled into Arizona's picturesque landscape, like an anchor being lowered into the sea. Just as a fish glowing in a coral reef finds safety nestled in hiding places, she feels tucked in, protected, and swaddled by Arizona's rich colors and vastness.

On her first night in Sedona, Jadyn and Teddy sat on the porch. Lights off, feet up, wine glasses in hand, watching the sky like a movie screen. Both were mesmerized by the intensity of repeating lightning bolts cutting through the dark, sliver-moon sky, a magnificent giant sword fight of dueling Gods. Each strike released an infinite number of bolts, colliding, breaking apart, and shooting out from massive, towering, and menacing thunderhead clouds. An instant deluge of the monsoon poured huge raindrops from what seemed enormous buckets, instantly saturating the parched earth, cleansing the already clean air, and changing the soil's complexion from sienna to a burnt sienna color.

She spent the greater part of her first-week painting Plein-air on canvas boards within Sedona's breathtaking landscape. The red rocks called to Jadyn, asking her to capture their essence. She felt a connection growing strong within her, a oneness, a familiarity filling her with a sense of well-being. Her heart celebrated. She knew this adventure would be far beyond anything she could imagine.

Teddy talked nearly nonstop each night about the Prescott Rodeo, proudly declaring it was the world's oldest rodeo, first staged as a Cowboy Tournament during the US 1888 Fourth of July celebration. Jadyn was interested to see what Teddy was so excited about. She loved horses but never really imagined spending time at a rodeo and wondered if perhaps it would inspire something new within her.

Chapter 31

Clowns & Cowboys

When Jadyn and Teddy arrived at the Prescott Rodeo Grounds, an organic, full-bodied, co-mingling aroma of manure, leather, fly ointment, mud, and dry dirt wafted through the sizzling-hot summer air. It was unmistakably pungent as they selected their seats. Thanks to the unusual one-hundred-two-degree temperature, and the monsoon's barrage of water the night preceding, they could literally see the stench rising from the hot steamy soil within the arena.

As Teddy's friend Gavin prepared to compete in this, his third bull-riding competition for the season, Jadyn gulped a cold beer, trying to relieve the dry heat braising her cheeks. Teddy bought her horse, Scultori, from him when Gavin was a new implant to Sedona. He threw in unlimited training sessions for horse and rider with each horse he trained and sold, not expecting she would continue for more than a few lessons. Two years later, Teddy was still coming to him for lessons, but Teddy was also the reason for his growing client list, and she never missed a chance to watch him ride in events, televised or local.

The softly playing background music abruptly turned up to let's party level, escalating the clamor of the exuberant crowd as the even rowdier bulls and pensive riders prepared to tear it up!

The announcer's thick Oklahoma accent increased the tension and excitement when he yelled, "Hurry up and take your seats Y'all! These bulls are about to bust loose! Every second counts! Show these hard-working cowboys and cowgirls some love!"

The crowd yelled out an almost choreographed, Yee-Haw! followed by lots of whistling, catcalling, and boots banging on the galvanized steel treads of the metal flooring in the stands.

Teddy hollered over the uproarious clamor, "Wait till you see the size of these bulls!"

Jadyn shifted in her seat with both hands on her cell above her head and yelled out, "Can't wait, Auntie! Woot! Woot!" snapping pics and filming video clips of the rodeo clowns entertaining everyone before the *real* action started. They mimed and spoke to the crowd with exaggerated facial expressions and comedic body movements. One acting as a bull with actual horns affixed to his head and poking another's rear, only to spin around pretending he hadn't done anything, was a crowd-pleaser! Their clowning around was a distraction preventing Teddy and Jadyn from grasping anything the announcer said as they laughed.

A slender and very tall cowboy named Granger Johnson could be seen beneath his black felt cowboy hat, dipping up and down behind the advertisement-covered chute. He set his rigging on the unsettled bull as the rusted and dented cowbells banged beneath the beast's belly.

The boisterous crowd combined with the announcer's banter and the bull's snorting and grunting sounds entirely muted the normally squeaky sound of his black and yellow wrangler glove rubbing against the stiff, golden-brown rope as he rosined it like a cellist rosins their bow hairs. He slid his left-hand palm up beneath the rope and crisscrossed over it several times. He was nearly ready. All the spectators could see were several white hats tipping over him. The rodeo hands wore matching hats like nametags. Their hats kept moving and shielding the hidden commotion, like umbrellas, a secret meeting visible to only them and Granger.

Watching their hats was like a drum roll for the audience to see, in addition to the clowns entertaining children lining the fence just above the arena. Small children, grouped by what appeared their age, were white knuckled, tightly gripping the fence. Their little noses poked through the chain links, and their eye-popping excited facial expressions showed they were all in and ready for this fantastic yearly event.

Hank, the announcer, yelled to the crowd, "Are you ready, folks?!"

The crowd collectively whistled, screamed, and cat-called louder and louder while they stomped with their boots, making it sound as if the earth herself opened up with the rodeo applause!

Hank taunted the crowd and yelled loudly at the next rider, "Granger! Are *you* ready?!"

Granger tipped his black hat and nodded a couple times, signaling he was ready! As his left arm shot up, the chute broke open against the fury of the bull's bulging girth! Granger's spurs repeatedly pushed into the bull's tough leathery skin and swung out again. Snot discharged from the downward-facing muddy snout as the bull's hind end thrashed for what seemed minutes. Sadly, Granger only lasted a disappointingly brief six seconds.

The crowd screamed, "Oh!" as his lifeless-looking body hit the ground with the bull still spinning and kicking! Granger had angels watching him along with the clowns! Proof of their presence was seen as the bull's hooves repeatedly cleared his face and stomach and came way too close to his family jewels! The crowd's voices resounded in supportive, pulsating waves.

"Oh!"

"Oh!!"

"Oh!!!"

It was impossible to not get caught up in the excitement! Jadyn found it all disturbing. It was flustering. She found it challenging to sit still after seeing him come so close to what could have been a terrible end.

Granger got his chance to escape! After fidgeting, her heart still pounding, Jadyn stood up and yelled in unison with Teddy, "RUN!!!"

Jadyn giggled and said, "Run, Granger, run!" with her voice sounding like Jenny in Forrest Gump, she went on playfully screaming, "Run, Forest, run!"

Teddy slapped her shoulder, laughed, and said, "good one!"

Granger crawled fast, knees up, like a baboon to safety. The crowd cheered louder and banged their boots until the clowns finally tricked the still-raging bull into the pen.

Hank compassionately exclaimed, "Oh, no! What a disappointing start for Granger; he's leaving today with a no score, but don't you worry, he gets another crack at it tomorrow, folks!"

The next rider, on Spinmeister, a latte coffee-colored

bull, lasted a short 2.6 seconds after the bull's horn struck the face shield of his helmet and spun him around like a helicopter blade through the air! The crowd gasped and held their faces watching the bull's still spinning, bucking, rearing body dance around and over him as he lay there knocked out cold. The clowns hopped and jumped near him to distract the enraged bull as best they could. Their arms banged against his mass, and after several attempts, Spinmeister wouldn't let any of the clowns close enough to remove the flank strap. He kept charging the men until finally being roped by a cowboy on horseback, only to break free, running and bucking his way back to the now-sitting Austin Sumner. He was pulled up by his belt just in time by one of the spotters.

Teddy was beside herself with excitement and fear, "I simply do not understand what makes these men do this!"

In a flirty voice, Jadyn said, "Yeah, but it sure is sexy!"

Teddy gave her a wink and an elbow nudge, "Yes, it is!" They kept laughing, releasing the stress of seeing Austin ride like steam escaping from a teapot.

Jadyn fell hard on her keister and blurted out, "Holy Moley! I need another beer. Want one?"

After a nod, Teddy handed her a twenty and said in a matter-of-fact tone, "Hurry, you don't want to miss any of the rides."

Jadyn raised her eyebrows and playfully replied, "Don't I, though?!" Then she walked off a bit awkwardly in Teddy's borrowed boots, blue jeans, and white camisole. She wore an also borrowed, and slightly tattered straw Aussie cowboy hat she decided was never being returned. Teddy was also in jeans, a white snap-up western blouse, and around her neck, she wore a bright red scarf to help Gavin spot her in the stands.

Gavin was sitting on the chute looking at Crusher, with heels on his back, helping to keep him from climbing out as the clowns struggled with Spinmeister. He couldn't set his rigging with him banging against the wood separating them.

Spinmeister was removed from the area, and Gavin prepared his rigging on Crusher, a primarily white Brahma with what looked like black paint splattered on his sides. Teddy could see it was getting close to his ride and didn't want to watch alone. She looked for Jadyn, urgently repeating under her breath, "Come on, come on, come on, Jadyn."

She hurried, spilling spurts of foam as the clear plastic cups flexed in her grip. She sat as they showed Gavin's picture on the large screen, and just before the chute flung open, releasing all six feet, two inches of him into the arena. She kept switching her gaze back and forth from him riding to the larger-than-life picture displaying his amber eyes and matching vest and hat.

Gavin rode the full eight seconds! He sprung off Crusher's bucking back like he'd been shot out of a cannon, landing on his feet, and running to safety.

Teddy stood screaming, "Yay! Gavin!"

Jadyn couldn't resist laughingly shouting, "He literally hit the ground running!"

Astonished, impressed, and drawn to the rodeo experience, Jadyn felt exhilarated by its unique sights and sounds. She sprang to her feet beside Teddy, cheering, and clapping. She intently stared at Gavin, now perched on the top rail of the pen with his bull rope over his shoulder. He smiled and talked with other riders as they watched the clowns deal with Crusher.

The announcer started talking louder than her thoughts, "Give it up for Gavin Michaels! The first cowboy here tonight to make it through to the buzzer, and what a ride it was! An 86.4 score ain't nothing to cry about, folks! If he can do it again each day, he might just take the prize!"

As soon as Crusher was secured, Gavin jumped behind the fence and out of sight. Several other bulls took their cowboys for wild rides, and after an hour, Teddy said, "We need to head downtown and find a place to park."

With eyes fixed on the arena, Jadyn pouted, "I'm just starting to have fun!"

Teddy banged her shoulder against Jadyn's, saying, "What you really mean is you're enjoying your beer buzz, and you don't wanna stop staring at these cowboys. But I'm fifty-two, feeling old, and all I want to do in these boots is dance!"

Jadyn pouted playfully, pushing out her bigger-than-average bottom lip and rolling her puppy dog eyes as Teddy smirked and said, "Trust me, Jadyn, you'll have fun."

Jadyn didn't attempt to get up, so Teddy baited her by saying, "All these cowboys will be downtown."

Jadyn finished her remaining beer, bolted up, banging her boots on the metal tread, asking, "Whatcha waiting for?"

Chapter 32

Porta Potties & Beer

Prescott was packed with people dressed in everything from shorts and tees to full-dress cowboy attire as dogs tugged their owners around the courthouse lawn and motorists inched their way through jaywalking pedestrians. Jadyn was falling in love with the quaintness of this smaller-than-small town.

She poked her head out the open car window with the same enthusiasm as a puppy. She loved feeling the breeze moving across her face and through her hair. Jadyn cheered, "I like this kind of traffic! Look at this! Oh, I love this town. Thank you so much for bringing me here!"

Teddy proudly said, "Told ya! There's even more fun to be had. Wait till you see those cowboys dance!"

Jadyn turned to look at Teddy with raised brows and a devilish smile as she imagined them moving on the dance floor in their tight, painted-on Wrangler jeans. She searched her memory of movies from her past and let go fast of those scenes because she knew she'd witness it first-hand tonight. She felt anticipation build with a promise of new paintings and stories waiting to be birthed from this unfolding adventure with Teddy. Jadyn carried on with people-watching until Teddy pulled into one of the last spots remaining in the town's only covered parking lot.

After closing the car windows, stopping the wind's flow, and trapping themselves inside with the summer heat, they looked at one another with a *something stinks* expression. Both realized the rodeo's stench had followed them and was lingering on their clothes and in their hair.

In an instant, their eyes teared up. Teddy pinched her nose and asked, "Oh, my goodness, is that stench coming from you?!"

Jadyn looked at her with disgust and proclaimed, "No-wah! Ewe! I thought it was you! I thought you farted!"

Laughing their asses off and gagging at the smell, Jadyn emphatically denied responsibility, "Oh, Auntie T, you can't blame this on me! Stop making me laugh! I gotta pee!"

Teddy jokingly said, "It's what you get for drinking two beers, dear! All I know is I've never smelled like this after the rodeo. It must be you. Check your boots. I think you stepped in a wet cow patty and brought it along for the ride! Thanks a lot!"

She looked to see, tipping each of her boot heels, one after the other, and found the wet, stinky patty stuck on the bottom of the left one. She begrudgingly said, "I hate it when you're right!" Jadyn flung open the door and kicked the cow patty off the offending boot."

Teddy laughed, saying, "That's exactly why we call them shit-kickers!"

Jadyn wanted to laugh out loud but only brought one pair of pants. Growing concerned, she crossed her legs tight, begging, "Hurry up and get out of the car; I might not make it, and you'll have to buy me a new pair of pants!"

Teddy argued, "Oh, will I? It's not my fault you had too much to drink."

Jadyn defended herself, "I didn't have too much to drink. I haven't even started yet."

Knowing how it sucked when you really have to pee and enjoying teasing her niece, she described the scene, "Porta potties all lined up in a row is the bathroom for the dance."

Jadyn winced and said, "ewe!"

Teddy took a deep breath of fresh air as soon as she swung her door open and explained, "Matt's Saloon is the closest; let's go. Let me be clear, we are not there to buy beer."

She rolled her eyes walking fast behind Teddy, insisting, "I just need to pee and fix my hair and makeup."

She reassured her, "Well, their bathroom isn't great, but at least it's a real bathroom with running water and mirrors."

In the bathroom of Matt's Saloon, Jadyn liberally sprayed perfume all over herself and her boots, hoping to cover the lingering cow-poop odor. It wasn't the badge of honor she wanted to bring back from her first rodeo experience. Even though Gavin was deep in the stink of it and probably wouldn't notice, she wanted to be sure the first whiff he had of *her* smelled sexy, not stinky.

Jadyn was distracted by her thoughts until she noticed they were walking away from all the action! Walking away from Whiskey Row and the Courthouse Square. She'd imagined the dance would be in one of the bars or at least where the art and crafts were displayed and furled her forehead, asking, "Do you even know where you're going?"

Teddy chuckled. She expected Jadyn to think something was wrong and teased, "Hold on to your panties! One more block, and we'll be at the dance."

Chapter 33

The Rodeo Dance

They stood in line at the entrance of a chain link fenced section of an ordinary shopping center parking lot. She took in the scene, watching those waiting in line, thinking this was more than a little hokey. Jadyn doubted she'd have fun seeing the young children waiting with them in line. This was a far cry from the hot young cowboys she'd been promised. She kept her doubts to herself and accepted she'd be her aunt's wing girl for the night.

After buying their tickets and donating at a charity table, Teddy smiled and pointed to a long line of mostly men, and said, "You're in charge of beer. I'll grab burgers and meet you at one of the hay bales by the dance floor."

Inspired by the music playing, Jadyn walked with a bounce in her step to the beer vendor taking pics and sending them to Kendall.

With beers in hand she carefully maneuvered over to Teddy through the growing crowd. She was distracted by the antics of a couple of kiddos dressed in full western garb running circles around her hay bale. Teddy held their plates like a server, trying to ensure they didn't knock the plates out of her hands. Jadyn mischievously surprised Teddy when she flung her leg over and straddled the hay bale like a horse.

Facing Teddy, she did a happy-dance sway and said, "Let's swap!"

They swapped. Teddy gulped, and said, "Eat! You'll be asked to dance all night and Two-Steppin' is a calorie burner!"

Teddy convinced her. She swung her leg around, brought her knees together, and tabled the flimsy, coleslaw-soggy paper plate. "Okey-dokey, Auntie! I'm starving anyway."

Teddy gave her a judgy-questioning look as she watched Jadyn overstuff her mouth. Jadyn felt her watchful eye and gave a Cheshire Cat smile with a full mouth, knowing full-well how much it would bother her. She couldn't care less about acting ladylike and loved taunting Teddy. She laughed inside. It was priceless to see Teddy's look of disgust in her peripheral vision as she watched mayonnaise ooze from the corners of Jadyn's chipmunk nut-stuffed-looking cheeks. Teddy stated, "Sure hope you don't eat like this on a date!"

Jadyn was secretly determined to devour every morsel before Gavin showed up and was thrilled when she swallowed the last bite followed by a swig of beer. Her loud burp made Teddy shake her head in disbelief, "Jadyn, must you?"

Another gulp finished off her beer, and Jadyn said, belching, "Yup."

Jadyn laughed hard and patted Teddy's shoulder, "Don't you worry, auntie."

Jadyn stood, clicked her heels together like Dorothy in the Wizard of Oz and said, "Okay, I'm ready for this honky-tonk part-tay!"

She looked at her stinky boots. "Just not sure how to dance in these-here boots."

Teddy knew how boring the dance appeared. She

reassured her, "I predict by the stroke of midnight you'll be loving this small-town country living." Jadyn had doubts and nodded.

An old worn-out cowboy in worn-out boots swaggered onto the dance floor. He had a trail of people following close behind as if they were cows being led to slaughter. One after the other, they lined up, side by side, all facing the crowd learning the steps of a line dance.

Teddy watched Jadyn analyze the line dancers and hoped she'd join in. She knew Jadyn would have a lot more fun when the cowboys got to town.

Jadyn went for another beer while Teddy talked to a couple she and her boyfriend, Luca, often socialized with. She admired the friendly attitude everyone displayed as she waited to order. With beer in hand, she skimmed the crowd and watched Gavin enter.

Seeing him made her react without her control. Realizing he made her feel off-balance she took a deep breath and let it out, "Ahh." She stood frozen, and flushed, watching Gavin walk. He was backlit by the dusky sky, looking even hotter than he had on his bull. She felt her neck with her hand as a rush of heat went through her, and with one hand holding her beer and the other capping the top to stop it from spilling, she walked fast to let Teddy know he'd arrived.

Teddy excitedly helicoptered her head around, smiling, "Where is he?"

Jadyn answered, trying to act like she didn't care one way or the other, and kept her eyes on the dancers, "I dunno, he was at the entrance a minute ago."

Jadyn walked through the dancers onto the floor and positioned herself as far back as possible to observe him from a distance, unsure why she felt so nervous. She only knew he stood out like an eagle in a flock of pigeons as he walked, tipping his cowboy hat and smiling at everyone in his path.

Gavin scanned the crowd until he found Teddy's red scarf. Their eyes met and she waved him over to their hay bale. Jadyn freaked when she noticed Gavin was looking in her direction, obviously for her. She pretended to be focused on the dancer's feet the entire time as she watched their intense and very confusing dance steps. With thumbs in the front pockets of her jeans she stumbled through the moves. Jadyn knew if she didn't catch on, embarrassment was coming if and when he asked her to dance. She needed to catch on fast! If Gavin danced as well as he rode bulls, she knew he was way out of her league!

When the dancers and music stopped, Teddy yelled, "Jadyn, Gavin's joining you!" Teddy, as usual, was impossible to miss. With her finger in the air and waving her arm around like a cowgirl roping a steer, she pointed at Jadyn as if throwing the rope around her. Teddy was thrilled with herself as she shot Jadyn a conniving, smartass grin.

Jadyn felt trapped and experienced a hot rush of fear as she watched him walk his cowboy walk over to her. When he reached her, Gavin's eyes were lit by a string of lights hanging over the floor, and he introduced himself, "I'm Gavin. Care to dance?"

She blinked and swallowed hard. She put her hand on his open palm and said, "I'm Jadyn and have absolutely no idea what I'm doing."

With his other hand around his back and hat tipped so only she could see his smile, he reassured her, "No worries. I've got you."

His words were alluring and reassuring, not I'll teach you, but I've got you. Jadyn felt safe and relaxed as he instructed her. They danced a couple songs in the middle of the floor with other inexperienced dancers. When he guided her into the stream-like flow of dancers, Teddy's heart filled with joy! Watching them reminded her how it felt to be young, with so much life and so many possibilities ahead.

They danced for over an hour before stepping off the floor and over to Teddy who was feeling more than a little pleased with herself as she questioned Jadyn, "Having fun?"

Jadyn read her eyes and gave back an acknowledging look, "Yes, Ma'am, but I gotta pee."

As she walked to the outhouses, Teddy asked Gavin what he thought about Jadyn. He looked past Teddy, keeping his eyes on the shiny rhinestone pockets of Jadyn's jeans. Smiling, he replied, "She's funny and very pretty, just as you said."

Teddy suggested, "If you want to show her around town, I can hang out with my friends, and you two could hit Whiskey Row. I know it's more fun than this."

When Jadyn walked up, Gavin excitedly asked, "Theodosia said we can break away and go have some real fun, wanna?"

She looked at Theodosia's winking nod and back to Gavin's waiting expression and exclaimed, "Hell, yeah, I wanna go!"

Jadyn felt a sensation; something within her forever changed as she smiled at Teddy with unsaid words of gratitude.

Teddy smiled when she noticed Gavin's hand

pressed to Jadyn's lower back as they pushed through the crowd away from her.

It wasn't long before Gavin texted Teddy to ask if he could be the one to drive Jadyn back to Sedona. Teddy texted back, *it's more than alright with me! Have fun & be safe!*

Teddy knew this meant they'd be out till closing time and was dying to say, I told ya so, to Jadyn but knew it was pointless to call. She couldn't compete with the loud music, laughter, and people talking around her as the dance floor flooded with people yet again for another popular line dance. With phone in hand, Teddy's face and eyes brightened as the screen lit up. It was a text from Luca, *hey babe, if you were here, I'd be rubbing those toes and kissing your neck! Winking face emoji. When are you heading back?*

With the long day behind her and a forty-five-minute drive ahead, she texted, *now! Followed by a blowing kiss emoji.*

Jadyn and Gavin more than hit it off. They spent the night singularly focused on each other, dancing like long-time partners with seemingly endless energy, and were the last to leave Matt's Saloon.

They held hands for the long walk back to Gavin's truck, and Jadyn thought back to earlier when he said, "I've got you." She smiled, knowing he really did.

Chapter 34

Vacation Brain?

Teddy's raw-sienna colored adobe-style home complemented the rich Sedona soil it was built on. Jadyn thought the smooth clay-like surface had a sexy feel, like sun-kissed skin, and it looked even richer as Gavin's lights skimmed across it as they entered the driveway.

Jadyn was impressed with the affluence her aunt's artwork afforded her and dreamed of being a successful artist one day. Jadyn loved Teddy's imaginative use of art in her yard and throughout her home. It reflected her free, fun-loving, yet mysterious personality. She especially loved the frogs, hummingbirds, snails, and flowers popping out of the cactus illuminated at night but felt working in metal would be too strenuous. Jadyn preferred the feeling of her soft brush sweeping the uneven surface of each canvas until it transformed by what she did to it. She also loved that a watercolor she gave Teddy as a child, hung framed above the piano she played each morning.

Teddy lit her art precisely, ensuring observers would see them as she intended. To Jadyn's delight, her favorite sculpture, standing eight feet tall and resembling a tree, twisted and turned as the warm breeze pushed through its shiny bronze openings. It was the most prominent of her pieces and the only one she duplicated. It looked majestic, standing tall like a totem pole, welcoming them as they pulled in and parked in the driveway.

Teddy was mindful of the fine details in life. She added hidden speakers throughout the terraced yard to enhance her guest's experience. There are unique sculptures to sit on in place of furniture, just a small sampling of the unique home and garden complimenting Teddy's equally unique personality. Jadyn fell in love with the idea of one day owning a home as special as this.

Each day during Jadyn's visit with Teddy turned into a day spent with Gavin.

Teddy correctly envisioned Sophia would soon have a new son-in-law. Jadyn's sixty-day scheduled stay quickly passed, and it was almost time for her to return to California. Gavin's insistence she move to Sedona finally convinced her. It wasn't difficult for him to persuade her. Jadyn loved Sedona, and she also loved Gavin.

A few days before her expected departure, Jadyn worked up the courage and sheepishly asked Teddy, "Auntie, would you mind if I stayed a while longer?"

She couldn't stop herself from teasing, "Oh, you want to stay, do you?"

Jadyn grimaced and nodded.

Teddy placed her hand on Jadyn's shoulder, "Sorry for teasing. How long would you like to stay?"

With eyes pleading and a desperate-sounding voice, Jadyn blurted out, "I don't want to go back. I don't belong there anymore."

Seeing the pain in Jadyn's eyes, Teddy didn't prod for details yet wanted to determine if it was a good decision for her, "Why do you want to stay?"

Jadyn explained, "Mom wants me to finish college and choose some safe major, leading to a safe job, leading to a safe, boring, normal, everyday life, and I'm an artist! If anyone should understand why I need to move here, it's you!"

Ensuring Jadyn considered everything, she pressed, "Sure you don't have vacation brain?"

Jadyn opened her mouth and curled her lip, "Huh?"

Teddy knew all too well what it was, having done it herself in Hawaii years ago, and described it for her, "It's like looking through beer goggles. About a place, not a person. People fall in love with an area, pick up and move, only to change their mind."

Jadyn scoffed, "Absolutely not! I know what I'm feeling... and Gavin."

Teddy opened her eyes and tipped her head, teasing, "Oh, so it's not just the area, and being an artist, you have another reason?"

Jadyn let out a frustrated heavy breath, "Come on, don't!"

Teddy was feeling rather good about herself and her match-making skills, "Sorry, love, can't resist teasing. Already suspected you'd be asking to stay. So, having had the time to already think about it and the fact you're no trouble at all, I can't say *no,* unless your mother says no."

Jadyn scowled, "What? Why? I'm not a child. I'm an adult. Why does it matter what mom says?"

Teddy sternly said, "Because we're family. You'll understand when you're my age."

Jadyn crossed her arms and argued, "I'm so sick of being told that!"

Teddy laughed, "Oh! If I had a dime."

Jadyn nearly cried, "Stop! Don't tease me, not now, not *you*, please."

Teddy embraced Jadyn and apologetically said, "Okay, I'll stop, but the condition stands. My answer is yes if you get your mother's approval. And to make up for all the teasing, I'll take you to my friend Winona's gallery and introduce you. Her assistant is expecting a baby and is taking maternity leave in a month. You never know; she may not return to work. I suggested she consider you for the job."

Jadyn hugged Teddy tighter, "Really? Oh, my God! You're amazing!"

She could feel the ties binding her to her mother breaking, one by one, with each decision she made. She could also feel her throat tighten at the thought of getting her approval.

Jadyn was nervous and excited when Teddy parked in front of the gallery to introduce Winona to her. They chatted for an hour or so, and seeing how much Jadyn knew about art, she decided she'd be a good fit for the gallery. Jadyn could barely sit still in the car as she anticipated her training day and how perfect it all seemed.

Four weeks is perfect timing! She thought *just enough time to go home, convince mom I'm old enough to make my own decisions, pack, and say my goodbyes.* Jadyn was anxious to tell Kendall about her move. She thought for sure she and her mom would try to make her feel guilty for leaving them. She didn't care; this was her chance for love, and no one would stop her.

Jadyn kept rehearsing what to say to her mother, but no matter how she rehearsed, it always sucked!

August marked the end of her planned visit with

Teddy. Her departure day was upon her, and Gavin was there to help her pack. It was awkward. He knew he didn't have the right to push her one way or the other. He was pensive as he watched her empty the drawers that had held her clothes for the last two months, hoping she wouldn't change her mind. He prayed she'd hold her ground and stand up to her mother. The more he thought about it, the faster he tapped his foot and bounced his knee. They both knew he was stressed even though he tried to make it look like he was moving to the beat of the music playing on her phone.

Each time she glanced at him, he tried not to look upset, but she could see right through him, so she stopped packing, leaned over, and gently kissed and comforted him with reassuring words, "I'll be back. Promise."

Once she finished packing, they rested on the bed and silently held each other. They were clearly falling in love, but neither wanted to be the first to say the words. She tried not to let him see her check the time on her phone, but he did, "Time to go?"

She put her hands on his shoulders and softly spoke, "Yes," then held her hand to help him stand for a hug.

Teddy thought they walked as if attending a funeral as they entered the living room. She held back a laugh, "Come on, enough with the sad faces. Time is going to fly by. You'll see. Think of the positive. You really like each other; you're so lucky, right?"

They both said, "Yes," in a low tone, though feeling what she said only made it feel worse.

Jadyn stopped herself from crying by excusing herself to go to the other room, saying, "I just need to grab my book from the den."

He followed her with hands open, "Another hug, please?"

Their awkward silence was cut by the sound of air being forced from his lungs when she squeezed him tighter than he'd ever been hugged. He dropped his arms from around her, took hold of her hands, brought them to his lips, and kissed them before saying, "Wish you weren't driving in the dark later."

Jadyn realized he was right. It was later than she wanted to leave, "I really gotta go."

She looked intensely into his eyes like she had opened a window into his soul and poured herself inside him. It was a look he would never forget, and few had ever seen. Her piercing jade-green eyes were so large on her petite face that he became caught in her gaze. The color was why her mother named her Jadyn.

Cole watched her drive away and waved goodbye, wondering, with an aching heart, if he would ever see her again.

Chapter 35

Quaking in Her Tires

J adyn's drive would've felt endless if not for the beauty of the ever-changing desert landscape blending into the massive Arizona sky. Far off, mountains overlapping along the horizon in varying hues of lavender and blue, contrasting the puffy white clouds suspended as if waiting to be colored by the sun's imminent descent, filled her with peace and calm.

She reminisced about her first sunset spent with Gavin, embraced in his arms while witnessing the indescribable beauty and warmth of the red rocks. She remembered thinking how hard it would be to work a regular job if she lived in Sedona. The intensity of the area and the colorful surroundings were simply too distracting. Now all she can think is it's becoming a reality! Living in Sedona! She envisioned taking her canvas, paint, and easel on the back of a mountain bike and disappearing for hours to capture and suspend in time the images of the red rocks forever etched in her mind.

She felt the last two hours driving on Interstate 10 were like not moving; it resembled a blank page, a relentlessly straight road, absent of buildings, no change in direction, and virtually no cell coverage. If not for the truckers periodically invading her lane, slowing her drive, she might have fallen asleep. It was dusk, the time when color seemed to not exist, and the eye begged for either more light or darkness to fall. She felt disconnected as she scanned for a radio station to help keep her awake and alert. She landed on a scratchy static-sounding country music station and let it play. It felt right.

Like a Twilight Zone scene, she passed hundreds of towering white windmills, standing ghost-like, some spinning, some not, and others with their blades dead and lying on the ground like tombstones, a cemetery of iron monsters. Jadyn's artistic tendencies helped even the mundane seem interesting, something to record or store in her mind for use in a future painting or story.

As she descended lower into the Inland Empire on Interstate 10 and into what remained of the orange-brown smoggy sunset, her SUV began thumping like it had a flat tire. She grabbed the steering wheel tighter and motioned to pull off the highway until she noticed other drivers were also breaking and acting like something was wrong with their vehicles.

Before Jadyn pulled over to stop, the sensation of flat tire thumps stopped. Relieved, she continued driving, and the music was abruptly interrupted by the D.J. saying, "Did you feel that!? Pretty sure it measured around 4.2 on the Richter Scale. Please call in and let me know if you have any damage in your area. As soon as I know the quake's magnitude, I'll be sure to let you know."

If she had doubts about moving, this erased them. She'd secretly feared for her life for as long as she could remember. Living with the uncertainty of when the earth would give birth to an earthquake hung like a dark cloud over her life. It didn't matter how hard she tried to ignore her fear. She couldn't. It was too unsettling.

Anytime a truck drove by and rattled the windows or whenever just about any other random rumbling noises occurred, Jadyn's heart beat hard, and her breath shortened.

Memories of past earthquakes flashing in Jadyn's mind were soon replaced with fear of approaching her off-ramp leading to the house holding her past. No matter how slow she drove, it was simply too fast. She longed for a little more time to settle herself before facing her mom, so she pulled into a gas station. Once parked at the pump, she picked up her phone and called her mother, "Hi, Jadyn; I was beginning to get worried. Where are you?

Jadyn felt bad she left her mom to wonder for so long, knowing she could have called sooner, "I'm just around the corner, getting gas. Want anything?"

Sophia dropped her shoulders, relieved to hear her voice, and softly said, "Just you."

Jadyn grabbed water from the ice-filled tub inside the store and said, "K, be there in a minute."

Jadyn's mother was sitting on the porch as she pulled into the driveway, put her SUV in park, turned the engine off, and closed her eyes tightly for a while before opening the door.

Sophia walked to Jadyn, asking, "Need help?"

They were both smiling but apprehensive as they grabbed her bags and walked into the house, knowing it was normally something her father would do, but he was gone. This only makes what Jadyn had to say more difficult. The house felt cold, empty, and quiet, and Jadyn's footsteps were even louder as she walked in her boots across the wooden floorboards to her room. She slid them off, thinking she never knew boots could feel so comfy.

Her mother came into her room and asked, "Join me for tea?"

Jadyn sensed her mother wanted to get right to business, but she wasn't ready to talk, so she stood up, gave her a quick embrace, and asked, "Tomorrow? I feel gross." She yawned and spoke in her defense, "I need a shower. I can barely keep my eyes open."

Sophia wasn't surprised. She knew Jadyn well enough to not expect anything else and said, "Sure, honey, I understand. The tea will keep. I've missed you so much and want to hear all about your trip."

Her mother kissed her on the forehead while holding her head with one hand and placing the other on Jadyn's cheek, and softly spoke, "See you in the morning, doll; sleep well."

Jadyn felt terrible. She knew if she talked tonight, as tired as she was, she would mess things up.

Feeling anything *but* emotionally stable, she texted Gavin, *Got here safe. Taking a shower. Going to sleep. Talk tomorrow, k?*

His stomach tightened as he read her brief text. He was hoping to talk till they fell asleep as usual. Getting such a short text worried him. Was she pulling away? It hadn't even been a day. He just texted back, *k, talk to you tomorrow.* She felt his disappointment through the lack of emojis but didn't have the energy to reassure him tonight; instead, she showered, put on a pair of Winnie the Pooh-boxer shorts, a cami, and slid into the recently laundered, soft sweet-smelling sheets.

Her tension caused a tightness in her stomach. She felt sick. It seemed like a thousand butterflies stirred inside her. It was the beginning of an endless night unless she could calm herself and find her way to sleep. When Jadyn reached to switch off the bedside lamp, she noticed a small envelope leaning against it like a canvas on an easel with her name written in her mother's handwriting, Anxiety built, and she reached for it. Wondering what her mom had to say, she removed the heart-shaped sticker sealing it, pulled out the fancy stationery, and began reading.

Dearest Jadyn,

This summer was so long without you to brighten up my days, and the house has felt so empty. I decided to write to you because I know how you always try to stop me from telling you how great you are, but I have some things to say, so here goes. I thank God every day I had you. No matter where life takes you, I want you to know you're the best thing that ever happened to me. It wasn't always easy for us through the years, I had to work a lot more than I wanted, and it often took me away from you when all I wanted to do was spend some mother-daughter time with my special girl.

You have grown into a wonderful young woman. I know you'll soon be leaving to start your own life, and although it will hurt to let you go, I will. I know you'll make decisions that are right for you. Your choices may not be what I would choose for you, but know I won't be controlling. I let you go, sweetheart. I sensed stress in your voice when we spoke on the phone earlier and thought I would spare you some of it by writing my thoughts and feelings in this letter. I did this just in case you were too tired to talk tonight. See, your mother knows you pretty well, huh?

I've spoken to your Aunt Teddy, and she let me know you have a special someone in Sedona. We are twins, you know – we can't keep things from each other very long.

I hope you're up to sharing some of the details of your relationship with me. I would love to hear all about him. I'm happy for you! I support your decision if you feel you need to move to give this relationship a chance. I'll support your decision should you feel you need to move to Sedona to give this relationship a chance.

I love you, my darling daughter, my girl, my sweet ray of sunshine, and I will let you go because I do. I know you'll continue to astound me with your talents and impress me with your strong will.

All I ask is a promise you will not lose yourself. Become the woman you want to be. When I say this I mean loving a man can suffocate you if you allow it. Be strong enough to not lose sight of the goals you set in motion before meeting him. Keep painting and writing! Take long baths and long walks, sing and dance with friends and always make sure you're happy with yourself. Never settle. You're the best! And because you are, you deserve the best. I wish I could promise the rest of your life will be pleasant, but I can't. You will have tough and challenging times in your life, times making you wish you could just cease to exist. So be sure this man is someone you can lean on, and allow him to lean on you.

A tear fell onto the stationery making the ink bleed, like when paint thinner is added to her oils. She enjoyed the look it created but quickly wiped it off; she wanted to keep this letter for future reads. Jadyn wiped away tears from her face, blinked away more that were forming, attempted to clear her blurry vision, and continued reading.

Some of my life's best and worst times were spent with your father. He was such a strong man; that's where you get your determination. He found it difficult to express his feelings and difficult to let me express mine. I spent some of my loneliest times with him right by my side. I really loved him but lost part of myself during our life together. I want to spare you those empty feelings, and although I know I can't, I can at least give you some of my wisdom to take with you.

I look forward to heart-to-heart talks with you, not as mother and daughter but as two women, like conversations I'm sure you've had with Aunt Teddy...

Enough said. I love you, doll. I hope this letter has given you some relief - the space you need to be you, and lifted your spirits, as you should be happy, not stressed right now. We'll chat in the morning.

All My Love, Mom

Jadyn was amazed and excited by her mom's words. They had instantly transformed her from daughter to friend and her fear to gratitude. She thought, *Boy, I was so wrong about mom.* She closed her eyes and fell asleep, her heart warm and her spirit calm.

Chapter 36

Sparrows and Parfaits

Jadyn awoke to shocking and alarming *"caw-caw"* screams repeating from a couple of prankster crows in the act of robbing the resident squirrels' loot. As they walked with cocky feet on the branches, an equally loud flock of angry sparrows swooped in beak-first, argumentatively insisting the obnoxious pair of crows skedaddle and hightail it away from their once concealed nests, covered within the Great Oak's canopy.

Jadyn was delighted to be a private guest in this vacant theater and to witness the show performed outside her open window. She likened the performance to watching a rehearsal for her eyes only. The crotchety crows took off, squawking louder, clumsily flapping their wings, only to be attacked again by the tiny, relentless sparrows swarming like bees.

Freaked out, the crows ran like hell and released the squirrel's acorns like bombs as they soared away. Jadyn, filled with delight, almost cheered seeing the squirrels chase one another around the thick, gnarled, and wildly twisted tree trunk.

Bubbling with gratitude for this heavenly awakening and with the memory of it, Jadyn took a shower and imagined her breakfast chat with her mom. She was grateful for the warm and fuzzy feeling growing inside about the upcoming conversation with her mother.

Jadyn's swift fingers twisted her hair into a French braid, wrapping around and hanging over one shoulder. A look of I need coffee, materialized on Jadyn's face. Ordinarily, until her first cup was in her hands, and she sipped and breathed in the deep rich aroma, it was all she could do to form even a tiny smile, and verbalizing anything was simply out of the question! Jadyn wasn't a grumpy gal today; she acted uncharacteristically happy. Today was a new day! Jadyn felt freer. Her mom's ordinarily mundane and familiar kitchen noises sounded musical! She moved quickly, shuffling her slippers over the wooden floor with a lovely, peaceful swelling sensation in her heart.

Jadyn's day got even better! Gavin texted, *R U ok?*

She replied, *Morning handsome,* smiling face emoji, *all good here, XOXO!*

She took a moment and sent a text to Teddy, *Good morning auntie; it's all good with mom, as you no doubt expected.* Jadyn added the *sticks-out tongue emoji. I'll be in touch, Luv U!*

Her phone chirped, announcing she had another text from Gavin. *Great! Told-ya so! Have fun with mom. Gotta Go muck the stalls. Miss ya! XOXO and a kissing-face emoji.*

Jadyn giggled and replied *S Happens. Hahaha! Ending with a winking face with tongue emoji.*

Gavin laughed out loud and came back with, *you are too cute! Way too much, poop emoji! I should cut out their oats lol.* He then asked *k gotta go talk to you tonight?*

She was happy to answer, *Yes, I'll call after dinner. XO!*

Sophia had coffee, fruit, and yogurts set out on the table. Jadyn walked into the kitchen in her boxer shorts and cami, yawning loudly, "Morning, Momma, thanks for the note. It means the world to me. Way to make me cry, by the way."

She smirked, "My pleasure. Which cup do you want?"

Jadyn's eyes opened wide at the full cupboard, "wow, been shopping for mugs lately?"

Sophia said with melancholy, "Your dad complained if I bought one. I figure I'll know I'm over it when I don't want to buy any more mugs." She stopped and said, "Sorry doll. I know our divorce has been hard on you."

Jadyn ached for her mom and said, "It's okay, momma. I understand better after your letter. I had no idea you felt so alone." She switched her gaze to the open cupboard and said, "The green one with the white top."

Sophia smiled knowingly, "Good choice. I knew this would be your favorite. This cup feels really good in your hands."

Jadyn resounded, "Perfect!" hoping to change the subject.

Sophia sat on the bench seat at the kitchen nook-style table, nested in the white paned garden windows. This is her favorite place to enjoy coffee, offering a clear view of the lush backyard, bird feeders, and rose garden off the patio. It was already too hot to sit outside, where they usually enjoyed breakfast together. Her mom patted the seat with her hand and said, "Now come sit and tell me all about Gavin, your new job, and show me some pictures."

Jadyn's eyes skimmed the table, and all the fruits and yogurts spread out, saying, "Yum, parfait time!"

Jadyn sat beside her mother on the bench seat and

in a large wine glass, each prepared her own parfait. They alternated between three different yogurt flavors on layers of blueberries, strawberries, bananas, and granola, a childhood favorite of Jadyn's. They turned and sat facing one another, each with one foot up, eating as they looked through Jadyn's phone.

Sophia had been waiting for this moment since she and Teddy conspired to motivate Jadyn. Her voice elevated, "Oh, you two make a beautiful couple, honey! He's got an amazing smile! I can see the love in your eyes in this picture."

She nodded, "He's perfect for me. He's so patient; and intelligent! You should see his ranch! He's amazing with his horses and takes me on rides into the red rocks. Oh, my God, mom, it's breathtaking in the backcountry. Have you been to Sedona?"

Sophia's eyes lowered for a second, and she lifted her spirit, saying, "Your father and I did some mountain bike riding near Oak Creek. It was gorgeous! Besides that and a jeep tour once on a freezing day, I haven't been to the area nearly enough. I'll definitely visit, but don't worry, I won't intrude on your new life."

Jadyn looked sternly, saying, "Come on, mom, don't talk like that! I'd love for you to visit! I know Aunt Teddy would too."

Sophia began feeling nostalgic and asked, "Up for looking through the family albums?"

Jadyn said with a smile, "I'm game." They moved to the living room with coffee cups in hand, reminiscing.

Sophia grabbed a gift bag beside the couch and sat it on Jadyn's lap, saying, "I bought you a little something to begin your new life."

Jadyn bounced in her seat and shouted, "I can't

believe you did this, mom!"

Sophia smiled big. She knew Jadyn was about to get even more excited, "Open it."

Jadyn couldn't resist teasing Sophia, "Mom, you do realize you don't need to wrap the box if you put it into a gift bag, right?"

With a quit-picking-on-me look, she insisted, "Yeah, yeah, just open it, smarty pants."

Jadyn could see the love in her mom's eyes and her look of support as she watched her untie the bow. Sophia rolled her eyes, saying, "Come on, Jadyn, don't take all day. Just tear the paper."

She teased, smiling big, "Oh, mamma, you know I love to stretch out opening presents; you'll just have to wait."

With a look of anticipation Sophia gave her a sarcastic punch, "Brat!"

Once the wrapping fell off, she exclaimed, "A laptop! Thank you so much! My old one barely works; this is so awesome! Thank you, thank you!" She hugged her tight and said, once more in a whisper, "Thank you, momma. I love you so much."

As Jadyn worked to open the box, Sophia said, "I've always been impressed with your writing, and there's a video camera on this one, so we can video chat."

Jadyn said enthusiastically, "We will. Promise!"

Sophia smiled and exited the room leaving Jadyn to herself with the computer. Jadyn ran her hands across her new laptop as if it had a life of its own.

They spent the better part of a wonderful day together. Feeling good about having given her mother what she thought was enough undivided attention, she texted Kendall, *Dinner?*

She responded in seconds, *Absofunkinlutely*!

Jadyn smiled with a silent chuckle and asked, *Sushi?*

Kendall sent a *rolling eyes emoji* and wrote, *duh*.

Jadyn thought about how long it would take to get ready and texted *7:00?* She made a reservation for 7:30. Kendall was always late.

Kendall, super excited to have her back, typed a quick, *see ya!* along with *the beaming face with smiling eyes emoji*.

Jadyn thought, *wow!* shocked, she responded so quickly! Typically Kendall took hours, if not days, to reply.

Chapter 37

Edamame and Sake

Kendall showed up right after Jadyn arrived at Kendall's usual time, fifteen minutes late. Jadyn teased, "It's about time K," even though she'd planned for her late arrival.

Kendall's typical self-absorption was all too familiar to Jadyn, "Sorry I'm late. I know the party doesn't start until I arrive."

Jadyn stood smiling and shaking her head, giving Kendall a tight squeeze. They held each other till the server arrived with their large hot Sake and two cups. Kendall's eyes opened wide, and they sat quickly, "Sake time!"

Jadyn teased, "You have to share this bottle."

Kendall wrinkled her nose, "What are you insinuating?"

Before Jadyn could answer, the server dropped off their menus, and Kendall continued, "I know last time we had Sushi, I got a bit...."

Jadyn yelled out. "Trashed! You were so trashed!"

They laughed. Jadyn snorted, and they both lost it! Jadyn struggled to talk through her out-of-control laughter, crossed her legs and said, "I'm gonna pee my pants. Stop laughing!"

Kendall cried out, "I can't!" They knew they'd still be laughing if the server hadn't walked up with their edamame.

Kendall's expression tightened, "You sure you want to leave all this and desert me for the desert?"

Jadyn looked annoyed and spoke defensively, "Sedona is *nothing* like a desert. It's breathtaking. Have you seen the pictures I've been sending you? It's a thousand times more beautiful than they show. You simply must visit."

She winked and toasted, "Sure, I'll visit. Kampai!"

Jadyn lifted hers and echoed, "Kampai!"

After taking her shot, Kendall leaned in, "So, are you going to marry this guy?"

Jadyn rocked her head and said, smiling, "I just might. He's the whole package, the perfect guy we conjured up over the years, and let me tell you...."

Curious, Kendall looked at Jadyn pour more Sake, "Tell me what?"

Jadyn lifted her cup of Sake and said, "Gavin is so much better than the man we imagined. Hell, if I'm going to ignore the connection we share. Hell, if I'm going to be her." She swallowed her shot of Sake, affirming the truth of her statement.

Kendall raised the empty Sake decanter indicating to the server to bring another. Then asked Jadyn, "Her who?"

Jadyn pointed at Kendall with edamame, bouncing it like a wet noodle, "The girl who says *I coulda had true love but was too afraid to take the leap.*"

Distracted by a plate of sushi being served to the table next to theirs, Kendall acknowledged, "Oh, her, well, you don't want to be her, I guess I approve, but I'm gonna miss... this."

Jadyn felt her stomach growl and assured her, "This doesn't have to end. We just need to make time for each other. True friendship never dies."

Kendall sassed Jadyn, "It may never die, but I'm dying to pee right now."

Jadyn shook her head, giggled, and said as Kendall walked to the bathroom, "I feel like I'm going to die of hunger; I'm ordering with or without you."

While waiting for the server, she texted Gavin, *about to order sushi. Can't wait to talk tonight! Followed by a smiling face and heart emoji.*

He teased, *tap, tap, tap... I'm waiting!* as if he would ever be impatient. There were no indicators he would ever be anything but kind.

Dinner ended, and she headed home to talk to Gavin as promised. They spoke for a few minutes before she drifted off to sleep.

Jadyn discovered she'd fallen asleep on him when she woke up to his text the following day. *If I didn't know any better, I'd think I bored you to sleep, but I know it was the Sake. Cheeky smiling face emoji, talk to you tomorrow, XO!*

She was tired but recognized last night was just the beginning of get-togethers, shopping, and packing. There wasn't much to pack, and Sophia cautioned her not to take everything, in case she changed her mind and wanted to come back home! This aggravated her to no end!

Jadyn shook off her frustration and switched focus to how excited she felt about this move to Sedona. Jadyn was grateful for her aunt Teddy letting her stay with her, arranging her job at the gallery, and introducing her to the amazing man anxiously awaiting her arrival just eight hours away.

She packed a cooler, filled her gas tank, set the radio

at maximum volume, and drove to her future, a future leading to some of the most intense times of her young life.

Chapter 38

Harvest Moon

Jadyn savored the enormous, surreal, cinnamon-orange glowing harvest moon sliced in half by silhouettes of red rock formations. Cautiously and slowly, Jadyn drove, avoiding the multitude of camera-toting tourists crossing the highway on foot in front of oncoming traffic. They ran mindlessly, hoping to capture the vivid and immense beauty unfolding. Jadyn knew the light-blue sky would soon fade to black. Revealing the moon's enormity on this lunar-like landscape. She couldn't resist the urge to join in. She pulled over, lowered her window, began taking pictures, and texted one to Gavin. *Guess where I am?*

He quickly texted back, *Bell Rock, you're almost home! Sick shot! Teddy and I are looking at it, too, and thinking how much better it would be with you here! Hurry up but drive safe! Heart emoji.*

Jadyn sarcastically replied, *you actually typed whole words and sentences! You know I'm always careful. Heart and winking face emoji. See you soon!*

Jadyn navigated her way through the excited onlookers and back onto the highway. She continued her drive with the passenger window open, allowing in the unusually frigid air. She kept raising her cell phone, pointing it out the window and snapping pictures, until the sound of gravel under her tires and a loud thud replaced the snap, snap, snap of her phone's camera. Jadyn shouted, "Oh, my God!" tightly gripping the steering wheel and slamming on her brakes! Her SUV slid to a stop on the loose, sandy embankment, causing her phone to slide off her seat and drop between it and the console. She stopped with a few feet between her bumper and a terrified woman holding her daughter's hand. Jadyn could see the color of her angry, disapproving eyes glaring back at her when she cried out, "I am *SO SORRY!!*"

With her maternal instincts on high alert, holding her daughter close with one hand, flipping her off with the other, she reprimanded Jadyn yelling, "Watch where you're going!" making Jadyn cower in shame. Her guilt was palpable as she passed the woman's husband justifiably yelling along with twenty or so witnesses who also screamed obscenities at her. Their collective faces felt as huge as the rising moon, making just as big an impact as it made in contrast to the sky. She took one more glance at them shaking fists at her and rolled up her window.

Jadyn drove away, in silence, with hands at ten and two o'clock, grateful to have not injured anyone, and vowed never to do something so careless again.

Jadyn pulled into Teddy's driveway and sighed with relief. Gavin stood tall in front of the door and smiled big as he walked to greet her. His much kinder look than those justifiably disapproving people was more comforting than he would ever know.

He opened Jadyn's door and pulled her out, hugging, squeezing, and planting a long, firm kiss on her neck, whispering with a heavy breath, "It feels so good to have you in my arms."

Gavin was unaware of her stress; he picked her up,

spun her around, and playfully said, "Yee-Haw!"

Jadyn giggled, "Silly man." He slid his hands on either side of her face and kissed her, a kiss more intense than any before. This kiss ignited tingles that spread over her entire body. Jadyn felt a burning inside, and a release of the energy built up from months of self-control. She felt safe and at home in his arms.

Not knowing what Jadyn was thinking, Cole said, "Welcome home, sweet thing. Hope your drive was pleasant."

She lifted her energy to match his, "The moon rising was something else!"

He grabbed her by the hand, "Wait till you see it from Teddy's backyard!" They ran into the backyard where Gavin's beer and aunt Teddy waited, seated in her chair. Teddy lovingly spoke, "Welcome home, sweetie." She outstretched her arm, and Jadyn leaned in to accept a one-arm hug as Teddy held her chamomile tea with the other hand.

Gavin easily saw Jadyn's warm smile beneath the brightly glowing, awe-inspiring harvest moon suspended and virtually taking up the entire sky. Its presence emphasized the blessings and gifts her aunt bestowed upon her as she settled into a chair, calmly saying, "It's good to be home, Auntie."

She still felt the road vibrating in her body and knew it wouldn't take much for her to fall asleep, especially wrapped up in Gavin's arms. Jadyn was determined to stay awake. This was a night she would never forget.

Once the moon was rinsed of its orange tint, they got up to go into the house. Jadyn was exhausted but wasn't going to let it stop her from going to Gavin's. She whispered in Teddy's ear not to wait up for her, gave her a goodbye hug, and turned to Gavin with hand outstretched. He took her hand, led her to his truck, and grabbed her overnight bag on the way. He opened the door for her, and once Gavin settled in, she slid over and rested her head on his shoulder, her legs folded and feet up on the seat as he drove to his ranch.

He happily wrapped his right arm around her and asked, "So, tell me how the goodbye sessions went? Is everyone upset like you expected?"

She smiled, looked out the windshield, glad to not be driving, and answered him, "It went much better than I expected, but my friends will kill me if we don't make a trip to visit them soon. They want to meet you and give their stamp of approval."

They laughed, and he reassured her, "Let's plan a trip after the rodeo competitions are over. I'll have money to spend on you and quite possibly a new truck to impress them with."

She argued, "You don't need to do anything to impress them."

Gavin loved hearing her defend him as he said, "I hope my cooking will impress you tonight. I made tri-tip and scallop potatoes. I wanted to see what veggie you'd like, so I didn't make any. I can make a salad, asparagus, or any canned veggie variety." When she didn't respond, he looked to discover she'd fallen asleep. It warmed his heart, recalling his mother asleep against his father's open arm on the couch nearly every night. He was caught up watching her until his tires rolled off the smooth concrete and onto the washboard hard dirt with a bumpy, thumping, grinding sound. The truck bounced and shook from side to side, and Jadyn sat up, grabbed hold of the handle alongside her door, and said,

"Rock and roll, baby!"

He laughed, agreeing, "Yep! Rock and roll!"

His truck screamed as the undercarriage squeaked, and groaned and unfastened items bounced around in the bed, and her suitcase slid across its uneven metal surface. They could be heard for miles on the road servicing the ranches in the canyon. Before his ranch was even in sight, they could hear the horses whinny and Chase, his yellow lab, bark which only escalated as he parked the truck.

Gavin grabbed her bag from the truck bed, hoping it wasn't damaged. He opened the door for Jadyn and grasped her waist with both hands to guide her feet to the ground from the above-average-height truck cabin. Gavin was surprised when she jumped to the ground and spoke with a spunky-sounding voice, "I can get out of this manly truck of yours a lot easier than I can get up in it." She gave him a quick kiss on his cheek and headed to the door.

Gavin's horses ran back and forth along the fence line bordering the left side of his house. He used railroad ties to create a lit walkway to his screen-covered front door. His larger-than-average gravel driveway and parking area appeared like a landing strip. He made another pathway on the far-right end of his parking lot. It led to a gate where his students entered for their riding lessons. Signposts guided visitors around the ranch reducing accidental knocks on his front door.

Once they entered the house, Chase flew through the doggie door inserted into the wall beside the back door and greeted them with a wet-tongued welcome. He was a young dog with boundless energy and alternated his front paws and concurrently looked at Gavin with tongue hanging out the side of his smiling mouth. He made whiny, grunting sounds until Gavin patted his head and offered him a biscuit.

Jadyn giggled, saying, "He sure did miss you."

Cole set her straight, "Don't mistake feed me, feed me, for him missing me!" Gavin filled his bowl with kibble, put it outside the back door, and said, "The moon is turning night into day; it sure is impressive!"

Jadyn stood warming herself next to his larger-than-average fireplace set right of the back wall and stretched almost as long as the living room, "It sure is. I've never seen the moon so big or been able to see the surface details so well. Even when camping, there is just something different about the Arizona sky.

Gavin confidently spoke, "It's because I'm under the Arizona Sky! Hungry?" he asked as he slid his arm around the small of her back and walked with her to the kitchen. Starving a split second before they arrived, now all Jadyn could think about was making love to Gavin. "I need a shower, big time."

He sniffed her neck, "You aren't kidding, whew!"

She hit his shoulder, "Hey! You're supposed to always say I smell pretty."

"Okay, you smell pretty, pretty strong!" They laughed as they entered the bathroom in the master bedroom. He pulled a towel from the cupboard, turned on the water, and turned back to see Jadyn had pulled off her top.

She tempted him with her eyes and invited him, asking, "wanna join me?"

With eyes wide, he asked, "You sure?"

She answered him by smiling and slowly pulling

his shirt out from his wranglers. She slowly kissed his stomach as he held her hair loosely in his grasp. He closed his eyes tight, took a breath, and said, "Come here." He gently pulled her head up and kissed her.

Still kissing, she reached behind to unclip her bra and slipped it off her shoulders. Gavin took a step back to gaze at her breasts and leaned in to kiss her neck. She put her open palm against his forehead stopping him. She leaned her back against the wall, then slowly unzipped and dropped her jeans. Gavin hypnotically watched as she stepped out of them, slid her thumbs into the waistband of her thong, and tempted him by shifting her hips side to side, slowly sliding the thong to the jeans.

Gavin had only managed to remove his shirt as Jadyn stepped into the shower and beneath the water. His boots were tight and slow to come off as he rushed, sitting on his hand-made, single slab, high-gloss, Juniper wood bench. He kept his eyes fixed on her ghost-like figure through the steamy glass. He was privy to segments, or slight glimpses of her naked body through water lines formed by little droplets, conjoining and trailing, some zigzagging, as others connected, slipping and sliding under their combined weight, creating increasingly larger lines and columns. These trailing lines of clarity on the glass were instantly veiled by more steam, taunting and teasing him. Cole squinted, hoping to see her through each droplet's path. He was surprised when Jadyn playfully slid her hand over the glass, clearing the steam away from her face, and teased, "What's taking you so long, Gavin?"

Jadyn, fully aware her actions were driving him crazy, decided to increase his impassioned torture by pushing her breasts and belly against the glass, finally supplying his eyes with the treasure he sought. He sucked in a deep involuntary breath! It seemed stuck in his chest as he dropped the last sock into his boot and wiped his hand across his face and over his hair. Gavin walked over to join Jadyn for the beginning of a long-awaited night of passion. He entered the shower and embraced her slippery body, with his desire fully revealed against her saying, "Oh, my God, you're killing me!"

She wanted to keep toying with him, "Am I? I don't want to kill you; I'm not finished with you yet." but once his wet skin slid against hers, it was his turn to drive her crazy. Gavin slowly slid his chest against hers, up and side to side, melding their bodies together. The purposeful long wait for lovemaking was sweet torture for them, and the reward sweeter because of it. Gavin had no intention of rushing now. He planned to savor each sensation, each pull from the nerves igniting beneath her fingers as she lightly skimmed them over him. She, too, wanted to delay the finality of this long-awaited joining.

They washed one another's hair and bodies, slowly caressing and kissing as the water poured over them until it lost its heat. Gavin wrapped a towel over her shoulders and sat on the wooden bench again, with her standing naked in front of him, wet, cleansed, and trembling with desire. He slowly, calmly, and passionately licked water droplets from her breasts. His gaze, looking up at her eyes and his mouth, igniting and joining their combined passion, made the outside world disappear.

Still looking at him, Jadyn touched his face, "I love

you, Gavin."

He swiftly picked her up and carried her to the bed, saying, "I've been in love with you since your eyes twinkled at me teaching you the two-step."

Gavin slowly set her on the bed. He laid her back with a gentle push of the palm of his hand and tasted her. He didn't allow her to touch him, holding her hands as she squirmed and wiggled until he brought her to climax. Gavin rose from his knees, "I love you so much." and slid his beard up her body ending with a kiss on her waiting mouth.

Her back arched, and her head followed as their bodies united. They made love slowly, with shared mindfulness and tenderness born only from true love. After the sweet release of their passion, Gavin said, "I thought I was going to lose my mind while you were away, and I must admit, I was afraid you might change your mind. I want you to know I was prepared to sell my ranch and come after you if you did."

With fingers digging in, Jadyn pulled him to her. She felt tortured, unable to get close enough to him. She surprised herself with her insatiable desire and unnerving animalistic behavior growing within, seemingly forcing her to pin his legs to the bed with hers. After joining together in lovemaking, she held tight to him, pressing her body against his to join them as one.

When long, steady breaths replaced her panting, followed by a light snore, he smiled and slid out from under her heavy head.

Cole quietly walked to the kitchen and prepared a dinner plate for them to share. His skin glimmered in the moonlight, reflecting the heat from his cooling shoulders.

He returned to the bedroom, spread open the silky white drapes using his free hand, and gently kissed her to wake her. With a content moan, she yawned, stretched, and reached her hand to grab him. He playfully swerved his hip to miss her reach and stepped over to a wooden table, where a bottle of champagne rested in icy water. Cole flashed Chase a, *you better not eat this,* glare as he put the plate on the table, lit a candle, and popped the cork! She watched him fill their glasses and expected him to come to the bed. He sat instead, with his left foot beneath his right knee, hand resting on the arm of his big blue tufted chair, and invited Jadyn to join him, "Come, sit with me. You've *got* to see this."

She slid Gavin's robe on, walked over, and slowly sat on his lap, "Oh, my God!"

Gavin smiled, "I know! Look at that moon! And there's Mars below it. It's like a painting, right?"

Jadyn loved to hear him describe it as a painting and said with a sigh, "I feel I've been transported to another planet. It's breathtaking! Thank you for waking me up. I would have hated to know I missed it. I'll never forget this night."

He held her tighter, "Me either. I wish I didn't have to go away this weekend."

Emotional and dreading his departure, she sighed and said, "Me too, babe, I know you're an amazing rider, but those eight seconds stop time for me. Promise you'll stay safe."

He wanted to lighten the mood, "Put your big girl panties on. I'll be fine, no whining, got it?"

She pushed a piece of meat into his mouth with a sassy expression, "okay," and another onto Chase's dripping ready tongue.

Jadyn's repeated yawns and head bobbing signaled Gavin it was time to end the night, a night they both longed for. This, their first night to sleep entangled after sharing themselves, an incredible night made even more delicious; they bathed in the glowing harvest moon's rays streaming through the windows and illuminating their sweaty skin.

The next harvest moon, a year later, was even more astounding, with Jadyn and Gavin set against its enormity, hands embraced and laced with an Irish Handfasting ribbon. Her gown glowed with an orange tint of the sunset's washing. Joined by a small gathering of family and friends, they faced one another and exchanged vows, promised to remain together, forever joined, with only death parting.

Chapter 39

Separation Anxiety

The sun rose with blinding clarity as Jadyn mucked the stalls, moody, feeling the rodeo was Gavin's mistress and the bitch stole him away again. Fighting December's chill, Jadyn wore his denim jacket. She walked to the horses over a light dusting of snow covering the red clay soil, like powdered sugar sprinkled on a cake. Jadyn didn't want to complain but missed his normal flirtatious play. How he slapped her ass when she bent over to fork the hay or teased her for being too short to get the fly ointment off the high shelf. She felt sorry for herself as she climbed on the wooden table below it, wishing he could grab it for her.

She closed the gate and pulled the heavy rope over the top of the post just as her cell vibrated in her back pocket. She flung off the leather glove and pulled it out to read the incoming text. *Love you, Darlin, can't wait to kiss your face! This is the last week of the season, and you'll be the present I unwrap!*

She smiled and replied, *could you feel me missing you?*

He shocked her with his quick reply, *I'd rather feel myself inside of you, winking smiley face emoji.*

Grinning, she took in a breath and messaged back *3 days and counting! Just get home safe & PLEASE wear the helmet!*

He avoided the topic with *Phone sex later?* And ending with a *Tongues out emoji.*

Chapter 40

December's Fall

Gavin's lack of response to Jadyn's request for him to be safe and wear the headgear she packed in his suitcase aggravated her. She sent him a rolling eyes emoji followed by blowing kisses emoji and heard Teddy's ringtone. Teddy's voice was soft; she knew it was stressful for Jadyn to watch Gavin ride, "Just calling to confirm our date this evening."

Jadyn came back with, "You, me, and the rodeo, I'll bring wine, see you around 6:00. Gotta go. I'm getting into the shower."

Teddy smiled with tight lips, "Okay, dear, see you soon."

Jadyn's day had been uneventful, almost too uneventful. She always felt conflicting emotions when Gavin rode, and today was no exception.

Jadyn locked up the gallery and drove to the store to purchase a couple bottles of wine and macaroons for dessert. Hiding the anxiety clinging to her like a backpack on her shoulders, heavy and unshakable.

Aware Teddy carried her own stress each time they joined together to watch Gavin ride, she looked in her visor's mirror and spoke to herself, "Get it together." She shook off the self-pity. Jadyn opened the front door. Teddy's garlic, rosemary, thyme, and lime marinated oven-roasted chicken aroma wafted over Jadyn. She let Teddy know she'd arrived, saying loudly, "Hello, Auntie!

Oh, my goodness, it smells like heaven. I'm drooling!"

Teddy smiled without looking up from peeling carrots as Jadyn pulled the cork, poured two glasses of wine, and set one beside her. With her chin lowered and eyes looking over the rims of her glasses on the tip of her nose, Teddy said, "Thanks, doll."

Jadyn washed her hands, rinsed and tore the romaine lettuce into a wooden salad bowl, and cut the remaining veggies beside her. They barely spoke, repeating their dining ritual, each quietly worrying about Gavin.

They took their wine and plates to the sofa. With music playing softly, the TV on and silent, they ate and watched the first few riders. They'd seen enough rides to know what the announcer would say and, between bites, enjoyed mimicking him.

Gavin walked up to the fence and watched the rider along with them. Teddy lowered the music, and Jadyn turned up the TV, releasing sounds of the rodeo into the room.

The announcers talked about his career wins, showing clips from his previous rides and falls. Jadyn's face tightened with each clip. No matter how often she watched, it always made her nervous when it was his turn. She hated that Gavin refused to wear a helmet and chest gear. He insisted he couldn't ride with them. Jadyn always packed them in his bag, hoping he'd change his mind.

Seeing Gavin choose not to wear his gear, she bit her nails, fighting her anger. He positioned himself on "Hellraiser," a white Brahma bull. Hellraiser had only been ridden for eight seconds a few times in his career, making them even more nervous as they watched.

The chute flew open with loud banging, clanging sounds mixed with the bull's defiant grunting! Gavin had perfect form right out of the gate! The crowd screamed! Jadyn and Teddy joined in, screaming in celebration and cheering as if they were in the stands! When the bell rang, they jumped up and yelled, "He did it!"

The announcers described Gavin's ride as *perfect!* And his 88.2 score guaranteed him a place in the final round.

When Teddy answered her ringing cell, she heard Sophia's voice. It was so loud Jadyn could hear her from across the room, saying how proud she felt about Gavin and asking Jadyn to congratulate him when they spoke.

A few minutes later, Gavin texted. *I finally made it, babe! Thanks for being you. I love you so much! Can't wait to see you!*

Other riders completed their rounds, and the finals started. No one rode as well as Gavin, making his chances for the big purse certain. When his turn came around, the cheers from the audience overwhelmed the announcers bringing them to laughter. One went as far as to say, "If it were up to the fans, Gavin would be wearing his World-Champ buckle already."

He mounted a black bull named Satan's Fury and rode till the bell sounded, riding even better than the first ride! He had won the purse! The crowd roared! Their cheers quickly changed to screams of trepidation when he attempted to dismount; he couldn't. Gavin's hand was stuck in the rigging! Everything was in slow-motion like minutes were passing instead of seconds. As time passed, Jadyn's face grew more anxious. Despite the clown's efforts, Satan's Fury dragged Gavin beside him into the metal fencing and back into the arena. When the rigging finally released, setting him free, he resembled a rag doll until finally landing motionless on the dusty dirt.

Jadyn cried out in terror, "Get up, baby, get up! Oh, God, please get up!"

Panic-stricken, Jadyn was helpless to do anything other than stare at the screen. Her mouth dry and frozen open, she watched the medics immobilize Gavin's neck before carrying him away on a stretcher.

When the cameraman zoomed in close to the medic's distressed expression, Jadyn hyperventilated!

She wrapped her arms around herself, her fingers digging into her flesh. She gasped, "No! Oh, my God, no!" Her self-soothing was an utter failure as she watched the ambulance speed away, with sirens blaring. Jadyn became unhinged when they cut to a commercial, and visual contact was lost.

Jadyn looked at Teddy with a pleading expression collapsing onto the couch. Teddy placed her hand on Jadyn's shoulder, kissed her forehead, quickly searched for the number, and called the person in charge. "Please let his wife know how sorry we all are; he was taken to Sunrise Hospital."

Teddy asked softly, "How is he?"

Her caring voice was soft, her words daggers in Teddy's ears. "All I know is they said the family should consider coming as soon as possible."

Jadyn's face was pale as she sat rocking her body with both hands over her heart and taking short, repeating breaths between soft, sobbing bursts. Jadyn wished someone would say it was all a dream. But it wasn't a dream. Their blissful marriage of six months is now polluted with the remnants of Gavin's unexpected and utterly avoidable choice.

Teddy left the room and called Luca, "Hi, Bella."

She fought back her tears, saying, "Gavin's injured."

Luca, caught off-guard, said, "What? How?"

Luca's heart ached with compassion when he heard Theodosia's pained voice, "Bull riding."

He spoke tenderly, "Sorry, Bella, can I do anything?"

Teddy fought back her tears, "Could you please fly us to Vegas? He's been taken to a hospital there."

Luca was quick to say, "Yes. Let me see if I can get the flight cleared immediately; I'll call you right back."

Teddy gave Jadyn a damp washcloth and told her to rest as she packed a bag and called a friend to arrange for care of Jadyn's animals. Sophia texted *I got a flight. Be there ASAP. Broken Heart emoji.*

When Luca called back, Teddy put the call on speaker phone, so Jadyn could hear, "Bella, I pulled strings; the Beechcraft is cleared for take-off when you arrive."

Teddy finished packing her bag and sat beside Jadyn. "Sweetheart, your mom's heading to the airport. I'm driving you to get your things, and Luca's flying us to Gavin."

Teddy's Cadillac SUV was spotless and still had a new car smell despite being three years old. Its leathery aroma reminded Jadyn of Gavin's chaps. The seats felt smooth and warm beneath her fingers as she traced the stitching with a slow, light touch while George Strait sang, *Carrying Your Love with Me,* one of Gavin's favorite songs. Packing seemed so unimportant to Jadyn. All she wanted was Gavin's promise to be fulfilled, for him to call, to hear his voice.

Jadyn packed a bag and gave Chase a treat, "Be a good boy. I... we'll be back soon." She gave him a soft kiss on his nose and a really firm hug.

Teddy questioned her, "Doors locked? Keys for the helper? Anything else?"

Jadyn just shook her head and walked beside her, holding onto her arm like a crutch, switching lights on, and setting the alarm.

Chapter 41

Clear the Runway

They arrived at the airport, parked, ran inside, and texted Luca. A gray-haired man wearing a jumpsuit with a Red Rocks Aviation patch, and mirrored shades, greeted them. "Hi, I'm Mr. Reynolds. Are you Luca Moretti's guests?"

Teddy stepped forward with hand outstretched, "Yes, I'm Theodosia. This is my niece Jadyn."

Mr. Reynolds' calming words, "Pleasure to meet you. May I take your bags?" helped keep Teddy grounded.

Jadyn was silent, hiding behind sunglasses, nodding in response to his questions, and relieved Teddy took charge, handing over their bags.

Mr. Reynolds led them to Luca's twin-engine plane. "Safe travels, ladies." Once they were inside, he informed the air traffic controller he'd cleared the runway.

Luca welcomed and encouraged them, "I'll fly you to Gavin as fast as these wings will take us."

Jadyn slid into the back seat wearing Gavin's jacket, looking tiny in the space he normally filled.

Teddy questioned Jadyn, "Do you want me to sit back there with you?"

She shook her head, "No. Sit up front with Luca. I'm okay."

They jumped when Luca yelled out the open window, "Clear!" announcing to bystanders to stand clear of the props.

The plane's engines turned on with a loud purring sound. Burning fuel fumes filled the plane's cabin, reminding Jadyn of a morning at Lake Powell. She and Gavin witnessed close to a hundred bass fishermen gathered near the dock before a high stake competition. Boats floating side by side in foggy fumes, engines idling, contestants readying their fishing poles, fantasizing about their win, and sharing big fish stories.

This isn't Lake Powell. This isn't a boat. This is the sky, not a lake. They're in flight, Vegas bound, only ninety minutes since Gavin's horrific fall. Jadyn's head resting against the window couldn't put her mind at ease. Navigation lights flashing from wing tips and her blank stare reflecting back were all she could see from her darkened window. Replaying his fall and hoping the engines and Luca's headphones muffled the sound of her sobbing.

Fifty-five minutes of tears flowing made the flight seem like hours. Jadyn held tight to her box of tissues, battling with wanting to know Gavin's status yet being afraid to actually learn about his condition. Feeling unequipped for this, never wanted her mother's support more.

Luca arranged for a driver to take Teddy and Jadyn from the airfield to the hospital and let them know he'd follow after he'd taken care of storing his plane for the day.

Chapter 42

Hurry up & Wait

The driver sped, aggressively out-maneuvering motorists clogging up the road, making it to the hospital in less than fifteen minutes. Jadyn and Teddy quickly entered the E.R. and anxiously approached the reception desk in the waiting room.

Jadyn hadn't spoken a word since leaving Sedona. When she told the nurse, "I'm Gavin Michael's wife," she was taken aback by the gravelly sound of her voice. She cleared her throat and said, "I was told he was brought here by ambulance."

With no expression and virtually no eye contact, the nurse standing before them spoke as she motioned with her forehead over to a line of chairs, "Take a seat. We'll have his doctor come out and talk to you soon," and continued to type with eyes fixed on her monitor.

Jadyn begged, "He's alive, isn't he?"

The nurse dismissed her, "Yes, Miss, but please take a seat." The cold, lifeless expression on the wretched nurse's face was impossible to read. Jadyn decided the nurse was a heartless bitch after telling her to sit like an f-ing dog! She questioned herself, thinking, *Me sit?! How utterly ridiculous! I need to help! I need to see Gavin! I need answers!*

Each person in the waiting room sat awaiting their turn, suffering their own reality, chained to their own bubbles of misery. Yet somehow, it felt as if the room was devoid of emotion. Jadyn's fight or flight instincts engaged; she felt the molecules in the air pushing against her skin and the room closing in around her. *The damn clock! Those damn hands, clicking along its white glass-covered face! Tick-tock, tick-tock!* She could hear the low clicking sound growing louder as her senses intensified with each passing minute.

Jadyn's rapidly bouncing knee and painfully tight grip on Teddy's wrist signaled she was overloaded and about to lose her mind. Even the slightest sound made Jadyn jerk her head in its direction. Her heart raced with expectant, fearful thoughts of the doctor's evaluation. Even the rise and fall of each breath was exhausting.

Jadyn's head rested on her aunt's shoulder, and Teddy finished reading Sophia's text and softly spoke, "Your mom's waiting to board her plane. She should be here in a couple hours, honey. I also arranged for Samuel to stay at the ranch with Chase, so you can focus on Gavin."

Jadyn pushed her head hard against Teddy, "I couldn't handle this without you. I'm so scared. What if...?"

Teddy pulled her hand from under and placed it over Jadyn's. She gently patted it and said, "Jadyn, think good thoughts. Picture him on his horse riding beside you in the backcountry, the beautiful life you've created, your favorite places, and remember, this too shall pass."

Almost growling, she said, "I know, The Laws of Attraction. Not easy to do right now."

Teddy dropped her head and let it bob a couple times before compassionately responding, "Yes, I know, but..."

Jadyn begged, "Please, not now. Gavin's hurt, and I

choose to be a mess."

Teddy knew to let it go, and they sat silently in the hospital's stiff, uncomfortable chairs, cuddling beneath the warm wind blowing in from the dust-covered vent. It didn't have a chance of actually warming the room. Maybe it could, if not for the constant opening and closing of the automatic doors continually triggered by the smokers outside, pacing and talking on cell phones; hearing their worried voices trying to console the person listening made Jadyn appreciate Teddy's comforting touch and soothing words.

Darkness fell during the two stagnant hours since they accepted they had to be patient and wait. Finally, the dreaded double doors of hell opened, and a short, stocky sweaty-haired man wearing surgical blues entered, remaining near the waiting room entrance. Two nurses followed behind him, intently listening as he spoke in a tone frustratingly much too low for Jadyn to hear. Unsure he was Gavin's doctor, Jadyn quietly watched, grinding her teeth and fidgeting in her seat.

Jadyn thought about how the nurses acted like they were his maids. One nurse held a bag open for him as he removed and dropped in his gloves, shoe covers, and cap, while the other offered him a cloth to wipe his sweat. Their unreadable faces looked at him until one looked out into the waiting room. In a pleasant, warm tone, she spoke in a whisper, barely loud enough to hear, "Michael's family?"

Jadyn and Teddy stood and sat again as the nurse motioned for them to remain seated. The doctor and two nurses approached as a group, making Jadyn fear the worst. She gripped the sides of her chair to stay upright, awaiting the secrets only they knew and waiting as they exchanged looks at one another. She thought his salt and pepper hair and black thick-rimmed glasses framing his moist eye sockets made him seem more intelligent as he finally spoke from his round, afternoon-shadowed chubby face.

With eyes fixed on Teddy, he raised his hand in greeting but didn't offer it and stated, "Hello, I'm Dr. Brandt. I worked on Gavin," and questioned, "Your son?"

Jadyn leaned in and urged, "My husband."

As Dr. Brandt spoke, Jadyn thought his voice sounded deeper than she'd expected. The distracting ambient noise fell away as she waited. She felt sucked into a tunnel with no oxygen. Time slowed, slower than the wall clock's ticking. His words would eventually come out. She knew it. She needed him to speak so the merry-go-round-ish repeating fearful thoughts, sounding like a million whispering voices in her mind, would finally be silenced! His words stung when they finally broke through the chaos in her mind, and unbeknownst to Jadyn, what he said would play in her mind over, and over and over again, haunting her for months to come.

His mask sucked into his mouth with each inhalation as he nervously yet authoritatively spoke, "I'm in charge of your husband's care."

Jadyn felt he couldn't have been bothered to learn anything about Gavin before cutting into his body. Oddly, his awkward indifference comforted her. Somehow knowing he'd only thought of Gavin as a body as he worked on him made her feel he was emotionless and used only science to repair the damage like an auto mechanic would repair a car.

Dr. Brandt searched her face for approval and,

with Gavin's chart in one hand and pen in the other, continued speaking in a caring, sincere tone. "He had internal bleeding we were able to resolve." The doctor clicked his pen several times and placed it in his white coat's chest pocket. He flipped open the chart and read aloud, "Your husband also suffered one broken rib and a D A I."

Jadyn questioned, "D A I?" Her eyes searched the hanging jowls on his emotionless face for a look of concern, or comfort, or any emotion.

He looked up from the chart at Jadyn and sympathetically responded, "Sorry. It stands for Diffuse Axonal Injury. It's a type of skull or brain injury, a medical classification for severe head trauma."

Jadyn sharply asked, "And?"

He replied quickly, "Sorry, miss, I don't want to frighten you, but I also don't want to give you false hope. Brain injuries are unpredictable."

She angrily thought, *can he talk any slower?*

Jadyn begged for information, asked, "Meaning?"

He could see her eyes searching for answers and tears welling as he continued, "I know my words aren't comforting, but I'm required to be honest with you. Your husband arrived in a comatose state. The E M T reported he wasn't wearing a helmet. If he weren't wearing one during his fall, it would explain the severity of his injuries."

Jadyn closed her eyes tightly and turned away as he spoke about the damn helmet Gavin refused to wear! If only he was born after 1994 and was forced to wear one! He was so proud of the fact he didn't have to follow the *new* rules, no matter how upset it made her. Jadyn held in the anger she felt towards Gavin, replacing her emotion with compassion and hope.

Dr. Brandt waited for Jadyn to turn back around, and when she nodded, he continued speaking. "This type of injury can be mild, or you may need to prepare yourself for a prolonged comatose state. The next twenty-four to forty-eight hours are the most crucial. We encourage you to stay with him as much as possible; talk to him, play his favorite music, and hold his hand. We can bring in a rollaway bed for you should you want to sleep here."

Teddy answered for Jadyn, saying, "Yes, please, thank you, doctor."

Jadyn agreed, "I don't think I could sleep otherwise. This is all too surreal. Can I see him now?"

"Yes. I'll have Nurse Laundry take you in."

Chapter 43

Whiplashed

T he nurse's expression was compassionate as she looked at Jadyn's expectant face. Jadyn was blinking her eyes rapidly as if windshield wipers were fighting the rain, trying to erase the words flying out of the nurse's mouth, each like a dart piercing her heart.

"Before you go in, I need to prepare you for how he looks. His head is swollen, eyes are black and blue. This happens with this type of injury; we have a thin tube, called a shunt, implanted in his skull. It controls probable cranial pressure from forming and allows cerebral fluid to flow out of the brain. So the fluid doesn't buildup, reducing chances of further brain damage, not to say he has any. We won't know one way or the other for at least a few more days."

With a desperate look first at Teddy and then at Nurse Laundry, Jadyn implored, "So you're saying he has a tube sticking out of his head?"

The nurse seemed to ignore Jadyn and said, "You'll need a sweater or something to keep you warm because we keep the room chilly for patients with head injuries."

Teddy quickly texted Sophia, *Bring or buy blankets! The room is cold! XO.*

The nurse kept her composure and appeared robotic to Jadyn as she continued speaking, "His time in the recovery room is just about up. We'll be moving him into a private room in the ICU. I'll come get you in about a half hour. You're welcome to continue to wait here."

Her words were so foreign and frightening for Jadyn. She sat staring blankly at the nurse's face. She imagined her first look at Gavin as Teddy responded to the nurse, "Yes. We'll wait; thank you."

The nurse put her hand on Jadyn's shoulder, "Don't you worry; it won't be long till I or another nurse returns." She and the doctor said everything so matter-of-factly, so sterile, so void of emotion. Each of their statements made her feel like an outsider to some plotline. Their words left her nauseous, just like the sterile, damp floors emitting bleach-cleaner fumes into the waiting room turned her stomach and strained her lungs.

Jadyn's memories of Gavin and Nurse Laundry's words made her feel whiplashed! Jadyn's bittersweet memories came as flashes and kept feeding her emotions, flipping her from a state of joy to unimaginable pain. Their joy-filled life, their pleasure, the love building that virtually blanketed them each day was extinguished by her burning, stinging words. Like a flicker of a flame trying to remain lit, all but burned out, barely holding on. With only the nurse's words to go on, Gavin's life and her comprehension of his state of being made her feel the world was spinning out of control, like vertigo combined with heartbreak.

Chapter 44

White Soled Shoes

J adyn sat dazed, unable to recall the nurse's name or anything she'd said when the doors swung open. Nurse Laundry came to retrieve her as promised, but there was no joy in this, only apprehension and the promise of devastation. Her uncertain future seemed more than she could endure. A future forced upon her and one she would be forced to face. Her mind's struggle to hold onto the past was like fingernails scratching and clinging as she desperately longed to maintain control and not allow the scary reality to rip her away into the unknown.

As they walked, Jadyn could feel the nurse's glove-covered hand slipping over her bare skin with a sweaty lubricant-ish nastiness. Jadyn cringed at the strangeness of their hand holding, which only amplified the surrealness of this solemn, depressing walk. She shrank into some peculiar version of a lost child. This slow walk required nothing more than her attendance. Putting one foot in front of the other and her hand guiding the way afforded Jadyn extra time to disassociate from reality. She mindlessly pushed through the misty blur filling her head and the halls as they walked. Their footsteps fell silent, mixing with hospital sounds of bells and phones ringing, pumping blood pressure cuffs, and voices of doctors and nurses; sounds hidden behind curtains drawn on hanging silver chains. Passing by, each one concealing their own story to be told, was disturbing yet made her feel as if she belonged. When her eyes met those of a desperately frightened elderly woman holding tight to the bedrail, her chest ripped apart with sorrow, and her fear elevated to panic mode!

Their steps remained silent, floating through the nightmare until the floor squealed like a mouse being crushed beneath the nurse's white-soled shoes, waking Jadyn. The nurse's shoes seemed more like skates, sliding effortlessly over the shiny, cold, white floor as they rounded each turn in this maze of misery. Jadyn knew she should pay attention to where they were going and should have paid more attention to what the nurse said about Gavin's appearance, but everything was so unreal.

Pulling back the light-cerulean blue privacy curtain, and hearing the screech of the metal chain sliding over the pole suspended from the ceiling, ultimately exposed him and accosted her senses. Jadyn fell against Nurse Laundry. Using her latex-gloved hand, she coaxed Jadyn to a chair close to his bedside. Jadyn was stunned by how cold the leather seat felt as she forced herself to look at Gavin.

Nothing could have prepared her for the sight of him lying frozen in his bed, making everything about the room even colder. She blinked and saw the thick white bandage covering his bulging head. She blinked again, and the shunt sticking out of the gauze, which looked more like a helmet than a bandage, came into focus. It made her angry, as she privately yelled, thinking, *if only you wore your helmet, you wouldn't be wearing this gauze helmet from hell.* Jadyn stared at the ECG monitor tracking his heartbeat. Wires seemed to come from everywhere, each connecting Gavin to machines that prevented her from embracing him, breaking her heart.

Her incomparable desire to connect with Gavin swelled as she spoke, "Your Doc said I should talk to you. He also said I should touch you." She skimmed her hand just above his bandaged chest. "I'm scared I'll hurt you, babe." Jadyn squeezed her eyes closed, releasing tears. Holding her breath, listening to the ventilator pushing breaths for Gavin, his chest rising in sync with its hollow sound, she wished with all she possessed, his voice would fracture this mechanical, robotic cacophony. Instead, she heard the incessant high-pitched, head-splitting beep, beep, beep increasing and reverberating. She mournfully took hold of his hand and lightly rested her head on his bandaged chest. She thought *light as a feather* and whispered, "I love you so much. Gavin, don't leave me. I need you; Chase needs you. Wake up, babe. Please wake up."

She closed her eyes, spiritually connecting to him, and said, "Oh, babe. It feels so good to finally touch you." Exhausted from the longest twenty-four hours of her life and feeling somewhat at peace, she dozed off.

Sophia quietly entered and saw Jadyn's eyes were closed. Trying not to wake her daughter, she slowly set flowers and hot tea on the rolling table. She made up the rollaway bed with a soft chenille throw brought from home and then patiently waited, watching Jadyn sleep against Gavin. Heartbroken and wishing she could spare her this suffering, she prayed for them.

His Critical-Care nurse entered the room, waking Jadyn and Sophia. She switched on the light above

Gavin's bed to read the label on the I.V. bag. With skilled fingers, she set the drip, glanced at Jadyn's observing eyes, and whispered, "I'll turn the light off in a minute. Can I get you anything? I can bring you some crackers, Jell-O, or sherbet; if you like."

Jadyn examined her stomach's churning and shook her head, "No. Thanks." Sophia remained quiet as the nurse checked Gavin's vitals.

His nurse responded softly, "Should you change your mind, you'll find water, ice, crackers, and the snacks I mentioned left of the nurses' station. Oh, there's always coffee and tea as well." She made eye contact with Sophia and nodded, "You're both welcome to it."

Rubbing her eyes, Jadyn said, "Thanks."

Sophia, sitting on a recliner by the window, rose and walked over to Jadyn, saying, "I brought tea and chocolate." Sophia knew if she gave her too much attention Jadyn would cry and inevitably get pissed at her. So she stopped at the rolling table and pointed at the assorted box of candy.

Jadyn saw the bed was made, got up from the chair, and slowly laid down, her eyes on her mom's supportive, loving face. She reached out her hand, "chocolate sounds perfect, momma."

Sophia unwrapped and opened the box, handing it to Jadyn. Parking lot lights streaming in through the partially open blinds illuminated the room. The ambient light accentuated Jadyn; she was pale, and a mixture of mascara and suffering shadowed her glowing jade eyes. Sophia marveled at how bright they got when Jadyn cried as if they were electric and said, "Aunt Teddy and Luca are in the waiting room. We'll take turns with you. The hospital rules won't allow all of us in here at once, or she'd be here too."

Jadyn wanted to be alone with Gavin and insisted they all go get some rest. Sophia kissed her forehead, "We're staying at the hospital hotel next door. Call me if you need anything."

"Thank you, momma. I love you."

"Love you too, doll. Call when you're ready for company." Sophia walked out and quietly closed the door.

Finally, alone with him, she felt the tension leave her body. She slid beneath the familiar and comfortable chenille throw, placed her head on the pillow, and turned to look at Gavin. Jadyn held the tissue box beside her and noiselessly wept.

Chapter 45

Not Quite Home

Jadyn was starting to feel she really knew Dr. Brandt. With only him and the nurses to talk with for the last month of living in the hospital hotel, she was feeling one-dimensional. Jadyn's calendar reminder on her cell let her know Gavin's evaluation was the next day. Hopefully, their sentence in this cell-like room was coming to a close. Worried about him and fretting about his prognosis, she struggled with her thoughts until finally falling asleep.

Jadyn woke up, kissed Gavin, and spoke with her face close to his, "Love you, babe. I'm gonna shower and eat breakfast. See you soon," and headed to the hotel.

She was told to wait for their call, to give them time alone with Gavin, and that they'd be taking him for a brain scan and running tests looking for improvement or possible decline.

She was getting nervous, wondering if something was wrong? It had been several hours with no communication, so she questioned, *Has Doc even seen Gavin today?*

Depressed, knowing she was being impatient and hoping to make time move faster, Jadyn napped.

When she woke to the nurse's ringtone, Jadyn was glad to see it was still daytime and read the text, *Dr. Brandt's status evaluation of Gavin is in 1 hour.*

Standing beside Gavin, holding his hand, Jadyn

faced Dr. Brandt and Nurse Laundry as they talked while reading his chart. Their conversation brought back memories of how she felt on the first day of this month-long ordeal. She thought about how she hadn't seen Nurse Laundry since then, which made everything more intense. She had been so calming that night.

Dr. Brandt finally spoke, "Your husband made it through the most crucial time." He kept referring to the chart and speaking. "He's stable. There aren't any signs of decline." His long pauses between statements left her breathless. "He doesn't appear to have improved." Dr. Brandt's expression led her to believe he didn't mean to speak so casually. "It's hard to detect cognitive function in his comatose state, though." He referred again to the chart, flipped up the page, and then looked at his tablet. Jadyn wondered why anything was written on paper anymore as he continued, "That being said, I feel it's safe to move him, and he should be moved. There's not much more we can do for him here, so we're releasing him to a long-term care facility in Sedona. He'll be moved the day after tomorrow. You're welcome to stay here until then, but the transport vehicle can't take you."

Jadyn detested Dr. Brandt's words, the highs and lows were beyond disappointing and not even close to reassuring, but at least he was coming home to Sedona. She was concerned by the inconsistent statements and asked, "There's no improvement. Are you saying he's not healing?"

Dr. Brandt winced, hearing his miscommunication, and said, "No. He's healing. I was speaking of his brain function. His body is healing. He will always have the shunt to eliminate chances of brain swelling."

He shook his head and finished, "He's doing well and

is safe to go home. What I mean is to be watched over and supported by medical staff at a clinic. He's no longer what we consider a critical care patient. This is good news. Of course, we want him to wake up, but I don't see any indicators that he will since he hasn't already."

Nurse Laundry jumped in, "Don't you lose hope. There is always hope."

After that rollercoaster ride of positive and negative statements, her heart was pounding, and her head was spinning. Jadyn wished her mother or Teddy were there for support but found her strength and spoke confidently, alternating her gaze from Doc to the nurse, "I'll fly home. Thanks for everything." Dr. Brandt felt incredibly uncomfortable when she leaned in and hugged him. "I know you did all you could for Gavin."

Nurse Laundry stepped to Jadyn, gave her a firm hug, and whispered, "Doc's bedside manner needs improvement."

Once the medical staff left the room, Jadyn gave Teddy a call. She attentively listened as Jadyn repeated Dr. Brandt's words. Trying to say the right thing, Theodosia quickly responded, "Wonderful, Gavin's coming home! It's time for you to come home too. Luca and I will come get you tomorrow."

She'd gotten used to the sounds of the machines and nurses and wondered what the long-term hospital would be like. How would sleeping there compare to sleeping here, beside Gavin in this room? The room they've shared as roommates for over 30 days and nights. Jadyn tossed and turned all night, praying for the strength to be what Gavin needed as she longed to hear his voice break through the never-really dark room.

Upon waking the next day, Jadyn gathered her books, cards from loved ones, the chenille throw, and the sweater she'd worn nearly every day. She grabbed Gavin's bag of personal items that came with him from the rodeo and felt sick holding it. It was as if he was reduced to a bag of clothes like an urn. She ate breakfast in the hospital cafeteria, grabbed a coffee to go, and headed to the hotel room with her overstuffed tote bag over her shoulder. Jadyn had spent nights sleeping on the rollaway beside Gavin, a pins-and-needles kinda sleep. She barely slept in the hotel; she just napped there. Packing didn't take long. Jadyn's planning and organized state of mind prepared her to vacate the room at a moment's notice and made today a little easier. She'd resided there with constant cat-like instincts engaged, anticipating an urgent need to leave may arise and never really unpacked.

Jadyn was thrilled to finally check out of the hotel but was conflicted as she slowly rolled her bag into Gavin's hospital room. She spoke tenderly, "Gavin, my love, I'll see you tomorrow. You stay strong. I love you." She thought about staying until they put him in the transport vehicle, but Teddy's convincing words to come home a day early won her over.

She kissed Gavin's cheek, rested hers briefly against his, and then headed to the nurses' station, where she was to sign papers. Jadyn placed a dozen donuts on the counter, saying, "I hope y'all enjoy these; your support and kindness made this past month somewhat bearable. I can't thank you enough." Looking at the release forms, Jadyn asked, "Do you think I should stay?"

His nurse compassionately shook her head and said,

"We'll be in the room with him a lot today. He won't be alone."

Jadyn sensed she was sincere, said a quick goodbye, and rolled her suitcase out of the hospital to the driver's waiting car, who had previously texted announcing he was waiting to take her to the airport.

Teddy welcomed Jadyn with a warm embrace at the cafe inside the small-plane terminal at the airport. They sat for a quick bite to eat at a table in front of a picture window overlooking the quiet tarmac while Luca readied the plane for the flight to Sedona.

Once the plane was fueled and ready to go, Luca texted, *ready for takeoff.*

Teddy and Jadyn finished eating, exited the cafe, and headed to the plane. Jadyn sat in the seat behind Luca and stared out the window to the blue sky with white puffy monsoon clouds forming, thinking *if only Gavin were sitting beside me.*

Chase's breath against her arm was a long-waited and very welcome waking. She moved through her morning regimen slowly and deliberately as she anticipated the call from Gavin's new, temporary home. Jadyn washed off the mucking smells from the stalls and rinsed away the memories of the hotel's shower as well. She practiced yoga to mentally ready herself for an introduction to this new and foreign experience. It went better than expected. Jadyn felt a little guilty and extremely relieved to learn they didn't allow visitors to sleep in the patient rooms. She needed to work and was more than ready to resume her daily ranch duties. Her emotions were all over the place, having only one night outside of the hospital. She felt desperate to hold tight to the feeling of being home, yet knew not to let her guard down.

As agreed, Dr. Brandt continued to monitor Gavin's case with his local physician, Dr. Simmens. The doctors assured if Gavin awoke, he wouldn't be paralyzed. Whether or not he would wake from his coma remained to be seen; the doctors didn't offer much hope.

Jadyn took Nurse Laundry's advice; she held onto hope and visited him daily. The facility was between work and the ranch, which didn't feel like home anymore. She decided that without Gavin, the ranch was just that, a ranch. After all, Gavin was her true north, her real home, and he was simply not quite home yet.

Chapter 46

The Question

At the end of another long day divided by work, painting, and visiting Gavin, Jadyn stoked the fire and began writing. She typed fast, striking the keys with intent until the phone rang and nearly scared the computer off her lap.

It was Kendall! She heard her excited voice saying, "Levi asked me to marry him!"

This news should have brought tears of joy to Jadyn. Yet, all she could do was listen to Kendall screaming with excitement, "Will you be my Maid of Honor? Please Jadyn. Please say yes!"

Jadyn rolled her eyes, took a sip of wine, and asked, "When?"

Kendall could barely hold back her excitement! "Next month!"

Jadyn fought back the desire to yell at her, thinking, *have you no compassion! It's only been four months since Gavin's accident.* Instead, she spoke with forced joy, "April showers bring May flowers. Not too hot, not too cold. I'd say you chose the perfect month."

Kendall knew this wasn't easy for Jadyn and appreciated her response as she continued talking about her wedding plans, "I'd love it if you'd come. The week before if you can. You know, the bachelorette party. A party isn't a party without *you*. At least it's what you've always said."

Jadyn longed for the desire to participate in the wedding. But unsure she could conduct herself properly as the Maid of Honor yet, knowing how much it meant to Kendall, she typed to herself, *can I?* And responded, "I'll do my best."

After saying goodbye Jadyn fell asleep almost immediately. Something she found herself often doing, sleeping when she wanted to stay awake and not sleeping when she needed to sleep. Depression was wicked that way. Her nightmare was not in sleep but in waking.

Chapter 47

Molly's Willy

Two months of feeling guilty for the time she spent with Cole and abandoning Kendall at her reception added to the dread she felt each morning when she woke and realized Gavin wasn't there. This seemingly endless cycle of blameworthy memories plaguing her days was bad enough but today seemed worse than all the others. She desperately needed to talk to Cole and have him understand why she didn't tell him about Gavin.

Her repeated texts saying "sorry" weren't working, so she decided tonight she'd call and leave a message if he didn't answer. She didn't want anything from him but his forgiveness, even though she couldn't forgive herself.

Jadyn knew she had to get up and out of bed at some point and get on with her daily routine, but the moisture in the air was like a weighted blanket, and the drop in temperature was a welcome relief. This dreary storm dulled her senses, so she gave in to the rain's steady, rhythmic pattering and fell back to sleep.

Chase's frightened, repeated barking cut through the thunderclaps rolling through the canyon, waking Jadyn. It was too difficult for her to drift off now. Like all the other nights, she found it impossible to release herself into the vastness of real, deep sleep. Jadyn, disappointed to be awake, walked with eyes half-closed to the kitchen.

Chase's frightened whimpering lessened, and the rumbling of thunder continued. She prepared a cup of coffee and looked out the kitchen window admiring the artistic changes caused by the rain's kiss. It's as if a brush was taken to the trees, transforming the light greens into dark greens.

Gavin and Jadyn always enjoyed watching monsoons roll across the red rocks in the evening from outside under their mezzanine, but this was just an ordinary, mundane storm. Like a damp washcloth covering Jadyn's eyes, it blanketed all of Arizona until the following day. This storm muted most of the colors that generally broke through gaps between the vast fluffy clouds produced during a monsoon. A perfect day to stay inside and paint or write, but she had to go to work and needed to go to Gavin, so she chugged her coffee, hoping it would brighten her mood and wake her up.

She didn't know him, and he didn't know her. By his appearance, he looked old enough to have lived two lifetimes. His long matted, gray hair framed his rough, weathered, unshaven skin. His appearance was what you'd expect from a lifetime spent on the high seas. Jadyn thought his old and faded fisherman's hat was a perfect topping. Each time she passed his little piece of the planet, she created life stories for him like he was a character in a novel.

Jadyn deliberately drove the same route from Gavin to the gallery each day just so she could see him. He could always be found sitting on his rod iron bench, with an old, tattered blanket to pad his seat, waving and smiling as she drove past. The trees seemed to crown him as they hung like a tarp across the road. The shade cooled him in the summer months, and she admired the times when the sun would break through the spaces between the leaves to dance upon his face as he sat waving.

He was an eccentric man and a perfect fit for Sedona. This kind and selfless stranger waved at those who crossed his path. He just wanted to make their lives better. The locals loved Willy; he was an excellent example of how people should treat one another.

Today, and for the last three days, the bench has been empty. Jadyn figured the rain stopped him from waving, but as she got closer, she noticed an umbrella covering a sign sticking out of what looked like a sea of flowers. It read *Willy has left to join the angels. He loved you! His spirit will forever wave as you pass our home. God Bless!*

Heavy-hearted, Jadyn wanted to show her support and gratitude for this stranger. He brought joy to her during her otherwise dreary drive from Gavin to the gallery each day.

With tears blurring her vision, Jadyn approached a nearby pottery shop with a black, metal silhouette statue of a man sitting with a book in hand, leaning against a fence. She stopped and bought it without hesitation. Jadyn, nervous her gift was appropriate, drove back to present it to the family.

She parked on the road and carried it, walking over the pea-pebble driveway leading to a rustic, red front door. After three soft knocks, and a lot of barking behind it, the doorknob turned, and the rusty hinges squealed. Molly stood merely four feet five inches tall. Her also-short, graying hair wasn't brushed and didn't appear clean. She wore a faded housedress, purple furry slippers, and glasses exaggerating the size of her eyes. Her face, like her husband's, was deeply creased with smile lines around her not smiling mouth. She stared at Jadyn with a puzzled look and said in a meek and shaky voice, "hello." The tilt of her head and her strained countenance revealed her hearing was failing.

She awaited a response from Jadyn as an old long-haired white dog with dirt-stained matted hair sniffed at Jadyn's legs and feet.

All but one window had thick burgundy curtains pulled shut over them, and a motionless, also-white, long-haired cat was draped like a blanket on the sofa, bathing in the sun's warmth. A pungent mothball-litter box ammonia smell filled the room, and dust mixed with hair swirled around within a single sunlight stream. She appeared to be a doll collector, and, by the number of amateurish paintings hanging on the wood-paneled walls, she, or someone she knew, was a watercolor artist.

Jadyn also noticed a buildup of years of paint on the wood separating the glass window panes. She deduced the windows were likely permanently sealed shut. Anyone else might have found it displeasing, but to Jadyn, it was the home of a couple who shared a million stories.

The grief this woman was going through was painted on her face like the watercolors littering her walls. She thought she could almost touch the sorrow filling the room and never felt this much compassion for a stranger. Jadyn felt surprisingly connected to her standing there with shared pain.

Jadyn was silent longer than anyone would think was right after knocking on a stranger's door. So she raised the black metal statue in front of her and said, "I bought this as a token of my admiration and appreciation for Willy and was hoping I could place it on the bench?"

Molly's eyes welled as she outstretched her arms to embrace Jadyn, saying, "What a kind child you are. Do we know one another?"

Jadyn softly patted her back as they separated and said, "No. I wish I had taken the time to stop and meet Willy, now I will never know him, and he will never know how much he meant to me."

With twinkling eyes, she squeezed Jadyn's hand for a second and smiled with kind words, "I'm Molly. Now *we* are friends. My Willy would love this statue. Thank you. She searched Jadyn's face as she asked. What is your name, dear?"

Surprised to realize she'd not introduced herself, she replied, "My name is Jadyn. It's so nice to meet you, Molly. Can I set this up for you?"

Molly's face lifted and brightened as she joyfully answered, "By all means, yes. Do you need any help?"

Gavin had gifted her a toolbox for her truck, so Jadyn was well-equipped to mount the statue to the bench where Willie had sat for so many years. Another motorist stopped and introduced himself as Walter. He appeared to be her father's age. She felt comforted to have his help and companionship as they spoke fondly of Willy while placing this small token where he once sat. When Walter drove away, Jadyn remained to chat with Willy and talked aloud to him, "I want you to know how much you mean to me. I know you're still here, and now others will too. Rest in peace, Waving Willy." She kissed her hand and placed the kiss on the cheek of the statue.

Driving past a few days following, she noticed other statues had joined hers, and a new sign was posted stating, "Honk softly so Waving Willy can hear you wave."

A few weeks passed, and Jadyn was ready to tap lightly on her horn, only to discover Molly sitting next to the statue, waving at motorists. It was heartwarming and brought tears to her eyes.

Jadyn ached to share a bond of a woman and a man like Molly and Willie shared. She was aware she had it with Gavin, yet also aware he was becoming someone she only used to know, leaving her tortured with loneliness.

End-of-life smells of rubbing alcohol and Betadine solution emanated from Gavin's lifeless body. His once sun-kissed skin, now pale, showed no sign of him coming back to her anytime soon or maybe ever.

Jadyn found it increasingly difficult to feel his presence as Gavin's now soft hands grew more and more unfamiliar. The calluses he wore as gloves all but disappeared. Jadyn had spent hours rubbing her fingers over them, one by one, charting out a map to recall in her mind when he was on the road touring with the rodeo. She never imagined she'd need to refer to her memory when his hands were in hers.

Daily, Jadyn made a conscious effort to connect to Gavin. She repeated their shared rituals. She tried to smell him on his now stale clothes, she kissed their wedding photo, she spent time with Chase, and she imagined Gavin beside them in their bed, a bed that grew larger and larger each night.

She no longer felt any hope. It felt like a seven-month-long lie, and she couldn't be fooled by the tricks she played on herself anymore.

Chapter 48

Patio Puppy's

J adyn held her coffee cup and watched the horses dance around. She craved the joy her relentless sadness overshadowed. It was time to stop wallowing in self-pity! Knowing Teddy would have a solution, she picked up the phone and texted, *Lunch?*

Almost immediately, Teddy replied, *Creekside?*

Jadyn loved the Creekside. She answered, *Sure.*

Teddy noticed dogs the last time she ate there and told Jadyn, *Bring Chase.*

Seriously? Jadyn texted with a smiling face with sunglasses emoji.

Teddy encouraged, *Definitely, yes, they added a doggie menu for patio dining. woof!*

Jadyn typed, *LOL, 12:30?*

Teddy looked to see the time on her cell and quickly typed, *Yes indeedy!*

Teddy, squinting from the sunlight seeping through the branches partly shading the patio above Antonio, spoke to her longtime friend, "I'm so excited you added the doggie menu! My niece and her dog Chase are joining me any minute now."

Antonio smiled, "It was the wife's idea; now that we have a doggo."

Teddy searched the patio, "What kind of dog?"

He pointed to his precious Beagle puppy resting on brick pavers and spoke with pride, "little Lucy is cuddled up over by the side door."

Teddy's face lit up with adoration, and she almost stood up to visit Lucy until she heard Jadyn's voice encouraging Chase, "Come on, boy, we're having lunch with Auntie T."

Jadyn and Chase entered the quaint patio. Antonio observed them walk towards Teddy and pulled a biscuit from his pants pocket. Chase watched and doggie-smiled. Even though he didn't know Antonio, he pranced toward him with a dangling and dripping tongue. Chase excitedly and wildly wagged his tail, sniffing Antonio's hand and making him laugh. Antonio used a dog-friendly tone, rubbed Chase's head with one hand, and offered the biscuit, "Here you go, boy."

Chase quickly wolfed it down and looked up at him with gratitude.

Chase's Aunt Teddy felt left out and playfully asked him, "Does Chase love his Auntie T?" She repeatedly asked throughout their rubbing and kissing session. Chase turned away, sniffing the air behind a server walking by with a tray of sizzling fajitas. He'd have kept following right behind him if not for the jerk of the leash attached to the leg of Jadyn's chair.

They sat with sunglasses covering their eyes, sipping Mimosas beneath the gently flapping umbrella, partially shading them. Jadyn kept the conversation light, speaking of the gallery and art until she got up the courage to ask Teddy, "Do you have any suggestions for helping me get past this grief? I know I look pathetic. I'm becoming a one-dimensional person with very little to say other than talking about Gavin's coma. I need help figuring out who I am without him again. I honestly have no idea who I am."

Before answering, Teddy tipped her head to one side and gave Jadyn a look of disbelief, "Well, you sure do make yourself appear pathetic. No one can understand what your life's been like; upsetting for sure. It's been nearly a year; I'm sure you've thought about what you could do to help yourself feel better, right?"

"Hello? It's what I came to lunch for, I'm asking *you*."

Teddy squinted, "If you seek happiness, you must first figure out what you want. If you're struggling, I recommend practicing mindfulness." Teddy paused, knowing her advice pissed her off.

Jadyn, as Teddy expected, snapped, "I get it! Mindfulness! You're talking about meditating again, like always. I can't quiet my mind. When I try, Gavin's end-of-life request pops up. There's no way to quiet my mind. There's no "How To" book for dealing with a husband in a coma either!"

Jadyn turned to look at the water moving in the creek and barked, "let me try some mindfulness right now."

She closed her eyes with a sour look, ignoring Teddy, fully aware she was acting spoiled and talking childishly frustrated. "I feel so bored with myself. I've become such a bore." Not feeling any better, she looked at the ascending effervescent bubbles in her glass, waiting for something inspired to come from their conversation.

Teddy didn't like hearing Jadyn's self-deprecating

talk. She spoke encouragingly, "Jadyn, you're not and could never be boring. I think I get what you're saying, though. It's easy to end up feeling like you do, especially if you focus too much on yourself."

Jadyn felt attacked and fought back, "I don't only focus on myself!"

Teddy placed her hand on Jadyn's to assure her she had no judgment and said, "I think I get it. You wake each day reminded that your wonderful life is on hold. Each never-changing day replicates the day before. You feel stuck, right?"

Jadyn finally felt understood, "Yes! Like my own version of the Groundhog Day movie."

Teddy nodded and, choosing her words carefully, spoke, "Don't get me wrong, I'm not saying you're self-centered. I know this from my own experience; we can talk more about me another day. If you focus too much on yourself, the world you create becomes cold and devoid of form, a sheet of brass never to be made into a sculpture."

Jadyn felt Teddy was at it again with her lecturing, "More analogies?"

Teddy smirked, "Yes! More analogies. The path to self-worth is like tending to a garden. It would help if you had a variety of plants. Taking care of yourself is important. It's even better to help others. You know, like how you feel when you create a painting to enrich someone else's life rather than painting a piece just for your own pleasure?" Jadyn nodded and privately giggled, thinking the conversation was starting to feel just as boring as she was. She bit her tongue and continued listening to Teddy's long-winded advice, "Mindfulness and quieting your ego will help you figure out how to move forward through your life; at least it helps me process my issues."

Jadyn's long slender fingers were no match for the halved strawberry bobbing around in her flute. She fished for it, people-watching and feigning disinterest in Teddy's words. She prayed for something good and noticed the sun was casting shadows on everyone's faces, thrilling the artist inside her.

Teddy knew Jadyn was listening, so she kept talking, sounding more upbeat, "I took a class near here, or should I call it a retreat? Anyway, no one talked for three days, except for short scheduled time slots. We all meditated the bulk of the hours each day, and I recall how funny it was when I found myself thinking, I paid all this money to stay near where I live, so I could be in a place where no one spoke. I could have accomplished this at home!"

They laughed and sipped on their Mimosas. Teddy raised her glass to cheer the irony of the experience and went on talking as only she could. "I did, however, learn something. The happiest times of my life were when I was in the service of others, like right now, helping you. Any idea of something you can do in service to other people?"

Jadyn looked out at the red rocks and realized one of the most positive, uplifting, and joy-filled things she's done since living in Sedona was painting. She spoke as if thinking out loud, "Don't know if I'm qualified? I love seeing how people react to the art in the gallery. Some mention the desire to learn how to paint. When the topic arises, I've felt the urge to provide them with a class, except we don't offer any. It made me feel energized when it came up; I enjoy sharing my love of painting.

Teddy let her head fall forward, fishing for inspiration, and excitedly asked, "How about starting one of those YouTube channels? Allow people to watch you paint?"

Something in Jadyn opened like a flower blooming. Her eyes focused on Teddy, wide with wonder! Gratitude poured from her newly open heart as she exclaimed, "A YouTube channel! What a fun idea!"

Teddy proudly exclaimed, "Fun? Well, now I'll bet you didn't think you would be saying Fun today, and Fun is usually associated with joy."

Jadyn hated admitting when Teddy was right but gave her the win saying, "Yeah, yeah, I knew you would be helpful, but I'm sure even you didn't expect you'd suggest a YouTube channel, correct?"

Jadyn raised her champagne glass, and the two said, "clink," as they brought their plastic flutes together in celebration. Jadyn's face was full of joy as ideas formulated seemingly without her, and she said, "You know what?"

Teddy asked, "What?" leaning forward and expecting a "Thank You, Auntie T."

"I have the perfect name for my channel. I'm going to call it Beyond the Brush Strokes!"

"I can't imagine a better name for it, Jadyn, because you and I both know artwork is born from the artist's soul. I can't wait to see what you do with this!"

They said their goodbyes, and Jadyn drove away from Teddy filled with purpose, smiling all the way home.

Chapter 49

Easels and Cameras

Conflicting emotions churned in Jadyn as she accepted that the best room to use for her YouTube channel was the den she and Gavin shared. She also knew he might never come home, and she hadn't felt this good about anything since Cole. She kept brushing aside memories of both Cole and Gavin. She focused on the details needed for this new and exciting project to form.

Gavin's essence remained, lingering in the dust, blanketing his belongings as if a ghost, reminding her of him sitting at his desk working on ways to bring in more money, scheduling his rodeo events, and riding lessons as she painted across the room. She remembered the day before he left for Vegas, the last time she stood beside Gavin as he worked. He was super excited about a plan he hatched to ensure a more financially stable future. He planned to use his winnings to add stalls so they could take in boarders, and he would build a guest house for a vacation rental. He just knew it was a perfect plan. "Can you see it, Babe? Customers can trailer their horses here so they can ride the trails and sleep with their horses just outside their rooms. I'll bet we could charge a fortune!" When he got excited, he spoke with a horse's canter rhythm, nearly breathless and bouncing in his chair.

She thought about how she positioned her easel so

Gavin couldn't see her canvas from his desk. Nervous, he'd catch a glimpse before ready to be revealed. Now somehow, she'd be painting in front of strangers! She recalled calming her fears by focusing on his love for her. So Jadyn concentrated on her paintings hanging in a gallery to lessen her feelings of inadequacy.

Getting down to business, she first moved his antique cowhide chair adorned with brass studs. She carried it with a bull rider's straddle to the garage where his truck sat lonely if a truck could feel emotion. She thought it must miss Gavin's country music playing and the roads he took her on, stressing the metal underworking of the truck, making it groan as they ventured out into Sedona's backlands. The rusted edges below the driver's side door, scarred from his spurs, helped her imagine him cursing with each strike, and she couldn't resist the urge to run her fingers across them. She smiled a melancholy smile and headed inside for more items, more pieces of Gavin, possibly never to be reunited with him.

To appear cheerful as she talked in her videos, Jadyn needed to conceal items full of memories of Gavin. She pushed through the sensation of betraying him as she rearranged the room he had enjoyed long before she arrived. Feeling guilty excavating his belongings without his permission, she filled boxes with magazines he'd read and saved, only to set them aside. With each box she loaded, she felt their connection break a little more. Jadyn hoped he'd understand when he woke up from this insidious coma. She had to do something to keep her sanity and possibly make extra money. She knew she couldn't build his dream for their future without him and thought he'd appreciate her tenacity to take on this project. Jadyn hoped he'd be proud of her as the room transformed into her space, with her canvases and brushes in place of his projects and treasures.

After skimming the room, affirming she had successfully conceived and created a beautiful setting for her new adventure, she felt a positive shift in her mood. She sensed she, too, was transformed. Jadyn wasn't secure in her plan and could feel anxiety and a new sense of purpose building within her, like heartburn, she mused.

Jadyn stopped to admire her view through the large window she loved so much. She marveled at how the window framed the horses and the red rocks towering above them. This view had filled their lives with such richness and joy for so long.

Jadyn prepped a blank canvas for her first painting in her new space. She felt a sense of peace as the sun set and turned everything in the room a shade of pink. She joyfully sketched, blocking in a design yet to be painted on the pinkish canvas. She loved knowing darkness would soon follow, rinsing the pink tones from the room, returning its surface to white; leaving it renewed and ready for the future to unfold and ultimately reveal who she is as an artist and the beginning of what lies beyond the brushstrokes.

Chapter 50

The Candle

When Jadyn wasn't at Gavin's bedside, she tended to Chase and the horses or worked for Wynonna at the gallery. She divided her nights and weekends between visits to Gavin and her new obsession, painting in her studio. Her dreams were filled with dreaming-up artwork for what felt like another boss, her YouTube channel. With each squeeze of paint from her paint tubes, she squeezed a little more life back into herself. Her artwork, like a therapist, listened to her heart, creating smooth, silky colors for the world to witness. With each stroke of the brush beneath the lights shining over her canvas, the camera recorded much more than paint. The artistic process of her paintings was stored on memory cards and allowed her to leave behind fragments from the past.

Her intense, arduous schedule created an extraordinary stiffness in the muscles between her shoulder blades. The sharp, burning, stabbing pain, born from a dedication to her viewers, was a sacrifice for them and, it turns out, a gift to her. She was invigorated and driven like never before and wore her muscle spasms like a badge of honor as she built up a collection worthy of a gallery. She learned more than she imagined possible about painting, filming, and video editing and was nearly ready to launch her channel.

Jadyn burned her hypothetical candle at both ends and in the middle. She didn't mind if that was what it took to reach her goal, and if it meant she had to endure pain, well, that, too, was for the better. She finally understood the meaning of hard work, never having pushed herself to this extent before. She was filled with excitement and wonder learning this about herself. Her selfless act of love and sharing revealed she was capable of boundless achievements.

Teddy's text of advice arrived before she reached for her brush; *You've been burning the candle at both ends. It is your and Gavin's special anniversary. Smell the roses and pamper yourself today—heart emoji.* The text affirmed Jadyn's thoughts to take it easy today.

As an artist and creative force, Teddy understood what it took to paint twenty-eight paintings in thirty days, and Jadyn realized she was right. She felt an emotional pull at her heartstrings, admitted her back muscles felt like a rubber band twisted tight and decided to skip painting. Jadyn used her projects to fill in the empty spaces and generated her self-imposed solitude. The time would come when the need for rest would force her to stop and contemplate her actions. Her memories were becoming harder and harder to recall.

Jadyn felt like she was looking at her past through a bug-eaten hole in the Maple leaf she held, a miniature screen revealing her story. She peeked at the sunset through it before going back inside for the night. Jadyn sat on Gavin's big chair with her legs crossed beneath her and thought about her limited memory; remembering was complex and challenging after working so long on letting go.

The past ten months of Gavin being locked away from her physically and mentally, locked away with people who were never going home, created a complicated emptiness and longing. Gavin was lying there still and silent in a separate bed; the miles between them slowly scraped away her memories, like paint on a canvas, removed, leaving her with the hollow void of loneliness that resurfaced from beneath the brushstrokes as she flipped through the pages of their wedding album, trying to feel Gavin and his love.

Jadyn felt her patheticness looming, shook off her dismal attitude, and flicked the silver wheel of her lighter. She lit the candle's waiting wick, the candle Gavin bought for her, and stared into the hot white dancing flame. She closed her eyes, inhaled the sweet vanilla bean scent, and allowed the aroma to pull and release the memories she needed tonight. Jadyn was carried back to the anniversary of the day they made love for the first time. This would be the last time it burned; the wick was burning away, almost gone, like her memory.

Jadyn recalled watching the dust, ordinarily hidden in the shadows, dance through the evening light and how the matchstick smoked when he blew it out. She watched him open the sheet, which floated like angel wings gracefully onto the bed. Gavin set the scene like a director. She was eager to play her role as his actress.

He spoke of the wondrous and expansive harvest moon that took up nearly the entire sky the night she returned to Sedona and gave herself to him. He had said, "this night would be perfect if I could change the full moon's calendar so we could bathe in its light tonight."

She watched him standing with his robe nearly

open and smiled, "my heart is full of love for you." She started to stand.

Gavin told her to sit still and wait. She watched him prepare the bedroom as if setting a stage. He teased with flirtatious expressions, smiling at her, sitting with perfect lavender light streaming in and glowing on the robe he bought her for their first Christmas as husband and wife. With the memory revived and vivid, Jadyn allowed herself to travel back in time.

She ached to recall every touch, how it felt knowing he'd taken the time to purchase the candle, massage oil, strawberries, champagne, and instrumental CD from a local musician; how Gavin turned on the stereo, took her hand, and led her to the bed. She remembered how he brushed her hair from her ear and whispered softly, "Lay on the sheet, babe. I'm going to show you how much I love you. Don't you even think about pleasing me, understand?"

Jadyn got a chill from his wet hot breath on her neck and said, "Yes, sir," as he guided her to lay face down on the cool, soft, white sheet and slowly pulled the robe from her body.

He straddled her waist, dripping the warm massage oil in deliberate drops, "Every time I look at you, I thank God for bringing you into my life, well, God and Theodosia."

She remembered how turned on and grateful she felt as he massaged her for what felt like hours and how she never really knew how long he'd caressed her. Jadyn only knew the hours increased each time they spoke of it. Her massage became Gavin's *Big Fish story,* and he used it against her when Jadyn massaged him. When she wanted to quit, he'd tease, "Come on, Jadyn,

I massaged you for three hours," all the way up to six hours, "surely you can last longer than a measly half hour."

Gavin considered this day their real anniversary, and the candle he bought in celebration was about to melt away. The candle is now a painful reminder of his broken promise, a promise broken by his refusal of the helmet. His promise to replace this special candle each year would not, could not be realized. Jadyn couldn't help considering how the candle's wax would last only until this day. *What if this is an omen?*

She shook off the thought, closed her eyes, and enjoyed remembering his gentle touch, slowly sliding the robe from her shoulders, him kissing each, slowly and softly, as she squirmed beneath him. Jadyn submerged herself in the memories, soaking in the sensations brought back to life. Her heart raced as it did that evening, and her skin tingled like it was charged with an electrical current that he ignited and kept lit by unexpected touches and kisses. She smiled, recalling how his beard felt like feathers skimming over her skin, causing her body to quiver in preparation for lovemaking.

She remembered trying to touch and give him pleasure, of how he held her hands to the bed with his strength while moving his nakedness over her buttocks and the small of her back. She felt the outline of her body as he slid over her and his body's readiness to join with hers made her insane with desire.

He tortured her with his touch for over an hour, then slid off the bed, grabbed her hips, and pulled her to him. He kissed her neck and loved her with a powerful intensity surpassing all she had felt before.

This profound experience was etched deep into her soul. Jadyn would compare future lovemaking to this night, this setting, his thoughtfulness, his tenderness, and his complete desire to selflessly please her.

Chapter 51

For Sanity's Sake

Jadyn prepared and ate dinner sitting on the couch with Chase by her side. His sniffing sounded louder than usual. He tried to inhale her meal through his nostrils. She fought memories of Molly and Willy with an aching heart.

Jadyn left the dishes there, coaxed Chase to join her for bed, turned the music on low, and surrendered to her Muse with an increasingly strong desire to write. Jadyn brushed her teeth and hair and, without showering, slid between the sheets with Chase cuddled beside her. With her laptop on bent knees, she rhythmically typed and typed.

Each night, no matter how weary, Jadyn habitually reached for her laptop and journaled her thoughts of the day. She needs to write like she needs to paint. She's an addict, and art is her drug of choice. She writes to numb the pain amplified by night; like a river replenishes life along its banks, writing cleanses her mind, preventing the chronic unfathomable sorrow that plagues her and could pull her into the uncontrolled undercurrent. Without this daily release, she'd surely have fallen victim to its persistent, looming presence, and have been swallowed up until no remnants of her remained. There would be no sign of the woman she knew herself to be before Gavin's fall.

Jadyn's words released with ease from her fingertips

as she typed: *Memories of us seem to pop up everywhere, an enemy stalking my mind. These memories of us that once made me smile are now a source of pain I fear may one day kill me.*

Jadyn, tortured by her words, switched from writing to Gavin and chose free writing to clear her thoughts. She wrote to her laptop instead.

You are my solace and comfort each night as I fight to keep my sanity. The only warmth I feel on my skin other than Chase.

I feel alone in my once full bed... Oh, how I miss the weight of his arm draped over me, resting on my waist, my head lying on his shoulder. When will this pain end?

Feeling some relief, she continued writing to Gavin.

I sprinkled your favorite t-shirt in your cologne before slipping into it and sliding into bed last night. This morning it held me as I drank my tea and took in the beauty of the sunrise. I felt a presence as I sat in your favorite chair. Were you with me? Are you with me now? If you can hear me, I love you, babe. I long for your touch and will dream of you again tonight. I wonder what you dream about as you sleep in what seems to be an endless slumber. I love and miss my best friend. I will see you in my dreams tonight, my love, goodnight...

Chapter 52

Thanksgiving Invitations

J adyn thought it seemed like she didn't even live this day; time stopped on her days off. She spent most of her free time wandering aimlessly around the house. There was so little between chores and work to fill her with joy she spent much of it asleep on the sofa.

November's chill took hold of her, so she wrapped a blanket over her shoulders and caressed her arms through it. She snuggled into bed and welcomed Chase's body heat. His moist, even breathing comforted her throughout the night even though he occupied more of the bed than she did. It was better than waking to a cold and empty bed, and no matter how much time passed without Gavin, she wasn't sure she'd ever be able to sleep on his side of the bed anyway.

She closed the laptop, and the room fell silent, other than the sounds coming from Chase as he attempted to get comfortable enough to sleep. Her mind drifted to the last Thanksgiving she spent with Gavin.

It was quaint yet lively, and as she did every year, Teddy insisted each guest invite someone who didn't have a place to celebrate. Living a life of gratitude and sharing was her style and everyone entering her home was better for it. It was Teddy's desire for Thanksgiving to be a new beginning when strangers became friends while sharing a delicious meal.

Jadyn flashed on a conversation with Teddy about

how lonely the holidays could be for those who have lost their spouses. Tears began to descend her cheeks as she realized it would be her this year. She knew Teddy wanted her to find someone to bring, and Jadyn knew the right person to ask.

Before she could fall asleep, her cell phone vibrated with a text message from Cole. She was shocked; he'd finally listened to her phone message and was blown away that he'd asked her if she wanted to come to California for Thanksgiving! She entertained the thought; *no one would have to know.* Jadyn conceptualized: *I can tell Teddy I'm going to a Friend's Giving this year. No one would be the wiser. Of course, if mom knew I was in Cali and didn't come to her house, she would become suspicious.* These thoughts added to the big pile of guilt she juggled. Jadyn didn't reply. She decided tonight was too much for her, and Cole would have to wait. Now all she had to do was stop her mind from thinking about how nice it would be to spend time with Cole; she longed for him, just as she did Gavin.

Jadyn rolled over and hit the pillow to make it softer, knowing this would be another restless night. How was she supposed to sleep with this terrible decision hanging over her, a dark, looming shadow haunting her *day and night*? She prayed aloud, "All the angels in heaven, please surround me, inspire me, protect me and ease me to sleep." And, after a final groan from Chase, sleep finally took hold of her.

Morning broke as if the night didn't exist. Jadyn awoke with swollen eyes from the tears she'd released during the night. She felt old and grimaced at her face in the mirror, letting the water run until it was hot on her washcloth. She pressed it to her eyes, repeating till the swelling reduced and the whites of her eyes could be seen again. She went to the freezer, removed an ice pack designed for placing over her eyes, returned to bed, and laid it over her face until the cool became warm.

To confirm the puffy proof of last night's tears was gone, Jadyn felt her eye sockets, lunged forward in excitement, got up, and raced to get dressed. She decided to leave early for work so she could stop on the way and invite her guest to Thanksgiving dinner.

The road was unusually quiet, and the trees were in time with the season, colors beautiful; fallen leaves danced across the street in the wake of her SUV as she approached the statues where Molly sat as if a statue herself. She pulled into the driveway, got out of her SUV, and walked to sit beside her. They waved at the cars. "This, oddly, feels very nice." Molly smiled and nodded in agreement.

Jadyn asked Molly with sincerity, "I was hoping you would come to my Thanksgiving dinner."

Her smile grew larger as she turned to look at Jadyn with a puzzled yet warm expression, "Why do you want this old woman at your celebration?"

Jadyn faked a stern expression, "Well, because you're beautiful and kind, and who wouldn't want to spend time with you? Come on, Molly, please. I'm sorry, I shouldn't push. I can come back later for your answer."

Molly gently grabbed Jadyn's arm to stop her from getting up and said, "Your kind invitation is the answer to something troubling me. My kids are trying to convince me to let them pay for a plane ticket and fly me across the country. Honestly, my heart and this old body are simply not liking the sound of any of that. They've been worried about me since my Willy passed, and want to be with me, but they were just here helping deal with the funeral, and I would be the albatross in the room. I don't want them to walk on eggshells as they worry about my sadness, so I say yes to your most gracious invitation and look forward to it."

Looking at Molly's shaky hand on hers, Jadyn turned her hand, their hands now palm-to-palm, and gently squeezed. With moist eyes, she raised her head to look at Molly, "You're sure your children won't be angry or hurt if you don't show up?"

"No, dear, my children want me to be happy. They don't want to say it, but they're concerned about me flying alone. None of them can really afford the ticket after losing work and being here for weeks. I know them pretty well; they can video chat with me on the computer on Thanksgiving, so we feel connected. I will be your guest. Can I bring anything?"

"Bring your beautiful self. My Aunt Theodosia and I will spoil you. We'll have more food than we can eat, delicious mouthwatering food. I'll come by tomorrow with her address, and I look forward to spending this time with you."

"As do I," Molly said. She smiled, adjusted her knit shawl over her shoulders, and carried on with her morning waving.

As Jadyn sat in her SUV on Molly's driveway, she noticed the trees lining the property had lost only half of their leaves. Each tree was all but vacant on one side and the other half barely alive, still hanging on to the branches. She took a deep breath and realized she felt like those trees, half alive and half dead. She wiped away the tear escaping her left eye, turned the key, and headed for work.

She could hear her mother's voice as she drove, "be sure to always find something to be thankful for every day." She closed her eyes to squeeze an inspirational thought out of her tired brain and remembered the laptop. She smiled as she realized her life would be unbearable without it. Jadyn felt gratitude for her mother's love and the gift she gave her. She got on a roll of thinking of all she had to be grateful for.

"Hmm. Let's see, I'm grateful I have to stop for gas because it means I have a car. I'm grateful I was awakened many times last night because it means I'm alive. I'm grateful I have to decide his fate because it means I was truly loved and married! I can't do this! Dear God, how do I make this decision? Why did he have to leave it up to me?"

Tears altered her vision, so she pulled over, parked on the side of the road, and reflected on a conversation she and Gavin had about death. He had reached out his hand for hers and held it tightly as he spoke, "Honey, it won't be a big deal, God's in charge. All you have to do is let him decide. Chances are slim-to-none; either of us will end up this way. I want you to know if something does happen, if I'm ever a burden, lying there unable to move, eat or breathe, just let God decide. Take all man has set into place and undo it. Unplug the will of man and let God decide. Understand, sweetie?"

She nodded, and Gavin continued, "Baby, I think we should set some kinda time limit on this. Like we give each other a year to overcome it. What do you think?"

Jadyn said, "I think I hate this talk and never want to have it again." She begged Gavin with her expressive eyes to end the conversation.

He relented, saying "Deal."

Chapter 53

Unveiled Desire

I t was clear to Jadyn; Old Man Winter had officially arrived as she walked beneath the hovering canopy of snow clouds veiling the usually vibrant colors of the foliage. Even the red rocks' intensely deep and rich colors were all but erased from the landscape. She felt isolated by the thick, foggy-brightness of the wall-like cloud cover, drifting ever so slowly over and through her property. This misty white also muted the normally audible, ambient sounds anchoring her to Gavin and the ranch.

A dreary deadened silence created by the cloud cover and fog muffled commonly ignored but ever-present melodious sounds of the neighbor's and wildlife surrounding the ranch. This eerie silence contrasted with the over-amplification of every sound she made, reminding her of swimming underwater. Jadyn's memories began floating to the surface. Snorkeling with Gavin on their honeymoon in Hawaii, how she could hear bubbles, her heartbeat, and a static sound seeming to come from inside her head rather than her ears. It was an above-ground underwater feeling. The loud crunching of pea gravel covering the pathway beneath her boots reminded her of walking behind Gavin the first time they mucked the stalls as husband and wife, stirring unsettled emotions.

On days like today, when Mother Nature forced the

world to delay its start, her memories of Gavin seemed to yell and rip her heart out. They both loved foggy mornings when the world slowed, carving extra time for cuddling within their own private winter's pre-storm cocoon, coffee cups in hand, and a fire burning.

Chase's breath and excited panting was a comfort breaking through the dead silence. She felt the need to connect with someone. Jadyn stopped walking, bent to the ground, one knee following the other, her right hand touching the ground first until ultimately lying on her back, completely still on the cold sandy red dirt. Chase rested his head on her shoulder and looked at her with a curious and confused gaze. She smiled but remained still, looking up at the white misty, heaven-like sky, recalling Cole. She allowed herself to drift off to the beach; to the day he taught her to surf, the cold bite of May's crisp air on her cheeks and the goosebumps covering her skin. She had tried to act warm, talking about their lives and dreams for the future. Jadyn recalled hoping her nipples wouldn't call too much attention. She simply couldn't bear it if he noticed them. She ached for his touch, more for the freedom to touch than to be touched.

She recalled the sound of his voice breaking through the pauses between waves, the smell of salt mixing with his cologne, and how her hand felt empty and awkward until she felt his cover hers. Jadyn relived the emotion washing over her. It felt as if she was the tide herself. She recalled opening her eyes to witness equal emotion looking back at her through his sincere, wanting eyes.

Jadyn softly touched her cheek with the back of her glove-covered hand. She attempted to reinvent the touch of Cole's hand on her waist when he saved her from those wretched men, his powerful and firm hold, his touch still lingering and pulling her to him. She was lost in thought until Chase pushed at her hand, checking for signs of life, urging Jadyn to get back to the regular routine. To end his coaxing, she kissed his nose and whispered, "Okay, Boy. Come here and let me use your back. Getting up isn't as easy as it once was." He was glad to help and smiled at her with his white-toothed open mouth when she was off the ground. Being a crutch for her delighted Chase and reminded Jadyn how Cole supported her through the parking lot the night they met.

She patted her jeans to remove the dirt clinging to them. Jadyn tipped her head to one side, shaking dirt from her hair, and smiled, seeing Chase's mirroring head tipping to one side, questioning her strange behavior.

After tending to the horses, she soaked in the tub for a couple of hours with music playing and Chase on the floor beside her. Following her third glass of wine, she exited the tub and blew out the last of six candles set along the bathtub's rim.

Jadyn was clean. Her thoughts, however, were anything but. She clicked *send,* emailing her words, asking, or more accurately, begging Cole to come to visit, and they couldn't be unsent! A quick rush of heat enveloped her as if getting too close to a recently stoked fire! Jadyn's tight chest and short breaths amplified the disgraceful thoughts she had brewing when she read his reply, *When?!* She sat staring at the screen, listening through the static to her rapid-fire thoughts screaming - like a thousand judging voices.

Chapter 54

One Beer Won't Do

The instant Jadyn pressed send, she knew her words were rocketed, unreclaimable. Her request for Cole to come to her, those words sped away, joining the multitude of other careless words previously flung by her. Jadyn envisioned them flying away like ravens into the murky night sky, scared and scarred by past self-inflicted disasters created by her. If words could feel emotion, she knew hers carried more suffering than most. With only herself to commiserate this action she'd taken, her stomach churned, and her heart pounded.

Cole's visit will put an end to her self-inflicted solitary confinement and isolation. Both were created by her own doing, but did she want to allow him into her life and her home? Berating herself she thought, *If only I was a better person,* and despite knowing there was still time to reverse Cole's invitation, she pushed that realization aside. A disturbing realization surfaced. At very least, she was capable of emotionally cheating on Gavin.

Stunned, she debated these acts; her angel and devil battled it out for her soul as guilt rose like heartburn into her throat. Excited and relieved she'd initiated this meeting was shining on her, shining bright, like a spotlight on a stage. Jadyn felt exposed, showing the world how despicable she truly could be. The once-locked door flung open to reveal an unknown side of her, a side that lurked and waited to surprise the *good girl* she thought she was until now. The floodgates of her past judgments opened. She allowed forgiveness to spill out, flowing over anyone she'd ever judged guilty. Even her father's infidelity was now undeniably relatable.

She relaxed into the warm, comforting vision of his touch. Cole's arms replace Gavin's, intimately blending their lives, in a way to reach the man lying lifeless in a cold and separate place, out of sight, out of reach, but never out of mind. Her love for Gavin is protected, suspended in a cocoon, awaiting new birth, safe, and would never die.

She and Gavin's uncertain, possibly bleak ending hung looming, like the dark abyss her words split through to become a light on Cole's face as he read Jadyn's invitation, "Will you come to me? Come here? To my home in Sedona? Want to?"

Jadyn giggled with his speedy reply, "On my way!"

She imagined him driving, heading in her direction, even though only a short thirty minutes had passed since his instant reply. She thought about how fast men could get ready. Cole is most likely packed and on his way.

She estimated six hours before he'd show up, or maybe it was seven? Unsure, she planned on six, slid on her rubber boots, and went out to bathe the horses.

Jadyn's horse Kharibia was shocked by the cold touch of water pouring on her withers making her almost buck! Kharibia shifted her weight and leaned hard against Jadyn for protection. Jadyn pushed back with her firmly rubbing, shampoo-foamy fingers, ultimately pleasing Kharibia. She made nickering sounds, a horse's version of purring in appreciation for the massage-like bath. Bathing Blaze, Gavin's much taller horse, required a crate for her to stand on, but the horse was so mellow he'd fall asleep while getting his hooves trimmed. Jadyn was conflicted by the thought of having Cole ride him, hoping he would, though, because Blaze hadn't ridden hard since her and Gavin's last ride together. After Chase's soapy turn under the hose, Jadyn left him in the sun to dry and went into the house to wash the floors and declutter.

With three hours to spare before his arrival and their agreement sex was not part of the plan, she showered and prepared herself for the possibility of intimacy, anyway. The wheels were in motion, and Cole was on his way. Her conflicted thoughts eventually resolved and transformed into a singular calming voice saying, "You deserve this time with Cole."

Cole exited the highway onto the main road heading to Sedona and pulled off to the side of the road. He called Jadyn. She answered, feeling mixed emotions fluttering in her belly, and asked, "Would you be a sweetheart and pick up some meat for our dinner at the grocery store? I've got veggies and potatoes."

Nervous yet excited to see her, Cole replied, "Sure thing. Got beer?"

Jadyn was saddened, realizing she'd stopped buying beer since Gavin's fall, "Wine drinker, I think I have ... 'A' ... beer."

Cole's voice sounded light, "Well, ... 'A' ... beer ... won't do. I'll grab a case."

Jadyn teased, . "An entire case? Scared of me?"

He playfully responded, "Terrified! I'll call you back

after I shop."

Twenty or so minutes passed, and Cole called back. Before he could say anything, Jadyn asked, "Where are you at?"

"Back on the main road, you said people miss the turn even with navigation. Ready to be my navigator?"

Feeling like a cat on a hot tin roof, she answered, "Sure. If you haven't noticed, everything in Sedona looks a lot alike. Even McDonald's blends in; it doesn't have golden arches! People have been told to go the wrong way, so when your navigator says you're going to turn left in a quarter mile, she's wrong; you need to turn right, and after you turn, you'll see a pile of boulders on the right-hand side. She'll tell you to turn left. Don't! Go right instead." She giggled in her private thoughts. "Once you turn right, go left." She ended with a couple of snorts, laughing, "I know it's crazy, right?"

Cole closed his eyes tight, trying to remember the instructions, thinking she sounded like the mother in a Charlie Brown cartoon. "Okay, tell me again, and only one instruction at a time. I'm a guy, remember."

Smiling, she knew he meant she had given too much information, "Okay, see the big boulders coming up on your right? Turn there and turn right, not left."

Jadyn continued instructing Cole until his headlights were visible, "I see you. Look straight ahead; you'll see the light on my front porch. Don't drive too fast, or you'll destroy the rack on your truck; it's a washboard road once you drop onto dirt."

Cole forced a southern accent, "Yes, ma'am."

She played along with a flirty-sounding voice. "Thanks for listening, cowboy."

They laughed and stayed on the phone as he pulled

onto the red dirt driveway lined with railroad ties. It was more like a parking lot than any driveway he'd seen at anyone's home before.

After parking, he ended the call, opened and slid out his door only to hear Jadyn tease, "So this is your truck? Or is the purple Mini Cooper?"

He threw his hands up in the air, "You know it's Malika's! Quit busting my balls."

She had her hands in her back pockets, tipped forward and up in her boots, smiling as he slid his hand between her arched back and arms and pulled her to him. They embraced without kissing, and he smiled as he felt the deep push of her strong fingers pressing into his back. He let go of her, turned away, and grabbed his duffle bag and the groceries from the backseat saying, "I bought wine, one of the pre-cooked chickens, and some dessert."

She took the chicken from him in both hands and led him to the kitchen as Chase sniffed his legs, whimpering and walking with bouncy steps beside Cole.

Once in the kitchen, Cole set the bags on the table and allowed Chase to sniff his hand, saying, "Nice to meet you, Boy." Chase spun around, ran off, and returned with his wet, slobbery tennis ball.

Jadyn warned, "Just know if you start throwing it, he's not going to let you stop!"

He loved hearing this, "It's alright, we're buddies now."

Jadyn had already prepared a salad and handed it to Cole with the wine and opener. He opened the bottle, poured her a glass, and opened himself a beer.

They both felt awkward as they enjoyed their meal

in the living room, tossing Chase an occasional piece of chicken, drinking the wine and beer, and finally picking through a box of assorted chocolates.

Jadyn got up, slid off her boots, left them by the back door, and returned to sit next to him on the couch. Cole grabbed her foot and asked, "Do I have your permission? I'm a foot-rubbing expert."

She smiled, lying back, "Prove it."

It wasn't long before Jadyn's light snoring let him know she'd fallen asleep. He placed one of her blankets over her, let his head fall back against the sofa, and continued rubbing until he, too, dozed off.

Chapter 55

Smeared Paint

As the subtle soft morning light started peeking above the horizon, Jadyn woke. She was unaware Cole spent the last hour watching her sleep in the glow of the fire alarm's light from within a mirror set beside several pictures of Gavin. The frames stood perched, facing them on the reclaimed brick mantle. He was conflicted, spooning on the couch, feeling his morning wood pressing against her body's weight through his jeans. Cole grimaced as he observed the shrine to their love and felt the heaviness of the looming reality the man in these pictures was not really out of the picture.

Feeling more than a little immature, pretending to sleep when Jadyn awoke didn't stop him from deceiving her. Cole decided it was his best option; he wasn't ready to discuss any of it! To be even more convincing, he added some fake snoring.

Jadyn used her cupped hand to smell her breath, squinted at the nastiness of it and carefully slid out from beneath Cole's heavy arm, and headed to the bathroom.

When Jadyn returned to the living room and quietly turned the knob on the door leading to the backyard, Cole pretended to wake, yawned, and stretched his arms out, "Sorry, I fell asleep."

She smiled at him, "Pretty sure we both fell asleep.

I placed towels on the bathroom counter; gotta tend to the horses." The high-pitch squeal of the door's hinges made him want to oil them for her.

Photos and news articles of Gavin hung on the walls above a sizable collection of trophies. They were like those in his own place, simply different. Gavin's existence was staring in his face! He was real. Seeing her husband's life in pictures gyrated Cole's moral compass.

As if seeing those pictures wasn't enough, taking a shower in his shower, shaving his face in his sink, and drying himself off with his towel felt wrong on many levels. Out of the shower, standing in front of the mirror, Cole thought about how Gavin was probably someone he'd like to hang out with. Wearing the towel around his hips, he placed both hands on the counter and dropped his guilty head.

When he raised his head and looked into the mirror, the reflection of Jadyn walking towards him was the jolt he needed to shift his focus. She was smiling and coming closer, smiling and looking like a mud wrestler after a fight. His words spit out from his tight lips, "What the heck happened to you?" trying to hold back the laughter breaking through his words was impossible.

She said, "Go ahead, have your fun, laugh away! I gave the horses baths yesterday. Apparently, I didn't shut off the water all the way. Ask me how I found out?"

Laughing, he asked, "Okay, how'd you find out?"

She swiped at the mud on her cheek, saying, "Because you're here, I was rushing. I carried both flakes of hay at once, blocking my view of the mess I'd made. The heel of my boot was sucked into the mud, literally stopping me in my tracks, and well, let's just say, if I hadn't been carrying the hay, I'd look much worse."

He laughed loudly before questioning, "So you're saying it's my fault you fell face-first into the mud?!"

She gave him a frustrated yet playful look, "My boot was literally sucked off my foot!"

Cole grabbed his mouth and turned to face her as she said, "It took me a while to get it out of the mud."

His laugh escaped as his eyes widened, and he said, "Please continue."

She wrinkled her nose at the joy he found in her situation, "The horses kept bumping me with their noses, knocking me back down. Chase got confused and barked at them. He was trying to get them to move. They moved all right! They acted like kids playing in the rain, stomping and splashing me with the muddy water! He finally chased them away." She motioned her hands, showcasing her body, "And well, that's how I ended up like this"

Cole lost it, "Chase chased the horses, Hahaha!" He was consumed by laughter! It took Cole back in time to the night they met, how trashed she looked, and now this!

He was laughing hard, one hand gripping his belly and the other trying to cover his mouth, but the sequence of events she described was too hilarious! He was merciless as he repeated, "the horses pushed you over! You fell headfirst!" He was having a blast teasing.

She wiped mud on Cole's damp shoulder and slipped, saying, "Okay. Okay! That's enough, Ga – Cole!" Jadyn hoped he didn't notice; she'd almost called him Gavin. She pushed her shoulder into his saying, "My turn in the shower."

Cole ceased teasing and stepped aside. Pretending

he didn't notice she nearly called him Gavin, his laughter slowed.

She looked matter-of-factly at him, "I'd love coffee when I'm finished undoing this mess; if you don't mind making some, all the coffee supplies are above the coffee maker."

Cole understood how she could slip, with so much of Gavin all around, so he didn't bring it up and headed to the kitchen. After entering, he imagined Gavin making coffee and couldn't bring himself to use anything else belonging to him. He grabbed his keys instead and drove into town. He found himself focusing on how the last day they were together was oddly familiar to this morning.

While showering, Jadyn considered her muddy morning and thought, for sure, it was karma, payback for teasing Kendall when they were kids after her pony knocked her to the ground during a hoof-picking session. She thought her skin felt softer from the mud as she turned off the water, wrapped herself in a towel, and yelled, "Cole, how's the coffee coming? I don't smell anything! Hello? Cole?"

Cole wasn't in the house or on the back patio, so Jadyn looked out the front window to see his truck was gone. Her first thought was he'd heard her almost call him Gavin and left angry like he had when he found the ring. She said, "Oh good," when she saw his duffle bag where he had set it last night. Even better, it was unzipped and open. Jadyn checked to see if he had texted. She smiled while reading, *Went to town for coffee. BRB—cowgirl emoji.*

Jadyn texted back, *Thanks!—coffee cup and cowgirl emoji.*

Jadyn turned on classical music, dropped her towel, and changed into a white, paint-splattered men's dress shirt hanging on a coat rack. She picked up one of Gavin's brushes, slid her finger across the tips of its bristles, perched herself on her wooden stool, and began to paint. She sat with one bare leg in front of her, the other foot resting on its wooden cross post, and blended yellow highlights into the white and gray clouds she'd already painted into the light blue Sedona sky of her painting. The still-moist pliable oils easily moved beneath her brush.

Jadyn was a site for sore eyes when Cole entered unbeknownst to her. He stood motionless near the closed door holding their coffees in a carrier and took in the scene. Jadyn's wet hair slowly dripped onto the already-drenched shirt. He saw the color of her skin where it clung tight, making him long to be that close to her.

Chase's whimpering broke through the blaring cello music, ending his silent witness to her beauty. His paws shuffled as he excitedly stood and trotted over to greet Cole. Jadyn kept her feet in place, twisted, and looked at him, smiling from through her dangling wet hair, and continued painting. When upbeat piano replaced cello music, she started swaying in tempo, and he knew he wouldn't be able to resist her like he had when he woke up. If she wanted him, he wouldn't fight it; he'd surrender to her desire. She lowered the music's volume, and Cole asked, "Get my text?"

She smiled, still painting, with her back to him and said, "Obvi."

Cole walked to her, looking around the room at the easels, cameras, and lights, "So, this is where you film your videos," surprising her.

Jadyn asked, "You've seen my videos?"

He nodded and said, "Some."

Jadyn was delighted knowing he took an interest in her work, yet teased, "So you're still stalking me?"

Taking in Jadyn's sexy appearance, Cole set the tray on the table beside her, placed his hands on her cheeks, and kissed her. Her shirt opened as she stood. They voraciously kissed and touched each other, moving as if dancing until the intensity of his touch made her react, causing her to fall against the canvas. He quickly drew her back to him, "Oh, my God! I'm so sorry!"

Cole was mortified as he slowly pulled strands of her hair free from the thick paint, thinking she was upset for sure. But she wasn't. She said, "It's okay; think of this as performance art."

Jadyn was hot, thinking how he caught her again, keeping her from falling, and how his hands were strong holding her waist. She was brought back to the night they met. Cole's pained expression as he held her paint-stained hair in his fingers made her laugh. He shook his head, "You're not upset about this?" She tightly grasped his forearm and drew him back to her.

She reassured, "Maybe you'll feel better if you get some paint on you." Entwined, they sank against the canvas, and she impassionedly begged, "Don't stop!"

Her unbridled behavior excited Cole, and as their bodies smeared the paint with their movement, he wondered how she couldn't be upset about the destruction of her painting. It reminded him of how concerned he felt knowing her drawing in the sand would be washed away by the rising tide.

She sensed Cole's apprehension, "Screw the

painting. Make love to me!" He pressed his foot on the easel, anchoring it to the floor, and gave in to her passionate, yearning eyes.

Jadyn smeared a little paint on his face, "There. Now we're even."

Cole loved her playful reaction and wondered how hard it would be to clean up after this. He was glad they were in her studio, a room all about Jadyn, and only Jadyn, her art, her talent, the same, unforgettable talent he captured on his cell of the drawing she drew in the sand. He finally accepted that if Jadyn weren't freaked out by them ruining her painting, he wouldn't be either.

Cole's desire for Jadyn had grown and intensified over the months of their separation, so when she begged, "I want to feel you inside of me." He immediately searched his pockets for a condom.

Jadyn unbuttoned his jeans and insisted, "Take me now!"

Cole said, "Okay, I'll pull out."

He let her pull down his jeans, and he let down his guard as they joined together for this fantastically bizarre, passionate, and unforgettable lovemaking! They fulfilled their need for one another with a simultaneous climax, bonding them forever.

Jadyn sat naked on the stool as Cole tenderly cleaned the oil paint from her body and hair with a turpentine-soaked paint cloth. She returned the favor thinking it was a very intimate experience that would forever resonate in the room.

Once as clean as they could get, they returned to the shower to wash each other and spent the remaining hours of the day out of sight of anyone who might judge.

Cole and Jadyn fell asleep on the couch. He wouldn't take her to Gavin's bed. He couldn't bring himself to cross that line. Cole felt a little better about himself for staying out of their room, fully aware his actions were still unforgivable.

He worried on and off most of the day and night about the timing of their lovemaking. It was time for him to head back to California. He didn't feel right about leaving without discussing his concerns, "Do you want me to take you to get a morning-after pill?"

She confidently responded, "Didn't you pull out?"

He argued, "Yes. But...."

Jadyn shrugged it off, saying, "Then stop worrying."

Cole pretended he wasn't worried and attempted to convince himself their indiscretion wasn't eating at him. They were in love and had shared themselves, and as the oil paint stains showed on their skin and in Jadyn's hair, they shared the stain of unimaginable guilt.

After saying their goodbyes in the house, she watched Cole get into his truck. She continued watching as he faded into the horizon. Jadyn returned to her painting and hung it out of camera range.

Jadyn looked at it thinking this painting represented better than any other, precisely what 'Beyond the Brushstrokes' meant to her.

Chapter 56

Cherry Tobacco

Surfin' USA broke the silence in the house. Jadyn's emotions swelled with excitement when she answered Cole's call. "Hi, Crutch."

Cole's voice sounded frantic! "Breakers caught fire!"

Jadyn stood straight, held her breath, and dared to speak, "Oh my God!"

She could hear Cole's deep tight breaths catching in his throat as he forced out the words he dreaded to say, "They found Drake." Jadyn sucked in and held another breath with her open palm firmly pressed against her chest, bracing herself for his next release. "His pipe."

Jadyn felt she was staring at water swirling down a drain, flowing steadily and slowly. She was afraid to guess what he'd say next but couldn't help anticipating as she offered, "Want me to come?"

Cole dropped his head with tightly closed eyes and said, "No point. He's gone, Jay." His short soft sob made her heart palpitate. He's been... Father... They got him out."

Jadyn's spirits rose! She quickly said, "Oh good!"

Cole shook his head and winced, realizing he hadn't said any of this well and apologized, "No. Sorry. Drake had a stroke."

Jadyn's heart fluttered with compassion, "Oh, no, Cole, I'm so sorry! Want me to come there?"

Cole's voice was barely audible, "No. No. Drake's

gone. He died at the hospital."

Jadyn reached deep for the right words, "I'm so sorry."

Cole said, "I need to go. I can't even…."

She said, "Call 24/7."

The call ended, leaving Jadyn with her memories of Drake and the restaurant where she and Cole shared their first meal, their first dance, and their first kiss. Breakers and Drake, the beautiful, larger-than-life man she grew to love, and the beautiful restaurant were both erased from PCH but not from her mind.

Jadyn watched her cell dim to black.

She wanted to comfort Cole. She wanted to tell someone. She wanted to share her grief and sadness. But no one could know about Drake. No one could know about Cole, about her sin, their combined sin.

Later that day, Cole texted Jadyn an update. *Drake apparently suffered a stroke at Breakers. His pipe was lit. It fell out of his hand and landed on the floor. The reclaimed oily wood he used to build Breakers erupted in flames, burning with lightning speed. Luckily, the kitchen crew heard the fire alarms blaring and went to tell Drake. They found him unconscious, slumped over in his chair with Sinker beside him. There's not much left of Breakers… Ashes… devastating….*

Cole followed with a broken heart emoji and told her he'd be busy for a few days.

Jadyn, grateful not to be in Cole's shoes, comforted herself on her sofa by pulling her blanket over her. She cried herself to sleep, fearing it would soon be her turn to orchestrate the passing of Gavin. Another nap, born out of depression.

Chapter 57

The Gift

J adyn checked her cell for the date; it was November 16th. Her mind reeled as she realized December 10th was nearly here. The date felt creepy as if stalking her, a dark figure lurking on the road of life. The dreaded date was peering out from unlit alleyways, from behind trees, and from windows that reflected the fear on her face, the fear she concealed from the world. It seemed to whisper taunting words of doubt, challenging her capability of the irreversible decision bestowed upon her. December 10th, a day associated with holiday glee, traditions, shopping, parties, and snowflakes, marked the anniversary of Gavin's accident. December 10th, from now on, would remain branded on her brain like the brand burned into the fur of the beast who took him from her.

Like a movie of the tenth of December, Jadyn's memory played in a loop in her troubled mind. All the violence was in focus and replayed in slow motion as if her mind needed to examine the finer details for some future debate on his fall from the sweaty, snot-oozing animal. This larger-than-life date marks the fall that caused his mind to fall into his insidious coma.

Jadyn knew the day was coming, she couldn't stop time, and the decision was hers and hers alone to make. She had to decide whether to keep him suspended in what felt like a still-life painting, a sedentary, broken, and separate life. She knew he didn't want that. Or she could let him disconnect from the living world, so he could ultimately fall deeper into oblivion... to his final breath. December 10th will force her decision, forever change their lives and could never be reversed!

She was exhausted from the guilt of the time spent with Cole and an unaffordable ten-pound weight loss since the month before. Drained, she rubbed her sore, sensitive eyes and prayed for strength to make it through another day. Jadyn drove to work, mindless of the obnoxious static sound screeching from the speakers, her eyes fixed with a corpse-like empty stare. Filled with guilt, absent of hope, and nearly lifeless, she arrived at the gallery.

She parked, a bit concerned she couldn't recall most of the drive. She knew buildings, rocks, and trees had surely whizzed by as she drove, yet they couldn't be seen or found in her befuddled memory. She shook her head and tightened her face before grabbing her coffee and heading to unlock the gallery doors.

Only a few leaves remained in the canopy of trees covering the Tlaquepaque Arts & Shopping Village. Fallen leaves gathered like children to a pet store window in front of the gallery's glass doors. Teddy had been hired to fabricate a custom copper trim to frame the doors, and it gleamed with green highlights where her torch scorched it. This added touch increased the gallery's artistic ambiance and set it apart from the other merchants inside the Village. This unique art gallery houses some of the finest art from a select group of local artists. It is positioned alongside an outdoor metal art garden visible through its picturesque window. And when the wind blew, Jadyn enjoyed watching and hearing the musical whimsy of the differing sizes of wind chime tubes swaying and colliding in differing tones within the courtyard.

Smells of fires warming nearby homes and thoughts, as flashes, of Cole's weight against hers on the painting, were making her feel warm and cozy for the first time in an awfully long time.

Jadyn sat at the reception desk conflicted, watching the last leaves of fall dance outside the door, and noticed a box among the leaves apparently too large to slip through the mail slot. She wondered if it was so small she didn't see it when she arrived or so distracted she missed the mail carrier.

Curious, she stepped outside and picked it up to discover it was addressed to her. She looked to no avail, back and forth for anyone who may have placed it there. But it was stamped and mailed to her at the gallery's address. Why would anyone send something to her? I just work here; what can it be?

Back inside, she set her things on the high-gloss carved flagstone and wood counter and blew long, hot breaths into her cupped, cold, shivering hands. Wondering, *Who's this from? Is this Good or bad?*

Steam rose from her coffee cup's opening; she wrapped her hands around it to finish the warming process and finally picked up the box. She flipped it repeatedly, pondering its contents and wondering who could have sent it. She knew anyone watching would be annoyed she hadn't opened it immediately, but she continued waiting. *Why are people in such a hurry to reveal a surprise?* Jadyn loved surprises and couldn't stand it when someone didn't wait until Christmas to open gifts and simply hated when a present giver ruined the surprise by blurting out the content's identity before the unwrapping process ended. But this wasn't a gift, *or was it?* Jadyn bounced in her seat. She loved surprises and puzzles. This appeared both rolled up into one.

She set it on the counter again, sat back in the chair, and held her cup with both hands, sliding the rim along her lips, continuing her evaluation, attempting to guess the contents. *Hmmm… what measures ten inches long, two inches wide, and only one inch thick? Who could have sent it, and why?* A young couple holding hands and wearing heavy clothing walked in as Jadyn reached her frustration limit. "Oh, forget it, Jadyn, just open it!" Their curious eyes skimmed the gallery, wondering who this unbalanced young woman was talking to.

Embarrassed, Jadyn said, "Enjoy your visit. Take your time and let me know if you have any questions."

They spoke in unison, "Thank you. We will."

With Jadyn's gaze on her package rather than the couple, they reached for a brochure on the counter. It spoke of the gallery, its history, and the artists represented. She finally looked up and saw them walking slowly, intently looking at the artwork and holding each other as if just married. It was all Jadyn could do to keep from crying. If not for the puzzling gift, she knew her tears would flow.

There wasn't even a tiny slit of an opening for her to insert the silver letter opener, and the tape seemed unbreakable. Determined to succeed, Jadyn searched the drawer and found a safety pin. Its sharp point sliced right through the untearable tape. With eyes focused on the slit she'd created, she began tearing until she heard the sucking sound of the door opening. Jadyn raised her gaze and saw the newlyweds exiting, and through the glass doors, she watched them head for their car.

Happy to be alone, Jadyn let the paper fall to the counter. As the outer wrap fell, it exposed a gift-wrapped inner box with a note attached. Jadyn looked disturbed. She looked around and felt someone was playing a trick on her. She ran her finger over the message and read, "Enjoy this special gift from Gavin Michaels." Jadyn dropped the box! She immediately tapped her cell and instructed, "Call Aunt Teddy."

Her aunt answered, and Jadyn tried but couldn't speak, prompting Teddy to ask, "You there, Jadyn? I can't hear you. Did you pocket-dial me?"

Jadyn attempted to speak, only to release a sobbing garbled snotty sound instead.

Teddy said in a concerned motherly tone, "Where are you, doll? I'll come to you right now. Tell me where you are."

The sound of Teddy's compassionate voice made her emotions worse. Jadyn was able to say only one word. "Work."

She continued sobbing and coughing from the tightness she felt pressing against her chest and gasped for every labored breath. Jadyn dashed to the door, flipped the Open sign to Closed, secured the bolt, turned off the lights, and ran back to the counter to hide. Jadyn pushed her back against the floor-to-ceiling picture window overlooking the statue garden and slid to the floor, hiding behind the counter.

Each second gave rise to her grief, like a leaky faucet, drip by drip. Her anxiety, like water, rose higher all around her making her feel trapped. Surely she would drown in her guilty grief if Teddy didn't arrive soon.

Jadyn waited there, emotionally paralyzed, clumsily wiping away her tears with her soggy-tissue-holding-right hand, as she embraced a tissue box with her left arm.

With all she had, Jadyn attempted to persuade herself she should be happy about this. No matter how she tried to convince herself, she couldn't shake the morbid feeling attached to Gavin's unexpected and unreal gift. *He's alive now, but what-if?* She stopped thinking about it and begged God for the thought to be lifted from her.

Jadyn's long sigh of relief made her dizzy as she released it. Some of her stress evaporated when she heard the welcome sound of Teddy's key turning the lock. Teddy walked over to Jadyn with her arms and hands outstretched. Teddy pulled Jadyn to her feet and gave her a comforting embrace.

Jadyn placed the gift in Teddy's hand. Her eyes flashed from confused excitement to shocked concern as she awkwardly announced, "Sweetheart, an ancient philosopher named Zeno once said, "The Goal of life is living in agreement with nature."

Jadyn knew not to expect anything else from her aunt. Of course, she didn't answer with an answer Jadyn wanted or could understand; she always had to make her think. "What the hell does that mean?"

Teddy sensed her disgust yet remained in character, saying, "What it means to me is unimportant. What does it mean to you?"

Jadyn grimaced and rolled her eyes, "I knew you'd help me climb out of my pity party, but must you make me work hard too?"

Teddy didn't have to speak; Jadyn didn't expect

a reply. Annoyed, she stared at her last painting, *Abeyance*, hanging behind Teddy. Jadyn felt squirmy as she contemplated its meaning. She said, "I need to be with Gavin."

Teddy nodded, "Go to him. I'll cover your shift." She tried but couldn't forget what she and Cole did the night before and prayed for the strength and insight of how to behave once she got to him.

Jadyn arrived and sat beside his bed as if in a confessional. She stared at her broken man in disbelief and had little hope of ever hearing his voice reply to hers.

The sound of Jadyn's chair leg growling in resistance to the hospital's shiny linoleum floor was punishing to her ears as she slid it close to his bed. Her lips quivered as she kissed her fingertips and gently placed them on his lips. She slid her fingers over the stubble growing, where his soft beard once was, recalling how proud he was of it and how she loved to feel it skimming over her skin.

Pained by his absence of mind and motionless body, she thought about Teddy, Molly, Willy, and Kendall. She mostly thought about Cole and realized what the quote meant to her. Nature would always prevail no matter what she tried to do or force.She considered the words, *living in agreement with nature,* and then spoke aloud in a whisper, "Living in agreement with nature."

A look of determination replaced her look of depression, and she reached for the present, talking to him as if awake and understanding her every word. "Gavin, baby, I received a package from you today. I brought it with me." She shook the box near her ear, listening. "Maybe I can guess what's inside. Hmm, could it be bath salts, soap, perfume?"

She sniffed loudly and continued, "Well, it doesn't smell girly, so that can't be right. Okay, here goes, sweetheart. I'm opening it."

She removed the safety pin from her jeans pocket and slit through the wrapping. A small, folded brochure dropped onto the bed. She read, "Please enjoy this recurring gift from Gavin Michaels. For the next eleven months, you will receive five red sable paint brushes each month." She pulled the enclosed brushes out with excitement. "She joyfully exclaimed, "Oh, honey, what a thoughtful gift!" She removed the largest from its protective plastic sheath and gently stroked Gavin's once-tan face with its soft red hairs. "Baby, this is the softest brush I've ever felt; amazing, isn't it? I promise to use these all the time! I can't wait for you to see the paintings I create!"

She searched his room for angels, "I wish you'd wake up and talk to me, baby. I miss you so much." Tears formed as she went on to say, "Chase looks for you every night from the front window. He really misses your walks, and I can't replace you."

With a longing to be close to him, she dabbed some of his cologne on the nape of his neck, unlocked and lowered the bedrail, rested her head upon his chest, and fell asleep to the sound of his beating heart.

Jadyn was startled awake by the nurse's soft voice informing her it was time for his bed bath. She looked up and out the window rubbing her eyes, "What time is it? Is it really about to get dark?"

The nurse nodded, "Mrs. Michaels, we tried to wake you several times, but you were out cold. You've been asleep for six hours, and well, there are things we simply must do for Gavin and haven't been able to because you've been in bed with him."

Realizing Gavin had been in one position for far too long, she abruptly sprung up and out of his bed. "Please do what you need to. I'm so embarrassed! I've not slept well in months."

His nurse spoke compassionately, "We understand; don't you worry. This was probably a wonderful experience for Gavin, to have his love beside him for so many hours. We were all touched by it."

Her southern accent was calming to incredibly embarrassed Jadyn. She was disoriented after losing most of her day to much-needed sleep. Jadyn, forcing a smile, said, "Thank you for being so kind." Jadyn slid on her sweater, laid the throw on top of Gavin's feet, and kissed his cheek, saying, "See you soon, darling. I love you more than you will ever know."

Chapter 58

Too Many Boxes

J adyn drove home in quiet introspection, trying to comprehend it was now night. She was glad to see the setting sun still glowing from below the horizon, proving she hadn't slept the entire day.

Jadyn's mind swam with guilty thoughts of Cole and guilty thoughts about Gavin's gift. She didn't think she could take anything else, so she focused on the sound of her tires moving beneath her, like a driving meditation. She planned to practice actual meditation after dinner to bring order to the chaotic thoughts she'd birthed. The vibration of the tires moving beneath her SUV was settling until her cell vibrated and loudly rang, making her almost jump out of her seat! She pushed the button on her screen to accept Kendall's call, "Hello, Darlin!"

Kendall was anything but calm, so Jadyn added, "Woah! Take it down a notch, will ya?!"

Kendall refused to let Jadyn be so serious, "Okay, granny! You sound like an old woman! My God! Where are you right now anyway?"

Annoyed and groggy, Jadyn rolled her eyes, "Driving home after a long visit with Gavin. Why?"

Kendall lowered her tone and said in a bratty manner, "Cuz I could swear you just passed the Circle K."

Jadyn grabbed the wheel tight with both hands and raised up in her seat, craning her head to look back over her shoulder, "I did! Oh my God, where are *you*?!"

Kendall flicked her headlights on and off. "Hello? Circle K, of course." Feeling proud of herself, she teased, "Do you realize I've never been invited to your house? I find it a bit rude, don't you?"

Jadyn made a U-turn yelling, "I see you! I'm going to pull in and lead you to the house! Follow me, baby." She loudly thanked God for Kendall's surprise visit. There was a piece of Jadyn, wondering if she could handle her after all this day had dumped on her.

Kendall coaxed Jadyn using a playful teasing tone, "Hey Jay, I brought wine!"

Jadyn wondered if everything was okay with Kendall and her marriage, "How much wine?"

She yelled back, "Enough! More than enough, and there'll be no talk of bedtimes or tasks needing to be done. You're not allowed to act all grown-up and mature while I'm here, understand me, missy?"

Imagining what it would be like, to not have all her responsibilities, and recalling their past wine nights, she fished for help, "I actually do have chores to do, and you're more than welcome to do them for me."

Kendall thought about how she had the life she'd always dreamed of. She loved having little to do other than what she considered fun, "What kinda chores are you talking about?"

Jadyn looked in the rearview mirror, knowing Kendall was questioning her offer. "Did you bring boots?" Jadyn flashed a mischievous grin, "I mean shit-kicking kinda boots!"

Kendall's expression kept shifting as she asked, "Ewe... me? Course not! Don't you have a ranch hand for that?"

Jadyn shamed her, "My God, we can't all drive

around in black Mercedes' and pay people to do the dirty work. Some of us actually do chores and enjoy it!"

Kendall's body stiffened, "Alright, I get it. We wear the same size boots. Got an extra pair of SKs for your new ranch hand? And I work for free! In fact, how about I pay you — in wine — to work for you! You can't beat that!"

Jadyn loved the sound of that! "Yepper! I most certainly do have an extra pair of boots for you, and I love the sound of your currency!" She smiled, recalling when they were kids. Kendall let her ride her pony, followed by grooming and stall mucking. Loving the roles were now reversed, she said, "I'll drive real slow, so you don't hurt your rich-bitch buggy on my Hillbilly dirt road."

She didn't want Jadyn to think she'd lost her good nature, "Hey, don't judge me for being rich. It's not my fault; it's Levi's, and this road ain't dirt."

Their laughter grew loud as they turned off the main road with a hard thud to dirt. It was smooth and firm beneath them as they drove with only headlights to guide them. "Okay, well, this dirt road doesn't feel much different than the concrete."

Jadyn giggled, aware Kendall was about to learn what a real dirt road is all about. "Just you wait!"

She turned onto the next road, which quickly descended, changing from smooth, hard dirt to a washboard surface created by the summer monsoons. "Holy speed bumps! This road feels like someone laid out a thousand speed bumps in a row!"

The sun officially set. Its once faint glow faded into complete darkness. Like a light switch, the sun's absence instantly turned on the stars! Trillions of stars!

The sky was a vision Kendall had never witnessed. "Wow! I've never seen so many stars!"

Jadyn, aware Kendall wasn't going to like what was coming next, said, "It'll be over soon." She almost felt guilty and couldn't wait to hear her reaction!

The late fall moon wouldn't rise for at least an hour, leaving only their headlights to guide them. And once the road went soft, Kendall couldn't clearly distinguish the shape and distance of Jadyn's taillights. The space between them was instantly engulfed by a thick, swirling cloud of red-clay dust.

Kendall squinted, searching for a break in the wall of dust. "Guess the car wash I got in town was a bust!"

Jadyn said with delight, "I warned you!"

Without Jadyn's help, Kendall knew she'd never find her way back. "Don't be asking me to run any errands unless you're my escort. How do you even know where the road's edge is with zero streetlights? I feel like I've landed on the moon!"

Jadyn reprimanded, "Don't exaggerate!"

She knew Jadyn stated the obvious, but she was spoiled. "It's what I do best!"

Jadyn rounded the corner, "This is our last turn, Kendall. Careful of the right side, there's a deep culvert, and you don't want to end up in it."

Kendall wondered what Jadyn was talking about, "What the heck...? Oh, that! Holy culvert!"

Jadyn laughed, "At least we're back on hard dirt, right?"

Kendall leaned all the way forward, looking over the hood of her car, hoping not to drive into it, "Words I didn't expect to hear tonight!"

Still laughing, she rounded the turn, the air

cleared, revealing Jadyn's taillights again and Kendall, lightening the mood, childishly repeated, "Are we there yet? Are we there yet? Mom, are we there yet?"

Jadyn spoke motherly, "Yes, dear, see the bright light straight ahead? It's my, our place."

Chase's barking could be heard from the road, and he sounded anxious. He knew she was coming home later than usual. Jadyn expected Chase to knock them to the floor with a wet-tongued, dirty-paw welcome if she didn't go in alone to calm him first. She texted Kendall, *Stay in the car till I give the all-clear signal XO.*

Kendall parked alongside Jadyn's SUV, soothing her still vibrating body from all the dirt-road drama, waiting till Jadyn flashed the front porch light several times. As Kendall pushed open her car door, she watched excited Jadyn walking with hands outstretched and ready for a hug. Kendall prepared herself for the crush of one of her intense dig-in-until-it-hurts kinda hugs. Jadyn squeezed hard, "I can't believe you drove all this way by yourself to see me!"

Kendall felt a rush of guilt as she said, "And I can't believe you're surprised! You mean the world to me! I'd have been here sooner, but my honey deserved some after-wedding time alone with me. I didn't want to hear him suggest the Honeymoon was over."

Jadyn smirked, "I'll bet you didn't."

Kendall went on, "I spoil him as much as possible, so he'll spoil me right back. And, as I mentioned earlier, I wasn't invited."

Jadyn swung her hips as she walked in front of Kendall, leading the way to her front door, saying with a smart-ass-sounding voice, "I wasn't invited."

Kendall defended herself to Jadyn, saying, "Hey! I'm

not trying to make you feel bad. I wouldn't have wanted a bunch of busy-bodies coming around, either. Not to say I'm a busy-body, nosey perhaps, but not busy about any-body."

Jadyn shook her head, "Okay, goofball, whom I love dearly, finished?" Jadyn invited her in and pointed to the couch. She grabbed wine glasses and set them on the coffee table. Chase came inside, wagging his tail, calmly greeting Kendall, and curled up in a ball beside her.

Jadyn's heart throbbed, "He must sense how much you mean to me."

Kendall put her feet on the table, ready for rest after the long drive. As she closed her eyes, Jadyn tossed a pair of filthy boots on the floor in front of the couch, "Here ya go. Put these on so we can be done with the chores and start in on one of those bottles."

She laughed hard when Kendall wrapped her arms around the three bottles she'd already set on the coffee table and said, acting like the witch from The Wizard of Oz, "You mean these, my-pretty?" Kendall switched her black leather boots for Jadyn's, stood up, with shoulders back like a soldier and said, "Okay, I'm ready for dooty-duty."

Kendall actually owned her own horses, so Jadyn didn't buy her act of being grossed out as they cleaned the stalls and fed the horses.

Once finished, she escorted Kendall to the guest room. After showering and changing into jammies, they met back in the living room, where Jadyn had a fire burning. Chase had waited contentedly for them, all curled up in a doggie ball on the fur rug in front of the rock fireplace.

Kendall started immediately on the cheese, cracker,

and sandwich meat platter Jadyn prepared, along with her homemade salsa and chips. She moaned in approval. "I have so missed your salsa!" Kendall talked about married life. Jadyn shared her experience with Molly and Willy and Gavin's freaky gift.

Jadyn cried a little as Kendall poured more Malbec into her glass and gulped it, "That is so...."

Jadyn knew Kendall wasn't sure what to say, so she offered comfort, "You don't have to say anything. It's even tough for me to verbalize my situation. I don't know how to feel right now." Jadyn swirled the wine in her glass, looking into its dark reddish-brown color, and slowly sipped, enjoying rich vanilla and blackberry notes.

Kendall impatiently pushed up on the bottom of Jadyn's glass, forcing her to drink faster. "You'll never get a buzz slow-sipping!" Jadyn squirted wine out of her nose, making Kendall laugh!

Jadyn caught some of the wine leaking from her nostrils with a tissue and yelled at Kendall, "Screw you! Don't do that again! Wine stains! I barely drink. I'll fall asleep, or worse, fall into a drunk sob fest."

Kendall placed her hand on Jadyn's knee, "Speaking of crying, and, just so you know, this was your Aunt Teddy's idea.

Jadyn looked confused, "What?"

Kendall reached from beside her and under the blanket, slowly revealing a small blue box with angels covering it. "It's a gift of sorts. Give me your hands." Kendall set it on Jadyn's open palms. "It's called an Angel Box. It's full of little messages written by various people, some you know and some you don't."

She glared at Kendall, at the box, then back at

Kendall. Jadyn slammed the box on the table. It tumbled as she shot up and started walking out of the room, harshly yelling, "Don't follow me!"

Kendall begged, "Please don't be mad. We all love you so much."

Jadyn stopped in her tracks! "Love me?! You conspired against me! You went behind my back! You tricked me into believing you're here to be a friend, but had this hidden agenda! Love me!" She shook her head and continued walking away from her, leaving Kendall shaken and feeling guilty.

Kendall was concerned she and Teddy only made things worse, and nervously texted her. *Jadyn freaked! Never seen her this pissed! I think this was a bad idea.*

Teddy reassured her, *I know my niece. It'll be okay. Just wish the other box hadn't arrived earlier today. Too many surprise boxes for one day! Hang in there. You're a good friend for doing this – even if she can't see it yet.*

Jadyn was unaware of how much weight she'd lost and the lackluster appearance of her once-glowing skin. She appeared terminally ill, with sunken-in, dark eye sockets. She spent most of her time walking around with a blank sorrowful stare. Although Jadyn knew sadness leaked from her, she believed to have it under control and thought no one could tell the depth of her suffering. Jadyn wasn't going to take this intrusion lightly. She returned to the living room with a worn-out look and yelled, "Go home!"

Kendall fought back. "Go home? I just got here. I can't find my way outta here." And with sad, begging, nearly tearing eyes, she asked, "You don't really want me to leave, do you?"

Jadyn felt betrayed and accused her of conspiring

against her, "Go to Aunt Teddy's. Apparently, the two of you are good friends now." Kendall, afraid to speak, remained silent and Jadyn kept yelling, "I know I look wrecked and feel like death warmed over! But do I look that bad? So bad Aunt Teddy felt she needed to go behind my back? Really? How pathetic do you think I am?"

Kendall reached out her arms. Jadyn stepped in for a much-needed embrace, sobbing heavily.

After a minute or two, Jadyn pulled away, exposing a wet-black mark on Kendall's silk blouse. "Well, you look a whole hell of a lot better than my blouse! Look at it; it's the Shroud of Turin! You left your face upon my chest!" Only Kendall could pull laughter out of Jadyn with so few words spoken.

Kendall patted the couch cushion, "Come sit. Let's think of reasons to toast." She tugged Jadyn's sleeve and pulled her down; this was Kendall's version of focusing on gratitude. A more dangerous version than her mom's, and more fun! Jadyn smacked the Angel Box with the palm of her hand, causing it to spin and slide away. Kendall caught it. "Don't you wanna know what's inside this pretty box of angels?"

Jadyn gave a disgusted look and changed the subject to how dirty her pretty Mercedes was, sitting outside looking like a dust magnet. "Wait till you see your car tomorrow! You'll wonder what color it is! Oh, and you can't just wipe this dirt off. You have to soak it off."

"Okay, fine. I get it. You're clearly pissed. Remember, this was Teddy's idea. A plan born from love, and you know it. So, play along or don't. Read the messages alone, with me, or not at all. It's up to you. I'm here now, so let's eat! We have cheese and wine, and we can pretend we're young again. Like when we drove up the coast of Cali and weren't allowed to drink wine. Remember when we liked Boone's Farm Strawberry wine?"

Jadyn yelled, "We loved the wine but not the brutal hangovers!" They laughed.

Kendall began doubting Teddy's assumption this box would somehow bring Jadyn back to them when Jadyn surprisingly picked it up, saying, "This is so Auntie T, forcing people to communicate. She knows me so well, doesn't she? She knows I can't resist a puzzle. My question for you is, can I bear to read these? Do we have enough wine?"

Kendall's eyelashes fluttered like butterfly wings as her expression switched from concern to joy, "Yes. I believe we have enough wine. Are you ready to begin?"

Jadyn sipped her wine, "There's only one way to find out! Go ahead, hand me one."

Kendall reached in, randomly pulled one out, and handed it to Jadyn, "I'm here for as long as it takes."

Jadyn brought the folded light pink paper to her face, rubbed it against her skin, and smelled it with her eyes closed and her hands shaking. The room was poorly lit. Her eyes, unable to focus, were starved for light, so she leaned toward the lamp beside her and clicked it on.

As if it was the last Christmas present to unwrap, she unfolded it with the speed of a snail until it was fully exposed. Kendall was dying to know what it said. She had her eyes tightly focused on Jadyn's hands. Jadyn toyed with her by not reading it, saying, "The fire's going to go out if I don't add some wood to it." Jadyn dropped it back into the box and shot up to rekindle the flame. Kendall took a swig from her glass and fell back against the sofa, knowing full well this was punishment for scheming with Teddy.

Jadyn walked and opened the back door, reached for one of the logs Gavin cut last winter, returned to the open fireplace, and placed it on the ash-covered rack. Kendall watched, puzzled when Jadyn lit the end of a dry spaghetti noodle with her lighter.

Jaydn turned on the gas and used the burning noodle to ignite paper loosely crumbled beneath the log. Kendall giggled, "Your ingenuity never ceases to amaze me!"

Jadyn remained, seemingly frozen, kneeling with her eyes fixed on the fires' ever-changing, flickering flames. Kendall remained respectfully silent, waiting and watching as her friend suffered seemingly endless suffering. Kendall was there for the duration, no matter how long it took. For Jadyn's sake, she hoped the process would be quick; but she didn't know the extent of the pain and self-loathing Jadyn held.

With lips tight, hands clenched, shoulders raised and rigid, Jadyn finally moved. She reached for the knob and turned until the hissing gas ceased. She looked to be sure the flames were well established and got caught in the red and yellow glow of the dry bark burning with thoughts of Gavin and Cole, both ghosts to everyone else. Memories of them lingered in her private thoughts like the smoke in the room.

Jadyn knew Kendall would understand about Cole, but could she trust her to keep it from Teddy after they conspired against her? What if her mom found out she'd been unfaithful to Gavin? She pulled her shoulders back, pinched them together, tipped her head to one side, and attempted to massage away the tightness.

Kendall felt the heat of her anger and the sharp sting of her avoidance. Jadyn was avoiding her, not just the notes inside the box, but her.

Jadyn bent forward, hands on her knees, allowing the heart locket she'd worn nearly every day since Gavin gave it to her to swing free of her chest. It caught Kendall's eye as it reflected the firelight, and she watched it sway until Jadyn finally stepped back from the fire. Jadyn quickly grabbed it! The fire's heat trapped inside the locket burned her. She privately said to herself, *Good, I deserve the pain. How could I sleep with Cole while Gavin lay in his stale hospital room?*

She finally spoke to Kendall, "Did you see that?"

Kendall nodded, afraid to talk, and Jadyn went on saying. "My locket burned me. I got too close to the flame."

Kendall asked, "You okay?"

Jadyn, visibly humored, shared a fond memory with Kendall. "It reminds me of a night Gavin and I spent at a bar in Prescott called Coyote Joe's. It was Open Mic Night, snow was on the ground, and they heated the outside stage area with firepits; man, were they hot! And so was my zipper after standing in front of it for a few minutes! I had a zipper-shaped burn mark on my belly for over a week, and Gavin mercilessly teased me!"

Kendall brought Jadyn's wine glass to her and encouraged her to sit beside her in front of the fire. They sat on bent knees, and Kendall raised her glass to Jadyn, "Here's to the memories that make you blush and those we pray aren't caught on video." Their laughter grew even louder as they both held their stomachs, begging the other to stop. The harder they tried, the deeper their laughs became until Jadyn released one of her snorts, and they fell, rolling on the floor.

Their contagious belly laughs dissolved into silence, and they calmly faced one another. Chase watched them questioning their odd behavior from the couch with his ears up and head tipped.

Kendall and Jadyn's unshakable friendship allowed them these moments where words were wasted if spoken; they both knew the box, their hearts, and their tear ducts would open when the time was right.

A song came on and reminded Jadyn of Kendall's wedding reception. She spoke softly with eyes wet with pain, "I'm so sorry for leaving the reception early."

Kendall pushed Jadyn's shoulder, "Stop, already. I forgave you that day. In the bathroom, remember? I literally gave you permission to leave."

Jadyn rolled over onto her back looking up at the ceiling, "I thought you were just being nice. Thought for sure you've been mad at me ever since."

Kendall was sick and tired of Jadyn questioning her forgiveness and sat up, "Come on, Jadyn, don't you remember me telling you to go?"

Jadyn could feel Kendall's frustration, "Yes, but."

Kendall wanted this to be the last time they talked about this, "No buts, Jay, why can't you let this go?! I have. I've even forgiven Brittney." Kendall smiled, knowing Jadyn was about to be shocked by her words. "The truth about that came out. Turns out she hated you because Greg is madly in love with you."

Jadyn sat up, facing Kendall, "What? Who? Not Greg from middle school... that Greg?"

Kendall nodded and smiled at her with a Cheshire

cat smile, "Yes, apparently, he's holding a torch for you."

They both laughed, feeling a little guilty Jadyn sympathized, "How sad! Poor Brittney. He's an ass for telling her, don't you think?"

Kendall had reconciled her feelings for Brittney, "Unrequited love is apparently pretty powerful. Brittney got suspicious and guessed something was going on with you and Greg. She overheard him at the rehearsal dinner asking Levi lots of questions about you. You never dated him, did you?"

Jadyn's face was hilarious to Kendall as it twisted with each word she spoke. "Oh my God! No-wah! I never dated anyone younger than me back then, did you?"

Kendall shook her head, "Course not," as she chewed on a piece of saltwater taffy. Jadyn went on, "I can assure you I did nothing to lead him on. I don't even remember seeing him at your wedding."

Kendall loved how uncomfortable Jadyn looked about this discovery. "Well, he definitely saw you! Apparently, he kept staring at you, which drove Brittney nuts!"

Jadyn grabbed the taffy Kendall had just unwrapped out of her hand and plopped it in her mouth, saying sloppily. "Ouch! Sucks for Brittney."

Kendall knew it was in bad taste but said it anyway, "And this box sucks for you." With the conversation back to Jadyn's decision, Kendall begged, "I love you, Jay. Talk to me, please talk to me. I can't stand seeing you in so much pain."

Sitting on opposite ends of the couch, Kendall was a captive audience. She stared at Jadyn's mouth, anticipating her words. She unfolded the note Kendall previously gave her, "I feel a lot better knowing you don't hate me for my pathetic blubbering at your reception and for bailing early."

Kendall said, "Good. Now never bring it up again."

Jadyn teased by delaying reading it. She scrunched her nose and asked, "Have you read these?"

Kendall responded honestly, "No. I only know what I wrote to you; it didn't seem right - kinda like reading your diary or something."

Taunting Kendall, "Then you must be on pins and needles and dying for me to start reading these."

Kendall wanted to smack her and snark back but restrained herself, "No one should push you to read them. They're yours. Keep them to yourself if you want." Jadyn searched her face for sincerity. "I'm here to support you. I want you to be glad I'm here. It broke my heart when you told me to leave." They leaned into each other and hugged, trying not to spill their wine.

Jadyn's emotions loosened with each sip of the wine, "I didn't really want you to leave. I've missed you terribly. I'm sorry I've been keeping to myself. I didn't want to bother you or screw up your newlywed glee."

Kendall sounded angry but wasn't, "Oh, my God, I wish you wouldn't talk like this. You never bother me! I want you to be happy, and it may seem impossible to imagine right now, but I know one day you will be happy again."

She made it clear Kendall crossed a line. Jadyn pulled back, leaned her head against the pillow, and took a defensive pose with arms crossed, paper still in hand.

Kendall apologetically said, "I can be such an ass! I don't have a clue about what you're going through. I'll be more careful, promise."

Eyes closed, biting her lip, pillow tightly clutched, she struggled to say, "Okay, I mean, it's okay. I know you mean well. I'm just like a can of shaken soda waiting to explode. When I open up, I'm not sure anyone should be around. I'm glad you're here now, though. Guess now's as good a time as any to face this. So, you really think these little pieces of paper hold some magic cure for your crazy friend?"

Kendall cautiously said, "I honestly have no clue. Ready to find out?"

Jadyn smoothed out the folds on her knee and read aloud, "It's from Rebecca. Oh my God, I haven't talked to her since your wedding. How is she?"

"Her boyfriend, Ryan, recently proposed, so I guess she's better than fine. She sent her love and asked me to tell you she's waiting for me to tell her when it's suitable for her to call. She doesn't want to overstep."

With frustration, Jadyn said, "This is so stupid. All of us are holding back for fear of upsetting each other. How pathetic are we? Tell her to call anytime. Better yet, I'll call to congratulate her myself."

With a sigh, Jadyn began reading the note.

Dear Jay,

I remember the day I met your sweet self! I sat, probably looking pretty lonely, till you came up to me and asked if I needed a friend. I will always remember it. You showed me people are capable of extraordinary kindness. I've tried to mirror you ever since. You are deserving of happiness because you have given so much to so many, and I'm praying for you. My door will always be open whenever you want to talk or escape the desert for a little trip to Big Bear. Of course, right now, it's freezing here, and the lake is all but frozen over, so we could ice skate like when we were kids.

I don't feel qualified to advise you, and well, this paper is way too small, so... XOXO Becca

Tears pooling in Jadyn's eyes magnified and reflected the glowing, flickering fire's flames. Staring at Kendall, she swallowed, took several deep breaths, and reached into the box, "This could be deadly. I hope my Angels are here to help me go through this Angel Box of yours. I sure do miss ice skating; it is such an amazing feeling. I remember it as if it were yesterday."

Kendall playfully said, "I recall all the boys following you around."

Jadyn finished by loudly stating her opinion, "Ha! That's not how I remember it. Too bad we don't have a rink around here."

They took turns reminiscing about the past when they were the self-proclaimed "Rink-Rats." They ended up falling asleep, lying beside each other on the floor. Jadyn's snoring woke Kendall. She carefully got up and removed the tipping glass of wine from Jadyn's hand just in time; had another minute gone by, Jadyn would have had a rude awakening.

Buzzed and yawning, Jadyn and Kendall walked each other to their bedrooms, a drunk, leading a drunk, bumping hips and holding hands. Jadyn remembered when Gavin led her through the hall to the bedroom the first time they made love.

Chapter 59

Angel Box from Hell

Morning broke with a calm silence only snow can bring, and the fog was so thick she couldn't see the barn from the back window. She shuddered thinking about going outside, but morning feeding and stall cleaning had to be done, and by the look of the sky, she'd better hurry! Jadyn was taken by surprise, there was no mention of a snowstorm in the forecast, yet snow was falling and falling fast!

Jadyn gazed out the window contemplating how breathtaking the red rocks looked whenever it snowed as if sprinkled with powdered sugar. She was excited to see Kendall's reaction as she walked up to the window squinting, yawning, and with a haggard look. Kendall rubbed her eyes and spoke as if God was toying with her, "Is that what I think it is?"

Jadyn chimed back with energy, "It sure is! Wanna go for a walk?"

Kendall looked at Jadyn, blinking and shaking her head, "You're crazy! I didn't bring clothes for this!"

It was an hour earlier for Kendall; they were up late the night before, and to top it off, Kendall was not an early riser. Jadyn suggested she go back to sleep while she tended to the horses, but Kendall was determined to be there for her, so she borrowed an outfit, and with Chase by their side, they walked through the foggy mist and fluffy snowflakes to the stalls.

As they approached the stalls, feisty Kharibia began nickering loudly, swinging her head in celebration of the season's first snow. Blaze was usually calm, but got caught up in the excitement too! Chase, alarmed by their behavior, kept running to them, barking, and then back to hide behind Jadyn with his tail tucked tightly between his legs. "What a tough guy," she said, smiling.

Kendall had her hands wrapped tightly around her, and teeth visibly clenched as she begged, "Please tell me you've got coffee brewing. I'm going to need some thawing out after this!" They worked through the cold until their bodies became warm from the exercise.

Jadyn said, "It's so great having your companionship."

Kendall tried to lighten things up, "You mean my help, right?"

They finished mucking stalls, and Chase's training kept the horses away from the feed bins while they loaded them. Kendall loved seeing him work the horses, "Wow, he is so good at managing the horses!"

Jadyn proudly smiled, "Yeah, he's a great dog. Gavin trained him well." Her sad eyes made Kendall feel she had stepped in it and ruined the joyful mood.

She attempted to lighten things back up. "He sure did! Oh, my God, do you remember when my pony, Whiskey, knocked me over with his nose? We could've used a dog like Chase that day!"

She patted Chase's head and said, "Yeppers! Sure coulda, but that's what you get for bending over in front of a pony! Should'a seen it from my perspective!" They laughed uncontrollably, leaning over, gasping for air, and holding their stomachs. "You did a front flip! It was like you practiced that move! I didn't know mud could splash!"

It was as if a switch turned Jadyn's laughter off, and she switched topics, "I've got a confession to make."

Curiously concerned, Kendall asked, "Really? A confession, do tell."

She mindlessly spoke, "I know you're going to say something about Karma, but a few days ago, I had a muddy stall fall on my face kinda day! I was so embarrassed when Cole." She froze in place and stopped herself but didn't stop soon enough.

Kendall heard and leaned down to get her face as close as possible to Jadyn's bent-over face and quickly asked, "Cole?"

"I'll tell you later; the snow will bury us if we don't go inside!"

Swiftly falling, heavy flakes, mixed with lighter, thicker swirling ones, coasted on the wind's current. Jadyn knew when snowflakes began floating weightlessly, they would stick.

With a childlike whimsy, Kendall leaned her head back, outstretched her arms, and spun around with her mouth open, hoping to capture the delicate flakes on her waiting tongue. Jadyn tapped her forehead, "Sorry to disturb your fun, little girl, but the pooch and I would like to go inside."

Kendall walked into the kitchen to discover Jadyn sitting at the table with her head hanging, apparently hungover. She placed her hand on her shoulder and took charge of breakfast, "You rest your muffin. I'll make coffee and warm us a couple of pumpkin spice muffins I bought yesterday." She set the Angel Box in front of her and pulled out the thickest note, leaving it for Jadyn to deal with as she danced around the kitchen in her Eeyore slippers.

Jadyn saw it, rolled her eyes, and suspected it was from one of three people, Teddy, her mother, or Kendall, but as she unfolded it, surprisingly, she discovered it was from Molly. "How'd you get Molly to write? How'd you find out about her?" She scoffed, "Oh, never mind, I know, Aunt Teddy," remembering she had ambushed Molly when she confirmed her invitation to Thanksgiving Dinner.

Dearest Jadyn,

Sorry for my chicken-scratch handwriting. Long life and hard work have taken my girlish style and replaced it with what you see before you now. There was a time when both my writing and I were considered elegant, but it was another life and time....

Speaking of life, I want you to know I won't forget your kindness and the time you've so sweetly spent with me. You have a spirit about you like no one else, and I believe time will heal us both.

As for the decision you have to make, I think one of the hardest lessons I've had to learn throughout my life is that while we are all responsible for each other, there is a point we must "Let God" take charge and know we are not really responsible for anything except for how we treat one another. I know it probably sounds like a cliché, but this time shall pass.

I'm sure if you do as Gavin wanted, "God" will be the one in charge, and you can be at peace and of clear mind. Of course, ultimately, it is up to you, and this burden must be very hard for a woman with so little behind her. If you ever need to talk, the spot on the bench next to me is yours for the taking.

Consider yourself hugged by a mother's arms, Love, Molly.

Kendall turned to hand Jadyn her coffee and saw Jadyn reading. She hesitated to sit till Jadyn looked up with tears and a smile signaling it was safe to approach.

Kendall set her muffin on top of her coffee cup; it barely stretched the width of the cup's mouth. She sat beside her without comment, knowing the words would come once Jadyn was ready. Jadyn wiped the tears from her cheeks, grabbed the muffin, and began peeling back the paper wrapper, "What a nice surprise."

Kendall celebrated the emotional release that washed over Jadyn, her face seemed radiant, and her expression renewed. "You mean the muffin?"

Feeling annoyed, she said, "No, I was talking about her note. Molly's so sweet. Everything about her has been a nice surprise. She's like a gift from God."

Kendall couldn't resist, "Like me?" Her cheesy grin made Jadyn's eyes roll. Their playful chatter during breakfast continued, as they enjoyed the breathtaking view of the snow, still falling.

Watching the falling snow made Jadyn's eyelids heavy so they moved from the kitchen to the living room to wait for a break in the storm. They sat wrapped in blankets, sleepy and silent listening to cello music with heads bobbing, holding back sleep.

Once the sun appeared, they ventured out and discovered the clouds beautifully arranged as if by God. The heavens opened with light streams spreading across the towering red rocks. The scene seemed created for their pleasure! It was made even more spectacular when a magical and vibrantly-colorful-double rainbow appeared as if for good measure! Kendall thanked God.

She was delighted to see a glimmer of hope shining from Jadyn's once-vacant eyes.

Their second round of coffee no longer released steam into the air, so they went back inside to warm it. Jadyn's cell phone began playing a familiar ringtone. Knowing it was Cole, she set it down, unanswered, and her flushed face stiffened. Kendall recognized Jadyn was hiding something and waited, giving her a curious, non-judgmental look. Jadyn finally relented, "Okay, you caught me. Yes. I have something to say. But no way am I talking without more coffee."

Kendall thought, *three cups of coffee, this must be really good!*

Jadyn returned to the room and set her laptop on the coffee table. She was hoping Kendall would forget she'd promised to reveal her secret. It appeared to work as Kendall slid her hand over the laptop and asked, "What are you writing?"

She relaxed her shoulders and flipped open the screen, now on her knees, "I'm working on a book, and I write to myself every night; it helps me sleep. I write about how I feel each day to help me process my thoughts and emotions. I wouldn't have survived if I hadn't done this. Each release cleanses the wounds emotionally crippling me; without it, there would be no healing, no real understanding. Does this make sense?"

Kendall tried to relate and said, "I don't have to understand. You've always intrigued me with how you can do anything you try to do... better than those who've worked their entire lives and never come close to your ability. Like your paintings, how well you paint without any training. I'll always look up to you no matter what you think."

Jadyn drew Kendall's attention to the snow to get the subject off her.

"Okay, I'll drop it, but you promised to tell me about your mystery text. I've waited long enough."

Jadyn set the computer down, grabbed a blanket, and pulled it up and over herself, "Before I begin, promise my indiscretion remains our secret?"

With her nose and forehead crinkled, she questioned. "Indiscretion? Okay, now I'm on the edge of my seat."

Jadyn was too fidgety to remain on the couch. She felt like hiding as she slid to the floor and prepared to confess. She'd been dying to tell Kendall, anyway. Jadyn candidly spoke with one hand on Chase's damp fur, the other beneath her resting head, and eyes directed to the unmoving ceiling fan. "When I came to your wedding, I was despondent. I'm so sorry and feel so bad for how self-centered I behaved. It was your time, and my problems consumed me." Jadyn knew bringing this up again would drive Kendall crazy, but she was trying to buy herself more time.

Kendall rolled her eyes in disbelief, shook her head, walked, and stood over Jadyn, "Listen. I'm the one who should apologize!" Kendall couldn't hide her rising emotions. "I should've been a better friend and considered what you were going through. I should've thought about your feelings. I certainly could have waited to get married."

Jadyn considered her words. She felt better hearing Kendall confirm what she believed true all along. "It's okay; you waited years to marry Levi."

Kendall sat on the sofa and changed the subject, "Tell me about this indiscretion of yours." She held her coffee in both hands and watched Jadyn like a movie.

Nervously twisting her hair, Jadyn confessed, "I met someone after I left your reception." Embarrassed, she ducked and kept explaining, "I spent a couple days getting to know him."

Kendall was surprised, "You did what?!" She was amused at Jadyn's squirming.

Jadyn flashed Kendall a cringey-smile, "I didn't. I mean, I did meet someone. Cole."

Kendall couldn't resist singing a verse from the movie Grease, "Tell me more, tell me more." She was good at softening a mood.

Jadyn snorted through her brief laughter and resumed, "We only kissed." Kendall looked disappointed.

Jadyn knew she had to come clean, "We stayed in touch. He was here two days ago, and I cheated on Gavin!" She rolled over, burying her head beneath a pillow.

Kendall, now lying on the couch and within reach of Jadyn, pulled at the pillow, "Take this stupid pillow off your head! Quit hiding! I'm not here to judge." Jadyn pulled the pillow away and looked at Kendall.

She pushed Jadyn for clarification, "So, are you saying you didn't sleep with him until the other day?"

Jadyn nodded like a Bobblehead.

Kendall continued analyzing, "It's almost been a year. His doctor said he's unlikely to wake up. Right?"

Jadyn nodded again, so glad Kendall was doing all the talking.

Kendall reassured, "Your secret's safe with me."

Jadyn cried, "I feel terrible having to decide his fate after cheating; I don't think it's my place anymore."

Kendall argued, "Come on! You're still his wife."

Cole popped up on her cell, "I told him to wait for me to contact him. Until Gavin...until I'm single for real. He just texted saying no matter what, he'd be waiting for me on May 9th in the parking lot where we met."

Kendall sounded out in disbelief, "Wow, such a long way off. Will you talk to him in the meantime?"

Jadyn replied, "I don't expect him to wait for me. I feel torn and hurt that God would take Gavin from me and bring me Cole before Gavin's even gone.

Kendall said, "When has God ever been fair?"

Jadyn agreed. "I've been teetering with being outraged with both Gavin and God and also wanting their forgiveness."

Kendall felt the mood getting too intense and said with excitement, "I brought some old movies for us to watch. Ready for a break from reality?" She held up the Grease DVD and asked, "Sound good?"

Jadyn's eyes widened as she swallowed her wine, nodding.

Kendall couldn't have picked a better movie. It was just what Jadyn needed, and she said yes by saying, "Grease is the word! It's been on my mind since you sang it. How many times have we watched it?"

Kendall placed it into the DVD player and said, "At least a hundred times." Memories flooded in as Jadyn recounted their younger days and how simple life seemed.

They settled in for the remainder of the day, snacking, watching movies, singing along, and recalling old boyfriends.

Chapter 60

Troubled

T he low-lying sun was fierce but not warming. It was one of the typical, sunny, after a snowfall, bitterly cold mornings, and the first of the season. Sedona was expected to stay below the freezing mark until at least noon. The horses were hungry now, so she pushed through the desire to return to the warmth of her blankets.

The deathlike silence was abruptly broken by the brash, harsh, screeching sound of her rake scratching the wet, cold, hard-clay soil as she collected still warm and steamy rock-size deposits the horses left for her.

Kharibia whinnied and snorted, with steam shooting from her nostrils like a dragon's fire, trotting with head nodding and black mane moving, like a fire's flame. Nickering lovingly, Kharibia rubbed her head against Gavin's fur-lined denim jacket that Jadyn had worn this morning.

As she wiped Kharibia's muddy kiss off the sleeve, she fondly recalled similar mornings when Gavin told her to stay in bed, and he did the chores without her. Jadyn lovingly hummed along with their nickering as she tore hay flakes apart, sending particles into the sun's slowly rising rays.

She spared Kendall from the drudgery of the morning chores, then went inside to read another of the Angel Box notes.

Jadyn brewed a pot of coffee and worked to decide what to make her too-good-for-morning-chores friend for breakfast. Kendall was apparently never going to wake up, at least not without some help from Chase. She smiled mischievously as she quietly walked with him to the bedroom door and told him, "Go give Aunty Kendall kisses," then ran back to the kitchen with giant sock-quiet steps and animated arms, leaving Kendall to believe he'd woken her on his own.

Hungover and messy-haired, Kendall shuffled into the kitchen wearing Eeyore slippers and Levi's torn t-shirt. She was faced with a bitchy, annoyed Jadyn shooting her a fast and false smile. Kendall had seen this before and knew Jadyn had no good reason to be angry at her, so she pretended not to notice and said joyfully, "Good morning, Jay; Chase woke me up with kisses, and now it's your turn."

She stepped up behind Jadyn and started kissing her cheek, saying, "kissy-kissy, are we feeling bitchy?" pissing Jadyn off even more.

Jadyn slapped Kendall away and didn't give in to her. There was no way she would give her the satisfaction of a smile. She continued peeling the sweet potato in her hand and slicing it with onions and fresh herbs. With the food simmering, she carried plates and utensils to the table. Kendall watched her move as if invisible, wanting to help but unwilling to be the brunt of Jadyn's frustration.

Kendall grabbed napkins and set them on the table before reaching for the Angel Box. Jadyn lunged and grabbed her arm tightly, saying, "Seriously, Kendall, finally, you slither out and immediately start in on me! I've been up for a couple hours. I've got breakfast going, and you push me before we even eat! You can go home if I'm taking too long for you!"

Kendall was taken by surprise, "Woah! I was just moving it to the other side of the table. Chill out! I haven't had my coffee yet!"

She snapped back, "I haven't had mine, either!"

Kendall pulled Jadyn's hand from her arm, "Clearly!" and walked to grab Jadyn's teal and lavender blanket off the couch. Knowing she'd be angry if Jadyn had surprised her with a box filled with emotional bombs, she composed herself before returning to the kitchen.

Kendall sat silently with Jadyn's blanket over her shoulders, resting her head on her bent knee and slippered foot sticking out toward Jadyn, defiantly ignoring her while she cooked. Jadyn had her emotional walls up standing with her back facing her and Kendall was slightly aggravated till she heard Jadyn sniffling.

She couldn't stand the silent treatment any longer, "Jay-baby, come on, you know I love you madly. I'm sorry I overslept. I'm sorry you were forced to do all this by yourself. We both know I've done much worse than this. You've never been this mad at me before. Is there something else bothering you?"

Before turning around to face Kendall, she snapped, "I already opened that damn Angel Box! That's why I'm crying! It should have little devils on the outside, not angels! I never knew it could physically hurt to know how much I'm loved."

Still afraid to move, Kendall sat and tried to comfort Jadyn, "I get it. Sadness hides inside true happiness. It's unexplainable. To feel it, you have to stand naked before it. You'll feel free once you work it out.

Jadyn thought she sounded a lot like Teddy,

"Whatever you say, Auntie T."

Kendall kicked her foot out as if to kick Jadyn, "Hey! I'm being nice. You should try it!"

Jadyn shared, "I thought I knew my mother." She handed Kendall her coffee cup. "I already read her note! It threw me. Like the letter I read to you before I left California.

Kendall said, "Ya. I remember. It deeply affected me too."

Jadyn said, "It's interesting how moving out changed my relationship with mom."

Kendall picked up the folded paper from the counter, "May I?"

Jadyn said, "Mom thinks of you as a second daughter. She'd want you to read it."

Kendall read:

My sweet, sweet loving Jadyn, my baby, my love,

I wish I could take this pain from you, and the decision was mine to make. Not so you would do what I think you should, but to shield you from the pain.

I'm here for you with open ears, an open mind, open arms, and of course, an open heart.

I don't have any real tangible idea of exactly what you're experiencing. No one does. All you have to do is call, if and when you need me, I'll drive to you and stay for as long as you wish.

Please know you don't have to be strong. It's Okay to let others embrace you and take care of you or to simply drink wine with you as you make this distressing decision.

Love. Mommy

With tears resting along the inner brim of her swollen eyes, Kendall said, "Your mom's proven to be more than we both imagined her to be. You're so lucky to have her in your life. I miss mine so much."

Jadyn chimed in after seeing Kendall's pain marking her face, "See, I keep feeling sorry for myself. I didn't even think about how it would make you feel."

Kendall yelled, "So what! It's your turn to be a bit selfish, my God. If not now, when?"

Each time she read one of the letters, Jadyn realized her perception of how they felt about her differed from her reality. They all appeared deeply caring and appreciative of her. They found a rhythm of love's outpouring building until she read Melissa's note; it blew them away! Kendall nearly spit her coffee out!

Jadyn,

You rarely talk to me, and now you ask me for help? Honestly, I find this request for me to write to you beyond comprehension. I don't think it's fair of you to ask me how I feel about your troubles as if we all don't have our own trials to deal with. I wouldn't bring my baggage to you, so I won't be telling you what to do with yours. You have a lot of nerve!

If you ever really cared, feel free to ask me what I'm going through or continue to do what you've done, and we can continue to pretend to be friends.

Melissa

Kendall was shocked, "Wow! I didn't see that coming!" she pressed a napkin against her mouth, holding back the coffee she thought would come out of her nose.

Kendall laughingly said, "In her defense, she's pretty perceptive; I can't say I ever considered Melissa, a good friend. She never reached out or responded. I finally stopped calling."

Kendall felt bad. "I had no idea!"

Jadyn laughed hard, "You should call this the Angels and Demons Box!

They both needed a break from the Angel Box so they showered, and drove to the Sedona, Tlaquepaque Arts and Crafts Village. She brought Kendall to her gallery, where she purchased a carving for herself and wind chimes for Levi.

Kendall loved the village and felt like she was on vacation, "Next on the agenda, wine tasting!"

Jadyn agreed, "What an inspired idea! The Art of Wine is the perfect place!" Kendall and Jadyn shared flights of red and white wines and gourmet chocolates. Then Kendall purchased several bottles to go.

They went to lunch at Hudson's, a restaurant nestled in Sedona's red rocks and one of Gavin's favorite spots. Kendall drank in the view as the hostess led them out the glass doors to their table. She took her seat and said, "Oh my God, I get why you moved here; it's amazing. The red rocks are so inspiring. It's the perfect place for someone like you. It's pulling out artistic impulses from me, and I'm not creative at all."

Jadyn expected her reaction and said, "It's the magnetic pull of the four vortexes. That's what you're feeling."

Kendall said, "Have you turned into a metaphysical crystal ball, tarot card reading guru type?"

Jadyn mischievously said, "Wanna psychic reading?"

Kendall asked, "You serious?"

Jadyn, bored with the conversation and missing Gavin, continued, "This is the only place Gavin would give up his precious beer and share a bottle of wine with me. Of course, you and I don't need any more wine!"

Kendall defended herself, "Hey, speak for yourself. I'm not driving, and I'm on vacation!"

Jadyn acted like she didn't hear her, "They would practically have to force us to leave, especially in late spring or early fall when it's not too hot or cold out here."

Kendall looked up at one of the blazing faces of the robot-looking heaters standing lifeless above the tables and said with arms around her shoulders, "Yeah, thank God for these heaters, or I'd be like those people looking out from inside, wishing I were tough enough to eat outside. I'm so glad you made me wear my sweater under my coat!"

Jadyn smiled, "Well, you're always colder than me, and how many times did we have to stop what we were doing because you forgot or chose not to bring a coat?"

Kendall crossed her arms defensively, "Alright, when did this become a pick on Kendall session? But hey, Jay, I hate to say it. I am starting to feel the cold air as if it were water rising under the table! And there I go again, sounding like a poet!"

Jadyn rolled her eyes, "I wouldn't go that far, but it actually did sound pretty cool, and I agree, it's getting too cool for school out here. Let's go."

Back at Jadyn's, they retreated to the living room with the wine, chocolates, and the ever-looming, extremely annoying Angel Box.

Jadyn's voice raised, "I want this angel box to be empty already!"

Kendall said, "Then I suggest you start reading."

Jadyn rocked her head side to side defiantly, pushed her shoulder, extended her middle finger, and said, "Read this."

Kendall gave her an, oh, you did not just flip me off look and said, "I'll still be here tomorrow. Don't be sneaking out without me. I'm here to help, and help I will! If it also means I scoop poop - I scoop poop. Deal?"

She smiled and nodded before dropping her arms into her lap and banging her head back against the couch, "Oh, great, it's from dad. Where are those tissues?"

Kendall slid the box over, "Here ya go, read."

She gave her a pissy-teasing expression, stuck her tongue out, and read.

Dearest Jadyn,

I'm not very good at sharing my emotions and fear because I don't, you aren't aware of how much you mean to me. The day you were born was a rebirth for me, and I've thanked God each day since. You have this way of turning around even the most stressful of times.

I understand you have a major decision to make, and I know, just as you've always done in the past, it'll be one best for all involved. You must have a line of communication with the Angels. You always seem to know the answers for any situation. Of course, it can also be a bit annoying at times for this old man anyway. I hope you never took my feigned annoyance as anger because I'm very proud of you!

On a serious note, I'm not sure what I would do in your place, darling, but through prayer, I'm positive you'll be guided to the correct path. Your mother keeps me posted on what you're up to for the most part. There's nothing better than the sound of your voice on the other end of the phone. It ignites a warm fire feeling in my chest. Please call me anytime, honey.

Love you, Daddy

She leaned forward, reached out her hand to pass

the note to Kendall, grabbed her pillow and buried her face into it, and cried.

The day turned to night. They tended the horses, fed Chase, and ate their leftovers from lunch. The wine bottle and the Angel Box were finally empty.

Jadyn was disappointed to not see one from Teddy and let Kendall know by saying, "Wow, the one person I thought would surely have written is Aunt Teddy. I'm surprised she didn't."

Kendall stood up fast, "Oops! I forgot, hers didn't fit in the box. I'll be right back." She ran to the bedroom and grabbed it from the suitcase. She walked with a bounce in her step, almost falling as she entered the living room, and presented Teddy's letter to Jadyn, with hands outstretched and smiling, "Here goes, we saved the best, or worst for last."

Jadyn playfully said, "I guess I'm ready." She squirmed and wiggled until her butt was against the sofa cushion. With the fire now just glowing embers, Jadyn felt the chill of the snow seeping in through the glass panes of the French doors. She slid a blanket from beneath Chase and wrapped it around her shoulders like a scarf. He grunted and renegotiated his position, resting his chin on her thigh and begging for bed. "One more note, Boy, promise." She looked at Kendall, aware she was dying to know what Teddy had to say, "I suppose you want me to read this one out loud, eh?"

She pretended not to be affected, "Only if you want to. You know I want to hear what she has to say. She's special to me too."

Jadyn cleared her throat as if to make homage to her aunt and took an exaggerated deep cleansing breath.

My Dearest Jadyn,

You've always meant the world to me, and it warmed my heart when you chose to not only spend your summer with me but to have you move here. I know what a sacrifice it was for you to leave your friends and your parents, and I'm sure it is not easy for them to be without you, either.

I hope you sense I am here for you no matter what. I am here when and if you want to talk. Should you be keeping your thoughts to yourself because you don't want your mother to know what you're feeling, I won't tell her, or I should say I'll do my best to keep anything you say between us.

I hope you're not mad at me for arranging this intervention with Kendall. I've seen you dwindling away along with Gavin and couldn't let it go on any longer. Kendall's a wonderful friend, and I hope you've read enough by the time you're reading my letter to understand you're loved by many. You're more than a niece to me. You're my friend. XOXO

I hope you'll push forward in your life and never let anyone or anything stop you from doing what you feel is right. It feels like you're trying to spare me from helping you to make this decision, and all I can think about is I don't want you to think you need to carry this burden alone.

I believe we're guided through our lives and get help making decisions. These guides nudge us along the roads we travel. They take us through a door leading us to a person we're supposed to meet. They help us see butterflies we'd otherwise have missed. If you attempt to control your destiny too much, you could miss out on a beautiful and wonderful surprise destined to take your life in a new, extraordinary direction.

Don't fight your life. Remain in harmony with nature, always. Eat when hungry, drink when thirsty, walk when antsy, and move when inspired to move. Open every door blocking your way and listen to the voices guiding you. If you listen really hard, I believe you'll know what to do and know with certainty and inner peace.

Gavin told you his desire. Now all you need to do is be a woman who supports her husband and grants him his request. The private, intimate request he placed in the hands of his best friend at a time when his mind was clear and he was healthy.

I am weary as I write, weary from the weight of your pain. I try my best to help carry it for you, wishing I could lift it completely away. I'm sure there's a lesson in all of this, and it will lead you to more amazing experiences.

When you're my age, you'll have so many life experiences to share with those who will come after you.

I love you, doll, and hope the universe opens up and takes care of everything for you. I pray for serendipity, for magic, for legions of angels to stand in your defense, for fairies or any other mystical help to wash peace through you. I pray this experience leaves you refreshed and ready for all life brings.

Enough said, from your non-stop talking, Auntie T XOXO

As day turned to night, Jadyn began to experience a metamorphosis of spirit and yearned for change, so when Kendall said, "I think you should follow me tomorrow. You can stay with Levi and me at the beach." Jadyn imagined her toes in the sand and let her mind run with the thought.

Chapter 61

The Last Mile

It was easy to say yes to Kendall's offer to stay for a few days. It was another thing to up and do it without planning, but there was something about Kendall, like Teddy, which made her think it was possible, and there she was, waking up in their guest room. It filled her with warmth, hearing Levi tease Kendall, "Well, the honeymoon has definitely ended. You didn't even ask before bringing home a lost puppy." She knew he was loudly talking so she could hear him and took it as her cue to get up.

She caught a glimpse of Kendall and Levi bumping each other's hips and dancing around the kitchen. In that moment, Jadyn was grateful for the Angel Box process, because she no longer felt the strings of jealousy pulling at her. Their newlywed glee was no longer upsetting, it was uplifting. She had renewed hope for her own future of happiness.

When Levi turned to see her standing at the kitchen's entrance, he said, "Darn, you're awake. I was about to knock on your door and sing, 'wakey, wakey, eggs, and bakey, but here you are! I made lots of bacon. Hope you're hungry." Jadyn gave his arm a hug. It felt good to feel normal, and he had a way about him that always felt like home.

She knew better than to offer any help. Kendall and Levi were obsessed when they cooked. The table was loaded with a variety of food, and even the lox looked good to her today. She was starving and hadn't made bacon since Gavin. It was too much of a Gavin smell, but today it smelled like Levi, and she was more than ready to partake!

Kendall didn't say her name or look at her when she walked in. She knew Jadyn was watching them. It all felt familiar and happy, and she was about to present her delish French Toast and wanted Jadyn's reaction to be the first thing she saw on her friend's face this morning. When the tray landed before Jadyn, her eyes opened she bounced excitedly and said, "Ooh baby! Is this all for me? Smells so yummy!" Kendall's one-inch thick bread, fresh ground cinnamon, and nutmeg egg batter was made even better from a splash of heavy cream and extra vanilla and made Jadyn's mouth water,

Kendall's heart fluttered with joy. She was delighted by her reaction, and relieved Jadyn looked like Jadyn again.

As Jadyn sat waiting for them to join her, she flipped through her cell for her daily notifications and saw Cole's text. She felt a nervous, excited rush build in her chest; she was only a few miles from him. She heard the two of them talking along with her little Devil and Angel. She knew who was winning when Kendall, as if reading her mind, said, "So, are you going to go do that thing you talked about yesterday?" Her wink let Jadyn know she was telling her to go see him.

Breaking bread with old friends was what she needed, and seeing the two of them even happier than before they were married was thrilling! Levi did his best to keep things light as he teased them, inciting laughter with every bite. Jadyn compelled them to allow her to do the remaining cleanup; there wasn't much because Levi had cleaned up behind Kendall. They were harmony in-motion when they were in the kitchen. Breakfast was complete, a walk on the beach a memory; Levi and Kendall cuddled up on the sofa, and she was antsy. It was just days since she'd seen Cole; she knew he'd be shocked as she texted, *"I'm in the area and on my way to you if you want?"*

Her screen didn't have the chance to dim before he responded. *"OMG! Meet at our beach?"*

She smiled, texting back, *See you in thirty—big smile emoji.*

Jadyn packed all her belongings, hoping to spend tonight at Coles, said goodbye to Kendall and Levi, and stopped for coffee before heading to him.

As Jadyn drove, she conjured up the repeating scene of their bodies sliding over the oily surface of the canvas. She convinced herself she had the right to the guilty pleasure of it but knew this visit was to support Cole's loss. Drake's funeral was set for the morning, and there could be no joy this time.

Jadyn thought *one more mile* as her cell rang. Her face suddenly tightened. The ringer was unmistakable, and like a fish being yanked from the Pacific, the sound jerked her out of the reverie she'd been swimming in. It was the sound she'd set for Gavin's long-term care hospital, where he lay in his coma. And when she heard this tone, it always made her heart palpitate with a mix of hope and fear. She questioned, *why are they calling so early in the morning?* "Hello." The seconds it took to get a reply confused Jadyn. She created several reasons and scenarios before answering again, "Hello?"

The woman on the phone spoke like a panting dog,

"Mrs. Michaels?!" She sounded more excited than upset, confusing Jadyn.

The caller's tone was foreign and frenzied as Jadyn offered a simple "Yes."

The nurse screamed out, "It's Gavin! He woke up not five minutes ago, and he's asking for you! Isn't this amazing?!"

Jadyn immediately slammed the brakes, pulled off to the roadside, and attempted to digest the nurse's statement. Thoughts raced and crashed into her guilty mind as she sat frozen, listening to the nurse's joyful and consoling words. "Ma'am, are you still there? You okay? I'm sure this is a shock. Sorry I was so loud. I was too loud, wasn't I?"

Jadyn sucked in a deep breath and responded with a sorrowful, frightened, and shaky voice, struggling to mask her feelings, "No, no, you're fine. I'm going to get things together and come to him. Unfortunately, I'm in California right now. This is horrible! I need to get to him! Tell Gavin I'll arrive this afternoon. Please."

His nurse felt compassion, "Yes, I will. Sure, Mrs. Michaels, I'm sure this is difficult. I could tell him we need to monitor him and do some tests before he can have visitors if you like?"

Jadyn was tempted but answered, "No, tell him the truth. Tell him I'm in California with Kendall. Tell him I'm on my way to him. Tell him I am leaving right now. Bye."

The nurse hung up the phone with a look of judgment, tipped her head to one side as if to shrug the negative emotion away, and regained her jovial, excited persona, nearly dancing to Gavin's bedside.

Jadyn felt the black-gloved hands of judgment

squeeze the guilt in her throbbing head as thoughts rushed in like a dam-breaking, mixing up a year of her memories, stirring up sediment and garbage in its wake.

She gathered the courage to call Cole, and when he answered with expectant joy. "Hey! Are you almost here?"

She cautiously replied, "Cole, this is so difficult."

Cole, concerned, impatiently pushed, "What? Jay? You okay?"

She went on, "I can't believe I'm saying this, Cole, but Gavin's nurse just called to say he woke up."

Cole felt the blood wash from his face as he pushed aside his self-pity and offered, "How amazing, Jadyn! I'm happy for you. Drive safe."

She felt the joy of the morning wash away as a tsunami sweeps away everything in its path. Driving past what remained of Breakers and knowing she would be passing their beach in less than a mile, she looked out at the Pacific with wanting, spying eyes.

Time stood still as she drove past Cole, standing on their beach, with his back to the ocean, cell phone in hand and shoulders dropped. He was defeated and knew he didn't have the right to feel bad. Cole strained to see Jadyn's face, and she waved her hand as she tapped on the horn and slowly drove away.

She felt boomeranged, returning to who had tossed her. Each mile rinsed away pieces of their near miss, unpromised relationship. It was never meant to be. She drove, wiping tears leaking from her jade-green eyes. With music barely audible, Jadyn coached herself for her return to Sedona, to Gavin, and to re-establish her role as wife.

Jadyn called her aunt and told her she wasn't even close to Sedona. Teddy's heart broke for both Gavin and her. "Jadyn, I'm sure this is hard, you being where you are, hearing about Gavin waking. I'll do my best to help him understand. I'm worried about you driving. I know how you wish you were here; please be careful driving."

Jadyn nodded, "It is so hard. I should be with him. I feel terrible."

Teddy knew she couldn't do anything to fix this. "I'll be here when you arrive. I texted your mom. She'll be here tonight."

When Jadyn called Kendall, she said, "Gavin woke up."

Kendall came back with, "Now that would suck since you're here."

Jadyn spoke sternly, "It's not a joke. Gavin woke up. I'm on my way home."

Kendall thought, *holy shit! No way!* And felt sorrow for her. She knew the fewer words, the better. She knew the secrets they shared, and she knew Jadyn's guilt would be louder than before and would surely never leave her. Kendall also knew her friend was on a personal journey no one would or could fully understand, as she offered. "I'm here for you whenever and however you want. I'm praying for you."

Jadyn ended by saying, "Thanks. I wish prayer could wash off the guilt covering every inch of my flesh." Kendall cringed in agreement.

Jadyn drove with a year of memories swirling around her, mixing with the music playing as she came to grips with the reality she no longer had to decide Gavin's fate. If only she had waited and not asked Cole to come to her; if only she'd waited a week, one tiny week, if only she hadn't cheated, she'd be deserving of the joy awaiting her at home.

Chapter 62

Happily Sad

Jadyn's drive to Gavin ended as she entered the rehab's parking lot. She had to think to control each and every breath walking with guarded steps to his doorway. Upon entry, she saw Teddy and several friends sitting and whispering with strained expressions, their heads hanging.

Jadyn questioningly looked at her aunt as she approached to hug her. Teddy said, "Go in, Jadyn, he's asleep, but I know he'll want to see you.

She kissed her cheek and whispered through her hair into her ear, "Why does everyone look so upset and sad?"

She didn't answer, "Go to him, darling. He's been asking for you." She squeezed her hand tightly several times and pushed Jadyn's hand as if sending her off to Gavin. He lay sleeping, his eyes darting beneath closed eyelids, breathing steadily and rhythmically till her hand touched his.

Gavin's eyes flashed open, and his hand clenched onto hers. A rush of emotion pulsated through her in waves. Lightheaded and heavy-hearted, Jadyn spoke in a voice shy of a whisper, the first words he'd heard her say in just under a year, "Sorry I wasn't here when you woke up, babe," followed by a gentle kiss to his cheek.

Her expectation of this long-awaited moment couldn't have been further from the reality of Gavin's cutting words, "Some wife you are! Get out!" His disgusted glare and disdain for her touch felt violent and accosted her senses.

Longing to connect and unwilling to accept he really wanted her to leave, she begged him, "But babe."

She recoiled as he rolled his head away from her trembling lips, "I said, leave. Leave me alone!"

Jadyn slowly walked out, her head lowered, feeling embarrassed, dejected, and confused. Glad not to see any nurses when she opened the door to leave his room, she walked toward the waiting room. Jadyn hesitated to enter, remaining out of sight as she looked through the waiting room window rubbing her arms and shifting her weight from one foot to the other. Her attempts to self-soothe stalled the inevitable, ultimately failing her, just as she failed Gavin, and she felt unworthy of the love that awaited her inside.

Jadyn looked around, trying to recall if there was another room she could hide in while she took in what had happened. She wanted to fall onto a chair and cry or lay down and curl up for a sobbing session but couldn't come up with a safe place. She was sure if she entered and saw their compassionate faces, she'd lose any semblance of control.

There was nowhere to hide. She couldn't hide from herself, the only one who knew why she was late to arrive and her true intentions for going to California in the first place. She thought the guilt was heavy before, but now it was as if she carried an anvil on her shoulders and wore a scarlet letter for all to see. She felt trapped, staring at the window just a few yards ahead and to the right, the window that revealed a room filled with the compassionate faces of the people longing for her to enter with good news.

Strangers were approaching, and she had to either walk out of the building or go to her family. She could sense desire building in everyone, and despite knowing how intense the experience would be, she finally opened the door. The small waiting room felt huge. It once felt warm and inviting to be inside its dark blue walls and lounge on the dark-toned furniture; the colors only made her feel heavier and depressed. Her mom's open arms heading for her felt like an anchor to her sanity, and even though she wanted to cry, she felt disassociated and emotionless.

Jadyn felt like a fly with no wings circled by a thousand ants, even though everyone was silent. Their silence was loud; she filled it in with the questions she imagined forming in their private thoughts. Luca sat with Teddy, their eyes on her as they watched her fall into her mother's embrace, which made their chests ache. Sophia's soft whisper was tangible. The words blanketed her cold-feeling shoulders, "Love you. It'll be okay, doll."

Everyone sat frozen, wondering what would come of Gavin's awakening as Jadyn said, "He's so angry at me."

Sophia spoke cautiously, "He's confused; he yelled at all of us. Gavin's doctor said this happens sometimes."

Jadyn wrapped her arm around her and cried, "Oh, momma!"

She tried to help Jadyn comprehend his behavior, "It's hard for coma patients to accept they've lost months or years of their lives; he suggested we come back tomorrow."

Jadyn covered her face with her hands. "My God,

when will this end?"

Teddy said, "They're giving him a sedative. He won't be waking up until tomorrow. They'll call you tomorrow when the doctor arrives for his evaluation."

Sophia embraced Jadyn and whispered, "Ready to go home? I'll make you something to eat, or we can get a pizza. You might have a lot of demands on you as he goes through this change and before he comes home."

Jadyn said, "You mean him, or some stranger comes home? What if he's a jerk forever? Can I survive this, Momma?"

Sophia motioned with her head to Teddy for help, "Come on darling, let's get you home." She never let go of Jadyn as they walked as one to her car.

Jadyn's mind raced through memories of their life together. The joy they shared, paused for nearly a year, shadowed by the decision now lifted from her, was too much to take in. She was unsure which emotion to hold on to. This sudden and abrupt change from fear of his once looming death, replaced by fear of his growing anger, shined a light on the fact their relationship remained fragile, making her feel vulnerable. All her lonely days and nights, her dreams for a future destroyed, all because he was too proud to wear that damn helmet! Her mind was a forgotten, cluttered, and filthy closet, holding thoughts as items and memories as spiders. Since the door to Gavin's brain opened, they were all falling on her at once, making her wonder what would come of all of this. She couldn't deny her guilt, but she wouldn't have sinned had he not started all of this by resisting following their more than reasonable rules!

As Jadyn's mom drove them to the ranch, she held

her emotions tight in her shallow-breathing chest; her ribs, the bars holding them inside, caged and imprisoned. Her angry, short breaths released in small spurts making her light-headed and dizzy. Sick of the mixed truths she privately questioned made Jadyn want to escape, to run away, to be a little girl again, to not have ever gone to Sedona, and to never have married Gavin. She stopped her self-righteous thoughts, disciplining the babbling baby inside of her, "Grow the hell up! Gavin is the best thing that's ever happened to me!" She secretly feared his confusing rejection was born from the fact he'd somehow discovered she'd been unfaithful.

Jadyn felt cheated by Gavin's rejection. He stripped away her dream of his long-anticipated awakening. Her warm bedroom and thick comforter didn't stop the shivers shaking her; shock had settled in and wasn't going anywhere. Jadyn was contemptuous of her weak, pitiful-self, her actions, and her selfishness. She begged for mercy and forgiveness before surrendering to sleep.

Chapter 63

The Morning After

J adyn's first thought was that it wasn't a dream. She stated it as a fact. She prayed, "Please, God, forgive me. Heal him. Heal us."

Her prayers went unanswered.

Gavin grew angrier with each passing day and insisted for space, so she left him alone in their bed while she slept on the couch. She wondered if he should have been released from the extended care center. He was improving physically; walking with his walker and refusing her helping hand. Even though only a few days passed, Gavin went so far as to tell her not to do anything for him, not to cook or even do his laundry. He stripped from her all it is to be a wife.

They once shared a loving relationship full of giving, and now he won't allow her those simple pleasures. It was hard to cope with the thought of living with this bitter-angry shell of a man. A man she once loved more than life itself wouldn't even let her bring him a glass of water and seemed repulsed by her. His once-loving gazes were replaced by avoidance and distance.

Jadyn asked him several times, "What did I do to make you so angry?"

Gavin was defensive, "There's nothing wrong with me. It's you."

Jadyn reacted, "I understand it's not you! Please,

Gavin! What have I done?"

Gavin's response was no response at all, just silence. Frustrated, she wondered if taking over the den for her YouTube show was the problem; if it was, she couldn't blame him for being angry.

Jadyn sat on the sofa with Chase beside her, feeling calmer, and resumed analyzing his recent angry behavior. She was deep in thought, folding clothes, gazing at the fire burning, and listening to soothing, softly playing music. She sat frozen and fearful when Gavin's face nestled against hers, and he tenderly kissed her cheek. Even though he'd never been violent with her, she was afraid. It felt like the night she met Cole when he saved her from those dreadful men on the beach; she didn't know who was holding her and couldn't move. This time she couldn't move, fearing what he might do.

Her fear diminished when he finally spoke, "Good morning, my love."

Jadyn was pensive seeing Gavin walk around the couch and nervous when he sat beside her. She wanted desperately to trust he was back to normal as he spoke with loving kindness and looked adoringly at her, "My memory's so screwed up. I'm not sure how long I've been home. I don't remember much. I haven't been very nice to you lately, have I?"

She wanted to celebrate! She reassured him, "It's okay, babe."

He continued speaking sincerely, "I'm sorry for how I've been acting. My thoughts have been jumbled; I feel pretty good today."

She faced Gavin, looked at his hand on hers, and said, "I'm glad you're feeling better, Babe."

He took his hand and moved her hair from her face, "I want to put a smile on your beautiful face. How about we do something fun today?"

She was concerned about him doing too much and wanted to say it but let him talk uninterruptedly. "What would you like to do?"

Still guarded and anxious, she accepted that Gavin was Gavin again and asked, "How about we start with breakfast?"

They shared breakfast on the couch and remained together for most of the day, holding each other, watching movies, talking about his accident and what transpired during his coma, and reminiscing about their past.

When the colors of the red rocks faded into darkness, they moved to the bedroom. It was a nearly moonless night. Jadyn lit some candles, turned on the CD he bought for her, and they settled into bed. Jadyn tenderly touched his face and massaged him, envisioning the body she once knew, and started feeling safe again. Jadyn had renewed hope for their marriage and happiness. She sincerely said, "I love you so much. Let me know what you want."

Gavin's desire for her was reborn, "I want to make love, but I don't have the strength."

She whispered, "Want me to do the work?"

He rolled over and looked at her as she straddled him, "You think it's work?"

Jadyn smiled with her entire being. His humor was back! She leaned onto and kissed his chest, then gave him a flirty smile saying, "Making love to you is anything but work."

She slowly moved in unison with his body's

readiness and tenderly made love to him.

Only a sliver of the moon was visible through the gap in the slightly open curtains reminding Jadyn of their first night together in this room, which later was a prison for her pain and suffering. Tonight, their bedroom was restored to a serene, loving space, and for the first time since they last slept together, she easily found her way to a deep restorative sleep.

Dawn's early morning light barely lit the room when Jadyn woke filled with the excitement of their renewed love. She rolled over to kiss Gavin only to feel the chill of his lifeless skin upon her lips.

The color washed from Jadyn's face. Fearfully she willed herself to find the strength to search for his pulse, touching and doubting her ability to judge if she was doing it right. She gently shook him, begging, "Gavin, wake up. Babe, you okay? Wake up, please! No! God no!"

She found the resolve to grab her phone, prayed to God for the courage to say the words she had no clue how to say, and called Teddy. Not crying and still questioning if she was awake or dreaming, she stated, "Gavin's gone."

Teddy said, "Gone?"

Jadyn tried again, declaring, "He's left us."

Theodosia questioned, "He left? What do you mean? What are you saying?"

Jadyn let out the words that followed as if intertwined with one long cry, "Gavin's gone. He died."

Teddy instructed Jadyn, "Call 9 1 1. I'm on my way."

Jadyn slid on a comfy sweatshirt and yoga pants before reluctantly dialing 9 1 1. Suffocating anxiety instantly kicked in as she waited for a voice to confirm she'd dialed correctly. A calm female dispatcher answered, "9 1 1. What's your emergency?" Jadyn wasn't sure her voice would come out, "Gavin... My husband. He died." She was surprised she didn't cry. She wanted to cry. Hell, she wanted to scream!

The dispatcher took control of the conversation, "Are you with him now?"

Disturbed, Jadyn nodded and said, "Ya-es, I'm with him."

She spoke slowly, "We show you're at this address... Is that correct?"

Jadyn nodded again, wishing she could see the dispatcher's face as she forced out more words, "Yes. That's my address."

Jadyn was glad not to have to think.

"I've called the EMTs, the local police, and a crisis care person. I'll remain on the phone with you until you no longer want me to. Jadyn forgot what she said when the dispatcher spoke; the only words she recalled were she'd remain on the phone.

She was comforted by her support, this faceless, nameless stranger who shared this insanely tough time with her as she waited for Teddy to arrive. Gavin's big chair cradled her as she stared at him lying on the bed, questioning if she was dreaming or awake.

Jadyn heard the sound of a vehicle traveling down the dirt driveway and said, "I think they're here."

When she heard the door open, she figured it was her aunt, but asked, "They'll ring the doorbell, won't they?"

The dispatcher quickly responded, "Yes. They won't enter without your permission." Jadyn sensed it was Teddy, so she remained sitting with a blanket over her shoulders and eyes resting on Gavin's stillness.

Teddy entered, and Jadyn told the dispatcher, "It's my aunt. I'm no longer alone. She'll be with me. I am hanging up. Thank you for helping me through this."

Teddy prayed the right words would come when she spoke to Jadyn. She privately grieved Gavin; he was like a son to her. Stoic and graceful, she confirmed he'd passed away by checking his pulse. She took a deep breath, held back her tears, walked to Jadyn, sat beside her on the chair and said, "Sweetheart, I'm so sorry."

Jadyn rested her head against Teddy, "Thank you for being here. The officials are on their way."

Teddy kissed her forehead, "I'll get the door when they arrive."

They sat holding hands, staring at Gavin, stunned, heartbroken, each focused on their memories of him.

Jadyn, not crying, sucked in deep breaths. Too tormented to release tears that were sure to emerge at some point. She was shivering, yet her face was hot to the touch. Jadyn was privately suffering flashbacks of his cooling skin beneath her kiss and how her hand felt touching him when she searched for a pulse. Everything about the scene bombarded her senses. This relentless merry-go-round of unceasing flashbacks was brutal and numbing; she wondered if they would ever fade away.

Jadyn rambled, "It was magical. Yesterday, he was back to being Gavin again. I just wish you got to see him acting all sweet again."

Teddy remained silent, holding Jadyn, and gave her a brief squeeze confirming she was listening before continuing her own grieving in disbelief.

Jadyn glanced at Teddy and started again, "It was

a magical day. He came back to me. I feel like I'm dreaming."

A fire truck's siren and loud humming engine alerted Teddy. She slid from under Jadyn's resting head and met the emergency personnel at the door. She led them to their bedroom. "This is Jadyn... Mrs. Michaels." With a sullen face, she motioned with her arm pointing and said, "Gavin's wife. My niece."

Jadyn sat, rocking and embracing herself with begging, watery eyes, watching all the different uniforms filling the room with unseen faces. It was all too much for her to take in, too surreal.

Still unsure if he was dead or alive, she requested, "Can you please check to see if I'm correct? See if he really died?"

An ambulance attendant pulled out a heart monitor and asked, "What time was it when you last spoke to him?"

She searched her memory for hints to help her determine the time. *What time did we finish making love? Seven-ish? How long did we lay there before falling asleep? About an hour.* She stopped thinking and said, "We fell asleep around seven-thirty."

The EMTs talked among themselves, trying to determine the time of death as police officers approached with their own questions. "Sorry, miss, do you have his driver's license?"

She pointed to Gavin's wallet on the dresser. Teddy pulled out his license and passed it to the officer who asked for it. He looked about Gavin's age, making Teddy's heart tug. He then asked, "Was he on any medications?"

Jadyn nodded and pointed to the tray holding

several pill bottles at his bedside. Another officer retrieved and listed them on the form held to her clipboard as he asked, "When was he discovered? What time?"

Jadyn took a deep sorrowful breath, "I woke up and kissed him at or around six this morning. He didn't respond to me and felt cool." Teddy squeezed Jadyn's hand. "I searched for a pulse and couldn't find...."

One of the EMTs approached with a stinging statement, "We've confirmed you were correct and listed five a.m. as the T O D, time of death."

The finality of his words hung in the air as Sheila, the crisis counselor, asked, "Which mortuary would you like us to take him to?"

Teddy answered for Jadyn, "Red Rock Cemetery in Sedona." They had previously discussed this when Gavin was in the care facility on life support.

Jadyn held his wallet in her hands. When she slid his ring on her finger, tears locked away from the shock of it all, flowed! With trepidation, Jadyn watched Gavin's body, bagged and rolling away! She had a foreboding sense of fear. She was his guardian, his wife, and they were stealing him from her! When the van doors slammed shut, she felt slapped in the face with reality and awakened from her thoughts. Right before they drove off with him, she asked Sheila, the crisis worker, "Aren't I supposed to go with him?!"

Sheila put her hand on Jadyn's shoulder and responded, "No, dear. He's in our hands now. He'll constantly have someone with him. I promise he won't be left alone."

Jadyn was hesitant to trust her thinking, *Is she right? Is this how they do this? Is this how they take my love, my friend, my Gavin?* She inhaled, surrendered, and cried with her whole being! Gone was her brave facade. She gave up her fight for Gavin's life. She relinquished her responsibility for his life, his well-being, and his body to their control and accepted her role as a grieving widow.

Sheila asked, "Are you ready for me to leave you now?"

Jadyn was comforted knowing Auntie-T would remain for as long as she needed and said, "If what you said is true, yes."

Sheila waved, got into her car, and drove away following behind the milk-white van that looked like any other van.

Jadyn felt sick watching them being swallowed up into dust kicked up by their tires on the powdery-dirt road.

Jadyn looked at her aunt, "They took him away again! Like the night he fell." Teddy reached out her arms, and Jadyn collapsed into her embrace. "Oh, Auntie, Gavin finally found his way back to me and they've taken him away... again."

Chapter 64

The Explanation

D r. Brandt's name appeared on Jadyn's cell, and she answered, "Hello?"

He spoke, "Hi, Mrs. Michaels. It's Dr. Brandt. I'm checking in to see how my patient is doing today." The levity in his voice stabbed her heart, and, once again, made her head feel as if it would burst with confusion. Her thoughts scrambled as she questioned whether or not Gavin had died. *Was this all a dream? Certainly, Dr. Brandt should know!* She pulled at her memory like the rope of a hot air balloon, planting herself in reality. *One of them was wrong.*

It had been five days. She knew she was right and felt odd having to explain it to him, "Weren't you told? Gavin died."

She could hear his exasperated breath, "No. I'm so sorry. I wasn't informed." He was embarrassed and knew how confusing his call must be as he considered what to say next.

Jadyn interrupted his thoughts, "He was doing so good. He slipped away in his sleep. I thought you called to explain what caused his death. It's been five days."

Dr. Brandt felt the sting of her words, "Sometimes coma patients come back just before death. Many believe God allows them this time to say goodbye to their loved ones."

Relief washed over her as she said, "I thought we

shouldn't have had sex. I thought I was responsible. I thought I killed him!"

He comforted her, "Oh, no, Mrs. Michaels. It isn't your fault. You mustn't blame yourself.

Jadyn placed her fingers over her lips and whispered, "Are you sure?"

He quickly said, "Yes. I'm sure."

Feeling she needed more reassurance, he decided to share one of his cases with her. "I had a patient with a similar prognosis as Gavin. She was comatose for over a year and suddenly awoke. She sat up and said, "Tell my family I love them." And just as abruptly, fell back on the bed and died."

Dr. Brandt's office door opened, and his assistant walked in, "Doctor, pardon me for a moment. I've been handed Mr. Michaels' chart."

Jadyn's chest was tight as she braced herself awaiting his evaluation.

With Gavin's chart now in-hand, Dr. Brandt said, "Mrs. Michaels, the Medical Examiner's findings reflect Gavin died from a pulmonary embolism. You didn't cause his death."

Two weeks later, on a bitterly frigid day in Sedona, when snow kissed the mesas, family and friends joined Jadyn for Gavin's memorial service at Red Rock Cemetery. Guests came from several states to bid him farewell.

Once the ceremony ended, many guests moved on to Teddy's for his Celebration of Life get-together. Jadyn tearfully listened and cherished their words as they took turns telling stories, many unknown to her. Their stories warmed her heart and filled her with pride for Gavin and his good deeds, yet, Jadyn couldn't imagine feeling any colder.

Chapter 65

A Touch of Molly

J adyn knew it was time to brush herself off and get beyond the loss of Gavin or give up and live a solitary life like Molly. So she got off the sofa and said, "Now's as good a time as any." She reached for her purse and headed for the door.

She figured Molly had a lot to teach her about loss and she always seemed so happy. Jadyn wanted to learn how to more than cope with her circumstance, she wanted to be truly happy, even if she had to spend her life alone.

Molly lived a full-life, married to one man, raised children who bore grandchildren for her to enjoy, only to choose life alone, rather than to move closer to her children. Jadyn knew with certainty only someone with a secret to tell could have the strength Molly owned.

Jadyn's timing was perfect. Molly was sitting where expected, waving, and smiling at all the motorists traveling Route 260 on their way to who knows where. Jadyn pulled into the gravel drive, stepped to the bench, and sat beside Molly. "How do you do it, Molly?"

Watching the motorists waving back at her, she answered, "One breath, one moment, one wave, one day, and one night at a time."

Jadyn wanted more, "But."

She palmed Jadyn's hand and said, "Time passes, and one day you and I will pass, like my Willy and your

Gavin have."

Jadyn grew frustrated with her negative words and waved along with Molly, "I'm not liking this chat."

Molly smiled, "If you care enough to spread love to others, as I know you do, nothing else matters, and nothing else feels as good."

Jadyn didn't want to lose her new friend. "I'd feel better if you'd stop talking about dying."

Molly's persistence scared Jadyn, "You can't stop death." She smiled, reassuring Jadyn, "Just like you can't stop these cars from coming."

Jadyn laughed as she raised and lowered her hand, "And they sure do keep coming. My arm's getting tired."

Molly put her hand on Jadyn's now-showing belly and turned to face her. "True love has a life all its own. Roots grow, spawning new life from their branches, and they ultimately break away from the tree. If you lead with love, your life will be bountiful."

She grew to love Molly like an aunt and confided in her saying, "I've been searching for happiness and feel much better today, but I'm not sure I'll ever be as happy as you."

Molly could see Jadyn was conflicted about the life growing inside her but didn't push a discussion about it. She figured if Jadyn wanted to tell her she was with child, she'd have told her and let the thought go, looking forward to that conversation in the future, and said, "I choose each day to live my life in joyful service. Although I reside alone in my home, it once held many. I'm not one person. Rather, I'm a collective of all who came before and all who follow. Live your life understanding you too will depart this world one day. Make sure to create a map for those you leave behind, allowing them to benefit from your failings and grow from your good fortune."

Molly's moving testament fueled something in Jadyn, and she wanted to hear more. Their conversation inspired Jadyn to write about Molly and Willy. Molly's philosophy on life intrigued her and birthed her curiosity to learn from others. Jadyn's new mission, seeking people with admirable lives and investigating the processes they cultivated to overcome obstacles and persevere, deeply affected her. Jadyn's maturity and character grew with each story, making her feel stronger and happier than ever imagined.

Each night she sat listening to recordings she'd taken on her cell, playing their conversations, and transcribing the stories in diary format. She planned to publish it, hoping it would help others overcome their challenges. Did she feel driven or pushed to complete it by God, herself, or perhaps her Muse? Maybe her out-of-control feeling is the writer's Muse? All she knew was she didn't feel this project was hers to abandon. Jadyn understood it required her to complete it, this incomprehensible force, and to publish, making it available to others.

Chapter 66

Trucks and Bucks

Jadyn tipped her hat to the men unloading Gavin's prize, a black and silver Ford F-150 Special Edition Ranch PBR custom truck. Once she signed the paperwork and had the keys in hand, they gave her the grand tour, explaining various features and all the bells and whistles. It was a bitter-sweet moment. She reminisced a bit, knowing Gavin would have loved driving it. With Chase riding shotgun, Jadyn took a quick celebratory drive into town and back to the ranch, loving the automatic drop-down steps that made it so easy to get in and out.

Chase sauntered, and Jadyn waddled back to the house after their drive. Wishing she could have coffee, she made a cup of tea and tossed Chase a treat. He settled at her feet, and she picked up yesterday's mail from the basket on the table where she'd placed it the evening before. Clouds drifted, hardly moving, as she slid the silver letter opener under the envelope's lip; it was addressed to Mrs. Gavin Michaels. The return address was from the life insurance company that insured the Professional Bull Riding Association riders.

To her astonishment, it was made out for $200,000 and payable to Jadyn Michaels. She thought *this day keeps getting better!*

Gavin's $80,000 purse and this insurance payment gave her a sense of security and freedom from financial worry.

She gathered both checks and a deposit slip as she read the enclosed letter. The PBR explained they'd make a special tribute to Gavin at this season's close and extended their condolences.

Chapter 67

Completion & Celebration

It was 2:04 a.m., and to Jadyn, it sounded like a million voices were discussing the conclusion of her book, making it impossible to sleep. It didn't matter what they were saying or where the voices came from; they were talking and guiding her to write the ending. There was no point trying to sleep or make notes for daytime writing; this was way too exciting, so she decided to join in the conversation!

Jadyn leaned over and picked up her laptop. It sat perched and ready inside the partially opened bedside table drawer, standing like a guardian in sleep mode, fully charged and prepared for battle with her Muse and the editor. She, too, was ready whenever inspiration struck, like an expectant mother, days from delivery, on high alert, prepared to be called into action by new words, like children awaiting their birth. They were coming with or without permission and needed her to guide them into the story. She pulled the screen open, and although her eyes attempted to close from the sudden change from dark to light, she pushed through until they accepted their plight.

Jadyn figured she might as well write; after all, there was only Chase to annoy with the screen's light breaking through the darkness. She reassured him, "I won't write long, Chase-boy," and rubbed his head as he settled beside her with his head resting on the crook of her elbow, occasionally moaning no doubt at the tapping sounds of her fingers on the keys.

More often than not, it seemed Jadyn's nights were divided into segments of writing and sleep. She no longer fought the process. Jadyn lived two lives. By day, artist and grieving wife; by night, writer and creator of a private world all her own.

She wondered if other writers shared her odd sleep pattern, that is, if it can be called sleep with all the action and discussions playing. Jadyn imagined thousands of authors typing away through the night along with her, each on a river of words, caught in the flow, unable to escape. She was comforted by the thought of their shared yet separate experience. Words floating and swirling all around her would not be lost by her tonight! The ending was right there for the picking.

Now 4:10 a.m., with the moon far from the horizon, and stars still visible in the predawn sky, Jadyn was awake and writing. The tips of her fingers were sore and her hands cramped from feverish typing. As long as her eyes remained open, she wrote and wrote. Sleep would come later.

She screamed from somewhere within her, *my book is complete!* She celebrated the momentous occasion with her Muse. Jadyn wasn't kidding herself. Today, absolutely, positively, for sure, was the day to mark on her calendar. There were no edits remaining, nothing left to do; her book was indeed finished, and a part of her was replenished, healed, and ready to embark on a new adventure!

Jadyn avoided contact with everyone for the better part of the last month, believing the slightest distraction might prevent her from finishing her book.

She figured Teddy and her mother were dying to know she was alright and couldn't wait to show them how happy and fulfilled she is. She would no longer feel like she was a burden or child to them. She longed for them to stop worrying about her and figured all the good news she had to share with them would silence their concerns once and for all.

Jadyn looked forward to standing before her mom and aunt as an equal. She finally identified as a self-sufficient woman on her own path, with a plan for her future, cut from the stone that made up her life till now.

It was 6:12 a.m. when she typed *"The End."* She slowly closed her laptop and held her hand on it. Her heart beat wildly and she celebrated like a parent after their child marries and embarks on their new life.

Jadyn accepted she'd accomplished what she'd set out to do and declared this day a day of completion and re-birth. The universe shifted in this life-changing moment, the moment she evolved from *person* to *author*!

Chapter 68

Preparation

It was 10:20 a.m. as Jadyn, filled with excitement, drove to Teddy's with a copy of her finished manuscript on the seat beside her, safely enclosed within a manilla envelope. Chase's head and tongue hung out the passenger window, and he whimpered in excitement for their shared adventure. His eyes focused on the world whizzing by, and she held her hand on top of it in case he flipped around and stepped on it.

Jadyn had previously tucked an envelope with a note into the thick collection of pages, letting Teddy know she'd be away for a while, and told the story of the unexpected insurance windfall so she'd be sure to accept the $10,000 check made payable to Theodosia Rizo. She asked her to keep $5,000 as back rent for the time she stayed with her before her marriage to Gavin, and the remaining $5,000 was for her ranch hand, Samuel's pay, and any expenses that may arise. She ended the letter with Love You! XOXO.

Jadyn called Teddy, "Hi, Auntie! Can you come outside? I have something for you and can't stay." She walked out front and waited for Jadyn. Her surprised expression made Jadyn smile; she knew the truck was confusing.

Jadyn rolled the window down. "This truck is part of Gavin's purse."

Teddy stood on tippy-toes and placed her hand

on the ledge of the open window. "Is that my lover-boy, Chase?" Chase stepped over Jadyn to reach Teddy's wiggling fingers and kissed them before bowing his head for petting.

Laughing at the undying love and adoration they shared for each other, she said, "Okay, Chase Boy, that's-enough." Jadyn patted the seat, pushed him back to the passenger side of the bench, and pulled the manuscript out of the manilla envelope just enough so Teddy could see the smaller white envelope containing the check and letter sticking out. She pointed to it, flicked it with her fingertip, and slid it back inside. She handed the manilla package to Teddy, smiled at her quizzical eyes, and lovingly kissed her cheek.

With genuine gratitude, Jadyn whispered into Teddy's ear, "I can't thank you enough for all you've done for us. Love you. I'll be in touch soon."

Jadyn looked at her with an *I'm proud of myself* grin and drove off. Teddy looked at Chase's happy face staring at her from the truck's open window, and yelled, "You be a good boy for your momma, Chase!" Teddy blew kisses and waved as Jadyn and Chase drove away.

Jadyn yelled back, "Love you, Auntie." Teddy stood hugging the envelope until they were out of sight and walked inside to read it.

Teddy sat with a cup of steeping tea. She read the letter with a pleased and comforted heart; she shook her head, thinking, *oh, Jadyn, you shouldn't have.* With a longing to have gotten one of Jadyn's long-lasting hugs, she began reading the manuscript.

Jadyn headed home to pack for their trip to California, truly a free woman. She debated calling Cole or just show up. She felt bad for not checking in with him after Drake's funeral and hoped he wasn't upset. She thought about how she'd feel if he appeared with no forewarning or invitation and shrugged off the ethics, thinking, *I can't change things.*

Sleep was restless as doubts about Cole showing up kept running through her mind. After all, they hadn't spoken in months; why would he show up? Jadyn set her plan into motion, and nothing was going to stop her from going. She had more money than she possibly needed and didn't care when she'd return. She convinced herself if they were meant to be, he'd be there, and their new life would begin. With a longing to see him and happiness in her heart, she drifted to sleep.

Chapter 69

Promises Kept

The sun was setting with intense orange and red hues as her truck crested Sandpiper Hill. Jadyn's anticipation reached its crescendo after hours alone singing, biting her lip, and steering wheel drumming. Unsure what to expect and filled with mixed emotions, she held tight to the wheel and slid her butt back in the seat. Mimicking Chase, Jadyn pushed her chest up and out and sucked in the salty, moist air swirling in and around them, deep in through her nose, like Chase sniffing bacon, with the same look of anticipation. Right before the Santa Monica Freeway changed to Santa Monica beach, she said, "A promise is a promise," and drove up the Pacific Coast Hwy.

Jadyn's long blonde hair slapped and stung her face, but she didn't mind. She continued her drive with windows open, rocking her body as if on a dance floor, singing along with Miranda Lambert, singing her song, Gunpowder & Lead.

Now on the other side of twelve months of hell, Jadyn felt feisty, empowered, ready to let loose, let go, or grab onto something or someone. No one, not even herself, was going to stop her. She had doubts about taking this journey, at times almost turning her truck to head right back to the Arizona sunsets she loved so much. Her desire to begin a new life with Cole, if he wanted her, kept her focused and on track. She had an astoundingly awesome week of surprises and accomplishments. She prayed this meeting would be the beginning of even more. Rubbing her baby bump, she hoped Cole liked surprises as much as she did.

The shoreline opened up as she descended onto PCH, and not long after, she pulled into the weathered parking lot where it all began. She thought it looked even more ancient than the last time she drove over it. It hadn't aged well. The concrete crunched loudly beneath her tires as she entered a space bordering the sand. If the seven-hour drive was for not, she at least had an unobstructed view of the sun's inevitable descent into the azure water. A stillness formed as the engine's idle ceased. Windows still open, Jadyn managed to place her feet on the dash, rested her head, closed her eyes, and took in more of the salty air with slow, calming breaths. After checking her cell for the umpteenth time, she started talking for Chase; he said, "Well? Aren't we going to get out of the truck?"

Jadyn knew he wanted to take off running, and she couldn't keep up. "We'll go for walkies in a minute. Promise." Chase whined and stuck his paws out the passenger window. He wagged his tail, watching seagulls pecking at a slightly inflated white paper bag. It was teetering on top of an overfilled pea-pebble-covered concrete trash container as the gulls dodged dive-bombing yellow jackets and fought for their portion.

She began matching cars scattered around the almost vacant lot with people meandering about, "Okay, this will be fun." She raised her sunglasses for a moment, observing. "I'll bet the shiny blue Chevy truck goes with the shirtless man tossing a frisbee with his wound-up Australian Shepard. Yepper. Easy-peasy.

Who in their right-mind would put that filthy, dripping, foamy-breakwater, sandy dog in any of the high-priced Richie-Rich cars?"

"Oh, we have another candidate!" She blurted out, giggling, looking at a beat-up white and bluish Chevy van with surf racks perched on top. "No doubt the van belongs to those diehards!" She framed a group of surfers bobbing in the ocean like fisherman's floats, using her hands like a photographer, preparing to shoot the perfect shot before judgingly saying, "Just look at Y'all, waiting like sea lions on a dock for a perfect wave, as if it's a fish. I must tell you, I'll take a beach towel and Mai-Tai over sitting out there any day! Thanks for the entertainment, boys. You have more patience than me! I'd given up on those pitiful waves a long time ago. Can't help but wonder how long you'll continue this futile fight with Neptune. I know it's fun when you catch one, but seriously, the ocean looks tired."

She enjoyed recalling the day Cole taught her to surf but was too nervous about falling too deep into the memory, so she continued skimming the shoreline to make another match. Jadyn set eyes on a man not quite sitting on an old rotting wooden and paint-peeling picnic table. He was having a heated discussion with hands flailing and face tight. She giggled and judged, saying. "With your attitude and business suit, sir, you belong to a pretentious car, yes, the black BMW, and look how you so carefully parked away from anyone else. Okay, so you're no fun!"

"Awe, these two adorable babies are much more entertaining, with their little hats, buckets, and shovels, and awe, look at that sandcastle, and its lumpy-bumpy, slippy-slidey construction, how sweet are they?"

She got lost watching them play under the watchful eyes of their mothers, chatting on a nearby blanket. Jadyn was thinking about how their umbrella rocked rhythmically to the music playing in her truck until one of the toddlers fell back against the castle in a diaper-leading-squatty fall. Their mothers wore t-shirts to fight off the cool pre-summer breeze and had towels draped over their laps. She knew it wouldn't be long before they gathered up their belongings and undoubtedly drove off in the metallic blue mini-van parked only a few feet from them. This thought led Jadyn to say, "Too simple."

She patted Chase and turned back to match up another car, only to be distracted by the sound of bike tires crunching sand against the concrete and Cole saying, "Jadyn?"

She held Chase back from climbing over her and responded, "Forgot what I look like already?"

He wasn't surprised at her smartass remark, "You? Never. This is a badass truck, and you've got a badass co-pilot. Hi Chase! How are you, Boy?" She bounced and smiled, agreeing the truck was awesome, protecting her belly from Chase's excited wiggling as he accepted Cole's pettings that felt like Gavin's.

He continued, "Wasn't sure you'd show."

Jadyn pushed Chase to his side of the seat and then looked to see Cole's eyes dancing along the surface of her truck until finally resting on her tiny face. He was amused at how cute she looked behind the wheel of such a manly truck and maintained his gaze as Jadyn slid her legs from the dusty dash. She erected her body from its previous slumped position and turned to look at him, grinning at her. She returned his grin with an even bigger grin of her own. Cole pushed his chin out and up, and Sherlocked, "Who's truck?"

Her nose wrinkled. "It's mine, brat, all mine."

He figured it was her husband's. "It doesn't exactly say I belong to a short blonde chick."

She was concerned about how Cole would feel knowing she hadn't told him Gavin had died months ago. It felt weird to lead with it, so she put the subject on hold, playfully saying, "Well, I'm not just some blonde chick."

Of this, he was sure. Cole nodded, "Agreed," knowing he'd never met anyone quite like her and paused to think about it.

She filled the silence, "So you actually showed up."

He showed no mercy, "Way to state the obvious."

She said, "You know what I mean."

He said, "We haven't talked in months."

Jadyn's eyes widened, "You're blaming it on me?"

Cole fidgeted. "No. I was..." Looking at his feet, he said, "I'm nervous, aren't you?"

She taunted, "Awe, whatcha nervous about?"

He said, "Why are you always busting my balls?" Cole gave her a little-boy look, his eyes changing to slivers of blue, reigniting the familiar and undeniable craving she had for him; just as a flick of a lighter instantly lights a fire, making it impossible for her to form an intelligent sentence, so she smiled and hunched her shoulders.

As he smiled back, she grabbed his arm, "These look bigger. Working out?"

He proudly announced, "Yep."

She looked at his hair, "Apparently, you've been

riding the waves. Your hair looks bleached blonde."

He flashed a quick white-teeth, crooked smile, "Geez, I feel like you have me under a microscope. Life's been good."

They both jumped as a speeder's tires screeched on the extremely congested highway causing Jadyn to scream-out laughing, "Holy shit!"

Cole laughed with her, "Holy shit is right! His day nearly turned to shit." He placed his hand on the ledge of her open window, balancing himself on his bike.

She looked at it before restoring eye contact and asked with a flushed impassioned face, "Remember when we met?"

He almost whispered, "I'll never forget."

Jadyn was surprised by how intense the moment was when she was no longer joking, and her eyes met his. It had been a little over five months since he'd visited her in Sedona when they made love, five months and a week since Gavin took his last breath after renewing his love for her, and just about five months since her last period. And during these months, she hadn't told Cole of Gavin's demise.

With everything building in her, Jadyn readied herself to tell him about the baby. She sensed he'd accept the child as his own, no matter who the father was. Cole was a kind man, and not having a close relationship with his own father spoke of how he'd be a better father to his own children. Yet, she couldn't shake their talk on the beach the night they met when Cole mentioned he wasn't sure children were a part of his future.

Her anxiety was suffocating; rapid heartbeats, short breaths, and unspoken words pressing against her diaphragm dug in, clinging on for dear life needed to be said. She was beyond scared to tell him. But there he was, standing in front of her one full year after their first meeting. She wondered, *does this mean he still has feelings for me?*

Amazed at how much her feelings for him stirred within her as he spoke, she struggled to silence the voice in her head long enough to hear his words. Her body temperature climbed higher and hotter by the second, and her eyes focused on his mouth as he spoke. Jadyn couldn't hold back her desire to kiss his lips any longer! With pursed lips and eyes closing, she reached her hand out toward him. Cole quickly pulled away! The look of shock and surprise on his face made her sick!

Cradling her growing belly with the rejected hand, she held back the rising vomit in her esophagus. Her heartbeat raced faster! It pounded so fast and hard that she feared for the baby. It was beating at an insane rate! So incredibly high it seemed to stop her lungs from sucking in the air! Jadyn didn't comprehend that his words sparked a full-blown panic attack. She feared she might be dying of a heart attack!

She was thrown off-guard by the growing realization he wasn't expecting this to be more than a casual meeting of two friends, not lovers. Just friends. Friends with a shared past. Each moment seemed endless! Jadyn wished she could blink and magically be back home, at her mom's, 'Kendall's, or in the desert. Anywhere but here, trapped in her truck, staring into the now-distant eyes. Eyes that once held the sparks of love's promise. Her heart was breaking with each word cutting through the panicking thoughts racing in her mind. Cole, confused, could tell he upset her, so he got off his bike and ordered her out of the truck. "Come out so we can talk without this metal beast between us."

With the sliver of hope she held on to, Jadyn obliged. It took all her strength, but she got out and stood before him with a vacant, unfocused gaze. Chase celebrated being out of the truck and getting the full-body petting he desired as she struggled to maintain her composure. She was determined to hide that he'd upset her and to hide her growing belly beneath her oversized sweatshirt.

Every passing second made her feel more foolish for showing up! She wondered if it was even possible to gather the pieces of herself she felt breaking off. Grasping at some semblance of dignity, confused and devastated, Jadyn refused to show him any vulnerability. He couldn't know. Him knowing how hurt she felt would be far worse than the cutting pain piercing her heart!

Her armor was like tissue paper ripped into shreds as he explained his resistance to her dejected kiss. "Not sure you remember the hostess at Breakers that night? Her name's Christina. She's over there." He pointed to the parking lot entrance where Christina stood, holding her bike, smiling, and bouncing. She appeared as if awaiting her entrance, an actress backstage waiting for her cue and her part to begin. Cole beamed, and Jadyn sank deeper into her grief. "I was hoping you two could officially meet. We're engaged." Jadyn's disappointed, dejected, broken heart exploded and oozed her unseen pain.

She forced herself to look at Christina standing beyond the last remaining car in the lot beneath the now-lit streetlight where Cole hid to spy on Jadyn one year ago, to the day, at this time. She stood smiling with a wanting look and hand raised, resembling a dog in a pound hoping for a new home.

Jadyn felt betrayed and wounded, wondering how he could bring someone, bring her, to their pre-planned meetup. She fought back the desire to run. She couldn't bring herself to feel anything for Christina. Cole was hers!

Everything in Jadyn seemed to overreact! Her confusion about this shocking reality conflicted with the anticipated story she'd written during the thick silence between them for those painful months since Gavin died. She knew it was her fault. Her silence created the space and time needed to make Cole seek the touch of another woman. She couldn't blame anyone but herself. She knew any woman would jump at the chance to have a man like Cole.

Jadyn's anger at herself and feeling trapped between Cole and her opened door made her calculate an escape. She slid from beneath his strong hand on her shoulder and asked him, "Can you take Chase for a piss and then put him in the truck? He nodded, and she watched as they walked over to some palm trees looking so good together and then climbed into the truck's cab. She looked chubby to Cole, but he wasn't sure if he should think anything of it as he picked up Chase and set him on the seat beside her, smiling and looking at her.

Jadyn nearly lost the ability to see at all. She was blinking and clenching her hand tight enough to draw blood again, this time because he wasn't holding her. She feared she would lose her mind and, quite possibly, the baby if she didn't get the hell out of there. She asked him to close the door he held open. Cole closed it softly.

She looked at him through red eyes, "Tell her I

couldn't stay and hope you're both happy." Jadyn's eyes, wet with unborn droplets of tears, ready to fall without her permission, were coming just as the baby, now fatherless within her, was coming with or without Cole.

She looked at her key, started the engine, and without another glance at Cole, drove away past the nervously smiling Christina. He was stunned by her behavior and looked lost as she sped off! Her sobbing was loud enough for Cole to hear over the noise of her truck racing away at full speed, kicking back stones in his direction. Christina feared what would come of this and watched Cole stand there looking bewildered and, most concerning, abandoned.

Chapter 70

Jadyn's Call

Jadyn couldn't focus through tears flowing from her pained green eyes. The road, unclear, smudged, and looking like a Monet painting, was disorienting, so Jadyn pulled to the side of the highway and called Kendall. The begging sound of her voice echoed in her cell and compelled Kendall to ask, "What's wrong? Jay? You okay? Talk to me." All Kendall could hear was Chase whimpering in the background.

Words wouldn't come as she loudly sucked in air between uncontrolled gasping sobs. Now that she could hear Jadyn breathing, Kendall sighed with relief, saying, "Oh, Jay, I'm so sorry it didn't go well. Just get here."

Jadyn let out with mostly breath, "Coming now."

Once she arrived at Kendall's, Jadyn explained what had transpired and said, "Before this baby gets any bigger and I become a mom, I'd love one more road trip."

Kendall enthusiastically responded, "As you wish!"

Levi, all in favor of the trip, said, "Go. You two have fun." And, turning to Kendall, winked, "I'll be A-Okay on my own. Anything not to be around crying women." And with that said, they planned to drive up the Pacific Coast Highway with no particular destination in mind. They made trips like this when they were teens, unbeknown to their parents, and it was what Jadyn needed now: time to be carefree and chill.

Anticipation of reliving past experiences filled them

with excitement as they fell to sleep with plans to venture out early the next morning. Levi woke them with his fabulous breakfast cooking and offered, "If you want, I could keep Chase here with me, while you do your girly things." He rubbed Chase's neck and slipped him a piece of bacon.

Jadyn thought about how much fun he would have exploring but then considered it was bad enough she had to pee all the time, and it would be nice to know he could walk the beach with Levi instead of being stuck in a hot car. "Are you sure?"

He turned and let Chase jump on him, and with both hands rubbing his neck and chest, he said, "You wanna go hike with Uncle Levi don't you?"

Chase's entire body wagged in excitement over his invitation and after they all shared another delicious meal, Jadyn and Kendall ventured off with Levi waving his hand and Chase wagging his tail.

Chapter 71

Secret Crush

Jadyn wasn't the only one who didn't want Cole to marry Christina. Randy secretly held a torch for her and thought Cole knew, making the shock and betrayal he felt seeing her enter Cole's apartment with a bottle of wine cut deep. But Randy hadn't let Cole know, and now he's paying for it.

Christina walking into his apartment replayed continually in Randy's head. If only he'd shared with Cole how he felt about her. If only he'd explained they shared a connection. If only he had admitted he'd been cultivating a relationship with her. If only he had the confidence to speak his feelings aloud before Cole stepped in with his successful surfer persona. If only Cole hadn't stolen her heart. So many if-onlies....

Randy was angry with himself, not with Cole. The fault was all his. He owned it. He continued to admire Cole and considered him a friend and mentor. And after Drake died, he couldn't bring himself to come-clean and fess up.

Nearly all summer, the three partied on Cole's deck, and Randy barely spoke to Christina. It was blatantly obvious to Randy that he and Christina were a better match than she and Cole. After all, Christina was Randy's age. They never ran out of stuff to talk about. They shared similar dreams for their future and were politically in line with one another. On the other hand,

Cole was six years her senior. Randy suspected Christina was a substitute for Jadyn filling the lonely hours. He figured Cole wasn't even aware of how little they had in common.

Cole talked about Drake and Alannah often and ached for a marriage like they had. It was so clear to Randy that Cole missed Drake and was still in love with Jadyn. He had to figure out how to help Cole see he didn't love Christina before it was too late!

So when Cole came home with his own six pack, looking frustrated, searching his pockets this time, he came out of his apartment and asked Cole, "whatcha digging for?" It was a flashback for sure, a flashback to the night he met Jadyn. Randy thought perhaps he could show Cole the parallel and help him see that he was replacing Jadyn with a look-a-like.

Cole looked at Randy, "My damn keys."

He baited Cole, "Remind you of anything?"

Cole was distant and gave Randy a *come-on dude* look.

Randy knew how much Cole missed Drake. He was aware he'd been his sounding board and more of a father to him than his own. Cole had stopped by Breakers nearly every night to hear Drake tell his stories and to share his with Drake. He was consumed by loneliness without Drake in his life, and after losing Jadyn, his unhappiness set it in big time!

Randy wished Cole could find his way back to himself, find his free spirit, and rid himself of the dark dullness lurking behind his sorrowful eyes.

Cole pulled out his keys, opened the door, and invited Randy in, offering a cold brew on his deck. This was Randy's chance to save Cole from marrying the wrong woman. Given another chance with Christina, he wouldn't hesitate, he wouldn't doubt himself, he would make sure she knew exactly how he felt about her, and rekindle the embers to create sparks to fuel their budding romance.

Chapter 72

Selfishly Spoken

The beers were cold, and Randy popped the tops as always. It was officially his job, bestowed on him by Cole.

Randy handed Cole an open beer and sat back, saying, "I guess this is my payback beer from the night you found me searching for my keys, and I shared my six-pack with you."

Cole seemed not to hear him and didn't acknowledge his remark. "Remember, it was the night you met Jadyn."

Those words woke Cole from his distant thoughts! "I can't believe you brought up her name."

Randy faked an apology, "didn't know it bothered you, sorry."

He was pleased with himself. He got Cole thinking about Jadyn; now he had to get him to see Christina was nothing like her.

Randy asked, "What did you see in Jadyn?"

Cole's eyes brightened, and he couldn't stop smiling. "She's artistic, unconventional, and full of moxie, and oh yeah, and married." Cole frowned.

Randy pressed, knowing Christina would be here the rest of the week. This was his last chance to have Cole all to himself. His chance to wake him up. His chance to save everyone from following the wrong path. "What happened?"

Cole looked pissed off, "Thought you knew already."

Randy pretended not to know, "Nah, I don't really know much."

He reached for another beer and held it in front of Randy and his lighter to open it. "It was tragic, really. Her husband was in a coma for almost a year. Long story short, he woke up the day before we buried Drake's ashes at sea."

Randy could see the pain raw in Cole's eyes. His attempt to ignore or avoid the subject was his MO. "Talk to her lately?"

Cole flashed on her taillights, driving away from him a few days earlier. "Ya. We planned to meet up on the same day and time we met. Corny, I know. Thought she'd bring her husband, so I brought Christina. She got all weirded out."

Randy figured she had to be jealous. She had to have feelings for Cole to act like that. This was his opening! He decided some passive-aggressive manipulation wasn't beneath him and asked. "Try calling her?"

He lowered his head, "Not sure I should. She was whacked. Pretty sure I saw her crying. I hate making women cry."

Randy grew concerned, "She cried?"

Cole said, "Ya, she looked hurt when I didn't let her kiss me."

Randy grew even more hopeful, "Kiss you?"

Cole looked at him. "Ya, she tried to kiss me. Not sure why. Her husband's back home."

Randy planted the seed of curiosity in Cole, asking, "You think she divorced him?"

Cole hadn't even considered the possibility and felt a twinge of hope thinking. *Does she want me? Is there still a chance for us?*

Randy kept going, "Still have her number?"

Cole nodded. "She drove like a bat out of hell to get away from me. Pretty sure she doesn't want to hear from me."

Randy's hope was growing stronger by the second. "Only one way to find out." He figured asking, "Love her?" would push him to react. or nothing would.

Cole couldn't deny his feelings for her. "Ya." Seeing Jadyn instantly took him back to Sedona, and—the painting.

Randy smiled inside, "Text her. See if she's still around. I mean, I would if I were you. Love doesn't come easy. Sure seemed like she was the one."

Cole realized he couldn't marry Christina. His heart belonged to Jadyn. "I guess I should at least find out what's going on with her."

Randy felt he'd succeeded on his mission, stood to leave, and said, "Sounds like a plan. Better than wondering the rest of your life."

He knew his young friend was correct, he knew he had to hurt Christina, and he knew Jadyn's hot temper could be as unpredictable as the day they messed up her painting when she didn't get pissed at all. Cole realized he needed to concoct a brilliant plan to minimize the pain he was about to unleash by opening this pandora's box, or he could end up looking like Inspector Clouseau and make a mess of it all.

Chapter 73

Road Trip

T he shoreline was breathtaking, and though they'd taken this drive many times before, they stopped the car repeatedly to take pictures and to let Jadyn pee. The aquamarine water was heavenly and precisely what Jadyn needed to fill her spiritually and artistically. They recalled times spent at different locations.

Jadyn stared out the window and asked Kendall, "Remember when we saw those migrating dolphins surfing the waves?"

Kendall nodded and said, "It was incredible! They kept jumping and were following our car! I'm sure of it!"

Jadyn laughed, "I'll never forget that day. Remember when we saw hundreds of sea lions and thought they were dead?!"

Kendall laughed along with Jadyn, "Hahaha! Ya! It was hilarious! We weren't the only ones! I'll always remember when we walked down to the sand to check on them, to see if they were alright, and one was blowing bubbles from his nose in a puddle of seawater!"

Jadyn crossed her legs, resisting the urge to pee, and went on, "I was so relieved to learn they were pups sunbathing."

Kendall said, "Me too! They looked like logs jammed in a river, all lined up. I'll never forget that or being chased out by the park ranger!"

Jadyn continued reminiscing, "Remember laying naked on those big rocks by a waterfall in the canyon?"

Kendall flirtatiously asked, "Naked?"

Jadyn enjoyed the memory and said, "I think it's after the next curve. Let's go, please! Please!"

Kendall laughingly said, "That place we accidentally found? As if! You think we're going to just magically find it again?"

Jadyn scrunched her nose and said, "I'm sure it's close. I can feel it! It's right around the next bend!"

With more than four hours and a lot of road behind them, they both hoped she was right. Jadyn's recollection was correct! Her rememberings didn't fail her. They arrived at the same coastal rainforest they'd accidentally found all those years ago, their secret treasure.

Kendall yelled, "You were right!"

Jadyn raised her chin and said, "Per usual!"

They laughed as Kendall parked the car, and Jadyn wiggled in her seat, anxious to pee again.

This tropical locale was secluded, and they were pleased to be alone. Most motorists driving distracted along Highway 1 were focused on the vastness of the aquamarine ocean and missed it.

Time may have passed, but their memories were intact and remained vivid. Camouflaged just across the street from the sea, they entered through a broken gate held open by overgrown blackberry vines. Jadyn and Kendall felt the cooling spray of the waterfall's mist as they walked in to rediscover their hidden treasure, concealed behind lush ferns and shrubs. The cool mist made her need to pee even more urgent. Jadyn grabbed the gate's moss-covered, dark-brown wood and squatted to pee behind it. "Oh, my God! That was close! I almost peed my pants!"

She pulled up her shorts, and they continued up the pathway. They could smell the freshwater as they pushed away overgrown lush-green foliage blocking the path. When they reached the stream's edge, they stepped over river rocks in the cascading water and crossed to the other side. Just a few yards up the wet-dirt path, they could see the fall's crest, and as if planned by God, the sun streamed through the trees, casting a rainbow in the water's cool misty spray.

It was a little after noon, and the sun's position was perfect for laying out on the same boulders they'd laid on all those years ago. After stripping down to their bathing suits, they stepped onto the bedrock to swim in the crystal-clear plunge-pool water and then stood beneath its flow.

Feeling safe and serene, Jadyn removed her top and lay exposed on a wide, flat, and smooth boulder. The cool feel of the stone beneath her and the sweet fragrance of wild jasmine from the jungle-like surroundings soothed her broken heart.

Kendall joined Jadyn sunbathing on the rocks and looked at her, saying, "Aww, look at your adorable little baby bump. And Wow! Those girls have gotten huge!"

Jadyn grinned and said, "One of the perks of being preggers. It won't be long before my tummy changes forever, and I give birth without a man."

Kendall tried to save Jadyn from future regret, "I think you should tell Cole."

Jadyn fought, "I think you should mind your own damn business."

Kendall snapped, "Fine!"

Jadyn pressed, "I swear! If Cole gets in touch with you, don't you dare tell him. I only want him in my life if he actually wants me."

Kendall assured, "I won't." with fingers crossed.

Jadyn didn't trust her after the angel box fiasco! "He said they're engaged! I don't even know if it's his baby." She looked at her hand resting on her belly. "How the hell did he fall in love with Christina? I can't believe they're engaged. It's only been five months!"

Kendall argued, "Did you tell him Gavin died?"

Jadyn shook her head. "I don't think he ever loved me."

Kendall asked, "Did you guys ever talk about love?"

She shook her head.

Kendall said, "No surprise."

Jadyn argued, "I was married. Duh."

Kendal defended Cole, "He asked someone else to marry him because all he knew was Gavin woke up. He thought he'd lost you forever. He doesn't even know you're pregnant."

Jadyn was tired and said, "I wasn't going to send some lame text or call him. I wanted to tell him in person. Yesterday was the first chance I got!" Kendall blurted out, "He deserves to know!"

Jadyn looked at Kendall like a lion cub being swatted by his lioness mother and yelled, "Butt out!"

Kendall pushed, "I think you're being unfair to Cole."

Jadyn yelled, "You don't even know him! You should be on my side! I don't need this from you! Let's go back! Now!" She put her top on, gathered her gear, and wobbled over the river rocks saying, "I need to do this in my time, on my terms. It isn't only me anymore."Kendall yelled, "Raging hormones?!" and then cringed, knowing she'd ignited Jadyn's fury.

Jadyn walked faster, and Kendall yelled, "Wait!"

In slow motion, Kendall watched Jadyn slip on the mossy rocks! Jadyn fell face-first into the water. Kendall thought, *if only the water were deeper.* Seeing Jadyn land hard on her stomach made her mind scream, *oh, no, the baby!*

Pulling Jadyn from the water, Kendall faked calm, seeing the fear covering her scraped and sullen face. Upright, Jadyn said nothing. She cried, crossed her arms over her midriff to support the baby, and limped with bleeding knees back to the car. Their silence was thick. Neither was brave enough to speak for fear their words would be the final straw that would end her pregnancy.

Jadyn felt nauseous. Not unusual, considering, and frightened by all the what-ifs running through her mind. *What if it's Gavin's? What if I lose the baby? What if it's Cole's, and he never even knows I lost his baby?*

Kendall knew Jadyn's berating mind was running at full speed. "Think positive. I'm taking you to Urgent Care. We'll get you, and the baby checked out. I'm sure you'll both be fine, other than bruises and scratches."

Jadyn wanted to believe her, "If everything isn't okay, you're the only one that knows I'm pregnant."

Kendall was surprised. "No one else knows? Not even Teddy or your mom?"

Jadyn shook her head, "No. Pretty sure Molly suspects I am." Jadyn shifted in her seat and placed a rolled-up towel against the window as a pillow. "I wanted to wait til the second trimester. After Gavin... I didn't want to break anyone's heart. You know..." She closed her eyes tight, "It's a good thing I waited."

Kendall said softly, "Go to sleep. I'll wake you when we're close." Jadyn wished she could talk to her mom, but this was a complicated secret that had to remain a secret, at least for now. It felt like a funeral as they drove the last hour in the dark, fearing the baby might die.

Jadyn and Kendall were exhausted after the day's adventure, their argument, the long drive cut short, and an hour-long wait in the ER after learning Urgent Care wasn't open. The ER doctor said if she didn't have any breakthrough bleeding, there was a good chance the pregnancy would proceed, and the baby would be viable.

Nervous and unsure they could trust the doctor's confidence in their well-being, they drove mournfully to Kendall's.

Levi's first night sleeping without Kendall in over a year, cuddled up with Chase instead, was interrupted by their whispering, "Jay, I'll bring you some water."

Jadyn said, yawning, "I've got a bottle; you go to sleep."

Kendall hugged her, "Sorry for being bitchy. I'll pray for the baby. Love you."

Jadyn, still wrapped in Kendall's embrace, rested her head on her shoulder and said, "I did my share of bitching." They separated, and Kendall remained in her room in case she needed anything as she changed into a sleep shirt. Kendall flicked off the light and quietly closed the door as Jadyn said, "Love you."

She said, "Love you too," and walked to Levi with worry in her heart. He was concerned, sitting up in the bed, waiting for her to enter their room. He figured they'd be in some hotel in Monterey or Carmel and knew something had to be wrong for them to unexpectedly return on the first day at 2:40 in the morning. She walked in, and he immediately and softly asked, "What's wrong? Why are you guys home so soon?"

Chase jumped off the bed, sniffed Kendall's legs, and got his petting from her. She sent him off, saying, "Go to your momma." He walked out knowing where to find Jadyn, and sniffed under her door, whimpering until she let him in and joined her for sleep.

Kendall knew she wasn't supposed to tell anyone about the baby and searched for words. "Jadyn slipped on mossy rocks and fell."

Levi loved Jadyn like a sister and asked, "Is her baby all right?

Kendall's look of surprise let him know she thought he'd missed the growing belly, and he wanted to mention she must believe he was blind if she thought he didn't know, but he remained silent.

"Jadyn isn't bleeding. I took her to the hospital, and the doc said everything should be okay, wish he had said it would be okay. I'm worried."

He reached for Kendall as she slid under the covers, clearly shaken by the whole experience, "Sorry your girls-only trip didn't go well." He held her and kissed her head, not sure what to say.

Kendall felt his compassion and whispered, "Babe, Jadyn can't know you know about the baby. And when she finds out, you need to tell her I didn't tell you. She'll kill me."

He squeezed her into his chest, "She's not fooling anyone. But, I'll be good." Kendall's shivers slipped away as she fell to sleep in the warmth of his embrace.

Kendall woke to the sounds of Levi listening to rock

music and filling the house with maple bacon and coffee aromas. Feeling groggy, Kendall texted Jadyn, *How are you 2?*

Jadyn texted back, *No blood but sore and looking pretty shitty. I smell bacon—tongue-hanging emoji.*

Grateful and relieved, Kendall replied, *meet you in the kitchen. He knows you're hurt. He also knows you're preggers. He guessed. I swear!*

Jadyn looked at her protruding belly and knew she was telling the truth. There was no hiding it any longer.

Chase rushed past Jadyn to the smells coming from the kitchen, skidding to a stop when he saw Levi. He sat like the perfect dog at his feet, hoping for a portion of bacon.

Levi's eyes widened for a split second as he caught a glimpse of Jadyn's face, pretended to be a complete fool, and acted like nothing was wrong. "You look like you need some tea." She knew he didn't want her drinking coffee while pregnant and smiled when he set it in front of her.

They enjoyed breakfast, and hoping everything was going to be okay, Levi loaded her bags into Jadyn's truck, "You take care of yourself." She could feel his brotherly concern through his gentle yet firm hug. He usually just bumped her shoulder with his; his hugs were few and far between.

Her animated smile couldn't disguise Kendall's worried look as she said, "Bye, Chase. Bye babe. Be safe and call when you get wherever you end up."

Jadyn only knew she was headed back to Sedona but not to her ranch or Teddy. She didn't want to face her mother with her face looking like she'd been in a fight. She'd skip a visit despite being so close. All she knew was she was staying at a pet-friendly hotel with room service until her injuries healed. She didn't want to explain all of it to anyone. She felt better knowing she would be close to home if anything went wrong.

Chapter 74

Freedom Ride

Jadyn's wounds had taken longer than she'd expected to heal. She was optimistic, on the mend, and home once again.

She let Samuel know he no longer had to sleep at the ranch but asked him to increase his hours working the horses. She was home, but only Samuel knew. She felt empowered by keeping it to herself until she was again centered and grounded to the ranch. She also knew her job at the gallery was at risk if she postponed her official re-acclimation into the real world much longer.

After her month away, Jadyn entered the musty stalls for the horse's morning feeding and grooming regimen. She slid her glove-covered fingers through a thick layer of dust covering Kharibia's saddle and reached for her bridle. Since she hadn't asked Samuel to ride the horses while she was away, she wasn't surprised at this dusty evidence of her extended absence. Jadyn pulled the soft-black leather reins from the post with her left hand and slid them over her right shoulder.

Jadyn decided to keep what she was about to do her little secret. She'd finally moved past having dizzy spells and tossing her cookies. Today was the long-awaited first day of her second trimester! Only Kendall, Levi, and likely Molly knew she was pregnant; she'd managed to keep this little secret too.

She spoke aloud, "Once I tell everyone I'm pregnant, they're going to helicopter all over me." She looked at her belly and said, "This may be my last chance to ride till you enter this world, little one." Jadyn followed her instincts, aware people who loved her and strangers alike would disagree with her doctor's opinion of riding while pregnant.

Her doctor had explained during an early exam, "Skip riding the first trimester. Odds are you'll be too queasy to ride during that time anyhow. Keep up your normal exercise program and keep paddle boarding for balance. I recommend riding your horse only during the second trimester."

Gavin had given her a paddle board on her last birthday, and she loved the escape it provided. During her bouts of desperation, she wasn't sure if she would've survived the days without it. Time spent at Watson Lake in Prescott, lying down on her board, floating among migrating Canadian Geese and a variety of ducks all swirling around her with their babies following behind, filled her with hope and connected her to God.

She always felt sure-footed and well-balanced on her board, having never fallen off like other people she witnessed taking a splashing butt-first cannonball into the lake water. She felt confident, strong and full of life. Everything inside her said it was safe to get back in the saddle and ride Kharibia; the window of opportunity would soon close.

Jadyn melodically spoke to her belly, "Baby, today we ride!"

Chase knew the word "ride," like city dogs know "walk."

As soon as she said ride, Chase began spinning around, tail wagging and whimpering. He smiled his doggo smile, with tongue dangling and loud panting. Chase could barely stand waiting for her to saddle up Kharibia. Jadyn felt powerful as she slid her boot into the stirrup, pulled herself up, whipped her leg over her hindquarters, and mounted easily. She surprised even herself! All those hours of paddleboarding had paid off!

She was excited to be able to wear her hair down after months of dust-blowing, braid, or ponytail-only weather; the wind had finally calmed. It was shaping up to be a sizzling-hot summer day in June, and her long, loose hair moved inside a wind tunnel created by Kharibia's cantering gate.

Jadyn never felt more alive than when she and Kharibia became one! This free and exuberant spiritual feeling is experienced only by those who ride.

She respected the immense power of this beautiful animal beneath her.

Despite Kharibia being over a thousand pounds of muscle, the two flew with grace and fluidity through the world when she rode. Their spiritual bond and unconditional trust gave Jadyn true freedom of movement. She let go of the reins, raised her arms above her head, and screamed, "This ride's for you, Gavin!" Her heart and soul cracked open!

Kharibia glanced back to ensure Jadyn was seated and took off in a full gallop. It was as if reaching to the heavens when they tore through the red-clay dirt, with Chase lagging behind and barking as if to say, "Wait for me!"

She'd never gone into the backcountry without Gavin. But today, unafraid, she felt blessed and protected. She heard Gavin cheering her on, encouraging her to go farther, and so she did. As they climbed higher and higher, she felt lighter and stronger. They reached the summit and stopped to gaze at the indescribable beauty before them. Jadyn slid off Kharibia's back, raised her arms, and screamed, "Yes!" Sedona's mountain spirits resounded in agreement in repeating echoes.

Jadyn's spirit awakened. And like the dust on her saddle was wiped away, leaving it polished and appearing new, she felt fresh and reborn, free of grief and heartache. She felt the life growing within her, begged Gavin's forgiveness, and asked God to release her from the guilt of her sin.

She remembered Gavin saying he wanted her to move on when he died, but until this moment, she never really believed him. She felt him with her as she overlooked the valley floor from the top of their mountain. They had made love here and had watched sunsets when life was sweet and Jadyn pure.

Jadyn mounted Kharibia, and they descended from the mesa. With the sun's heat hot against their backs, she knew she'd received forgiveness from God, Gavin, and most importantly, herself.

Back at the ranch, Jadyn bathed Kharibia, walked to the next stall, and reached to stroke Gavin's horse, reassuringly saying, "Blaze, you'll get to go next time. Promise."

She walked a bit sore-legged to the house, gently brushing her belly in small circles like a child finger-painting repeating her new affirmation, "Today is the first day of the rest of our lives, and I will create it wisely."

Chapter 75

Delayed Reply

J adyn,
    I feel like such an idiot – such a fool, to not have considered your feelings more, but in my defense, last I'd heard from you, Gavin had woken up! In my mind, we were not to be.

I suppose I should have confirmed with you, but you hadn't contacted me in such a long time. I was left with only my own thoughts. I forced myself to accept us as a couple was simply not possible. I gave up.

I suppose my hopeless romantic personality made me come to the beach. How fantastic to think two people could plan something a year before and both show up.

In all honesty, I didn't think you'd appear; I thought for sure you and Gavin were doing great! So, what happened with you and Gavin? I can only guess you didn't want to disappoint me, so you showed up, or something else has happened, and I'm dying to know because my feelings for you have not died. In anticipation of your reply, Cole"

Jadyn repeated his words aloud. "My feelings for you have not died?" She continued parroting his words within her private thoughts. *My feelings for you have not died. My feelings for you have not died. My feelings for you have not died!* Jadyn fell back on the bed in disbelief, thinking. *Now what?*

Chapter 76

The Chair

Jadyn stood in the doorway of her bedroom, rubbing her sore back; she knew it was time to stop sleeping on the couch. Although she removed their bed and replaced it with a new one, it didn't alter reality; it would forever be the room where Gavin died, just as painting over the paint that covered the canvas of her secret didn't erase her guilt.

She's tormented by flashbacks each time she catches a glimpse of Gavin's oversized chair, the chair he loved so much, the chair he'd sat on watching her sleep, the chair they sat on together after consummating their love, the chair where she sat alone the morning he took his last breath, after making love for the last time, the chair that seemed larger than ever as she observed the emergency personnel prepare to take Gavin away.

Gavin's last moments flood in every time she enters their bedroom, like a rerun of a movie she can't turn off. She can't shake the memory of him lying there, motionless, in their bed with all the commotion, whispers, and chattery voices of strangers preparing his body as she sat in shock, grieving.

She felt the chair knew too much as it witnessed their lovemaking sessions. She also felt its presence judge her as she made love to Gavin for the last time, with Cole's body still resonating on her skin. Each time she sees the chair, she is reminded of the brutal reality of the closeness of the two events. It will forever haunt her, the two memories blending into one.

His chair takes up so much space in the room, drawing attention and reminding her of when they watched the Harvest Moon after making love for the first time. Seeing the chair now makes Jadyn's emotions bubble to the surface like molten lava flowing, burning her heart, and punishing her guilty mind. His chair sits there as a reminder of the morning he died and how she shuddered at the realization some of her still clung to his flesh; some of him remained inside her when they rolled him out in the black body bag on the gurney with its squeaking wheels. Even now, a reminder of that scene is still blurry through her tears and reminds her of how tight her chest felt and still feels from the weight of all the sadness pressing against her.

Yet she knew after waking up this morning and struggling to get off the couch, last night was the last night she would call it bed. After five months of hibernating and hiding, it was time to face her demons and make peace with her failings. She spoke aloud, "If you're here, Gavin, I want you to know I love you and hope you're happy wherever you are. I hope you ride horses and fly as you'd imagined death would allow. I'm sure you're aware of my betrayal, and I hope you can forgive me."

She felt a light pressure on her shoulder and a movement of air across her cheek. Her heart clenched, and she sucked in a breath of wonder, asking, "Gavin?" And expelled the air, whispering, "I love you so much, and I'm so sorry."

Jadyn felt his forgiveness surround her and a soothing release of some of the guilt that burdened her soul, and she said, "Thank you, Gavin. Thank you for your forgiveness and for the life we shared. I love you— forever."

For the first time since his death, Jadyn felt a sense of gratitude and peace as she dressed before going out to tend the horses. She slid the chair to the front door. Once she was ready to disclose her pregnancy, she would ask Samuel to put it in the garage where the rest of Gavin's treasures sat. Still, it was time to let go of him and the memories that clung to the cushions of Gavin's big chair.

Chapter 77

Truth & Consequences

J adyn welcomed each rise and fall of the morning breeze as she walked, leading the horses up the trail. Feeling hot was her constant state of being for at least the last six weeks. Until now, Jadyn never thought she'd be able to say with certainty how it felt to be cooked from the inside out.

Sedona's summer heat sucked oxygen from the air, making her feel dizzy as she held tight to Blaze and Kharibia's leads. Climbing the red clay sandy trail behind the ranch with the weight of her growing belly was becoming more exhausting each day, but the horses needed exercise. She knew the time would come for her to have Samuel exercise them in place of her, but she fought like a bull to keep control.

Jadyn poured water over her neck to cool the insane heat building inside. It felt wonderful but wasn't enough to reduce her body's heat. She felt lightheaded, and her breaths were louder. Chase's heavy panting and whimpering reflected his growing concern for her, so she turned them around and headed back to the ranch. "Okay, Boy, I hear ya. Let's go home." Chase and the horses walked with hesitant steps and slowed to match Jadyn's gate. Now walking between the horses, shaded by them she could see Kharibia's huge brown eye reflected back, watching her.

Chase suddenly stopped in his tracks, making the

CLARE ROWLEY

horses and Jadyn stop. She'd thought he wanted water till she noticed his tail wagging and tongue-hanging exuberant smile. Jadyn squinted beneath her cowboy hat to see what was exciting Chase.

Jadyn wondered, *is that Cole?* Then said, "What the heck?"

She tried to make sense of his visit. He hadn't said he was coming, hadn't asked to see her. She considered that it might just look like his truck; it could belong to someone else. She instructed Chase, "Keep going, Boy." Chase led, and she and the horses followed. Jadyn occasionally slipped on loose pebbles beneath the smooth leather soles of her cowboy boots. Her unbalanced, heavier body made it challenging to stay upright and made Chase extremely nervous.

With over sixty yards between them, Jadyn walked, peeking between the two horses which blocked his view of her. Jadyn slowed down when she decided it was unmistakably Cole! He was walking to her front door with a dog by his side.

Cole was unaware Jadyn had her eyes on him when he knocked. It was reminiscent of the night they met, but the tables are turned today. She was now the spy.

She knew Cole would be able to see them once they passed from behind the scrub oak. He walked back to his truck, looking disappointed, staring at his feet until Chase barked! He didn't want Cole to leave. He looked at Jadyn for permission before running to Cole, whimpering and enthusiastically wagging his tail.

Cole raised his arm to block the sun with his hand and waved to her. She peered over Kharibia's mane with a puzzled look and continued leading the horses to the ranch.

When Chase reached Cole, he passed by his welcoming hand to sniff Sinker. Chase looked up at Cole, wondering why Sinker didn't run around with him. "He's an old dog, Chase. Don't worry. I think he likes you. Maybe you're just what he needs. He's been sad lately; think you can cheer him up? Where's your ball?"

Chase took off running for his ball, and what do you know, Sinker ran after him! It was a delightful sight and reminded Cole of when he blasted through the doggie door the night he met Jadyn and Drake gave him fatherly advice. Cole wasn't sure which emotion to deal with first and opted to go to her instead.

They reached each other on the trail. Jadyn kept her distance from Cole by maintaining her position between the two horses. She spoke over Kharibia's back, "What are you doing here?"

He felt like a loser. "Kendall pretty much demanded I visit you. She said I owed it to both of us."

Jadyn rolled her eyes, "Damn her. She can't keep her nose out of my business." Jadyn lowered her gaze to her fingers, combing Kharibia's black silky mane. "Aren't you about to be married?"

Cole shook his head to say no.

Blaze, Gavin's horse, pushed Jadyn, urging her to take him to his oats. When she did, his gaze lowered to her feet. Cole noticed Jadyn's shadow being cast by the morning sun, a pregnant belly shadow! "You're pregnant?"

She nodded.

He blinked a few times and stepped over to her, mumbling, "How pregnant are you? Who's. Is it mine? Where's Gavin? Is it his baby?"

She snapped at him. "What difference does it make?

You're getting married."

He fought back, "I told you I'm not. After seeing you on our beach, I knew I was still in love with you! It wouldn't be fair to Christina, to me, or you. My heart belongs to you. I did not and will not be marrying her."

She looked at him angrily, "Sure didn't take you long to replace me."

Her words provoked him, making him irritated and growing more confused. "Oh, my God! What a load of crap! What difference does it make now? Were you ever going to tell me?"

Jadyn was utterly embarrassed; she didn't know if the baby was Cole's or Gavin's, and she couldn't hide it any longer. "Walk with me; let me put the horses away."

Cole didn't want to wait for answers. "What happened with you and Gavin?"

She stopped to look at him and said sternly, "He died!"

The tears in her eyes made him question his irritation. "I'm sorry. When? How?"

She preferred to have good eye contact when talking about serious matters, "Please wait till the horses...."

He felt terrible, "Oh, crap. Ya, sure. Can I help?" Jadyn handed him Blaze's lead.

Cole followed Jadyn through the gate, where she unbuckled their halters. She fed them handfuls of oats, and when they were done and sniffing for more, she slapped their hindquarters, sending them out to graze on the grass with the dogs running after them. Jadyn wondered about his dog. "I didn't know you had a dog. What's his name?"

Jadyn searched Cole's sullen face as he answered, "That's Sinker. He's Drake's..." Jadyn felt her heart skip a beat, filling with overwhelming sadness, yet simultaneously joyful to learn he hadn't perished in the fire.

Cole continued softly, "He's a good ol' dog."

It was nice to see Chase have a buddy and entertaining to watch Sinker's electrifying fear as he sniffed the horse's legs. He kept bolting away, barking, and looking to Chase for reassurance before returning to continue his investigation of the horses, dodging their fly-swatting, wildly swishing tails. Cole's gaze was alternating between the animals and Jadyn's belly. They left the dogs to enjoy the yard and walked to the house.

Jadyn looked at Cole, with the sun illuminating his ice-blue eyes, and asked, "Coffee?"

He kept looking at her face and back to her tummy with worry and excitement beating up his heart like a fighter hitting a punching bag. She led him through the French doors off the back patio and into the house. Cole looked around and noticed subtle changes making him wonder how long it had been since Gavin passed.

She handed him a cup of coffee, poured herself tea, and sat in front of Cole's serious and handsome face. "First, I'm sorry you're learning about my baby now. I was going to tell you when I showed up at our beach. My thought was I should tell you face to face. But you told me about Christina, and I lost it!"

He was upset and frustrated, "Let's forget about all that and start over."

Jadyn's face loosened, "Gavin died a week after he came home."

She fidgeted and played with a string hanging from a hole in her blue jeans. "We made love, and the next morning, he was gone."

Cole reached over, wrapped Jadyn in his arms, and hugged Jadyn, "I don't have words..."

She rested in his warm, consoling embrace and continued, "I know I should have told you sooner that he died. First, I had to deal with the memorial. Then everything else... Then I skipped my period! Devastated doesn't even begin to describe my emotions!" She sobbed, "I don't know if the baby is yours... Or if it's Gavin's. I feel so cheap!"

He wasn't surprised she was crying and desperately wanted to find the right words to comfort her. "I don't care about the baby." He stopped and shook his head, "What I mean is I don't care if he, or she, is mine. I love you Jadyn. There's no way I wouldn't love your child."

She wanted to take his love and cling to it forever. "I don't know how to handle this! If the baby is Gavin's, no one will judge me. If it's yours, everyone will know I betrayed him."

Cole rubbed his hand gently on her baby bump and said, "You don't have to go through this alone. I'm here for you. I'm your crutch, remember? I want us. I'm in if you love me and want to pick up where we left off! All you have to do is say yes."

The End.

Let's Stay in Touch

I'm working on the second book of the
Beyond the Brushstrokes series!

Sign up for updates at www.clarerowley.com

About The Author

Clare Rowley

About The Author Clare Rowley Clare Rowley always felt called to the mountains, where she currently resides in northern Arizona. She was inspired to create at an early age, spending her tender years writing and painting, never without a pad in hand. Her call to an artistic life led her to paint as a reproduction artist, creating hundreds of paintings a year, and inspired her to embark individually as a fine artist, favoring oils as her preferred medium. Combined life experiences led her also to invent a line of sewing machine products, instructional education videos, and online school which integrated and contributed to what is now Creative Feet, supporting her while raising her two children.

Her lifelong dream of being an author is indisputable, with many more books unveiling what lies beneath the brushstrokes of her life.

www.ingramcontent.com/pod-product-compliance
Lightning Source LLC
Chambersburg PA
CBHW020418030726
47495CB00006B/1572